# NK3

# NK3

## MICHAEL TOLKIN

Atlantic Monthly Press
*New York*

First Grove Atlantic hardcover edition: February 2017

*Published simultaneously in Canada*
*Printed in the United States of America*

FIRST EDITION

ISBN 978-0-8021-2543-9
eISBN 978-0-8021-8984-4

Library of Congress Cataloging-in-Publication data is available for this title.

Atlantic Monthly Press
an imprint of Grove Atlantic
154 West 14th Street
New York, NY 10011

Distributed by Publishers Group West

groveatlantic.com

17 18 19 20    10 9 8 7 6 5 4 3 2 1

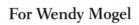

For Wendy Mogel

It really was as if the so-called "human" qualities had been characteristic features of a period of human history long past and were now only to be found on tombstones, as inscriptions for the dead.

Joseph Roth, *The Silent Prophet*

# NK3

# Colonel Lee, Sergeant Jun

It was a warm night in the bunker and Colonel Myung Lee was worried about money. "Boarding school is expensive, Sergeant Jun," said the Colonel, but Sergeant Jun knew it really wasn't the money. The Colonel's son had been accepted at Daewon Foreign Language High School near his home in Seoul and expected to go there, but a space had just opened up for him at Korean Minjok Leadership Academy, the boarding school a half-day's drive from the city. His best friend was going to Minjok and the boy wanted to go there with him. The Colonel rattled with indignation. "Daewon costs five thousand dollars a year and Minjok costs fifteen thousand. Ten thousand more for food and a bed? Does that make sense, Sergeant Jun?" Jun agreed it seemed excessive.

The Colonel had been in charge of this outpost since before Jun had enlisted. Due for a transfer to the capital, he wanted nothing more than to stay at home and see his son every day. But if the boy went away to Minjok, the Colonel would never again have the time to be close to him since most of the graduates of both schools went to university in America. Before he departed for such an exciting world of opportunity, Colonel Lee wanted to leave his son solid memories of good days together and was scared that this would never happen if the boy went to Minjok Leadership Academy.

"I told my wife, if he's going to get into an American university, I don't want him going to one of the schools on the Atlantic side of the country. I want him in Los Angeles or San Francisco. Berkeley and Stanford are there. Those are very good schools. Apple, Google,

Microsoft, Oracle, Facebook, these are all in California. My wife says, 'But what if he gets into Cornell? What if he gets into MIT? You want to hold him back from a great university because the flight is five hours longer?' Then I say, and Jun, I know this is wrong, I say, 'America doesn't matter so much anymore. A Korean education is in many ways superior, especially in technology. Remember, the Americans buy the TV sets we make here. We don't buy theirs.' And she says, 'Just admit to yourself that you're going to miss him. I'm going to miss him too. And if he didn't score so well on tests, if he wasn't such a strong tennis player, then he wouldn't be accepted by Minjok, and then he wouldn't be on his way to a great American university.'"

It was Sergeant Jun's burden that the Colonel confided in him. He worried the Colonel might one day regret this late-night fraternization and find some excuse to punish his subordinate for having answers to questions about the Colonel's private life that the Sergeant had never asked. But he had no choice about the assignment. On the nights when the Colonel was senior duty officer, he made sure that Jun was beside him watching the monitors for activity on the north side of the DMZ. Jun understood what the Colonel's wife meant about the Colonel's need to admit things to himself. It was Jun's experience of the Colonel that he exaggerated to the point of impersonation the stubborn skepticism of a career soldier for whom all problems are merely logistic as a way to pretend he wasn't in fact a complicated man. Jun had the passing thought more than once that the Colonel was infatuated with him for reasons the Colonel could not express without stirring up the cistern of his own emotions and that the Colonel found excitement, too much excitement, in the exercise of his restraint.

After a moment of quiet, the Colonel confessed, "She's right. I'll miss him. She's right. It doesn't matter if it's Boston or San Francisco. Why should I be cross with him for leaving home? You and I left our homes, right, Jun? We traded the warmth of family life for the glory of war. Look at how we traded family life for the dreadful machinery of war!" He pointed at the electric kettle, with its setting for herb tea, green tea, and black tea.

Jun laughed quietly at this. The Colonel used his rank to exercise irony, but it was risky for Jun to make humor out of their situation, not for fear of political reprisal. It was their opposites in uniform on the north side of the fence—along the mined strip of negative space that stretched from one coast of Korea to the other—who couldn't openly discuss the truth of their absurd situation for fear of dreadful punishment. No, the danger of levity in this bunker was that it would open these defenders of the free world to the pointlessness of their mission. And if their job was pointless, why weren't they home in Seoul adjusting, perhaps slowly, to the forfeit of rank, bored by mundane reality, but at least watching their children grow up? The North would never invade with its army because China, dreading chaos and refugees, would let the United States defend the South and the North would lose. Everyone knew this. No one could say it.

The command phone rang. Jun answered. Seismic detectors were picking up an increase in normal activity directly across from them, possibly from previously unknown North Korean tunnels. About this kind of alarm, the Colonel was never casual. And for all that Jun worried that their familiarity would provoke trouble in some form, Colonel Lee's response to an alert instantly turned every false alarm into an adventure.

Jun drove the Colonel the three kilometers to the scene. It wasn't a surprise to see a platoon of North Korean soldiers approaching the fence on their side of the empty zone; both armies played the same game of posturing. But there was something different about the shape of the North Korean soldiers.

Jun told the Colonel: "They're wearing hazardous materials suits, Colonel, enclosed circulation."

"Are any of them not wearing those suits?" asked the Colonel.

"None that I can see, sir."

"Weapons?"

"None visible, sir."

"No sidearms?"

"None visible, sir."

Lee asked for the field phone and woke up the General, who, like Jun, didn't for a moment think Lee's call was out of unnecessary caution. "Fifty men in hazmat suits across from Outpost Twenty-Three, sir. Consistent vibration suggesting tanks in a tunnel."

The opposing outposts shared a ridge. A fire truck drove up to the North's outpost and stopped, leaving the motor running. The driver of the fire truck was also wearing a hazmat suit.

Lee narrated: "They're raising the ladder." It had a stainless steel water cannon at the end next to a long orange windsock that filled as the ladder lifted it into the breeze that came from the North.

The ladder extended five lengths.

"Jun, what is the angle of that ladder and is it crossing over the line of their fence?" asked the Colonel.

"At least seventy degrees, and . . . no . . . it's completely on their side. It might be a fire drill."

"Why wear hazmat suits for a fire drill?"

Two men in the suits carried a hose to the top of the ladder and twisted the fitting onto the cannon. Immediately they turned on the water, which came out in a wide spray, not a long tight stream.

Colonel Lee told the General: "They're spraying something into the air directly above them, and the wind is carrying the mist across the DMZ. I can feel it on my skin. It's an attack. It has to be an attack, but what's our response?"

## Hopper, Hopper's Silent Voice

Hopper was asleep in an underpass when the sound of the first bus entered his dream, and then the dream melted into one of those invisible mental tapestries he called Thought Pictures. His Silent Voice didn't talk about them. He saw a big yellow dog and a smiling woman in the Thought Picture. He didn't have many Thought Pictures like this. The dog, a group of boys playing basketball, Hopper shooting and scoring.

Another bus followed the first. He grabbed the binoculars from his bicycle's saddlebag, crawled up the embankment, and watched as the buses drove down the freeway off-ramp a hundred yards away. The buses then continued a mile down the road that led to the mountain. Furrows of rippled sand covered the blacktop.

Hopper read the words stenciled on the buses. **THANK YOU FOUNDERS FOR THIS GIFT—THERE IS NO EQUAL VALUE— LEAVE NO TRACE—INCLUDE THEM—YES YOU'RE HERE!— PARTICIPATE!—NO BRANDING—SUSTAINABILITY NOW**

The buses stopped and the doors opened. Two women left each bus and then stood by the door as the passengers walked out: more men than women, all of them quiet except for the times when they hummed in unison, one setting a random pitch and the others finding it. The women made the passengers form two straight lines, facing away from the buses.

The women then returned to the buses, the doors closed, and the buses returned to the freeway, driving west.

The two lines stayed where they'd been placed. Hopper asked his Silent Voice if it was safe to move closer.

"Leave them alone. You can't help them and they can't help you."

Ignoring his Silent Voice, Hopper rode his bike nearer to them, pushing hard to move through the sand.

A few of the Drifters looked at him, smiling with a blank familiarity.

Another four buses came down the road. His Silent Voice told him to get away.

The lead bus stopped and someone inside it pointed a rifle at Hopper and started shooting.

Hopper's Silent Voice said, "I told you it wasn't safe to stop here. Ride toward the mountain."

There was no straight line to follow between the rocks and the clusters of brush. Hopper didn't look back until he dropped down the side of a dry riverbed and disappeared from the view of the men who were shooting at him.

The Drifters scattered during the shooting. Their lines were broken and they spread out in all directions panicked, except for the Shamblers—the more degraded among them—who shuffled in small circles or stood in one place with no reaction to the noise. The shooter stood on top of the bus, scanning the gullies with his own set of binoculars. He took a few shots at what he thought was there. He climbed down from the roof and consulted with the others.

The sun was setting. They turned on their headlights and drove away.

Hopper had done everything the Teacher had warned him against doing.

"I trust you to do what's right and your Silent Voice will help you. Listen to him when he speaks."

He waited for the deep part of night and walked the bicycle back to the freeway, past Shamblers stumbling in the dark looking for something to eat.

There was sand on his chain and his gears slipped when he shifted. He wasted two hours walking through an outlet shopping mall, looking for a sporting-goods store and a new bicycle. The next town was five miles away. He would stay out of sight on a road parallel to the freeway. If he found a bike, in two days he'd be in Los Angeles, where he would look for his wife. If he found her and she didn't have a bicycle he would get one for her and they would ride back to Palm Springs and he could introduce her to his Teacher.

The Teacher had said it many times: "Your wife is in Los Angeles. If you want to find her, you have to go there. It won't be easy but I can help you. How long have we known each other, Hopper?" asked the Teacher. It was a question he asked often, and Hopper always had the same answer.

"Forever."

# Erin, Stripers, Seth, Seth's Silent Voice

When you are nineteen years old and pretty, every day in Center Camp is an adventure in advanced perfection. So how wrong was it for Erin to wake up angry because some rude person was banging on her door? She shouted a yawp of annoyance and then the door was open and Brin, Jobe, Helary, and Toffe—who never spoke—looked in at her. With Erin, they were Center Camp's first fivesome, and called themselves the Stripers for the white-and-red-striped stockings they took from Inventory whenever a convoy returned with them. Only last week, the sharp scouts from Inventory returned with a carton of striped socks from an overlooked Target distribution depot in San Bernardino. And while most of the socks were blue and white, instead of the preferred red and white, no one but Erin's squad was going to get any of them. Brin, always the first among equals below Erin, threw a Red Vine at Erin and said, "We're leaving for the DMV in fifteen minutes. Inventory found another eleven Drifters around Long Beach, and Chief wants them all processed today."

This would be Erin's third trip this week to the DMV—the Department of Mandatory Verification. This was sometimes called the Department of Mental Verification, or Manual Verification. Until four years ago it had been the Department of Motor Vehicles, Hollywood branch. June Moulton from the Mythology Committee, the committee's only member, said it was always a good sign when something that used to mean one thing could now mean something entirely new. She had no other examples. The heads of committee each had their own mansions in Center Camp, except for June, who shared this house with Erin, though claiming the master bedroom. Brin and Helary thought the room should be Erin's because the house had always been Erin's, not just in the new or recent now. It was where she lived with her father and mother, when she still had them.

Erin was nineteen by the old calendar, but by the only calendar that mattered she was four. In the known world, by the new calendar, four was ancient. The new calendar four-year-olds had been rehabilitated four years ago by the best doctors in the city. They had been given the kind of attention and thorough cortical stimulation—three weeks in a controlled coma—that was no longer possible since the best doctors themselves were gone and the replacements they had trained didn't understand the subtleties of the machines and drugs, or were forced to abbreviate the cure because the drugs had run out. The scale of the disaster obliged them to focus on the minimal rehab needed for the Systems Committee to continue without falling apart. Systems, the largest committee, meant Toby Tyler and her crew, the master civil engineers. They were granted the privilege of rehab even before medical specialists. There was no Medical Committee. Plus, and this isn't a small thing, no one can run a smashed rehab machine.

The daughter of privilege, born lucky, Erin's good fortune continued even when she was one of the first three hundred people in Los Angeles to be diagnosed with what was then called Seoul Syndrome

Release 3.0. The first puzzling and awful symptom hit her thirty-two hours after a long night at a karaoke bar in Koreatown. There she was, walking in a corridor at her high school, when she felt the unfamiliar awakening of her soul's recognition of God's love, and with that, galaxies of old resentments rolled out of her—memories of insults and bad grades and rejection and envy—like a movie reel unspooling into a fire, and in the empty space left by all that crap, she fell into an infinity of peace. She tried to explain this feeling to everyone around her in the school corridor, where no one ever talked about the love of God. In the school nurse's office, the first assumption was that she was high on ecstasy. But then she kept saying good-bye to memories, as she watched them take to the air like a flock of swallows leaving a disappearing barn and disappearing into a disappearing sky. She failed the basic mental status exam: time, place, count backward, who's the president. The evil of the syndrome was that the victims felt relief as NK3 swept through their brains, before wiping them out. When the area's emergency rooms compared notes after the first hundred cases, the Centers for Disease Control broadcast the description of the disease, which matched the epidemic marching through Asia. When Erin's father, the president of Warner Bros., understood what had invaded his baby girl he called UCLA hospital's chief of surgery and asked for the kind of favor typically and not covertly granted the charitable president of a studio, to put Erin at the head of the line for the first available bed in the SRC, the Syndrome Rehabilitation Center.

June Moulton was in the next bed, and after rehab, June—age not certain but probably in her midforties—kept close to the young Erin, who neither welcomed her nor pushed her away. It was possible June was her father's mistress.

June Moulton had tried to teach the mass of Drifters a story that would explain what they were doing and give them a sense of purpose that could be translated into devotion. She left out NK3 and told the story of a race of giants who built the cities and bequeathed the Gift Economy, all the food in the supermarkets and warehouses and the farms too, before they moved to a place behind the clouds.

She had trained a cadre of Inventory specialists to give lectures on the city's history, using the old churches after taking down the Christs and crosses. June hoped that giving the Drifters a history would make them loyal to an idea, and from there the Mythology Committee could elaborate a bigger story and transfer that loyalty to the First Wave directly. But like so much of the mental effort in this four-year-old world, there were gaps in logic, leaps of coherence. June believed that forgotten mythologies of the world before NK3 had done no better when the world lived on the Theft Economy.

The SRC started in a suite of three rooms in the main part of the hospital and then moved to the psychiatric ward, forcing the expulsion of all the teens in the eating disorders wing. It then moved to the floor of the basketball arena, which had room for an additional five hundred beds. Twelve weeks later, as the syndrome spread, no connections would have helped. After six months, no one remembered what Warner Bros. was, not even the president of Warner Bros. Before the senior specialists in the syndrome fell to the implacable rule of the disease, they named it NK3.

Toby Tyler and her crew of supervisors from the Los Angeles Department of Water and Power selected their best workers. Wind farm crews were put to work setting up power generation close to the city. All the phone systems were dead because they ran on central computers, but there were walkie-talkies in every film studio and the Systems crew set them up to work as far as sixty miles from Center Camp.

After two months, not even Erin's father himself could have taken a rehab bed away from a roofer who knew how to install solar panels. Rich men offered everything they owned to be saved, but without the highly specific skills that keep the world's wheels turning, the real wheels, their brains were abandoned to the mandibles of North Korea's weaponized nanobacterium. The doctors should have taken care of each other, but when they finally understood the crisis, most of them had forgotten what to do. Each freshly trained rehab specialist understood less about the process and the machinery and the tolerances than the one who came before, until finally someone with five days of training couldn't even ask for help from a doctor with twenty years of experience, because it was all forgotten. And then, so it was later told to those outside the Fence by June Moulton, the machines fell apart from so much use and no one else could be saved.

As June said, "It was not betrayal, no. The opposite. Thank them for this gift. There is no equal value." With the best intentions, the final wave of the Rehab Committee broke the machines trying to make them work. That was when the Founders showed Chief how to protect the saved from those who could not be saved. Following their instructions, Chief organized the construction of a wall of steel, concrete, bricks: anything a contractor could pull together with a rehabbed construction crew, a sixty-foot-tall barrier surrounding the range of low mountains that divided the basin of Los Angeles from the San Fernando Valley. Downtown Los Angeles was left to those not admitted to the society of the useful.

In honor of the Founders, the Playa was cleared and the statues of The Man and The Woman were erected so the Founders would never be forgotten.

Erin had photographs of her father so she knew what he looked like, but she didn't remember him. And she never had a thought about finding him—if he was alive—since he was a stranger to her. Indifference was the special cruelty of the syndrome's design. Erin's brain tossed up a few detached memories from the old days but they weren't felt as memories with an emotional connection, in the way she remembered sex with her friends the next morning. No, these fragments came in like the interference of someone else's conversation on walkie-talkies when signals were crossed on shared frequencies. She lived in the house in which she was born but didn't remember anything about it before she got sick.

She had been drilled by the leaders that her duty to honor her father was through dedication to doing something useful, but for the first two years she had been nothing more than the hub of the society of those other young orphans who were verified but had no skills to offer the community. Like everyone who was verified, since only the

First Wave was trusted with the food grown inside the Fence, she worked one day a week on the farm, where the oranges, avocados, lemons, persimmon, carrots, and lettuce grew, but Systems was in charge of the irrigation and there wasn't much for her to do there but pull out the weeds.

She wrapped an elastic band around her purple dreadlocks, put on a white ruffled skirt, striped knee socks, and cowboy boots. She crossed two Flintstones Band-Aids over her nipples and finished off the outfit with a fuzzy white vest. This is what every girl wears, but no one denies that Erin was the first.

Brin and quiet Toffe were verified university students who had forgotten their majors: math and history. They floated among whatever jobs amused them for however long. Jobe was verified but lacked an employment designation so no one was quite sure about what he had done. Helary, probably twenty-five, was a verified pharmacist, her usefulness diminished because most pharmaceuticals were past their expiration dates. The antibiotics were dead. The painkillers were unreliable. The antidepressants and antipsychotics might have been as fresh and effective as the day they were minted, but the brain damage suffered by the victims of the plague changed the synaptic switches the drugs were designed to fix. The serotonin and dopamine receptors as redesigned by the genomic-modification wizards of Pyongyang were invisible to the old remedies.

Erin was good at recognizing past social differences, a skill—if that's what it was—that no one on any of the committees (Systems, Verification, Security, Inventory, Mythology) regarded as having value until a squad from Inventory found the incomplete database of registered drivers on the computer at the Hollywood office of the Department of Motor Vehicles. The computers couldn't be moved because no one had the skill to trace the cables that linked the cameras with facial recognition software to the servers where the information was stored. The Fence's closest gate was two miles away, and the Security Committee, with Chief's concurrence, ruled that it was safer to build a strong barrier around the DMV than to expand the great Fence.

Center Camp, in the old days, had been Beverly Park, a private gated community of sixty mansions in a little valley at the top of the hills. Before the changes, the mansions cost thirty million dollars for thirty thousand square feet with ten bedrooms and fifteen bathrooms, and kitchens large enough to feed the wedding party of a billionaire's daughter. There were screening rooms and wine cellars. The wine cellar cooling systems needed too much electricity and were disconnected. The houses were assigned by rank and seniority. Chief lived in the redbrick palace on the leveled peak, the highest point over Center Camp. The view took in the long ridge that started beyond the Fence, fifteen miles to the west, at the ocean in Santa Monica. To the east, the ridge continued through Hollywood and ended a little north of downtown, at the LA Dodgers stadium and massacre site. Between the hills and the wall of the San Gabriel Mountains to the north were the Burn Zones of Encino, Van Nuys, Northridge, North Hollywood, Panorama City, and Sunland. They extended to the east, almost to Palm Springs. No one was allowed to explore the desert.

The view from Chief's terrace included all of this and more on a clear day, and most days were clear. The view to the south swept from Santa Monica south along the coast to Long Beach, forty miles away. The next controlled Burn Zone outside the Fence was still being prepared: from the USC campus to West Adams, Crenshaw, the Byzantine District, La Brea, the lower parts of Baldwin Hills, and Culver City. South of that was LAX, the airport. Chief had waited three years to attack the airport and after the coming Burn, he was sure he could face the airport's guns and, in a fast enough strike, keep the LAX crew from destroying the remaining twenty-three jets parked on flat tires around the terminals.

The van left through the Fence's East Gate into Hollywood, now mostly abandoned, bulldozed, and burned. Two blocks from the DMV, Erin waved at the shambling Driftette with the typically flattened expression who shook a broom to greet every vehicle going past the Honda dealership, which was now the DMV motor pool garage. The

Driftette had been the motor pool mascot for a few months, and Erin, usually indifferent to Driftettes but tickled by the mascot's dull-eyed enthusiasm, always waved back at her.

Then they arrived at the old Department of Motor Vehicles, a broad parking lot now surrounded by a cinder-block wall inside double chain-link fences wrapped with razor wire. They stopped beside the *Christina*, a sixty-five-foot wooden cabin cruiser built around a truck chassis. The stern of the boat carried a message: **THANK YOU FOUNDERS FOR THIS GIFT**.

The Inventory bus with the day's Drifters still inside waited for the DMV to open. Erin and her friends entered through the back door and she took her seat behind the registration counter with its computer terminal and camera. Brin and Jobe took their seats along the same counter. Quiet Toffe sat behind Jobe. There were only nine men and two women on the day's assignment sheet. They'd been picked up twenty-five miles from downtown, living together in the same house. The area had already been swept for Drifters, so they had either been overlooked, or had grazed their way up the coast from San Diego.

The Drifters were presented as they'd been found, not washed or shaved, in the clothes they'd been wearing.

Erin's first intake was like her second and third intakes, slow to answer the questions: Do you know your name? What's your first memory? Do you know where you are? And so on. Their pictures were taken, uploaded into the system, and if there was no match in the database, they were sent to live downtown, where they were fed and housed for as long as Systems or Inventory needed help. And then? The desert.

Erin's fourth intake was a man in short khaki pants and a T-shirt from a surf shop in Santa Monica. He was sunburnt, with long matted curls of light brown hair streaked with gold highlights. Erin saw Toffe look over at him with an expression that said she would kill, kill for those highlights. He might have been a surfer at one time, but a T-shirt was proof of nothing.

Like most Drifters, he needed to be told to sit.

"We go to the same barber," said Erin, shaking her dreadlocks. He didn't respond. Of course not.

She told him not to move while she took his picture and uploaded the photograph. He didn't ask anything about what she was doing or where he was.

"I'm Erin," she said. No answer. Few Drifters talk to each other and some of the newcomers had not spoken full sentences in four years.

"Do you know where you are?"

"They didn't tell me."

"Who didn't tell you?"

"Them. The people. The man in the bus."

"The bus driver?"

"Yes."

"He didn't tell you where you are?"

"No."

"Where were you yesterday?"

"The place. The house. Yes?"

"Are you asking me if I know where you were yesterday?"

"I don't know."

"There's no right answer. There's no wrong answer. Tell me about your T-shirt. Where did you get it?"

"A place."

"Did you ever surf?"

"What?"

"Did you ever go in the ocean and ride that board on the waves, and stand up?" Breaking the rule forbidding all but minimal physical contact, she poked the surfboard on the T-shirt.

"Is that me?" He touched the man on the board.

"It could be," said Erin. "What's your first memory?"

"I was walking this morning when the bus stopped and the people told me to get inside."

"That's your first memory today, but what's your first memory ever? What do you remember from when you were a little boy?"

He had no answer. She asked him to turn his face from one side to the other. He hesitated, and rolled his eyes to one side, looking over his shoulder without turning around.

"Do you have a Silent Voice?"

"What's that?" He said this without asking his Silent Voice how to answer her question.

"No one is sure exactly, but some people who were given short turns in rehab hear a voice that doesn't go away. No one understands more about it than that. Do you hear someone guiding you?"

"No."

His Silent Voice commended him: "Good answer."

"Silent Voices tend to tell their hosts to lie about everything. I'm in the First Wave, first of the First as we say, so I don't have one, but I have friends who do. It happens even to late First Wavers. No worries. You look pretty well fed. Where did you eat?"

"In a big building."

"I bet," she said, but not really listening to him because the computer had found a match.

This was always a moment that demanded caution. Erin tossed this question to him without putting emphasis on its importance. "Does the name Seth Kaplan mean anything to you?" she asked.

"No."

"One Forty-Eight South Windsor Boulevard, does that address mean anything to you?"

"I don't think so."

"You don't think so or you don't know?"

"I don't know."

"October seventeenth, nineteen eighty? Does that sound familiar?"

"No."

"You used to wear glasses. Do you know what happened to them?"

"No."

"MD. Do you know what that stands for?"

"Stands for?"

"Let me explain what's happening. My computer links to a database that belonged to the California Department of Motor Vehicles. It uses facial recognition software to find matches to the pictures we take here. It just found a match to your picture, proving that you are Seth Kaplan, MD. This could be good for you, but my supervisor has to look at this before we can be sure."

Erin called to Toffe to get ElderGoth, the head of the Verification Committee. She was the only committee head to live outside the Fence, but she'd been a computer technician before everything happened and Chief wanted her to stay at the DMV, on the chance that if the verification computer broke, she'd know how to fix it. ElderGoth spent most of her time in an Airstream trailer attached to the building. She came out, her corset loose over a tired black velvet dress, and she wasn't wearing her usual uniform of fishnet stockings and the angel wings made of crow's feathers stapled to an elastic harness around her shoulders. Erin had never seen ElderGoth without the black wings, and the committee head apologized before Erin asked why she was so informal today. "My three best dresses are all tearing at the seams like they were following a schedule. Vayler Monokeefe says Inventory has already gone through every vintage clothing store between here and wherever. My wings are falling off the thing that holds them together and there's nothing left for me to wear, unless I want to wear stuff that's new and you can imagine what I said to him. I don't believe they search hard enough, and this is not how to treat a committee head. What do you have here?" She looked at the Drifter and then at the photograph of Seth Kaplan, MD.

"Hold his hair away from his face." ElderGoth looked into his eyes and back to the picture on the monitor. "Good work, Erin."

ElderGoth took Seth's hands in hers. "Dr. Kaplan, I'm ElderGoth, head of the Verification Committee, and I want to welcome you. Because your face matches up with the system, and you have a skill that we need, you are now going to join the community of other verified people as though you were First Wave from the beginning. You will no longer have to sleep in cold houses and eat whatever you can scavenge from supermarkets and grocery warehouses. You will no longer have to run from packs of coyotes and wild dogs. No predators are ever again going to steal things from you or hurt you or do things to your body that you don't like. The Founders have left us with food for many years. Only Inventory knows for sure but it's somewhere between twenty and a thousand years. So instead of being what was once a Productive Economy, we are now, instead, in replacement, a Gift Economy. We give freely to each other expecting nothing in return. What you need you get and because of this, you are no longer greedy. How's that?"

"How's what?" asked Seth. "You said a lot of things. Which one of the things you said is the thing you said is 'that'?"

"The community is going to do everything it can to help restore your old skills. How does that sound, Dr. Seth Kaplan?"

His Silent Voice said, "You don't know yet."

He didn't answer. Erin said, "He's happy. I can tell. Thank the Founders! You're here!"

"I'm here."

"Yes," said Erin. "There's one more thing we have to do."

ElderGoth left for a minute and she returned with a metal rod, about two feet long, in one hand, and a butane torch in the other. She used the flame to heat the end of the rod.

Erin and Jobe grabbed the doctor's left arm and pressed it onto a table. Before he had the time to ask his Silent Voice what was happening, ElderGoth pressed the hot end of the rod into the inside of his left wrist. He cried out.

"It heals fast," said ElderGoth. Before Erin wrapped the burn in gauze, Seth saw the mark:

∴

# Marci, Eckmann, AutoZone, Tesla, Carrera

Two blocks from the DMV, the motor pool mascot swept the garage floor. She found two washers and a bolt and put them in the right containers on the tool bench. She almost never found anything small on the floor, because AutoZone kept the shop organized and had trained Carrera and Tesla not to get sloppy. But neither of his assistants wanted to sweep. The motor pool crew called her Hey You. Carrera wanted to name her Hey Stupid and Tesla thought Suck Me might be funny, but AutoZone disagreed. "If we give her a joke name and she ever figures out we're making fun of her, she might leave. And she sweeps up better than either of you. Or me. She answers to Hey You, so that's what we'll call her." AutoZone ran the motor pool. The decision was final.

Hey You picked up a flat-head screw and then got back down on her knees and pretended to feel for more in the shadow under a workbench where she used the screw to scratch off a line marking the ninety-seventh day she had been at the garage pretending to be stupid. Her real name was Marci, although no one had called her that in ninety-seven days, and ninety-seven was a guess. She might have scratched the same day twice, and she was sure she'd missed it a few times.

Eckmann and his crew of sixty had worked for four years to keep the Boeing 787 Dreamliner from Singapore Airlines ready to fly, lacking only a pilot who knew the plane. The Dreamliner in the hangar was the only functional plane at LAX. The twenty-eight planes still parked at the terminals would never fly again. The last planes to escape flew off over three years ago and even if they had landed safely somewhere, there was no way to let anyone know, or, as Eckmann said, no reason.

Then the Canadian showed up at the perimeter, in uniform, with airline identification. He hadn't sought verification at the DMV but said he wanted to fly away. Eckmann trusted that with enough time in the cockpit, the Canadian's skills would return, but he couldn't make sense of the cockpit no matter how many hours he sat in the pilot's seat and finally Eckmann gave up forcing him to try. Eckmann threw the Canadian off the hangar roof. With no pilot or prospect of escape, the hangar crew was afraid that Center Camp would send a raiding party, but Eckmann promised them that Chief knew Eckmann would blow up the Dreamliner before he surrendered. In the days of chaos, a battalion of national guardsmen had surrounded the airport with land mines and rockets—in the interest of national security—to keep anyone from hijacking a jet. Then the national guardsmen, without authorization, took two jets and left the airport to Eckmann.

Marci had been a flight attendant for United Airlines, based in Atlanta, and was on turnaround at the airport the day the first infected plane came in from Seoul. She joined the community of the hangar, sweeping up the floor.

After killing the Canadian, Eckmann told Marci to meet him on the runway when it was dark. "This isn't for sex."

Marci found him on a blanket in the middle of the long runway that only needed to be swept of debris to be ready for the jet to take off. Eckmann offered Marci a small bottle of Absolut Vodka. There weren't too many of those left and he never offered the Absolut except to reward someone for a great contribution to the community. Marci wasn't sure of what she'd done to deserve this. He was in one of those moods, she knew, in which it was better to let him speak instead of asking him questions. He told her to lie down and open her arms.

She expected a kiss, or more, but nothing followed. "Now look up at the sky and pretend you're looking down. And instead of thinking that you're held in place by whatever keeps us on the ground, you're about to fall off the ceiling and you're going to keep falling."

"I can do the part where it feels like I'm looking down, but not the part where I feel like I can fall."

"I always feel like I'm ready to fall."

"You knew Chief," she said. "Didn't you?"

"A little."

"Tell me about him."

"I haven't talked to him in four years. He wanted control. He wanted me to work for him."

"Why didn't you do that?"

"I have my team. He has his. He'd let me get the plane ready and then he'd kill me. For sure if he knew he could fly out of here, he'd handpick the best people in the Systems Committee, who could fix and run the machinery wherever they landed, and it wouldn't take long for everything here to turn back to desert. That Canadian wasted our time. He didn't want to do the work. He wanted to read the flight manuals, but reading the manuals isn't enough. Good ideas come slowly these days, Marci. And now I have a good idea."

She waited for the idea while he opened another small bottle of Absolut.

"I want you to go to the DMV motor pool, pretend you're a Driftette, work for them, and wait until a pilot is verified."

"Why me?"

"You're good at sweeping up. You'll be doing a lot of that."

"For how long?"

"I don't know. If a pilot does get verified, we have to grab him before he's taken behind the Fence. Once Chief has a pilot, he'll find a way to attack us and win."

"If they attack us, we'll just blow up the plane. Won't we?"

"We'd like Chief to think so. But if Chief gets a pilot, he can sit with him until we run out of food. We have enough for a year, maybe a little more. The Fence has food and supplies to last twenty lifetimes, forever."

Marci tried to feel the difference between a year and forever. "How do you know a pilot is going to get verified?"

"I don't."

"How will I find out working in the motor pool?"

"I can't get you any closer to the DMV and I can't get you into Center Camp. The DMV sends the verified to the Playa on the *Christina* and the driver comes from the motor pool. It'll be news. We'll set you up with radios and we'll always have a team nearby."

"I don't know how to be a Driftette. What do I have to do?"

"The weakness of the First Wave is that they're lazy about cleaning up after themselves and they're always happy to let someone else sweep up around them. Be eccentric in your work and endearing in your manner. Dance a jig to music only you can hear. Make them laugh at the way you move but don't let them see you connect the laughter to the gesture. Don't talk more than the chattiest Drifters, and don't be noticeably better at your work than the most competent Drifters around you and not at all better than any Second Wavers. Make yourself wanted by helping and not asking for anything. Amuse the First Wavers. Come and go at random times. Make them happy to see you again. Be their dog. Be their little puppy dog who likes to run away sometimes."

"Do puppies run away?"

"I saw it in a movie."

"This could take a long time."

He pointed to the sky. "One of those lights is a space station. There are six men and a woman in there, from America and Russia. After communications stopped with Houston and Russia that first November, they watched the lights of the cities go out. They watched planes crash and boats sink, saw the fires and the oil slicks spread over oceans. They had enough food and water to last eight more months and might have starved to death but after Earth's second silent month, one of them opened an airlock while the others were sleeping. We're in a space station here and we have to get away. I don't want to live in a world ruled by the First Wave."

"How do you know it's going to be different anywhere else?"

"Will you do the job or not, Marci?"

She didn't answer, distracted by the dead astronauts in the tomb of the space station, forgotten by the people who put them there.

"How do you know how the astronauts died?"

"That's a good question. That's why you're right for the job."

"But how do you know they died like you say if they couldn't talk to anyone on Earth?"

"It's what I would have done."

"Why did this have to wait until dark to tell me?"

"You're a Drifter now. Drifters don't ask questions."

Eckmann led Marci through the minefield the next night. She went downtown first, where she slipped into the crowds of Second Wavers and Drifters who were always out until dawn, and from there walked to Hollywood and the DMV.

When the motor pool crew arrived in the morning, they saw nothing special about the quiet Driftette in the hooded parka with the fake wolf-tail trim, sweeping the sidewalk with a broom.

After ten days of this, AutoZone missed her when she disappeared and was happy to see her when she showed up again. Marci came in early each day because she liked having the company. She let Carrera teach her how to pick up the metal parts that rolled on the garage floor. She jumped from one foot to the other, attempting a broken rhythm, her idea of what she thought Eckmann meant by a jig.

So it was on the ninety-eighth day, by Marci's markings—not by what was strictly accurate—that Seth Kaplan was verified. AutoZone took the call from Erin. "Fire up the *Christina*. They just verified a doctor."

"It's my turn," said Carrera, grabbing the white cap with the braided gold anchors above the black brim. He put on the admiral's jacket from the Paramount costume department.

# Seth, Dr. Piperno, Erin, Carrera

Carrera narrated as he steered. "The *Christina* is sixty-five feet long, and we are twenty-five feet above the road. It was made of wood in 1965 and was a pleasure craft cruising the Santa Monica Bay. I control it from where we are, which is called the bridge, just the way the owners of the craft controlled her on the water. The Founders brought her to the Playa and left her to us on the truck chassis."

"Dr. Kaplan was a surfer," said Erin. "That's what his T-shirt says."

Seth wanted his Silent Voice to tell him what to do, but the Voice was quiet.

"There's the Fence now," said Carrera as the boat turned a corner. "It changes color in different light. What color would you say it is today, Doctor?"

"I don't know."

"I couldn't tell you either." Carrera pushed a button on the control panel and the air was filled with the sound of three high notes in anxious harmony.

"You don't have to do that," said Erin. "It scares the newbies." She explained to Kaplan: "Newbies are new. You're a newbie. Did he scare you?"

Seth's Silent Voice woke up. "What was that?"

"What is that?" Seth asked Carrera.

"They called it a foghorn. And we call this the Fence, but it's really a wall, isn't it? Calling it the Wall, though, Chief says makes it sound too important. But look at it. A thousand miles around, ten thousand feet high, steel plates, cinder block, and reinforced concrete and protected from attack by poisoned electricity. What happened to the builders, you ask?"

"He didn't ask," said Erin. "And I think your numbers are wrong."

"Do you know the right numbers?" asked Carrera. "I don't think you do. June Moulton, Mythology Committee, introduce yourself, fascinating woman, she tells us to tell the Drifters that the Wall, or Fence, what have you, was built by whoever built the world. I say, 'Why isn't the Fence in any of the old pictures?' And June says it was painted out. This is my way of saying, the Mythology Committee isn't to be trusted, and you can quote me on that. It's like the numbers that Erin here says aren't real. Doctor, the truth is nobody knows."

"June says we need the Fence if we're going to hide the life inside from the eyes of the world."

Carrera took his hands from the wheel to applaud himself. "Erin is making my point for me, Doctor. June is just spreading this story for the benefit of the Drifters who aren't verified. She doesn't know who built it and we don't know. We're telling you this because you're one of us now, Doctor. Welcome to the East Gate. Life here is beautiful and you'll be an important part of it."

Carrera called out: "New doctor!" to the guards in the gun towers. The steel gate rolled sideways, Security let them pass, and the gate closed behind them.

They entered the Fence to the cheers of the Gatekeepers, Systems Committee members without assignment, Inventory Committee members back from search-and-collect convoys, and Security Committee members home from patrolling Figueroa. Systems usually wore their utility kilts, heavy brown cloth with deep pockets for tools and a few cans of beer, and the Inventory members usually wore the newest clothes because they were first to find them. This was the crowd that liked to gather around the gate and offer their cheers to the newbies, for fun and also to make fun of the idea of fun. Most were on bicycles, and as the boat parted them—as it once parted the waves—the gatekeepers biked alongside.

"Welcome home," said Erin. "Let me give you a Center Camp hug." She wrapped her arms around his back and put her feet between his and pressed her face into his chest, an embrace due a returning hero long thought dead. "You're home now. It takes a while to see the differences between what's out there and life in here. And I don't think a Drifter would understand them so I won't give you a headache by trying. We're on our way to the hospital at the University of California in Los Angeles, which is also called UkLa, which is spelled U-C-L-A, which is on walls and T-shirts and bumper stickers all over California. The area we're in now used to be a city called West Hollywood. The next city is Beverly Hills and after that is Westwood. But just before Westwood is the Playa. It used to be called the Los Angeles Country Club. It was a golf course and now the trees and grass are gone and it's an open field and in the center are The Man and The Woman. Drifters don't have anything like it."

"What man and woman?" asked Seth.

Carrera hit the foghorn button for a short blast. "He doesn't know about The Man and Woman, Erin. You see?"

Erin wasn't sure what she was supposed to see.

The *Christina* continued down the streets, where houses and smaller buildings had been torn down or the windows to the fifth floors had been sealed with cinder block.

They passed Barneys and Saks and Neiman Marcus, the old department stores—now empty, but kept open as party halls. And at the other end of Beverly Hills, Seth saw the head of The Man above a line of trees, and then as the boat drove past the trees to the cleared golf course, he saw the whole Man and, beside him, The Woman.

Seth touched the brand on his arm. Erin saw this. "That's right, it's the same thing, except he's six stories tall," said Erin. "And she's just a little shorter."

The Man was made of stainless steel, with unarticulated legs that anchored in the ground and arms raised overhead as though he was cheering. A staircase wound around his left leg, or the leg to the left of Seth, because The Man was the same on both sides; his face was a featureless oval. The stairs went into The Man's trunk, and then rose to a platform inside his chest. The Woman, beside him, was almost as tall, made of metal mesh, and, unlike the stiff Man, she was realistic, naked, and balanced on one foot, arms lifted in the posture of someone dancing alone, unwatched, and free. There was a door in her standing leg and small handholds leading to a viewing chamber in her head.

His Silent Voice said, "I've never seen that."

The bicycle escort left the *Christina* and rode onto the Playa. The riders left their bikes and joined the crowd around the base of The Man and Woman, First Wavers walking slowly, some bowing toward the statues, stiffly from the waist, palms pressed together in front of their chests.

"The Founders left The Man and The Woman for us," said Carrera. "June says no one could have built them without help from outer space. There's things she says that are wrong, but I believe she knows what she's talking about when it comes to The Man and Woman. And look, at the foot of The Man, isn't that Chief?"

"I think it is," said Erin. "You're nothing but lucky, Dr. Kaplan. Most newbies don't see Chief the first time they see The Man and The Woman."

Carrera said, "With Chief there, we can't stay. You see, everyone is outside the circle now."

"Circle?" asked Seth.

"When Chief visits The Man, everyone has to give him room."

Carrera and Erin were quiet after passing the Playa and in a few minutes the *Christina* pulled up to the emergency room of the hospital at UCLA.

"This is where you get off, Doctor," said Erin. "I may not see you for a while. You'll be busy with Dr. Piperno."

"Who?"

"Him." Erin pointed to the man at the entrance to the building. He had a long beard, mostly gray, and he wore a white coat and three stethoscopes around his neck.

Seth climbed the ladder to the ground and with a blast of the foghorn, the *Christina* backed up, turned around, and went wherever it was going.

# The Woman, The Man, Chief

Chief waited on the Playa until the sun set. He liked to wear his brown kilt when he visited The Man. Chief didn't carry tools and he didn't like beer, but to dress like a Systems worker was to look competent. He wanted to look competent for The Man. Before he approached The Man for help, he called for the Lamplighter Guild, who lived by themselves in tents on the far north side of the Playa. Their faces shaded by the deep hoods of their robes; they walked in double file carrying torches. They touched their flame to the oil lamps atop the tall poles that defined the perimeter. When they finished, they returned to their tents, and Chief talked to The Man. "I'm not sleeping well. Something is wrong. I can feel it. What do you think it is? I don't expect an answer right away but it's good to ask the question. It's good to hear myself ask a question I'd be afraid to answer if someone else asked me the same thing. People are watching me now. They wonder what I'm doing here. I thought of clearing the Playa so there would just be me and you and The Woman, but I'm afraid I would look desperate, and I'm afraid of enough things without adding new fears. Nobody knows what I know. And I'm not sure I do, either."

He felt The Woman trying to tell him about The Man, about something The Man didn't know. So it felt to him, and he wasn't sure but he had to trust in something.

*The disorder cannot last.*

That's good.

*Not for you. She is not safe.*

Who? Pippi?

*She is not safe.*

But I'm just talking to myself now, aren't I? I'm saying what I want to hear.

*Is this what you want to hear? How long could you get away with it?*
Away with what?
*Have you forgotten? Ask the mythologist. What is intuition?*
The organization of deduction from random evidence.
*Subconscious recognition of what is not recognized.*
Someone is coming. For Pippi or for me?

# Dr. Kaplan, Dr. Piperno

The man in the white coat introduced himself. "I'm Dr. Paolo Piperno, director of medicine here at UCLA Medical Center. How are you today?"

"Today?"

"Do you understand where you are?"

"No."

"Is your Silent Voice telling you not to answer my questions?"

"Silent Voice?"

"The alienated echo of who you were, reinvented by what remains of the circuitry of context. You were a whole man once, just as I was a whole man once. We were doctors, men of subtle skills developed over years of training."

"I don't understand."

"Do you think I do? NK3, North Korea 3, following the failures of North Korea 1 and North Korea 2? Never heard of them?"

"I don't think so, no."

"Well someone gave you a solid jolt or three on the rehab table. Otherwise you wouldn't be here with your Silent Voice, Dr. Kaplan."

"I'm a doctor? I don't understand."

"Who understands anything anymore? I can tell you that I know certain things but can I tell you that I understand them? Of course not. Some of us have Silent Voices that scream; some of us have Silent Voices that mostly keep to themselves. We have a saying in Center Camp: the earlier the rehab, the quieter the Silent Voice. Of course that's not much of a saying, not like: employees must wash their hands, or objects in mirror are closer than they appear. Generally, after we've been awhile in Center Camp, the Voice goes away. Theories why? Something to do with trust or exhaustion. Theory mine? Something to do with the way a plant dies if you don't give it water. The Silent Voices fade away after they've spent some time in Center Camp, because they get tired of being ignored. I'll just talk to you and if your Silent Voice has something to say, I'd appreciate your sharing it."

Piperno watched as Kaplan's eyes changed their focus from the room around them to something inside his head.

"He wants to know where we are," said Kaplan, surprised that his Silent Voice would give permission to speak for him.

"Excellent question. I'll start more slowly. Slower. Slowlier. This is the UCLA Medical Center. It was a great hospital, with thousands of doctors and millions of patients. Now there are only twelve of us: twelve doctors, with fifteen nurses. We're not what we were. The medicines are mostly past their due date. We don't know how to run a lot of the equipment. Most of the information that might be useful to us is on the computers. Most of the computers are working, but all of the computers require passwords and all of the passwords have been lost or forgotten. We hope that with your help, we will be able to get around the loss of data, Dr. Seth Kaplan. Do you know what kind of doctor you were?"

"No, I don't."

"A very important doctor. A pediatric oncologist. That's children with cancer, by the way. We looked you up. Here's the big surprise. You worked here. Apparently, I knew you. Yes. There's a picture of the staff and you're in it. And so am I! And your office was here. I'll show you. Let's go."

On the way, Piperno asked, "Do you understand the Gift Economy?"

"There's food for everyone. Forever!"

"They say it's a gift from the Founders, but I've seen some numbers here, the number of dead. I think maybe we're eating their food."

"Whose food?"

"The food of the dead! Massive fortresses with things to eat and wear, who was it set there for but the dead who once lived here. It's my theory and I tried my theory on June Moulton. She said I was contradicting the myth. I persisted; she said I was crazy. Two things can be true, do you know?"

Seth's office was in the medical school building. On the desk and wall were pictures of a man with a woman and two children, a woman and one baby, a woman with a baby and another child.

Piperno pointed to the man in each picture. "That's you, that's you, that's you. And those aren't different children. They're the same children, growing up, and that was your wife. She changed her hair color. We still do. My beard, you think it's black."

"It's gray."

"And so it is, today. Like your wife's hair."

"Where is she?"

"We have a saying: what the Fence forgets, no one remembers."

Piperno touched Seth's diplomas. "Can you read these?"

Seth's Silent Voice told him not to answer.

"That's fine," said Piperno. "Not important yet. But you went to the University of California at Berkeley, then medical school at the University of Vermont, and then you came back here, back home to California, for a fellowship in pediatric oncology— as I said, that's children with cancer—and never left. So you're not just a visitor to the Fence. You are one of those rare people, like me, who are of the Fence, too. It shouldn't be surprising, since the people left alive in Los Angeles were already living here, but so many things surprise us these days."

"What's cancer?" asked Seth.

"You can look it up later. Something about the wrong kind of cell things. Truthfully, I'm not exactly sure myself, but treating children with cancer is not a useful specialty now and may not be again for many years to come. Not many children, if you know what I mean. I was a heart surgeon, one of the best in the country, and I was lucky enough to be here at UCLA, in a position of power, when the damn North Koreans overdid their thing. So I got as thorough a rehab as anyone, and still, I don't have a memory. You had a very partial rehab; otherwise you'd be dead of course. Or a mindless Shambler. However, you're reasonably alive and you're here and let's keep it that way. How does that sound?"

"I'm a doctor?" The question was put to his Silent Voice, but Piperno took it as an insult directed his way, suggesting that Kaplan's Silent Voice doubted Piperno's credentials. "What does a doctor do?"

"Don't worry. We have videos. I'll watch them with you. We can start now. Why not?"

Seth's Silent Voice explained, "He asks questions but he's not expecting answers."

Piperno led Seth through the hospital corridors. They passed a room with an old man in a bed and a woman standing beside him. She had a hand around his wrist and she was looking at the wall clock. She wore tight leather pants and a leather vest with nothing underneath, a version of Erin's style.

Piperno introduced her to Seth. "Sarabeth, this is our new doctor, Dr. Kaplan." She nodded but said nothing until the second hand on the clock was at twelve.

"I was just taking his pulse. Thirty-eight. Blood pressure is low."

Piperno explained. "He's our best dentist but he's dying. We only have three more. We don't know the problem. Maybe it's cancer. You want a look? Probably better not. Thank you, Sarabeth."

They passed another five rooms with nurses tending patients. "You see all that medical equipment. Heart monitors, oxygen monitors, brain-activity monitors, blood pressure, we've got the best machinery ever made, but none of us are all that comfortable trying to make this stuff work and the manuals are confusing."

Seth thought about the place where he'd been found. It was when, yesterday? His Silent Voice said, "Always ask if you need to know."

They settled into a small classroom. The seats had writing tables that folded away, but two tables were set with food. "You must be hungry," said Piperno. "The Center Camp food isn't what you're used to, because you haven't had a Vayler Monokeefe and his Inventory Committee looking out for what you eat. We'll have a fresh salad of avocado and grapefruit, and spaghetti with a fresh tomato sauce. A far cry from making your way through the canned food at whatever Costco you suckled at. We all work a day on the farm here, and of course we trade with the farmers in the Central Valley. All in good time to explain."

Seth lost track of Piperno's words as he looked at a whiteboard with the drawing of a spiked ball cut away to show its internal structure of layers and squiggles. The spikes were labeled: NEURAMINIDASE, HEMAGGLUTIN, M2 ION CHANNEL, LIPID BILAYER, NANOCULES, and HORMONIRUPTORS.

"That's NK3, or a drawing of it," said the older doctor. "I don't know who drew it and it doesn't help us, but there it is, what they knew of it. We were just starting to talk about it. Why NK3 you asked?"

"I did?" Seth wasn't sure he'd heard himself ask anything.

"We know all this from the newspapers left to us by doctors who are probably out there drifting now, poor bastards. NK1 and NK2 were savage drugs with short lives, and not contagious. NK3 targeted the deepest links between genetics and sociology to create the new man to be ruled from Pyongyang. That's the capital city of North Korea. Language retained, check. Literacy, under limited circumstances, check. Connection to family, uncheck. Ability to care for children, uncheck, but not necessary because the children weren't going to survive. NK3 targeted the markers for hormones that don't get released until adolescence, and without those markers, most of the children died. As for more children: fertility, sabotaged. Follow the leader confused. Violent tendencies, uncheck. Without rehab, the people of the world wandered into starvation. There's a hint in this outline that the scientists who created this had designed a way to protect themselves, but if they did, it was only for them. So there may be a few thousand North Koreans with full immunity, with full memory. Completes, we call them. But they haven't shown up yet. The problem was that NK1 and NK2 were short-lived and NK3 was supposed to be short-lived, but, well, they made a mistake in the formula. That's the best explanation for what went wrong. So what was supposed to be a limited attack on South Korea— Excuse me, Dr. Kaplan, but are you listening?"

"No."

"Then let's get back to medicine."

Seth asked his Silent Voice to explain now, but there was no answer.

"While we eat we're going to look at some videos, Dr. Kaplan. They're not a substitution for the real thing, and we'll be getting to that soon enough." Piperno weighted his tone with the looming insinuation that everything from now on was a test.

In the first video, hands in pale blue latex gloves held knives that cut through isolated squares of skin framed by cloth and stained brown with disinfectant. Other hands in gloves joined to assist and the hole in the body was spread apart and held open by steel clamps as the knife probed more deeply into the bleeding wound.

"Bring anything back, Dr. Kaplan?"

"From where?" asked Seth.

"That's not the answer I was looking for, Dr. Kaplan. Let me explain. That's one sick appendix. I've done a few of these myself; the video is very helpful. Let's switch to this one. Here's an open heart." The next video showed a masked surgeon using an electric saw to cut through ribs and expose a beating heart. "Do you recognize the eyebrows above the mask? That's me doing the operation! This was my patient. I recorded this video because I was so important that when I changed the way an operation was done, the hospital sent the video to every open-heart surgeon in the world. That white stuff is fat," said Piperno. "I don't actually remember this, of course, but I have to say I'm impressed by my skills. This is a quadruple bypass. We haven't done one yet, but it could be that you'll get the honor if Chief thinks you're ready."

Seth put his right hand over his own heart, as he understood
the connection between the heart on the screen and the thing inside
him that he felt thumping all the time, the thing that thumped harder
when he was running or scared.

Piperno said, "Yes, you have one of those. We all have one. One
each. The heart. Didn't you ever wonder what was beating inside
there?"

"No."

"Now you will. This is your first lesson in anatomy."

They watched more operations: the amputation of an arm man-
gled in a motorcycle crash, a hip replacement, two more appendec-
tomies, a caesarian section.

"That's a baby," said Piperno, with confidence.

When Seth's right hand twitched in sympathy with the movement of the scalpel in the video of an operation on a cancerous lung,
Piperno grabbed his wrist.

"Do you see that?" he said. "Your hand, do you see the way it's
moving? It was moving while you were watching the operation. That's
a great sign, a powerful sign that you're going to do fine, that you're
going to pass the test, that you're going to do more than live, that
you'll thrive, that you're going to be a real doctor."

"Do I have to do those things? Do I have to cut people open?"

"That's what we're here for. Yes, you'll have to do the doctory
things that doctors do."

"I was a doctor?"

"I don't expect you to remember. None of us do, but I can still
perform operations because of the doctors who took care of me."

"Where are they?" asked Seth.

Piperno sighed. "If they're alive, they're in the same kind of place
you were when the Inventory people found you, drifting with the
Drifters and unverifiable because they're not in the database. Sad, sad,
sad. When it came time for them to be given the rehab, something
happened. It was too late; it didn't work. But that's all past. Let me
show you where you'll be sleeping."

Seth followed his new mentor through the hospital to the surgery ward, where Piperno turned on the lights in a large operating room. Trays in the middle of the room, under bright lights, surrounded a hospital bed with surgical knives and clamps, an electrocardiogram machine, an oxygen monitor—everything needed to keep a patient alive during a long operation.

"We set this room up for you."

"This is where they cut people," said Seth.

"Very good. Yes, this is an operating room. We'll show you more videos and help you read the books. Do you remember how to read?"

"Read?" Seth didn't know if the answer should be yes or no. Piperno pointed to a label on the wall.

"What does that say?"

"It's not saying anything." Seth lied. The label said "oxygen."

"It'd help if you could read, but we'll do what we can with the videos. Until you pass the tests, you'll sleep here to absorb the vibrations of the room, to bring back the feeling of your training by setting you in the place of your work."

"I'm supposed to become a doctor by sleeping in an operating room?"

"Do you know a better way?"

# Hopper

In a small dead city called Redlands, Hopper found a bike store across from a park. The front door and window were behind a metal gate locked with a chain and padlock. The back door was steel and flush to the wall and needed two keys. The batteries in all the cars on the street were dead so he couldn't drive through the gate or pull it away with a rope. He needed a tool to break the lock. He couldn't picture it, but he thought if he rode his bike around the town, the thing he needed would appear to him. His Silent Voice would tell him, when he found it: "This will do what you want it to do." He stopped at a looted hardware store, but there was nothing left for him to use. From there he rode into a neighborhood of small houses, with no direction from his Silent Voice, until he passed REDLANDS HIGH SCHOOL, a central building three stories tall between two low wings, behind a chain-link fence. The football field was now a nursery for tumbleweed except for the green circles around two manual water pumps. The front row of the home team football bleachers was obscured by rows of blue and white plastic outhouses. If they stank, the light breeze moving the shreds of the flag on the school's tall pole carried the smell away. There were children looking down at him from a second-floor class-room. He'd seen a few children in Palm Springs. Children were weak.

He locked his bicycle to the bike stand by the school's front door.

He waited for the children to come to him.

The children stayed in the classroom.

He looked back up at them for a few minutes and then took a Kind power bar, chocolate and coconut, out of his pack and ate it.

His Silent Voice spoke to him: "You're already a day behind schedule. Your Teacher expected you to be fifty miles down the road by now. Don't waste your time here. Find the tool someplace else. Get moving."

He knocked on the front door of the school. The light of three candles came from down the corridor, with a child behind each point of fire.

Hopper asked them: "Are there any older people with you?"

They didn't answer.

"How many are you?"

No answer, although one imitated the sound of the question the way he might have hummed or whistled a melody he had just heard for the first time.

"My name is Hopper."

A child, in the darkness, said, "Hah-puh."

Others repeated, "Hah-puh. Hah-puh HappoHah-poo."

"No, Hopper. Hopper."

"No. Hah-puh. Hah-puh."

He asked, "Who are you?" None of them could explain who they were or why they were there instead of someplace else.

Some of them smiled. Two boys pushed each other and laughed at the struggle. Others argued with the two boys, but not with words, only a few grunts and whistles. They sounded more like coyotes than children.

They blew out their candles and pulled Hopper by both hands, while some pushed him from behind. They walked him into the school's small gymnasium, large enough for a basketball court and bleachers on both sides. No candles here, either, but they pulled him to feel the hospital beds and smashed rehab machines in the middle of the room. He recognized the electrodes and the restraints.

The feeding tubes were crusty at the end. His Silent Voice spoke impatiently, returning from an awkward moment of reflection. "What are you doing here? You have a goal. You have a goal and you have forgotten the plan."

There were few children anymore between the ages of two and twenty. Rehab shocks killed the youngest and after the first month of the plague, the rehab process—two weeks in an induced coma during the neurocortical stim—was reserved only for adults who could do real things. Most children died.

They led him out of the gym into the locker room. They guided him cautiously not to trip over benches, not to bump into the sharp rusting edge of a metal locker door.

They walked him into the echoing tiled space. He felt along the walls, spigots, showerheads. He wanted to leave them and return to the road, but they took each arm at the wrist and pushed his legs from behind until he was kneeling on the hard floor, and at the same time they grabbed his hands from the other side and pulled him forward. As he spread his fingers to catch himself on the floor, he felt a body. He was pushed and pulled too far forward to stand up straight and his left hand pressed down on the body's ribs and his right hand on the body's neck. Some bodies rot until nothing is left but bones, but in the dry air of the desert, some bodies—like these—become desiccated, flesh still covering bones. He shifted his weight and when he put his right hand down again, because he had no choice, it slipped sideways into the body's mouth, scraping against teeth. He shouted in disgust and the children made the same sound, which echoed. Then they pulled his hands forward again and he fell across the body, chest to chest, as his hands settled on another dried-out body. One was a man and the other a woman, probably. The second body had breasts. The children imitated his heavy breathing.

And then there was light, from a cigarette lighter. The darkness of the room absorbed the flame's weak glow and the child walked with the light away from the bodies, to show Hopper the drawings on the wall.

The first picture: children, adults, cars on the streets, planes in the sky, and dogs in the yards. The next picture was the same picture, but most of the people were crossed out with X's: most of the adults, almost all of the children. "More light," said Hopper. They didn't understand him. He wanted his Teacher to see this, he wanted his Teacher to meet these children and be their Teacher, too. His Teacher would give them a goal and a plan.

He stopped in front of each picture even while they wanted to hurry him along. Adults dying, on the ground, eyes open; adults dead, on the ground, eyes closed. Children sick, with streams of black exploding from their opens mouths. Children dead, in piles. Adults and children in piles. Adults and children in piles, the piles burning, bright yellow and orange lines sticking up from the bodies. Rehab in the gym, two adults, and the children on the rehab beds. Then those two dead.

One of the children opened a door, letting in the light from the playground.

Another touched the single gold ring on Hopper's left hand.

"Ring," said Hopper.

"Wheen," said the child. Other children said it, too. "Wheen."

"Who are you?" he asked a girl. "Who is in charge?"

"Inch odge," they chanted. "Inch odge. Inch odge!"

A wave of heat advanced with the rising sun. His Silent Voice said, "It's getting hot. You can't ride during the day, not with the buses on the road. Use the day to get the bicycle you want. Find the tool here, then get the bike, then ride at night."

The children followed Hopper into the school; a swarm pressed around him and crowded the stairs to keep him from passing.

He found the tools locked inside a cage in a garage with a school district pickup truck and three lawn mowers. He found a bolt cutter. He knew the function, but not the name for it. He found the truck's tire iron and bent the cage's steel mesh until he could tear a hole to crawl through and easily snapped through the cage lock to get out.

His Silent Voice told him it was time to go and not to say good-bye. One boy called after him, "Hah-puh, Hah-puh," but stayed on the sidewalk and didn't follow.

# Marci, AutoZone, Tesla, Carrera

Hey You, the mascot, lifted each tire in its rack on the wall and gave it a quarter rotation when AutoZone came into the garage and told Carrera and Tesla to grab the keys for five Hummers and get them ready for Security. "They just verified a pilot and want to run him up to Chief."

Marci said, "Keys. Keys, I can get keys." Then she hopped twice from one foot to the other.

"Not this one, Hey You," said AutoZone. He went to the key locker, picked out the *Christina* keys, and, whistling to Carrera and Tesla, led them to the motor pool parking lot.

Marci let ten minutes pass and then wandered away, as she did twice a day. The first few times she did this, AutoZone sent Carrera to follow her, and each time he found her squatting in an alley, peeing, talking to herself.

Carrera complained to AutoZone that this was disgusting, and that they should train her to use the toilet. But AutoZone said, "There's only so much you can teach a Driftette in her condition, and so long as she's not pissing in front of the building, it doesn't make any difference to me and I don't know that we'll get someone else so eager about sweeping."

This time she squatted but only to reach the controls on the walkie-talkie hidden behind a loose brick. She spoke in code: "I missed the end of that. Could you say it again? I said, 'Could you repeat what you just said?' I can't hear you. Sorry. See you on Figueroa."

*Could you say it again?*

This meant a pilot has been verified.

*I said, "Could you repeat what you just said?"*

This meant Security is moving a pilot.

*I can't hear you.*

No more communication.

*See you on Figueroa.*

Good luck. Be careful.

It was the sort of nutty thing that Marci often said to herself while pushing a broom near the motor pool crew: "See you on Figueroa, see you on Figueroa, Figueroa." And it was also the sort of thing anyone tuned to that channel hears at least five times a day.

In a few hours, the *Christina* passed the garage on its way to the Fence and she danced her jig, for comfort. She was still dancing it when AutoZone and the others came back, sharing a bottle of rum. Carrera tapped on the bottle with a screwdriver, to make Marci dance more, but AutoZone made him stop.

"No bottle banging in the motor pool."

"It's fun. Everyone does it," said Tesla.

"I don't," said AutoZone. "I never go to Figueroa."

"Too good for it, I guess."

Marci returned to the tire rack.

"If you want to bottle bang, take yourself down to Figueroa," said AutoZone. "We're working here."

Tesla looked to Carrera for support, but Carrera shook his head no. "Don't ask me to back you up on this."

They heard an explosion just as AutoZone said, "Take a few days off and check in downtown. It's crowded and filthy there. You like that. Have some fun."

The three men ran to the street.

"Find out what happened."

They jumped into Tesla's Porsche convertible and drove away before AutoZone could say that he only meant for them to go to the Security detail at the DMV.

Marci swept the floor that she'd swept three times already. She heard AutoZone come in and counted to ten before looking up at him.

"It sounded like an old gas line or a propane tank that leaked near someone who lit a match," said AutoZone.

"Match," said Marci, though she knew it was more than that.

"But you're not scared," said AutoZone. "I don't know why you should be."

She said "match" again.

"You're really talking to me, aren't you?"

"Match."

"I don't want to call you Hey You anymore."

Marci wanted to turn around and tell him that he didn't have to, but she knew if she did the consequences would be ugly. "I want to call you something else but I don't know what. I want to call you something nobody else would know. So we'd have a secret. Do you even understand what I'm saying, Hey You?"

"Sweep," she said.

AutoZone put a hand on the broom to stop her.

"The person you were is still in there. You know that? Someone's little girl, someone who was loved." He took her face in his hands and kissed the tip of Marci's nose. She couldn't control her breath and he smiled as he drew out her excitement, but she didn't know how much she could respond without breaking character.

"Sweep."

"You swept plenty. You're beautiful," he said. "I think, anyway. And I like having you here. I really do. You make me happy every time you come back after you've been away. It's a good feeling. You give me a good feeling."

He slipped his right hand past the waist of her pants and probed for an answer.

"You're wet. Does that feel good? Does this feel good?"

She argued with herself: what would a real shambling Driftette say? The worst cases would say nothing, but she wasn't at that low level.

"Good," she said, looking into his shoulders.

"I'm glad." He traced the patterns of electricity that circulated over her skin like passing breezes on a pond. The lighter the touch, the better he could find them.

Too soon, he heard Tesla's Porsche. "I have to open the door."

"Sweep," Marci said, getting the broom. She followed AutoZone to the door.

"The *Christina* is wrecked," said Carrera.

"Why are you talking about the *Christina*? Forget the *Christina*," said Tesla. "The pilot is dead. It was an ambush. They killed all but one of ours and we killed three of theirs, but they lost what they came for. The pilot is dead. An LAX crew, no doubt about that, but they got nothing except for the righteous wrath of Chief."

Marci dropped to her knees and searched the floor for loose debris until she was under the counter where she scratched a line to mark another day.

☢

# Chief, Frank Sinatra, Pippi

"I blame you." Chief looked Frank Sinatra in the eyes, but at the head of the table, his back was to the city, always a distracting view on a clear evening like this, and Frank Sinatra, in charge of the Security Committee, forced himself to keep his eyes on Chief's. This was hard because Chief's woman/wife/sustainable lover, Pippi Longstocking, her own back to the meeting, looked through a telescope pointed at the airport. From where Frank sat, her left pigtail, dyed red and thickened with paste to stick out to the side, lined up with Chief's left ear. This was about as funny as things got for Frank and he wanted to share this with someone, but in his position, the radical gift of sharing a joke could get him into trouble with Chief.

Her name had been Gretel before she was Pippi and she was Heidi before she was Gretel. Gretel's messy blond hair had been covered in a dotted kerchief. Heidi's blond hair was tied in two thick braids that dropped over her breasts. But now that she was Pippi, the Heidi braids stuck out like handle bars on a bicycle. She dotted her cheeks with red lipstick, to look like the little girl on the wallpaper in one of the mansion's bedrooms.

Frank would have asked to move the meeting inside to the card room or one of the dining rooms, but Chief liked to hold important meetings on his terrace, precisely to test the attention of his heads of committee. His two closest guards, Go Bruins and Royce Hall, lived in the house with Chief and Pippi. Royce Hall had played football for UCLA; no one was sure about Go Bruins. They were on the Security Committee but answered to Chief. Chief looked like he might have been built like them when he was their age. He was tall with big arms, but the strain of being Chief showed in the creases in his face, and wherever he went, he walked slowly.

"When the DMV verified the pilot they didn't call me for extra security."

Frank Sinatra was not his real name, but most of the music on the iPhone he still carried, because it was the only thing he owned from before that stayed with him after rehab, was Sinatra. The phone was useless but the music was still there. The songs, which had as little effect on him as they would a dog, were directed at two different women, or, possibly, to one unreliable woman. It was either "I've Got You Under My Skin" or "I'm a Fool to Want You." If the head of Security were ever sad and lonely and heartbroken, a set of emotions lost like the passwords to the computers they needed most, he wouldn't sing about it.

Three years after rehab, Inventory found Frank Sinatra's identity papers in a UCLA administration building file cabinet. He was once Reynaldo Johnston, UCLA director of Security. That job would explain why he'd been included early in the First Wave, but not why his name had been changed. June Moulton, when the papers were found, told him: "You should believe that the doctor who was in charge of your rehab died and that the person replacing him didn't know who you were; that he looked at your iPhone and that he found all the Sinatra music and that he gave you that name. That's your myth, Frank Sinatra. It's a great Playa name. Live it."

"Vayler, do you have any evidence that Eckmann sends his own crew beyond the LAX perimeter for food supplies?"

"Still none, Chief. You have to understand things about the airport and its supply-chain management, Chief, sir."

Toby Tyler, the head of Systems, held up a hand. Drunk as usual, she was surrounded by her squad of subcommanders, all of them wearing their radios and headsets in case there was an emergency in the field. By rights each should have been given their own committee: Water, Power, Gas, Gasoline, Transport Service, Communications, Agriculture, Medicine. Toby claimed control of them all because a disruption in one system affected the others. She'd been General Mercedes Santos in the California National Guard, the coordinator in charge of civil disasters, and under the emergency rules, she was

the fifth person in Los Angeles to go through rehab. She was probably in her early fifties and had kept to her physical fitness regimen
after the reconstitution of her mind. Even with a hangover, she ran
five miles every morning.

"Whenever you're pressed about Eckmann, you go into this
supply-chain story, Vayler. We've heard it."

"Just answering the Chief's question, to me, Toby, to me."

Chief told Toby to shut up. Pippi laughed at this and Chief
reached back to pat her ass.

"Was it Eckmann?" Chief asked, then corrected himself. "That's
not a question. It was Eckmann."

"One of the guards is still alive. He's on his way to surgery now,"
said Frank. "But he's not expected to make it."

"And how did they know we had a pilot?"

"I am only too happy to answer that question," said Vayler Monokeefe. "They have a spy in the DMV or Security. No one from Inventory could have known about the pilot. It's an ElderGoth lapse. But
Verification isn't Security, so it's really on your shoulders, Frank."

"Prove it and I'll take action against the traitor," Sinatra said, "but
I don't think so. We only allow First Wavers to work inside the DMV
and it's not like a First Waver to sabotage what we have here. I think
it's a Second Waver who was rejected by Verification and heard about
the pilot. This is all a gesture of resentment. And that fits exactly with
what we face in the crew at LAX. Resentment and exclusion. Right,
Chief? Who's the more resentful, you or Eckmann?"

"We've never before verified a pilot who could fly big jets," said
Chief. "They shot that pilot at close range, Frank. They blew his head
off with a shotgun. They didn't want him for themselves. They knew
that if we had him, we could hold him until they starved to death."

"Are you saying they do have a plane ready or they don't?"

Pippi interrupted. "They have a plane. If they didn't have a plane,
they'd open the hangar doors. I've been watching."

"Why assassinate a pilot if you have a plane and no one to fly it?
What don't they want us to do now in response?" Sinatra asked this

out of deference to Chief's position, not because he thought Chief would have better insight.

Chief pointed at June Moulton. Standing alone, June Moulton looked north over the dark ash pit of the San Fernando Valley. She usually wore a sari. Today's was orange. Both Moulton and Chief made everyone understand that she wasn't to be approached by anyone. She almost never spoke up at general meetings without a prompt. Sometimes, after decisions were made, she might talk quietly to one or two of the others, but in ways no one could quite remember when asked what she had said. Even Chief rarely talked to her. It had been expected that she was going to have more to do if the children in the Fence lived, to tell them about the Founders. But children didn't live long. She flapped her shawl, the sign of inspiration. "They can't beat us. They have no story to tell. There aren't enough of them. They're goading us to attack."

Chief clapped his hands, something he'd seen in a movie. "Everyone be quiet and let me think about this."

This shut them up.

While they waited for Chief to break the silence, Pippi saw movement at the airport, a car, and she thought about saying so, but when Chief wanted to think, no one could interrupt him.

"June is right," he said. "They're goading us to retaliate. I think they've got just enough weaponry to hurt us badly. If they get an advantage over us, that'll go far. They can organize the Unverified Second Wave, because they can be persuaded, and they can cause trouble with the Drifters, dumb as they are. We won't get drawn into their fight. Just because we had a pilot doesn't mean he could fly whatever they have inside the hangar, and now he's dead. So, Vayler, we have the Burn coming up and we need to complete the inventory. Use all the Drifters you need."

"Thank you, Chief."

Vayler Monokeefe was a thin man with stringy gray hair to the middle of his back. He wore cowboy clothes and boots made from ostrich skin. In his early life, Monokeefe had been the managing director of the Los Angeles County Museum of Art. And in the photographs from those days his hair was cut short, and he wore black suits, white shirts, red bow ties, and no jewelry. In the new days he liked turquoise. Monokeefe had been married to a man before the plague. The man was gone, and now he sometimes had sex with either men or women, or men and women together. The rehab selection panel chose him for an early rehab so the future would have someone who knew the value of what remained from the past, **THANK YOU FOUNDERS**. At first he was in charge of collecting art and furniture. Then he took for himself the job of looking for and bringing back all useful material, everything that could be loaded on a truck and stored in a warehouse: drugs, weapons, sporting goods, running shoes, toilet paper. After he took charge of the trucks and the drivers, he took over from Systems the collection of food from the box stores, supermarkets, and warehouses that the Drifters—too weak willed for organized looting—could not break into. The bounty Monokeefe discovered and cataloged, June and Chief taught, could only be from the Founders, as a model for the organization of distribution for this new society. After Vayler's exploration of the city, he found warehouses and box stores with shelves full of enough food to support a metropolis of three million people, when now there were only thousands. Chief and the committee heads declared the new Gift Economy. There would be work to sustain the systems, work to gather the gifts from the past, but no one was allowed to trade or barter food for service beyond one meal for one session of work. The rule was stenciled on walls around the city: **THANK YOU FOUNDERS FOR THE GIFT, THANK YOU FRIEND FOR THE GIFT, FRIEND YOU ARE LIKE A FOUNDER TO ME**.

Chief had more to say. "The Drifters are spreading out from Figueroa and squatting in the old houses. Figueroa is getting out of control. After the Burn we're not going to need so many but we still need most of them, if not all of them, to finish the Burn all the way to the ocean. Vayler, the Drifters are going to get skittish or worse when they smell the fire. The day of the Burn, truck a thousand Drifters and

Shamblers to the storage depots and do us all the service of loading up the foodstuffs in the trucks, When the Burn is over, cart it all into town and we'll keep it warehoused closer to home."

"Chief, I'd like to honor that request but the quality of the material that Inventory is getting out of the Burn Zone now is high and I want to clear out the Burn Zone before it's too late to save what's valuable. I need that thousand as long as possible. We can move the other stuff after the Burn."

Sinatra intervened. "Vayler. What Chief is saying, which I support, is that we have to get the Drifters away from Figueroa. How much more time do you need for your treasure hunt?"

"Depends on the quality of the inventory. A couple of days."

Chief looked to Toby for her opinion. "Any risk in putting it off?"

"There's a lot of flammables waiting to be distributed. Best not to delay for too long but if we have to wait, we have to wait."

Vayler slapped the table in happiness. "That's a beautiful neighborhood, many fine collectibles, and we have to be methodical. Thank you."

"Just get your job done."

While Vayler and Toby quarreled about prep time, Redwings, Sinatra's number-one assistant, came up the stairs to the terrace, signaling to Sinatra that he had urgent news. Redwings—dressed as he preferred, in a slut nurse costume—was a verified Hells Angel, initiated into the First Wave because he'd been an electrician with a general contractor's license. Redwings's verified name was Robert Harnwood, but everyone called him Redwings because it was the name on his vest and it matched the name tattooed on his right shoulder. No one who came through the DMV ever had a Hells Angel tattoo without being a real member of the club, but they still needed official verification. When ElderGoth sent an Unverified Drifter with a Hells Angel tattoo on the one-way bus ride to the desert, the driver knew enough to call Redwings.

"ElderGoth," Redwings had said to her. "In respect of the club, I'm having Vayler assign him to an Inventory warehouse."

He whispered to Sinatra: "There's a Transport Service deverification driver saying he took shots at a Drifter on a bicycle in the desert past the outlet mall near the Indian casino on the road to Palm Springs."

Chief told Toby Tyler to stop talking. "Redwings, what's so important you can't let Frank listen to Vayler plan for the Burn to make sure Security is prepared?"

"Excuse me, but I have news." He waited for Chief's permission to continue.

"Speak."

"You've said before and made it a piece of your philosophy of the rules of doing things in an alert way that we should always be on the lookout for anyone coming through the pass from Palm Springs and I just want to alert you sir to the incident report from the last Drifter dump now that the buses are back."

"When did I order a Drifter dump? Don't we need them for Inventory? Vayler?"

"They weren't justifying themselves. Mostly Shamblers. We won't be shorthanded."

"You didn't tell me you were sending anyone out. I thought you needed them."

"Wasn't enough to bother you with."

"These things should be told to me."

"Yes, Chief."

"So Redwings, what happened?"

"Someone was at the site, a man, alone, riding a bike, and he saw the whole thing. They shot at him but, as it happens, he lost them."

"Why didn't I hear about this right away, Redwings?"

"You're hearing about it now, sir. As right away as is possible under the circumstances."

"Why didn't they tell me directly?"

"It isn't in the rules to tell you everything everyone sees."

"Show me where it isn't in the rules."

"That's a troubling but excellent direction, sir, seeing that I never saw the rules writ down."

Chief faced Sinatra. "Redwings isn't behaving."

"Redwings is always the same, Chief. He answers questions in his own way."

"I try my best, Chief."

Chief was quiet again before asking Redwings: "Was the man going to or coming away from Palm Springs?"

"They don't know."

"Did you ask?"

"Yes sir, Chief. I asked that very question, knowing you'd want to ask it yourself, sir, begging your pardon."

"Was there a description of the man?"

"Sir, Chief, sir, those folks who did the dump aren't possessed of the most clarified minds, so to speak."

"They're verified, right?"

"Verified, yes sir, yes sir. Verified, but there's verification and then there's verification. These folks was Transport Service workers, rehabbed late, because they was diesel mechanics, and the buses are diesel, you see. They saw a man. They shot at him as they're supposed to but they missed as they're not supposed to, so to speak."

"How far from the nearest town?"

"It was out by way of Banning, not far from the San Gorgonio Pass." Chief wouldn't let anyone go beyond the pass. He said that NK3 was still active in the desert and they needed to stay away.

"Where there's no reason for a man to be out riding a bicycle, and was it a road or mountain bike?"

"It was a mountain bike, sir. They're sure of that, Chief. But there is a reason. The sand drifts on the freeway make biking hard, and a mountain bike has the tires and gearing to power through."

"Vayler, is there still an Inventory run out to Covina tomorrow?"

"Yes. And where we just found an underground garage where an Audi dealer stored cars. Frank loves Audis. These are perfect. Top of the line."

"It will take at least two nights to pedal from where our man is. He won't travel during the day, so just establish a base camp on the 10, around West Covina."

Frank didn't like the way Chief was giving work meant for Security to Vayler, and asked, "What's the fear of a lone rider from Palm Springs?"

"A lone rider from Palm Springs could still be infected. We have to stop him. Do that, and bring home a new Audi."

Sinatra saw Redwings give him a "makes sense" signal with a tilt of his head. And it was true he loved Audis. Sinatra still had something to say. "Chief, I'm more concerned about the Drifters and Shamblers and how they'll be nervous around a big fire."

Chief smiled. "That was my concern, too, but then you may have heard that I went to the Playa and talked to The Man."

"What did The Man tell you?"

"The Man? He was implacable. It was The Woman who spoke to me in her special way, to say, 'Not to worry.' So what does that tell you?"

"It tells me not to worry, Chief."

The meeting was over.

Pippi wondered why no one had asked Chief why he was more concerned about a man on a bike than about the attack on the Security convoy and the murder of the pilot. She switched from the telescope aimed at the airport to the one pointed at the ocean. June said the ocean was full of whales but Pippi had never seen one.

Chief kept a dozen telescopes on the deck. Even the most raucous partiers settled down when it was their turn to look at the stars. At his orgies, Chief invited his favorites to the deck where—naked and drunk or stoned—they took turns at the telescopes. Mythology encouraged these night-sky parties. "This is the same sky we saw in the old times and the same sky our ancestors saw." Pippi was up at the telescopes most nights. East of Center Camp, on the same ridge, just past the H LYW OD sign, was a large telescope under the green copper dome at the Griffith Observatory, but the dome needed electricity to run the motor to open it and the power lines to the observatory were down. Pippi asked for help to get it started, but it was outside the Fence and Systems needed all spare power to keep Figueroa electrified because Drifters and Shamblers were scared of the dark.

## Marci, Eckmann, Tiny Naylor

Marci was peeing in the alley when Eckmann and Tiny Naylor, one of the LAX crew, walked up behind her. Eckmann never wasted time with greetings. "They think the pilot is dead, but we have him at the airport and he's hurt badly. If we don't get a doctor, he will die. Get me the keys to a Security car. We're going inside."

"You need a pass for that."

"We have them. From the people we killed. Nobody recognizes faces anymore. It's not a problem."

## Dr. Kaplan, Dr. Piperno, Sarabeth

In the operating room, Dr. Paolo Piperno showed Seth how to wash his hands with the sterile soap. "We've been through this before, Dr. Kaplan."

Sarabeth, the nurse, kept her shiny leather pants on but covered her breasts in a medical smock, to keep the blood off her skin.

The man had been the driver of the boat. He'd been cut up badly by the explosion but had been left for dead without being shot.

"The sign on my office wall says **DO NO HARM**. Let's get to work," said Piperno.

Seth didn't know what to do but he wanted to be polite, so he stood beside Piperno.

"Find the metal and glass that went into his skin."

"Really? I didn't see the video for that."

Piperno was angry. "Well, I've never seen a verified medical person, doctor, or nurse be so uncomfortable in an operating room. You should feel like this is home if you're a real medical person. Even with a lost memory, the environment in a hospital has what we call redolence. As we say, redolence leads to evocation leads to recollection. Recollection, Dr. Kaplan. Does being in here help you recall anything that would be of use to the community of Center Camp?"

His Silent Voice prompted him, and Seth repeated what his Silent Voice said. "Give me time."

"I don't think time is going to help," said Piperno. "When this gets back to Chief he's going to ask me: 'Paolo, did the only possible witness to an ambush die because you let an incompetent doctor learn his way around the body with someone so important?' If I answer yes, it's the one-way bus ride for me, Dr. Kaplan, the one-way bus ride to you know where. I'm beginning to doubt you even were a doctor. I'm beginning to think the computer made a mistake, and either you're not the Seth Kaplan who was a real doctor, or when you filled out your application for a driver's license, you thought it would be a big joke if you put down that you were a doctor. That's what I'm beginning to think, Dr. Kaplan."

"My picture is on the wall of my office."

"June Moulton teaches us that there are conspiracies, Dr. Kaplan, that can arrange the past to look like the present. But we'll talk about that later. For now, didn't you study those surgery videos?"

Seth hated the surgery videos. The doctors' hands moved too quickly inside the wet flesh, although it impressed him that everything inside the body wasn't just blood. When no one was looking, which was most of the time, he watched the movies he found in a drawer in the sleeping room where the interns used to go between shifts. The movies were stories about women who stayed home and had sex with the plumber and the mailman or the woman who lived across the hall, or everyone together. They were better stories than the surgery operations and no one was going to test him on them.

"I don't think I watched the right ones," said Seth.

"Then just stand there, out of Sarabeth's way. Sarabeth, are you ready?"

The nurse said she was. Piperno pushed a metal probe into the bullet hole and the patient pulled away from the pain. Seth watched the doctor and nurse, but his thoughts turned to the family he used to have when he was at the hospital in the old days. His Silent Voice told him: "Pay attention to the surgery." Seth did as the Voice told him, and Piperno did not push Seth away when he stood beside the surgeon to get a better look. Seth was pretty sure that the patient was dead. Sarabeth said what he was thinking: "He's dead, Dr. Piperno."

"I hate when that happens," said Piperno. "It's just so rude of people to die when you try to help them. Call for burial," he added, and Sarabeth got on the radio to find the burial crew. Piperno put a hand on Seth's shoulder. "We did what we could, and I apologize for my impatience with you."

"So it's over?" asked Seth.

"As we say, our lives go on, his doesn't. You're thinking, what do we do with the body, right?"

His Silent Voice said, "Just say 'yes.'"

"Yes."

"We take the bodies to Runyon Canyon, it's a ravine above West Hollywood, in the hills. We dig a hole for them and put rocks over them. It's kind of messy up there and I don't like talking about it."

Seth left the operating room, thinking again about his wife and children. So they were dead, too, like the man on the table. He'd seen death before but never with so much blood. He understood better now how death worked, what life needed to keep going. Life needed blood.

On his way down the hall from the operating room, two men walking toward him grabbed his arms as they passed.

"Come with us, Doctor. We need help. Our friend is hurt."

"How do you know I'm a doctor?"

"You just left surgery and you're covered in blood. This way, he's just outside, this way."

Five minutes later Seth was in the trunk of a motor pool police car, gagged, with his head on a clean pillow from an Emirates jet. He heard a woman talking to the men.

The woman said, "They're not going to miss this car. It wasn't part of the regular motor pool. But I should go back."

One of the men said, "No, Marci, your job is done."

"Sweep," she said.

Seth didn't know what he was doing there, but it was warm and no one was yelling at him. He thought about the letter he found in his office desk drawer.

> Seth, I beg you. The rehab takes ten days, two weeks, more. By the time the doctors give each other rehabs, the rest of us will be finished. I promise you, we all promise you, make a video of how to do it and once we're done, we'll do you, and you'll be fine. You were important and you can be important again. Please Seth.

The letter was signed, Marty. The name meant nothing to him.

# Hopper

The bike store lock yielded in two snaps of the bolt cutter.

Hopper tested the bicycles in the shop, for fit and weight, pumping air into the tires of the bikes he wanted to ride. Some were steel, others were carbon fiber, very light. There were energy powders to mix with water. He put them in his pack.

He compared two bikes outside, not sure if he wanted straight handlebars or dropped. Dropped bars pulled him forward, cutting wind resistance, but he wanted to sit up and look around. Better to lose a little time. He took the carbon fiber mountain bike, black. The price tag on the bike said:

$3,200 $2,900 $2,500 $1,750 MAKE OFFER

He picked a bike messenger bag on a strap and put his food, set of hex wrenches for the bike, binoculars, and his change of clothes inside.

On his way back to the road to the city, he passed a Ralphs supermarket. **THANK YOU FOUNDERS** was sprayed in white on the heavy steel plates that were bolted to the entrance and welded together. They were marked with a green triangle.

The loading dock was sealed the same way, but a side door was open. There was no food. The shelves were empty except for cleaning supplies.

He found his way back to the freeway. He didn't know how long he would be riding before the road brought him to the place that would tell him what to do next.

# Seth, Marci, Eckmann, Franz

The car entered the airport on the south side of the terminals, invisible to anyone—like Pippi—who might be watching the airport from the Fence. Eckmann wanted to tell Marci how sick he was of taking precautions for everything, of thinking strategically for however long they'd been there.

"Marci, was it hard?"

She didn't answer.

"Marci?"

"Marci. That's my name. I haven't heard it in a long time."

"So it was hard."

The car stopped at the hangar. She didn't want to say more; she didn't feel she owed him a report. She hadn't had a real conversation in a long time and didn't want to talk now.

"Push the trunk-release button and let's get him out."

When Marci opened the trunk and saw Seth, she thought he was dead, that she'd tied the gag wrong and he'd suffocated. She put a hand on his neck to feel for his pulse. His eyes opened, and he looked at her without anger or fear. She untied his gag. He said, "Thank you."

"For what?"

"For getting me out of here."

"But I put you in there."

"But then you let me out."

She held his hands as he swung his feet to the ground. "I'm Marci. Here." She handed him a bottle of water.

Eckmann took the water from him before Seth could drink. "Doctor, we're desperate. A mistake was made and someone was hurt. We need your help in surgery. If you won't help us, we have no choice. We'll kill you. You understand?"

"I think so," said Seth. "But if you want a doctor, why didn't you take Dr. Piperno? He's much better than I am."

"You're not Dr. Piperno?"

"No. I'm Dr. Seth Kaplan."

"Are you a surgeon?"

"A long time ago I was a children-with-cancer doctor, but there aren't any children with cancer in the Fence. And actually I don't know what cancer is, except it's not good."

"You didn't get surgery restored in rehab?"

"No."

"Did Piperno teach you surgery?"

"He was trying to."

Marci walked up to Eckmann and slapped him in the face. "You know what I gave up for you, pretending to be a Shamblerina, not being able to talk to anyone and have a normal conversation?"

"Not now, Marci."

"You don't know. I did my job, the one you asked me to do, and you had your job to do, and you messed it up completely, twice. First you shoot the pilot and then you get a doctor who didn't go through rehab."

"But what about the blood on his clothes?"

"Why should that be anything but a really bad sign?"

Eckmann gave the water back to Seth, to show Marci that he was merciful. "I'm sorry, Marci. You're right. You sacrificed for us. I asked you to do something difficult and you did it well. I deserve your anger. And now, we have a problem and your anger doesn't help us."

Eckmann led them into the hangar, thinking evil of Marci for making him feel bad for his mistakes, when no one else was stepping in to protect his crew from the life they'd have to live if they had no hope of escape.

Eckmann took Seth's left hand in his right and ahead of Marci and the rest led Seth across the floor of the big room to the other side of the jet and a red paramedic truck from the airport fire department.

Eckmann let go of Seth and opened the back door of the ambulance. "In here," he said. Seth followed him. His Silent Voice told him: "Do what they say."

The pilot was on the gurney, his shoulder wrapped in bandages and gauze over a spreading red stain. A woman held his head up so he could drink from a bottle of Fiji Water. The woman holding his head said, "He told me his name. It's Franz. He flew for Lufthansa."

Franz raised a weak hand and pointed to Seth. "You're a doctor?"

"They call me Dr. Seth Kaplan, yes."

"He's verified," said Eckmann. "Just like you."

"Am I going to die?" asked Franz.

"I don't know."

"Did they tell you who shot me?"

"I didn't ask," said Seth. "I'm sorry, though. It looks like it hurts."

Franz pointed to Eckmann. "These people did this to me. They attacked us and killed the others. I got shot. They switched my clothing with a dead man's and shot his head with a shotgun. No face. So Center Camp thinks I'm dead. Did they tell you that?"

"No."

"Did you get branded when you were verified?"

"Yes."

"You're really a verified doctor?"

"Yes."

"I don't remember anything about flying. Do you remember anything about doctoring?"

"Not really."

Franz grabbed Eckmann's hand, sobbing. "What are you doing?"

"We're going to get you better and you're going to get us out of here. Because Dr. Kaplan plays by the new rules, and the new rules are this: whether it's in Center Camp or Camp LAX, if the patient dies, the doctor dies."

The pilot took Seth's hand. "Get this bullet out of my shoulder. I don't want to die and I don't want you to die."

Seth's Silent Voice said: "Tell them to leave."

Seth told the Silent Voice: "No. I need help."

The woman said her name. "I'll help you. I'm Consuelo. I think I was a nurse. They found me in a hospital. I feel like I know what the things in this truck are for."

Seth turned to Marci: "I want you here, too."

"I'm not a nurse. I was a flight attendant."

"I want you here." He turned to Eckmann. "You can go."

"I need to watch," said Eckmann.

"Then stand back," said Seth.

Consuelo gave Seth a long squirt of hand sanitizer. "There are first aid manuals in the trucks. I read them. They have pictures of what to do for some things. Here, this is what you need to sew the bullet holes shut."

There was a tray of surgical knives like the ones Seth had seen at the hospital. Consuelo held up a short-bladed knife. "I think this is the right kind."

"You don't know?" said Franz.

Eckmann grabbed the scalpel from Consuelo and opened Seth's hand. "Take the knife."

Seth tucked the end of the handle under his palm and—watching his hand move without conscious intention—he curled his three outer fingers to hold the knife in place, pressing his thumb on the left side of the knife and his forefinger along the top of the blade.

"Close your eyes, Dr. Kaplan," said Marci. "Just close them and feel it, Dr. Kaplan." Piperno had never said something so simple. Seth closed his eyes and rolled the handle of the knife against his thumb. His Silent Voice said, "I watched Piperno. He was a good man trying to help you but you didn't try hard enough to learn. You were scared of hurting the patient. I saw what he did. I watched the videos. You were looking at everything except the operations. Let me do this. I can do this. Just let me do what I know I can do."

Seth put the blade down on the tray with the other surgical tools and watched his fingers dance through them, lifting them gently, testing their weight, studying the different shape blades, opening and closing the forceps and spreaders.

He liked the way they felt. Each brought up a different reason for appreciation: the craftsmanship of each blade impressed him, the way the blades made him think about the people who had forged them and how they were now dead or drifting. Then he stopped thinking about anyone else, and the world was reduced to the tools on the tray. He closed his eyes.

Consuelo pricked him with a needle. "Wake up, Doctor."

"It's easier this way," he said.

Eckmann whispered into Kaplan's ear, "Take the bullet out of the pilot, Doctor. Do it now."

Seth grabbed another tool, a long probe.

His Silent Voice said, "Go through his back."

"Turn him over," said Seth.

Consuelo said, "That's going to hurt him."

"Turn him over."

Seth used the scalpel to open the wound so he could see into the torn muscle. Then he pushed the small tip of the steel probe into the pilot's shoulder. Seth heard the screams but Franz's agony did not register to Seth as distress for which Seth might be responsible or suffering that Seth might have an obligation to relieve. The muscle memory that guided Seth as he searched for the bullet had nothing of the original mix of motives that brought Seth to study medicine in the years before the disaster, nothing of the call to heal or the hunger for prestige. Seth didn't understand the connection between his hand, the probe, and the pain. Did he want to save the pilot's life? Only his hands, searching for a bit of flattened alloy, could answer that question, but they were busy. The probe tapped the metal and with small forceps he pulled it out.

Seth showed the bullet to Franz. "Why should I be grateful for this?" asked the pilot.

"Because he saved your life," said Marci. Turning to Eckmann she added, "He did what he was supposed to do. Tell him that."

"Thank you, Doctor. You've done us all a great service."

Seth dropped the bullet onto the metal tray with a plink and unwrapped the needle and thread. His hands relaxed as Consuelo held the wound together. He pushed the fine needle through one side and then the next and pulled the two parts closer. He made a dozen loops like this in Franz's arm, on both the entry and exit wounds, and tied the knots. Loose ends dangled. Consuelo cut them.

There was nothing more his hands could do.

Marci saw that Seth was tired. "Is there anything else you need to do?"

"I don't know."

Eckmann put his arms around Seth. "You want a drink? I want a drink."

Franz tried to sit up but the pain pushed him back.

Consuelo said, "I'll stay with him."

Eckmann took Seth to a bench outside the hangar where they could see the lights of downtown, the smaller area of light around the Playa, and the thin line of lights along the top of the Fence.

"You can't see Center Camp from here, but you can feel it."

"Piperno is in Center Camp. That's where he said he was going."

Marci passed around small bottles of vodka from a rolling drink cart from American Airlines. Seth didn't know what to do with it and Eckmann unscrewed the cap.

"Drink?" asked Seth.

"Drink," said Eckmann.

"Drink," said Marci. "This is my first drink since I gave up my name. I didn't want to drink while I was a Driftette. I was afraid of giving myself away."

The vodka hit Eckmann quickly and he wanted to explain himself to Seth. "My memory is almost continuous, Doc. They got to me so early . . . They knew. They needed me so the airport would keep running. We were smart people down here, engineers, bright guys, and we set up our own rehab center in Terminal Five. We got the ECT machines, we got the insulin, and we got what was needed to keep NK3 from tearing deeper ditches in consciousness. I think it worked better than what they had at UCLA or the other centers. And did you figure out the truth about what happened to the machines at UCLA?"

"What happened at UCLA?"

"You saw the broken rehab machines in the gym, didn't you?"

"They were broken?"

"Yes. Guess who did it?"

"Guess?"

"It was Chief who broke them. It was Chief and Toby Tyler. Chief and Tyler locked the gym, only let in their friends, people who could do things, or were fuckable, and abandoned the rich, whose money was now useless, and the politicians, whose constituencies were dead in body or spirit. The old aristocracy died or turned into Drifters, and the new aristocracy tore up the machinery to make sure no one else could get through. I don't blame them. It was cowboy justice. We knew what they were doing and stayed away. We had our own rehab system here, and we did the same, in our own way.

We wanted a society of the useful. If you were an executive for the airline and had a pass for unlimited flying, but you never knew how to fix a jet, what good were you? The Drifters, this used to be their city, and we paid the rent on it. I don't miss them. Twenty-three planes managed to get away with the last pilots who remembered how to fly and the only rehab-trained mechanics, leaving the rest of us you see here to patch our collective training together. All we lacked was a trained pilot. In comes Franz. I'm sorry he got shot. How much time do we have until he's strong enough?"

"Strong enough?"

"To fly, to fly!"

"Fly where?" Seth asked.

"Away from here!" Eckmann opened another two bottles. This time he didn't have to force Seth to drink.

Seth asked for another bottle as soon as he finished the first.

"Feels good," said Marci.

"Yes," said Seth.

Eckmann sighed. "Do you understand how fucked up everything is in the world?"

"It's the only world I've ever known," said Marci.

"No," said Eckmann. "There was another world and it's still inside us if he can only find it. What do you think, Doc?"

"At the hospital, I saw movies about the before world. People got undressed as soon as they met."

# Chisel Girl, Frank Sinatra, Justin

She carried a woodworker's twelve-inch beveled-edge chisel in a leather sheath on her belt. Even if the two men chasing her knew what she could do with it, they wouldn't have stopped, because they were Drifters and didn't have minds supple enough to understand that if they grabbed her, she would kill them.

They started chasing her when she came out of the empty Costco. They thought she had food. If she got away from these two, she wouldn't bother with another Costco. Even with the green triangle, all of them were empty now.

She was fast, but not fast enough to get away from them if this kept up for the rest of the day, so she turned off the street into a five-story parking garage. She ran up the ramp, past cars on flat tires, cars never touched by rain, their color hidden under dust and ash.

She slowed down to let the men see her. She didn't want them to quit, because if they turned away and then saw her again the chase would start over, so she kept up her pace until she came to the open roof of the garage, where the cars had been washed by recent rains and where the chrome reflected the sun.

Stopping them with the chisel was the easy part. The first one to reach her blocked the view of the second, already dropping his pants, and the chisel was in his eye the moment he pushed her shoulders into the wall. As she pulled the chisel out of his face the other man saw the blood. The second man, with his pants around his knees, tried to run away, but he tripped and fell. She pushed the chisel into his neck. Her hands were bloody and using the blind man's shirt, she wiped away what she could.

After they died she searched them for food, but they had nothing but a few hard candies. She was hungry and the whispers came to her, like all the people in the world saying the same thing, but in words she didn't understand. The crows would find the bodies soon enough, and go for the bloody eyes first, but she was tired and no one could see her. So she slept. The crows almost never bothered the living. It could have been ten minutes later or an hour when she heard the van coming up the street. She thought it was in her dream and she stood up too quickly, without thinking.

Frank Sinatra was in the front passenger seat of the van. The driver, whose name was Pickle, saw her. He slowed down, pointing her out to Frank, and then stopped. "There's one there, a woman, see her, up top?" Frank stepped out of the van to get a better look. He hoped she would just go away and disappear so they could move on to the Audi lot, but she stood up taller.

"Forget about her," said Frank.

"I know you're in a hurry but rules is rules," said Pickle. "And this rule is yours." They were only ten miles from downtown, in Alhambra, just past the eastern ash moat, the remains of an early Burn, and it was Frank's order that all Drifters found this close to downtown had to be taken in and processed by Verification. "And there's something different in how she stays there, watching us," said Pickle. "I've never seen that before, Frank."

"How so?"

"She likes being looked at."

So Chief's assignment to find the fearsome lone Drifter on a mountain bike last seen near Banning, who was probably lost on his way to death by thirst or starvation, would have to wait.

Pickle went around to the back of the van and opened the doors.

The woman had seen this before, the van, the rear door, the folding table, the two-burner propane stove, and the cooler with food. The stove was lit; ramen from a package was heated in a pot of water. Everyone who ate the food ended up on the vans or buses—and she was hungry. She'd seen no food for a few days. Knowing that it was a trick, she could trick them back. She could take the food and then run. She could hide the chisel between her waistband and shirt, not let anyone see it. They might have a gun, though. Or more than one. She could stab two men quickly and run. Only if more Drifters showed up. There were Drifters around, hiding. She knew that without seeing them. They were watching the van, and watching her.

"Drifter baiting takes practice," said Pickle. "Everyone has to be quiet, but available. The food is not the best that Center Camp can offer. We give them Slim Jim sausages, vacuum-sealed logs of string cheese, sodas, jars of taco sauce, and ramen."

Frank was surprised the cooler held oranges. "Those are for us, too good for them," said Pickle.

The woman saw two Drifters, a man and woman, in torn bridal gowns, coming down one street and a third Drifter, a man in a blue Dodgers jacket, coming from the other side of the van. He had long hair and a matted beard, and his running shoes didn't have laces, so with each shambling step he almost lifted out of them. He kept his eyes down.

Keeping a hand on the chisel, the woman walked down the stairs, aware of every route she could take to get away from the van if someone, Drifter or van driver, attacked her.

She walked up to the table and in one fast move skewered an orange with the bloodstained weapon. She slipped the orange from the steel blade, pushed a finger deep into the entry hole, tore the orange in half, and offered one piece to the Drifter in the greasy Dodgers jacket.

Drifters almost never shared at these buffets and Sinatra studied the man, wondering what Chisel Girl saw in him that provoked her generosity. She wasn't giving anything to the other two Drifters, the man and woman, who looked to be in better shape.

Sinatra handed Chisel Girl another orange. "These are gifts. We don't expect anything from you. It's good, isn't it? When was the last time you had a fresh-picked orange?"

She could talk but decided not to give up that information until it had value.

"I'm Pickle. I'm here to tell you something you may not have heard. We're out here looking for people who might become our friends. You can stay here; that's your choice. Or you can come with us back to Los Angeles, where there's a lot more food, and safe places to sleep. But you can't carry the chisel in the city. I can't let you on the van with the chisel."

"I won't use it unless I have to." She took a bottle of Dasani water from the table, unscrewed the top, and then drank from it quickly.

"Do you have a name?" Frank asked her.

"No."

"Do you know what you were before?"

"Before what?"

"Do you remember anything of your rehab?"

"Rehab?"

"Well, you can stay out here and take your chances, or you can come with us and we'll see if there's a way for you to live a better life. Think about it."

The Drifter in the filthy Dodgers jacket had stopped his clumsy movements and Sinatra knew that meant the man had been listening to them. Sinatra passed him, brushing shoulders, and then introduced himself to the Drifter couple. "My name is Frank Sinatra. I invite you to get on the van and come with us to where there is more food and a warm place to sleep."

He said this without looking too closely at the Drifter in the Dodgers jacket.

The couple got on the van. The Dodgers Drifter stayed close to Chisel Girl, eating Slim Jims.

"You sure you don't want to come with us?"

Dodgers seemed incapable of understanding. "This is good," he said.

Frank tried again. "There's more food in Los Angeles."

"This is good," he said again. The man reached for another orange, and as his arm stretched, Sinatra saw the circle of pale skin on his wrist.

"Did your parents ever hire a clown for your birthday when you were a kid?"

"More food," said the Drifter.

"When you were too old for it, say, I don't know, fourteen, fifteen, did you go trick-or-treating on Halloween with your buddies for the free Snickers, without bothering to wear any kind of costume?"

The Drifter ate his food without turning his head.

Pickle said, "What are you doing? I don't think he understands you."

Frank persisted. "Cat or dog? Fish or turtle? Both? Hamster? Cockatiel? Xbox or PlayStation? Do you still remember your password to Facebook?"

The man stopped adding food to his plate.

"What was rush hour like? Cars so thick you couldn't move. And did you ever see the Lakers play? You weren't here when it hit; you were never sick. How'd you miss it? What happened? Were you out of town, sailing? There's a theory that the Completes were just passengers on a cruise ship coming back from Hawaii, and that the captain heard about what was happening and stayed a hundred miles off the coast. And when he finally landed, some of the people who made it to shore split up and went alone and stayed away from everyone else for, what?" Frank paused. "Well, you tell me, six months? And have you found others? Are you waiting until you find others to create a small army that can conquer us the way the Spanish conquered Mexico? That's from a book. I read them. History, it's interesting. We don't have it anymore, not like they used to. I've spoken to a few Completes. They say they've all gone crazy because there's no one to share with, unless they randomly find another Complete, but that's only happened a few times that I know of. There may be a community of Completes beyond the desert, but if there is, they're smart enough to stay away from us. Have you found any others?"

Sinatra tossed Dodgers another question: "Excuse me, do you know what time it is?"

The Drifter's eyes flicked to his left wrist.

"My guess is that the watch is in your pocket. My guess is that it's a good watch, too. And that you took it off because Inventory likes to claim good watches."

The Drifter sighed. "Yes, yes, yes, yes, yes. It's a great watch."

"And you know what time it is. You know what day it is."

The Drifter took a watch out of his pocket. "It's eleven seventeen a.m., April seventeenth, twenty twenty-one. That's the time; that's the date. I know you're out of phase because I've seen the clocks on Figueroa. Some are right, the ones with chips in them. The rest, no."

Pickle slapped Frank on the back. "You got him! You're amazing, sir, amazing. I don't think I ever saw a better demonstration of what makes a man head of Security than that."

Sinatra asked Dodgers: "Where do you sleep? Near here?"

"The fire station."

"Pickle, I'm going for a walk with our new friend here. You can pack up the van, I'll be back soon."

Pickle asked Chisel Girl for help and instead of stabbing his eye, which had been her plan; she put the uneaten food back in the cooler.

"I'm coming with you to the city."

"Of course you are. Why would you want to stay out here now that we've found you? And we might find out who you really are. Don't happen every day, but it happens every week."

The two men walked down the middle of the street between the long boulevards with all the signs in Chinese. "This was a big Chinese neighborhood. The food here was great, very authentic, typical of many regions of China."

"You live with any others like you?"

"No."

"Is it hard? Remembering everything?"

"There's no one to share it with. It's like remembering something that never existed. You go crazy."

"Why didn't you get on the van and take your chances?"

"Because in ways great and small, I would have tripped myself up. I'm too nervous. Too lonely. I can't fake it. I've been to Figueroa, but on my own terms."

"What's your name?"

"My name is Justin Ozu."

"Where's the fire station, Mr. Ozu?" asked Sinatra.

"Two blocks south, three blocks to the west." Justin knew Sinatra would have trouble with the compass. A trustworthy sense of north and south came from a continuously aware lifetime, not a reset only four years old. Rehabs Level 1, or whatever Justin felt like calling them on any given day, used other ways of keeping their place in the world. Rehabs Level 1. First Wavers. Semicompletes.

"Have you found others like me?"

"We've seen a few."

"And there may be others in the desert?"

"It's a rumor. Check it out."

"I never heard the rumor. Who do I talk to? I don't talk to anyone. Too dangerous. Not that it matters anymore. You're going to kill me now. With all my knowledge."

"Knowledge is power. You have more knowledge. We can't let you back, none of you. We're not making memory weapons—that was you."

"That was the North Koreans."

"I've heard that, Justin, but I don't *know* that. I know where I slept last night. I know where I woke up four years ago. I know a few things about me from a letter my rehab doctor wrote to me, but I only know those things from the letter. I don't actually remember them, and that's your fault."

"I'm half Japanese. My father. My mother was Mexican. I'm not a North Korean."

"You might just as well be. Really. You escaped this thing. I didn't."

"You're still alive. You're in charge of something, aren't you? You have your own kind of power. That counts for a lot."

"That's the way things used to be, right?"

"Human nature."

"Well let me give you a big round of applause for that. You're the only one with human nature, Justin, because you're the only one who's still human. I am a reinvention of the idea of the human. I don't know anything from before; it's all just a series of stories. I can't pick out the news from old movies, and you can. You can tell the difference between a movie and the news. And is the boat story true?"

"It wasn't a cruise ship. It was a Coast Guard cutter. We had full contact with the shore. They told us what was happening. We were called back to keep control at the port in Long Beach. We voted to stay at sea. A few took a Zodiac boat to shore because they had family in Los Angeles. They're gone. The captain wanted to stay at sea. I took my chances and I got off the boat in Santa Barbara and ended up here."

They were in front of the fire station.

"Why a fire station?"

"Good locks on heavy doors. If you look in the windows on the ground floor you can't see any evidence of life. Plenty of living space on the second floor. Iron shutters to block the light for the fire fighters who work the night shift and sleep in the station during the day. I keep them down all the time."

Ozu opened the door with a key. The fire engines were still there, polished, their tires full of air.

He led Sinatra up the stairs. "If you want to know what time it is, look at this," he said, opening the door to what had been the dispatch room. There were shelves and tables, and watches on every surface.

"How many?" asked Sinatra.

"Eight hundred and twenty-three, all set to the same time."

"What's the best watch you have?"

"Do you want to go three hundred feet underwater? Do you want a watch to measure your heartbeat while you're mountain climbing and know the rate of ascent, and keep a record of the climb that can be transferred to your iPhone? Do you want to impress an Iranian hotel owner with how much money you can spend on a quality timepiece? Do you want a watch that costs more than a Ferrari?"

"I like Audis."

Ozu picked up six watches. "These would be a fair trade for an Audi RS7. Which one do you think is the most valuable?"

"I know Rolex watches are expensive."

"Well, Rolex is nice, they actually . . . they kind of lived up to the promise in the ads. They work really well, but they're expensive to maintain. I keep them out of the dust. I don't abuse them. But they don't keep time without being cleaned every four or five years and they're starting to slow down. And I can't fix them."

"What watch did you take off before you came to the van?"

Ozu took a large watch out of his pocket. "It's an IWC. A Portugiescr Chronograph. About ten thousand dollars, at least. That Rolex Daytona, there, that was twenty grand. Some of them are more, way more."

"Who wore the IWC?"

"Men who had a lot of money, who . . . well . . . wanted to appcar too cool to wear a Rolex. But the more I look at them, and think about who wore them, the more I find a kind of dishonesty in the IWC and I keep coming back to your basic Rolex Submariner, a bit James Bond, even though he wears Omega, but the standard that everyone else is copying. It's sort of like a BMW compared to an Audi. No insult to Audi. You know what I mean."

"Well put," said Sinatra.

"Please, don't kill me. Don't you want someone to help you? I can be your secret weapon. You don't have to tell anyone what I really am. I can give you help with things that no one else even thinks about. I can even help you find passwords."

"We don't want to rely on memory anymore. Not your kind. You'd take the power back."

"No. I'd help you get the power for yourself."

"You'd end up killing us, or killing the leaders. You have a cleverness that we can't imitate."

"I'm not being clever with you now. I can help you. Take any watch you want. It's something I've learned from the Founders, how to give a gift."

"What Founders?" asked Sinatra, walking away from the watches and looking around the bedrooms.

"I like you. I let a few Drifters through but I can't live with them. They're stupid, too stupid."

"Women?"

"I've had a few."

"Did they ask for your protection or did you just take them up here?"

"It's nothing I'm proud of."

"Pride? I've heard that word."

"But you don't know what it means."

"There's a difference between feeling and understanding, Justin. Do you know what it is?"

"I think so, yes."

"I don't. And that's why we have to hunt you all down and kill you when we see you. Because you know the difference naturally and we have to figure it out for ourselves. Because you don't have the problem of a Silent Voice, do you?"

"No, I don't, but I have a lot more than one voice in my head. We all did."

"We were left with only our main thoughts and the Silent Voice. Two voices. Twenty people like you could take over."

"Everything you're saying is bullshit, Frank. Have some respect for me, and be honest to me about why you can't let me live. I know what you and Chief did. Anyone else who's Complete knows it, too. The people who ran the world put you in line ahead of them for rehab because without you, they wouldn't be able to fix anything that broke. They couldn't fight for themselves. You promised them they were next, and then when you and your friends had saved the right people, you broke your promise and you built a fence to keep yourselves safe from the people you didn't save. Then you made up the Founders to hide your crime. You're going to kill me, so please kill me for the truth."

Sinatra left the body on the floor and scooped twenty watches into an empty shopping bag. He would tell Inventory about his new trick: the next time they set up a buffet, lay out a spread of cheap watches with a Rolex or two among them. They make good bait.

While the van waited for Sinatra to return, Pickle talked to Chisel Girl.

"There's blood on your chisel."

"What's a chisel?"

"That sharp thing you carry, the thing that has blood on it."

Sinatra came around the corner with the shopping bag. He wanted to move quickly now. "Pickle, it's time to go. Run me to West Covina and then take them back to the DMV. Has she made up her mind? In or out, her choice."

"Chisel Girl," said Pickle. "You see? It's your choice."

While she thought about the offer, Frank grabbed her hands from behind, pressed her into the side of the van, and tied her hands behind her with zip ties. He took the chisel away.

"If you're not verified and you want to come back out here, we'll make sure that happens." He opened the door and put her in the middle seat. She didn't fight.

On the way to Covina they passed a food-storage warehouse marked with a green triangle and Frank told Pickle to stop. "Stay in the van. I have to see something."

Chisel Girl asked, "Why are we stopping?"

"He wants to," said Pickle.

All food-storage depots were secured with steel plates welded shut. Until it was time to release the larder, nobody could get into them without torches. But this one was missing a plate. Frank looked inside. The food was gone.

He needed to talk to Vayler and Toby Tyler, because if there were Drifters out there who could handle acetylene torches, then Center Camp was in trouble. This was news best discussed in person. Pickle drove him to the West Covina Audi dealership, let Sinatra out, and went back to Los Angeles.

The freeway here was straight for a few miles in each direction and no one on a bicycle could hide, but there were miles of parallel roads and not enough people to watch them. The Inventory crew had a room for Frank in a hotel if he was going to stay the night. "I expect I have to," he said. "Now show me the cars."

An hour later Frank was doing 155 miles an hour in an Audi A7—worth thirty watches—when the call came over the radio from Redwings. "A doctor disappeared from Westwood. Not Piperno. Name of Seth Kaplan. He was working on the driver who was shot in the ambush and the driver died. It's my opinion that the truth may be that knowing of Dr. Piperno's way of threatening new personnel with a punishment, which is promising death for failure, that is in truth not part of our Chief's arsenal, he went to the beach and drowned himself, but what do you think, Frank?"

"Nobody saw him in Santa Monica?"

"So far as we know, no."

"He might have gone for a canyon hike on the trails above Brentwood and fallen down a cliff, maybe. Broke his neck or leg, is out there now crying for help. But all that's coming for him is a pack of coyotes."

"You're a good man, Frank, and you may be right. If he wasn't a good doctor, I don't think Piperno wants him back."

"Do we have other things to worry about?"

"We do, sir."

"Such as?"

"Another Burn and not enough time to prepare for such problems as arrive with the frightened Drifters."

Redwings returned to Los Angeles, a happy man, an always happy man, grateful to the Founders for their gifts and for their wisdom as taught by June Moulton. "You're here!" That's what June said was their great lesson. Yes, and every morning he woke up, his first thought was: "I'm here."

# Hopper

Hopper stayed with the plan impressed on him by the Teacher and rode on the freeway but only after the sun went down. On the mostly flat road, with his light carbon fiber frame, he made fifty miles the first night and stopped in Pomona for the day. The Teacher told him he would find food in the box stores and warehouses with the green triangles painted on the walls. The doors would be locked and sealed but there would usually be a way in through the roof. He found a Mexican supermarket with the green triangle, but when he broke in through the roof, he couldn't find anything to eat except for a few boxes of taco shells.

# Erin, Chisel Girl, ElderGoth,

# Chief, Sinatra

With the death of the pilot, ElderGoth was sure that someone on the Verification Committee had sent word to LAX. She asked everyone if they had betrayed the First Wave and everyone answered that they hadn't. So that was that, a good question, no useful answers. She stayed close to Erin.

"How's the day going?"

"I've had nothing but Shamblers. Jobe and Helary both scored Oscars before lunch and they're done." Oscars is what they called anyone who had worked in the movie business. Jobe verified a film editor; Helary verified a writer. Film editors were valuable because they'd been trained for the minute examination of things. The rule about writers was not to tell them they were verified, and just ship them downtown and let them continue to drift.

"I don't think there's anybody left to verify," said Erin, only because she was having such a boring, boring day. "We've basically got everyone with skills that are needed except for another pilot and did you hear about the doctor? I feel bad for him. Maybe he drowned?"

It was the end of the day and about time to go when Pickle arrived with the Drifter couple and Chisel Girl. The intake papers said that a bloody weapon had been taken from the woman, which made her sound just interesting enough that Erin claimed her, although later Erin said the vibration of her real identity was clear just from the intake papers. Erin also later said that what gave her the feeling that history was being made wasn't the woman's face but a feeling of familiarity in the woman's posture. Drifters weren't angry or depressed; they were dull. This woman stepped through the door with an assumption of deserved attention, with an expectation for something that wasn't there, but it was something she wanted, something that had once been hers, something she missed.

She looked to be in her early thirties, but everyone who drifts looks older than they really are. She wore a hooded gray sweatshirt zipped to the neck.

Erin introduced herself. "I'm Erin. Do you know your name?"

"I don't know anyone long enough to get to the name part."

Erin took the woman's picture, from the front and from both sides, and sent them into the computer.

"You were found close to the city. Where have you been for the last four years?"

"What's a year?"

"Do you know where you are?" Erin asked.

"They said this is the city."

"Do you know the name of the city?"

"I forget."

"Where were you yesterday?"

"I forget."

The hint of a secret brought Erin's attention to something in Chisel Girl's responses that might sound to others like nothing more than proof of Drifter mindlessness. But to Erin it sounded like defiance. If she was defiant, she wasn't a regular Drifter. If she were pretending to be one, then Erin would probe until she broke her down.

"What's your first memory?"

"Lights. People screaming."

"Why are they mad at you?"

"I didn't say they were mad at me. I said they were screaming, but they were also smiling."

"Do you remember when you were a little girl?"

"I forget."

Chisel Girl lowered the zipper of her sweatshirt to let in air and Erin saw the top of an ornate tattoo.

"Could you do me a favor and take off your shirt?"

Modesty died with memory. The woman unzipped the sweatshirt. She wore nothing underneath, and at the first sight of the tattoo—a jeweled Russian Orthodox cross from her neck to her stomach, with gold trefoils around her nipples—Erin knew that if the woman had a tattoo on her back, and that tattoo was a portrait of Chisel Girl herself rising naked out of an eggshell beside a fire-breathing dragon standing on the bloody corpse of a vanquished Saint George, then the only proof necessary for verification of this woman would be the signature of the tattoo artist at the base of her spine.

"Stand up and turn around."

The woman stood up, dropped the sweatshirt, and showed her back to Erin. There it was, in Russian letters. Erin could now make sense of her suspicions about this woman. For the first time since the world changed, Erin thought the world had been restored. She checked the computer to see if the woman's face matched the database. No. But she didn't care. She told the woman not to move and ran to ElderGoth. "ElderGoth, I have to show you something. Right now."

ElderGoth, always steady, saw the woman with her top off.

"Why is she naked?"

Erin said, "Just look. You have to see this."

"It's against rules to leave a Drifter alone during verification."

"This is no ordinary Drifter. You've been in my room at home. You've seen the poster on the wall. Well, here she is. Shannon Squier."

"Who?"

"The singer."

"I still don't know her."

"I do."

"Did she verify?"

"No. She doesn't have to. I can verify. Redwings can verify. He has a tattoo from the same tattoo artist."

Erin's bedroom remained as it had been when she returned from the treatment at UCLA, and the centerpiece of one wall was the poster of a woman with silver hair, purple glitter streaks around her eyes (the same purple Erin chose for her own wild hair), upper lip painted black, lower lip blood red. The woman's parents were Russian and at the time the picture was taken she had the most famously wide Slavic eyes in the world. Erin knew the face on the wall better than she knew her own, since she had forgotten the first fifteen years of her life and with that disappearance went all the time she'd spent looking at herself in the mirror. It was a peculiarity of the rehabilitation: like most people in the Fence, Erin could never get used to the face that was forever jumping out of stray reflections. June Moulton declared this the "stranger effect" and for some people it was the hardest symptom of the plague.

ElderGoth walked around the woman a few times.

"The back," said Erin. "Look at her back."

"That's the tattoo from the billboards and the posters."

ElderGoth touched it and Chisel Girl turned around and punched ElderGoth in the face, knocking her down. The Security reps came over and grabbed Chisel Girl's arms while Erin cried for them to let her go.

"This is Shannon Squier. You don't treat her this way. She's the best person in the world and I found her."

ElderGoth asked, "How do you know she's really Shannon Squier?"

"The signature," said Erin. "You've seen copies of this tattoo on people's backs, never as good, and they never have the Smersh signature."

The sixth album of the most famous singer in the world had been released the week before the first case of the disease in America, and the advertising campaign had covered billboards and buses with a photograph of that tattoo. Shreds of the billboard were everywhere. Memories of the singer as a personality had disappeared, but the tattoo itself, and her music, rediscovered, not remembered, had become for the tribe that lived inside the Fence the anthem of and a requiem for the lost world. Some say that The Woman, on one foot, dancing to unheard music, was really meant to be Shannon. Other Drifters had walked in with versions of that tattoo: there were verified women and even some men with versions of that tattoo, but it wasn't the egg, the dragon, or the dead saint that gave immediate verification to this sunburned, scarred, and emaciated Drifter, naked without shame. No, it was the large block of Cyrillic letters across the base of her spine: СМЕРШ. Erin knew from the singer's authorized autobiography on her bookshelf, along with the unauthorized biography, that the word was pronounced *Smersh*, the acronym for the Russian words *Shmert Spionam*, or Death to Spies, which was the name of a spy network in the James Bond novels. **СМЕРШ** was also the name of the Moscow tattoo artist who had done the work and any ink genius with the talent to do work this fine would never copy Smersh's signature. This was the original. Shannon Squier was alive and Erin had found her.

Chisel Girl said, "What's my name?"

"Your name is Shannon Squier. You're Shannon Squier and everyone loves you." Erin started to cry, first from a gratitude she'd never known, not since waking from rehab, and then from something new.

For the first time in four years she could feel with certainty that a world was gone and, with it, people she had loved. She saw, just for a second—less than a second—that the great Fence that circled her world had the shape of the great fence that circled what used to be called her soul and that outside that North Korean fence, it was all a Burn Zone. Recoiling from the shadows of depthless melancholy, Erin wanted Shannon to be her best friend, her best sex-game partner, her best everything.

"Whatever you want, from now on, whatever you want, you're going to have."

"I'm thirsty. I want water."

ElderGoth said, "I'll get it."

Erin said, "Shannon, you can put your shirt on."

## Chief, Pippi Longstocking

Chief was on the phone and Pippi heard him say, "Who is Shannon Squier?" There was an explanation. "A singer? How would I remember that? If she's not verified, we can't take her, Erin. That's rule one." More talk from Erin. Then: "The same signature. If she's not in the computer . . ." Finally: "No, you've never asked me for a favor like this. And yes, I care about you but you can't bring her in without my permission. I'll come down."

He ended the call and told Pippi he might be back with someone special.

"Did I sound excited?"

"You sounded suspicious."

"Good."

"Are you excited?"

"The Woman told me someone was coming."

"And that's enough to verify . . . Who?"

"Someone named Shannon Squier."

"She's a little more than 'someone.' Erin has Shannon Squier pictures in her bedroom. And there are billboards with her name on them."

"Of course," said Chief.

"You haven't noticed."

"That's why I need you. Don't you know who we are?"

"Chief and Pippi."

"The Man and The Woman."

After Chief left with Go Bruins and Royce Hall, Pippi went to her bedroom, where she had a closet filled with cartons of cigarettes. She opened a pack, emptied the cigarettes into the trash, took out the silver paper that lined the box, and on the inside cover of the box wrote:

"*Darling, my new name is Pippi*" in the inside of the cover of the box. Then she went outside to find a black decorative garden stone that just fit inside the box, and rode her bike down the hill to the Playa. She parked her bike at the perimeter of the invisibly drawn circle around the two statues. Inside the circle, no one rested a bicycle, a Segway, or carried food. It was custom, not law, to cross the line in silence. Outside the perimeter there were usually a few clusters of people having sex, but today, except for one threesome blocked by The Woman's leg, she couldn't see any sex at all.

No one could explain why The Man and The Woman were down here on the Playa instead of on top of the hill beside Chief's house, but it wasn't a question that anyone asked except, perhaps, Pippi Longstocking. Why did The Woman dance and why did The Man stand there, so unbending? She climbed the stairs up his leg and into his chest. She had a view over the trees and looked for a particular place at the Fence. As she hoped, no one was close. She wasn't allowed outside the Fence, by Chief's orders, and she never went near the gates. She left The Man's chest and rode her bike to the Fence.

No one expected anything from Pippi Longstocking. June taught that Chief found Pippi her sometime during the early days and brought her to Center Camp. She was a First Wave rehab, original name lost. She finished the rehab wearing a T-shirt from a special effects company. This didn't prove she'd worked there, but if that's what she really was, it didn't matter. She had nothing to do. There were no movies being made with special effects anymore because there were no movies being made at all. Even watching old movies was difficult. There was a problem with understanding stories. June Moulton said it was a bad idea to watch movies, because the old myths died with the old brains. "In the hero's journey," Moulton taught, "the hero had to receive a call to his quest and then fight his father, and people in the audience found connection to those moments. If, as I believe, the Founders left some of us our Silent Voices to guide us, they never tell us to be heroes. Mostly they tell us to be frightened."

What mattered to anyone in Center Camp who watched the movies with the movie stars wasn't the story but the pictures of the old world. No one cared about the actors; they watched the cars on the streets, the crowds in the parks, and the downtown skyline at night, with all the windows lit up. War was interesting. And sex was more interesting, because it was something you could watch on-screen and then do with the person next to you.

In the leaves at the base of a eucalyptus tree Pippi uncovered a slingshot, with a leather pouch connected to two strips of rubber tubing.

She took the cigarette box out of her pocket, pinched the inside of the leather sling around it, pulled the rubber tubes back, angled them for the box to go high, and released the pouch. The cigarette box with the message that said

### Darling, my new name is Pippi

disappeared over the fence in a satisfying arc. She didn't see where it landed. Then she buried the slingshot in a different place.

# Frank Sinatra, Redwings, Chief, Shannon Squier, ElderGoth, Erin

At the hotel in West Covina, Sinatra wanted to get drunk on bourbon and talk about all-wheel drive Audis, but he called Vayler first, to warn him about the empty food-storage depot.

"No worries, Frank. We had that open, what, two years ago. Remember, lots of Chinese food?"

"It's marked for twenty twenty-eight."

"It was raining hard that month and I switched it out for a Costco in Simi Valley, too long a drive in bad weather. I have to say you have a good eye."

Frank didn't say anything.

Frank went to the bar, trying to remember if the season of Chinese food had been rainy. As he poured his drink, Redwings called and without introduction said, "Copycat tattoos don't fool me, Frank."

"I'm the last to quarrel with you on anything related to painted skin, my good friend, but why need my affirmation about that now?"

"You know the music Erin sometimes plays real loud at her house?"

"Redwings, I don't pay attention to music."

"The signatures match, and that can't be faked. No one good enough to fake it would fake it, Frank."

"I believe you, Redwings. What are you saying?"

"Guess who found Shannon Squier today?"

"I could use a hint or better for both."

"You did. And Chief wants you at the DMV, right now, toot sweet. It's her all right, identified by Erin and verified by me because I just saw the tat on her back, and her Smersh matches mine perfectly. Can you believe it? Two Smersh tats in the Fence now, two of 'em."

Three years before NK3, Redwings had traveled to Russia just to get a tattoo from **СМЕРШ** in his Moscow studio. Redwings kept a journal of his adventures on that trip, and by what would have been called a miracle if anyone still believed in God, the ten-page journal, printed for circulation among the members of his club, survived because he'd given it to his rehab doctor, who left it with Redwings before disappearing into the void of NK3:

> This is the story of how I got my smersh tat. How I wrote to Leonid "SMERSH" Sorokin in Moscow, with the help of Beria, a Russian brother from the Moscow charter, who I met at the funeral of the treasurer of the Encinitas, CA, charter, may he Ride Free Forever, who translated my request. I sent the word that I very much admired the smersh tattoo he had performed on the back of the singer Shannon Squier and I so admired the craftsmanship and the meaning of Death to Spies—or as we in the club would say, Death to Rats—that if it were at all possible that I could come to Moscow and have him tattoo nothing but that word across my shoulders, I would pay what he asked. Smersh sent back an e-mail not too long after I sent mine, also translated by brother Beria and therefore he could tell me: "You come, I do. €500." I thought he meant $ instead of €, but he preferred the € because it was worth more. It's only money.
>
> Thus began my adventure of first acquiring a United States passport and then it was off by Delta Airways to Amsterdamn, Holland, where I was met at the airport by a dozen brothers who had also brought a Harley Sportster for me, which normally I make fun of as a bike for women (although it's a fine bike as my ride showed me) but I was proud to join them on a great run across the flat land of Holland and then to the club house in old Amsterdamn. What a trippy place. Legal hash, just like home. Well time could not be wasted and after we partied in Amsterdam two of my Dutch

brothers joined me on a trip from Amsterdamn to Moscow, which took but three days. It blew my mind that the ride from Amsterdamn to Warsaw took a total of twelve hours of actual riding time, which we did in a day and a half. Twelve hours! I can say that I finally understand the Blitzkrieg. Europe is large on the map and small on the ground. And then another few days of easy ridering to Moscow through Belarus where I could see the partisans in the forest if I just squinted my eyes. Think of it! So close the distances between these famous cities and places and yet how many years did it take the Russians to defeat the Germans and get from point A in Moscow to point B in Berlin? I salute the soldiers on both sides of that mighty conflict.

The Warsaw charter included a few friends from a Sturgis run, which is sort of a bogus powwow in South Dakota but I have to admit draws an impressive number of dedicated bikers not including the dudes who put their bikes on a trailer, which they park ten miles away and ride the final ten miles. To each his own as we say, I guess.

Mighty mother Russia! I wish I had the time to visit what had been Stalingrad to see where the epic battle took place but I was there to get my tattoo. Smersh Sorokin could not have been a more regular decent guy, which was not a surprise because in my experience the real true artists with some exceptions—hello Bono and good-bye, you pretentious motherfucker—that I have met have been easy to talk to and not just about themselves. Do you hear me, Bono? Now Leonid, that man did not drink, not ever, nor take any drugs, because he wanted a steady hand and nothing fuzzy ever between his inspiration and his amazing touch. He also was a man not to gossip and when I asked him about Shannon Squier he told me gently that just as he would never talk about me to anyone he would not talk about her. A true Russian gentleman. I was surprised to see that he used the same inks as my tattoo artist in San Berdoo, CA, uses, but I don't know why it should have surprised me. This truly is one World.

*Leonid did keep vodka in the freezer for his customers and that was so cold it poured like motor oil. A shot of that with a cut-up slice of some delicious Russian black bread and then the pain is happening to someone you sort of know but don't talk to very often. You may well ask me how is it that I could cross the Russian border wearing my Hells Angel patch, but there's an answer. You would expect that even with the visa I had in my passport there would be resistance to admitting us, once they saw us, in the way that I could not get a visa into Australia because of the colors I proudly wear. But as explained to me the Russian Hells Angels are nationalists with support from nationalist elements in the Russian government and sometimes help out when a certain kind of help is needed. In America we are not political at all. We hate all government equally and they hate us. I don't think* **СМЕРШ** *himself was a political person, although in Europe I found everyone is more political than here in the sense that they vote. He liked hanging out with Hells Angels because everywhere in the world the club carries a mystique that adds some high-gloss metal flake shine to the impression made by anyone we call a friend. Ride Free.*

Shannon Squier sat next to Chief on the leather couch in ElderGoth's office, looking more like a Drifter past the threshold of even recognizing defeat than someone with a partial rehab and a will to live. Erin had a copy of *People* magazine with Shannon on the cover. Inside were pictures of her in a high school production of *Cabaret*, when her name had been Sandra Tur. But once she invented Shannon Squier, she buried Sandra Tur and never appeared in public as anyone but the character she played. When Sinatra arrived from Covina, Chief told ElderGoth to wait outside. "The room is small. It's getting crowded."

"Frank!" said Chief. "Look at what you found! And look at these pictures. It's her. It's really her."

Sinatra saw enough of the pictures to believe them.

"Do you remember me?" he asked her.

"When will you give me my chisel back?"

"Turn around and take off your shirt." He didn't say please and she didn't act like it was expected.

The tattoo was as good as Redwings had said.

"You used to be famous. People listen to your music. I'm not one for songs, but people do like your music."

"That's what they tell me."

"How did you end up in drifting?"

Chief stopped him. "Talk to her later. This is a lot for her to absorb."

"Security is my responsibility if anything goes wrong."

Chief nodded his head for Sinatra to follow him. "You're wondering what my plan is. She can be useful. People still listen to her music."

"Do you?"

"Erin does."

"This woman is not who she was, Chief. The way none of us are."

"You're wrong. She's still exciting. From what I hear now, she was one of the most exciting people alive in the Complete World, right up to the end, which is maybe why she's still exciting."

"She's not working on me."

"I think she is, just by the way we're all talking about her. The Woman promised me something and Shannon is the answer."

"If she's that powerful, you shouldn't just let me take her back to where I found her. You should kill her. We know why we're in charge of the city now; we know what we did to put ourselves on top. And we remember who we stole the power from. Here comes someone with what you say is power and you want to give her more. Introducing Shannon into our community is going to bring trouble."

"No sign of the rider coming from the east?"

"Chief, listen to yourself. The Woman told you—what? That someone was coming. Not that two were coming. There's either a rider from the east, or there's Shannon."

"You're not convinced."

"How can anyone be convinced of anything, Chief?"

Chief called for Erin to come back to the room and told Sinatra to just listen, and not interrupt or ask any questions.

"Am I in trouble?" Erin asked.

"Erin, you're a smart girl. You're important to life in the Fence because of how early you got the rehabilitation treatment and I know you worry sometimes that others might not like you for the way you haven't made yourself useful. But today is the day that you get to say to yourself, and I get to say to everyone else, that your value to the community needs no greater proof than the way you can be credited with verifying Shannon Squier. Let everyone know from this day forward that you recognized Shannon Squier when nobody else did, and that in appreciation of this service, you are now in charge of her. She stays with you. Get her cleaned up, make her comfortable, get her dressed, and be ready to bring her to a meeting of the committee heads when I call for her."

"Yes, yes!" shouted Erin. "I have the magazines, I have the pictures, and I have the music. I'm going to get her hair back to the way it was when she was Shannon. I'm going to teach her to talk like she used to talk, with an English accent, when she pretended that she came from Manchester instead of San Diego. She's going to be my new best friend."

Chief turned from Erin and then she stopped him. "Chief," she said. "What about branding her? She'd be the only person in the Fence who doesn't have the brand."

"What do you think?"

"No. That's not the way to welcome her home."

# Seth, Marci, Franz, Eckmann

After the pilot's surgery, Seth moved him to the bed in one of the Dreamliner's private first-class cabins.

"How soon can you fly?" Eckmann asked the pilot.

"I need to rest."

"We need to get out of here. We don't have a lot of time." Eckmann was scared. If Center Camp knew about the living pilot, Chief would probably attack, herding wispy Shamblers through the minefields. Eckmann wanted somebody to do something right and yelled at Marci and Consuelo. "Help this man. You two are nurses. Be nurses!"

Consuelo denied that she had been a nurse. "I worked in a hospital. My badge says I worked in a hospital. It doesn't say Consuelo Santos, RN. That's registered nurse. If I'd been a nurse, the ID would have said so. I probably just worked in the kitchen or mopped the floors."

Marci said, "And I was a flight attendant. I was trained in first aid, not medicine, and do not raise your voice at me. Not after what I've been through in the motor pool."

"I'm sorry," said Seth. "I'm really sorry. I'm pretty sure I used to be a good doctor. I worked with very sick children at UCLA and that means parents trusted me."

Marci put a hand on his shoulder. "It's not your fault, Doctor. And you got the bullet out and sewed him back up. You're not the one who shot him; you're not the one who screwed up getting him here and then screwed up getting you here. I don't want to make you feel bad."

"I have to say that I'm happy to be where I am," said Seth. "I've been given something to do that brings me back to what I was like before everything changed. Dr. Piperno didn't help me. I've made great advances in one night with you." He wanted to take care of his patient. Of all the things he could do, just being quiet around a sick man offered Seth the greatest protection from everyone else's expectations. What he said next surprised him. "I want everyone to leave me alone with my patient, and I'd like Marci to stay."

Eckmann protested, "She's not a nurse."

"No," said the doctor. "She's a flight attendant, and we're in an airplane. This is where she belongs, right, Marci?"

"He's right," she said, with an eagerness that was new to her.

Seth didn't know what to say to Marci after Eckmann cleared the plane and the crew went back to work testing the electrical and hydraulic systems while others swept the runway clear of dead palm fronds, dog bodies, gravel, strips of metal. Alone inside the quiet plane, with the curtains pulled down and the lights dim, they felt a pleasant instability, as the pilot's fate depended on powers neither of them could petition for help.

Seth looked through the magazines and newspapers that no one had cleaned out of the plane. Most of the newspapers were dated October 16, 2019. The magazines on the plane were all from October or September. It confused Seth that the plague was front-page news in some but not all of the papers. There was local worry but little global panic.

The *New York Times* had an article about the rehabilitation centers at UCLA and USC giving secret priority to people who knew how to run and maintain the central systems that society needed or would die without, and how this policy enraged some of the hospitals' wealthiest donors, who found that having their names on the hospital buildings didn't give them a free pass to the next empty bed. The rehab centers in New York denied they were giving privileges to anyone who didn't have skills. Hospitals in Chicago and Atlanta had no comment. It was noted that as the syndrome spread, social outrage diminished.

*Time* magazine's cover that week was a black question mark on a white background.

# ?

Why did the newspapers and news magazines, at least by page count, show that fear of extinction was in only one compartment of readers' minds? The magazine and newspapers did not devote all the news to NK3. They still printed reviews of movies and books, articles about new cars, ways to make inexpensive costumes for Halloween.

Something happened, though, on or around October 18, 2019, to keep the Singapore Airlines plane from flying again. On the planes at the airport that had arrived that day—the planes with the galley trash bags full—there were carry-on suitcases filled with clothes in the overhead bins, books and small tubes of toothpaste, still pliable. Jackets. Hats. Children's dolls. Why did the passengers leave their bags? Were they told to get off the plane quickly for fear of an explosion or fire or because the police knew that someone on the plane was infected and everyone had to be taken away? Or did the infection spread so quickly that the passengers forgot what they'd brought with them?

Marci wiped Franz's hot forehead with a cloth soaked in a bowl of water.

Seth showed her the *Time* cover and the articles about the rehab centers. She told him she didn't care.

"Why not?"

"It doesn't change anything to know. Do you feel bad that I don't want to know what you want to tell me?"

"Maybe a little."

"That little is all that's left of what we used to be like and I don't want to hear anything more about it. It makes me too sad. Is his forehead still hot?"

Seth cupped his hand over Franz's wet brow.

"That's the first time you've been gentle with him. You cut him open but you didn't touch him just to make him feel better."

"He's cooler now, isn't he?"

"I think so."

"How quickly can Eckmann have the jet ready to fly?"

"It takes two hours to fill the fuel tanks. A truck will tow the plane to the head of the runway. The engines won't be turned on until we're ready to go, because the sound of the jet will be the loudest thing anyone in Los Angeles has heard in four years."

"I think I can fly this plane," said the pilot. His eyes were open and clear.

"You heard what we were saying?"

"Yes. Yes. I don't want to fly with me any more than you do, Dr. Kaplan. But Eckmann won't let me run away."

Marci asked, "Do you think you can do what he needs?"

"I think I can get it in the air, yes. I don't know if I can bring it down so that we can walk away from the plane, even though the plane can land itself. Although it's not clear to me that it can land itself without the right signal coming from the airport we're approaching."

"Thank you for being honest."

"Is that what I am?"

"You're not lying," said Marci. "I know that much."

"I'm scared of my mind splitting into pieces. I hear two different sets of words, Doctor. I haven't told anybody. I hear a voice in my head that speaks a different set of words than the one I'm speaking with now."

"Stay here," said Seth and walked back into the cabin. He returned with a copy of *Der Spiegel*. The cover was the picture of a damaged brain cell. He handed the magazine to the pilot, who turned the pages, mumbling in German as he read phrases aloud.

"I can read this."

"Of course, you're German. And this is German. This is an article about the plague. What does it say?"

"This says, 'Scientists at the Max Planck Institutes are working on a cure.'"

"What else is there in the magazine?"

"Turkish skiers are advised to make reservations now if they're planning on skiing in Austria next January or February. The Austrian hotels are recruiting seasonal guest workers from Australia and Spain and are trying not to hire so many Turkish guest workers, because last year the Turkish guest workers at the resorts went on strike over housing conditions. The hotels don't want Turkish staff making the Turkish guests feel uncomfortable."

"I don't know why that story makes me feel calm," said Seth. "But I would rather listen to news from the past than eat."

"Eat what?" It was Eckmann coming up the stairs to the cabin, followed by the three senior maintenance crew. He put a hand on

Seth's forehead, then Marci's, then the others'. "I'm taking an average. My pilot feels normal. Am I right? How do you feel?"

"It hurts when I laugh."

"What were you laughing at?"

"Everything."

"Are you ready to fly a plane, Franz?"

"Yes."

"Are you thirsty?"

"Yes."

"Then we will feed you and be ready to fly away from here when they have the big Burn. It may be that they'll postpone for a few nights, but I don't want to bring the jet out to the runway until the moment we're ready to leave. And the Burn will add the cover we need. And I expect you to be scared. We're all scared. But what choice do we have?"

Franz asked if he could shower. Seth said the stitches were fresh and that Marci should bathe him with a wet cloth but that she should make sure to keep the wounds dry.

"Is it day or night outside?" asked Seth.

Eckmann said, "Night."

"I'm going for a walk."

He nodded for Marci to join him, but Eckmann saw this and told Marci to stay with Franz. "You were a flight attendant. He was a pilot. Read the flight manuals with him."

She wanted to go but she had to stay.

Seth left the plane. The door to the outside was ahead and he went to it, expecting to be stopped, but with the pilot now safely out of danger except for Eckmann's demented fantasy that what might go up will come down in one piece, no one checked in with the chain of authority to see if Seth needed permission to leave the building.

The air carried sounds that caught the uneven gusts of westbound wind, the distant thump of music from Figueroa and from the Fence. The weave of tangled beats reached him, interrupting the interruption of his interrupted life.

Marci was inside. Seth said good-bye to the night and went back into the hangar. He wanted to be with her.

# Hopper

The crew in the West Covina Radisson was busy fucking and they missed Hopper as he pedaled by three hours after sunset, tasting the lingering but not unpleasant air of the ash moat. He knew what to do, as his Teacher directed, when he came to the Los Angeles River on the east side of the city.

Hopper rolled his bike down the riverbank and then carried it overhead as he walked through the stream where it was slowed by marsh grass. He left the bike in a thicket of bushes and took his city street clothing out of his bag.

He walked through dark streets and alleys where he could follow the strange sound—new to him but intelligible, of people celebrating life—until ahead of him were the bright lights of Figueroa Street, where every night was a party, where no one was hungry, where everyone was drunk because the Founders had so generously left the survivors enough alcohol to keep the world buzzed for another thirty years or ten thousand.

Hopper walked slowly down the middle of the street, copying the unsteady weaving of a few drunks stumbling on their way to take a piss against a dead cash machine beside the entrance to a Bank of America. When they peed he took a place at the wall beside them, and also peed. They nodded at him and when they left, he followed them to the festival of light that was Figueroa. He was in the crowd now, and no one cared.

The First Wavers owned the night. Only First Wavers could ride Segways to roll and pivot through the crowd. They were the careless ones and also the most polite, with exaggerated good manners, stepping out of each other's way, or out of the way of the Second Wavers, giving their place in the food or liquor lines to those behind them.

His Silent Voice told him: "No one cares you're here. Eat something."

Hopper stood in line at a fish taco truck and took the plate the server handed him. His Silent Voice reminded him: "No alcohol."

Down the block, a hundred men stood shoulder to shoulder in a circle, knocking their bottles together in a steady pulse, and in the center of the circle were five naked women, skipping from foot to foot and shaking with no connection to the beat of the ringing glass. Their clothing lay in the street around them. Hopper's Silent Voice told him to walk away. Hopper asked the First Waver next to him about the women. "What is this?" asked Hopper.

"Where have you been?"

"I was in Long Beach." This is what the Teacher told him to say if he was asked.

"They don't bottle bang in Long Beach?"

"I forget."

The First Waver said, "Welcome to your better life, friend. These are what we call Shamblerinas. Barely any rehab or maybe even no rehab. The ones with the least rehab, they can't hold their booze. They get drunk but they don't have any inhibitions to lose because they don't have anything restrained by social convention. It's like no offense, but you would never understand a joke unless you'd been through full rehab, like I have. Like only a few of us have. We keep these girls around for giggles. They're nice to look at naked, right? They'll sleep it off and in the morning they'll be out here, sweeping up the broken glass. They don't mind being naked like this. And you can just fuck them."

"Do they like it?" asked Hopper.

"How could anyone measure that? I'm an expert in mechanical systems, especially electric motors. In advance of gas running out I have a specialty in electric cars. I'm Tesla, DMV motor pool, but

out here they call me Papa BangBang. Papa BangBang of the Bottle
Bangers. My boss doesn't like this, okay, fuck him. He's got a Driftette, borderline Shamblerina, to himself and thinks he's an important
man. Well, I was one of the first to go through rehab at UCLA." He
pulled up his sleeve to show Hopper his )'(. "I earned this. Doesn't
that make me an important man? Who are you?"

"Nole Hazard," said Hopper, as his Teacher told him to say.

"Nole, I'm drunk. Are you drunk?"

"Drunk enough," said Nole. "Good answer," said his Silent Voice.

Two of the women bumped into each other, knocking one of
them to the street. The others paid no attention, bouncing from foot
to foot, slapping hands to bare breasts, eyes scanning without focus,
without attention to the woman who fell onto the broken bottles on
the street. Blood dripped from the side of her mouth. She raised
herself to her hands and knees, face toward Hopper. He showed her
the ring on his left hand.

"Did you ever wear a ring like this?" She didn't answer and he
asked again in a louder voice, in case she hadn't heard him over the
ringing of the bottles as the men made the other four women dance.
He bent down, kneeling on one leg. "Did you ever wear a ring like this?
On that finger?" He squeezed the ring finger on her left hand. "Yes?
No?" She was too drunk to understand and one of the other women
tripped over his foot and fell across her. The second woman used the
first woman's head to steady herself. The bleeding woman couldn't
answer Hopper's question about the ring and collapsed once again to
the street. Hopper wiped her bleeding mouth with the T-shirt from
the nearest pile of clothes.

Tesla stopped him. "What are you doing? Don't mess with the
Shamblerinas, Nole. It's not how we do things down here. You should
know that, or tell Papa BangBang why you don't know that."

"I do know that," said Hopper, as his Silent Voice ordered.

Hopper left Tesla and looked for a hotel with an empty room.
The Ritz-Carlton had the best view to the south and west, but the
hotel was for verified First Wave only. The Marriott was for First and

Second Wave. He tried three hotels, the Marriott, Embassy Suites, and the Standard, and walked ten blocks up and down Figueroa and a few blocks to the side before finding a room at the Hilton.

His Silent Voice said, "Their hotels weren't supposed to be this crowded. Ask them why."

The desk clerk was in her twenties, with braided blond hair. She wore a hotel maid's uniform and a name tag that said CECILIA.

"Cecilia," Hopper said. She didn't respond. He said it again.

She looked up. "I forgot."

"Forgot what?"

"Forgot my name is Cecilia."

"It says Cecilia."

"I know."

Hopper's Silent Voice dictated what he should say. "My name is Nole Hazard. I failed verification."

"Oh."

"And I'm here to work."

"Oh."

"And I'd like a room. On a high floor, facing south."

"Twenty-sixth floor."

"I appreciate that. Thank you."

"How many keys?"

"One. Just for me," said Hopper.

"Housekeeping every three days. The room will be dirty. Sign." She gave him a ledger book.

He signed for the key card, Nole Hazard. She handed him a key card. "Put it in the door, wait for the green light, open the door."

His Silent Voice told him to ask a question, "Is it always so hard to find a room?"

"The Burn."

"The Burn what?"

She couldn't explain. He thanked her.

The elevator knocked and rattled on the way up. It smelled of Clorox and cigarettes. A placard from before announced that there would be live music in the bar on Friday and Saturday nights, from a band called Sausalito. There was no live music anymore because no one could play the instruments.

The hallway on the twenty-sixth floor was badly lighted. He found the room and opened the door.

The lights in the room worked. The sheets were stained; there were empty bottles piled in the corner. The shower was hot.

Hopper opened the sliding glass door to the balcony.

Something out there in the shadow, over West Adams or Crenshaw, cast an invisible hook on an invisible line, tugging Hopper's heart toward the center of the void. Nothing was any clearer except the command to follow the line to its source, or die.

He told his Silent Voice: "I'm tired. I need to sleep. I traveled hard to get here."

His Silent Voice said, "Go to sleep. You shouldn't do this at night, anyway. You need to see where you're going. It's dangerous enough."

# Franz, Eckmann, Spig Wead, Seth, Marci

Eckmann returned to the pilot's cabin with the oldest man in the crew. "Franz, this is Spig Wead, he's our electronics engineer and he's been in charge of the cockpit." Wead had sparse hair and a back that always hurt him and he walked slowly. He accused everyone of incompetence though his own had never been proven.

"I've read the manuals and run the tests and everything works. I could probably fly it but with you here I'm your copilot. I'm in the seat on the right."

The cockpit windows were covered in heavy black cloth. Seth watched from the cockpit entrance. They'd long ago removed the heavy security door. Marci sat on the flight attendant's jump seat, lost in the mayhem of her thoughts, because she missed AutoZone. He had almost given her a good name and she wanted that more than she wanted to be on the plane. She missed the adventure of the motor pool. She could look back on those days and remember different moments, as though they were tires on a rack, there for her to touch. For the first time since her rehab, she had a past to long for.

Franz sat in the left seat in the cockpit, pushing the controls for the wing flaps. He asked Spig Wead to continue doing this so he could step outside of the plane and watch what he was controlling. When he was behind the plane the signal was given to Spig Wead and the flaps moved in and out.

Wead explained, "This will slow your airspeed and this will also help you climb. And did you know that we shouldn't land with full tanks of gas? I read that in the manual."

"I hope we won't make that mistake," said the pilot.

"A full load of fuel can get us to Europe."

"Is that where we're going?"

"I don't know. Eckmann won't say."

Seth watched Franz with an expanding anticipation of doom, as under Eckmann's confident directions, the pilot believed that these simple rehearsals in a covered hangar would successfully translate into controlled flight. Doctors were intelligent people; he could see that from the equipment he once understood. Airplanes were complicated. Medical equipment was also complicated. He trusted that his brain, however degraded by NK3, was still better in proportion to the brains of those around him. Then he caught his thoughts and reversed them, impressing himself with his willingness not to hold to an idea to avoid feeling lost in the emptiness between one conviction and its replacement. If doctors are smart, so must pilots be smart, in proportion to the rest of the brain-damaged world. If so, and Franz still has brain power, then Spig Wead, a mechanic and also therefore a smart man, is acting prudently.

*So I should go with them*, he thought. *And be close to Marci.*

He looked at Franz as a scared and injured man. Franz needed his help.

Eckmann climbed into the jump seat behind the throttles, going through the manual to determine the function of every button and dial, puzzled by the way everything on the gauges on the screens above the pilot's seat was matched by the same instruments above the copilot's seat. They weren't sure what to do about this. Should they perform the same function at precisely the same time, or was it enough for one of them to make the change on his side of the plane?

When they met this kind of dilemma, Eckmann told Franz to close his eyes and feel his way to the answer. Franz then closed his eyes and waited for a moment of sudden clarity, something that made immediate sense of the confusing elements of the cockpit.

Wead thumbed through the manual. The manual's illustrations showed the correct alignment of the gauges, but there was no function in the cockpit to simulate a flight and show what the wrong positions looked like.

"Franz? Eyes still closed?"

"Yes."

"We're going into a stall. We should be at four hundred knots but airspeed has dropped because the speed sensor has frozen and without knowing it, headwinds have slowed us to two hundred and thirty knots. We're losing lift. What do you do?"

Franz steadied his hand on the wheel.

"We're slowing down, Franz, the tail of the plane is dropping. We're going vertical, about to fall tail-end first," said Eckmann calmly.

Seth pulled the lever to release Franz's seat, which flopped backward. Franz watched his hands reach forward to push the pillar away from him, still with his eyes closed.

"I think that's right," said Eckmann. "I know it doesn't make sense, but when the plane is falling, you push down on the nose to get lift again."

Franz pulled the pillar in and kept it there, as though climbing. He bounced a little in his seat, pulsing in time to a steady turbulence only he could feel. Seth asked him: "Are you tired?"

Franz nodded.

Seth put a hand on the wheel.

"He's flying," said Eckmann. "Why are you making him stop?"

"My patient is tired. He needs to rest. Ten minutes. I want him to drink some water and have some food."

Marci pushed a reluctant Eckmann from the cockpit to the stairs and told everyone else in the galley and first-class cabin to leave the plane.

Franz didn't want to talk after the others were gone. He just sipped water and ate three small bags of hickory-smoked almonds and then returned to the cockpit alone, closed his eyes, took the wheel, and pretended to fly.

# Shannon Squier, Erin

Outside her bedroom door, Erin told Shannon: "Close your eyes."

Shannon refused.

Erin said, "You have to."

"Why?"

"Because of the surprise."

"I don't want a surprise."

Shannon reached for the handle of the chisel before she remembered the chisel was gone. She wanted to plunge the sharp end into this woman's eyes, not deep enough to kill, just to blind her and kick her into the streets screaming. It was something she'd done a few times, and afterward walked in a foam of mirth.

"I don't want you to do anything you don't want to do, Shannon, so here." Erin opened the door to her bedroom and her shrine to all things Shannon. "After you, please."

Shannon walked cautiously into the room, prepared for a surprise that might be violent, but Erin stayed a few feet away, respectfully waiting for Shannon to respond to what Erin was showing her.

"This is you, Shannon," said Erin. The walls of the room were hidden behind pictures of Shannon Squier on magazine covers, in newspaper articles about her, in framed photographs of Shannon Squier in concert, along with framed stubs of concert tickets from Los Angeles, San Francisco, Chicago, New York, São Paulo, London, Barcelona, Rome, and Moscow, the CDs and the American, British, and Italian editions of the official autobiography. "I don't think I went to all those concerts of course, just LA and San Diego. I have pictures from those. My father was in the movie business and he could get me good seats but I don't know how I came to own the stubs from all those other cities. It's possible I went but I haven't seen any pictures of me in any of those cities at any of your concerts. Although my passport shows stamps from France, Germany, Italy, and England."

"You're saying this is all me?" asked Shannon.

"Now you get it!" Erin clapped her hands. "Yes, yes, this is you, all of these pictures, all of this music, here: this is you at the Grammys. And over here is the special picture, the most special picture of all."

On the nightstand beside Erin's fluffy bed was a photograph of fifteen-year-old Erin standing next to Shannon, with Shannon holding the three Grammy Awards she'd won that night. The picture was autographed:

*To Erin—Choose to Be You!*

*I love you madly, little one—kisses, SS.*

"Do you understand, Shannon, I didn't tell you about this before because I didn't want you to not believe me when I told you, but we knew each other. You loved me madly, you see?"

Shannon picked up the picture and held it next to Erin's face. "That's you?"

"And you."

Shannon looked at herself in the mirror and back to the picture. "That's me?"

"Well, with a silver wig and a dress made of plastic steaks, but yes, that is you, and that is me. It's lucky I have all of this. And I have your videos collected on a DVD because my father was head of Warner Bros. and Warner Records was your label." Erin put the DVD into her iMac.

"Was that your father who found me?"

"Frank? Oh, God, no, no, but forget about him. Look at this. This is you. The director of the video was David Fincher. He made a lot of famous movies. That's what it says in your biography. You worked with some of the best directors in the world just five years ago."

The video began. Shannon watched the woman on the screen, in a tinsel wig and a short plaid skirt, surrounded by stiff-legged marching robots, singing about life in a submarine.

"You have the most beautiful voice," said Erin.

Now she was outside the submarine, longer than the submarine, spreading her legs for the submarine, now she was inside the submarine, now she opened her mouth wide for a high note and the camera plunged into her throat and now she was on the stage of a large stadium with a hundred thousand fans dressed like her, dancing like her, singing along with her.

"I don't have those people inside me," said Shannon.

"Of course not," said Erin. "It took me a while to figure that out, too. This is all stuff they could do with computers. But it's interesting, isn't it? Everybody in the world knew who you were. And they will again. I'm going to bring you back."

# Hopper

Hopper woke up before dawn. His Silent Voice told him: "You have to do something important today." Hopper took the binoculars out of his bike messenger bag and opened the sliding glass door to the balcony. The house was out there, to the southwest. The Teacher had shown him photographs, and a map, and tested Hopper until both were certain that Hopper could find it even in the dark, but something was wrong. The map didn't agree with the city. There was a wall of rubble forty feet high and miles long between two of the boulevards that went from downtown to the ocean.

Throwing the messenger bag over his shoulders, Hopper went downstairs.

The receptionist this morning didn't look like the one from the night, but she wore the Cecilia name tag. Hopper checked his watch against the clock behind the Cecilia. His watch said 6:18; her clock said 6:52.

There were free bicycles on the sidewalk and he took a steel-framed road bike with straight handlebars.

Hopper pedaled south on Figueroa, past the hotels and apartments, past the parking lots of car dealers, the cars maintained by Inventory but not yet in service. He turned west on the boulevard that would bring him to the house and then south again, to the wall of rubble he'd seen from the balcony. The wall was three stories high, made of the buildings demolished by Toby Tyler's Burn Brigade. The buildings had been knocked down, crushed, and pushed together into a loose mound the height of the Fence, made from sections of roof, floor carpets, pink fiberglass insulation, staircases, refrigerators, and washing machines. Why didn't the Teacher know about this?

Hopper's Silent Voice said, "The house is on the other side of this, somewhere in there. You lived so close to where you are now.

A block to the west a gap in the wall was protected by an open gate that was guarded by Security. Two men and a woman, all of them in formal wear, with pistols in their holsters, sat under the awning of an Airstream trailer.

A line of Inventory trucks with Second Wavers sitting in front and Drifters in the back waited to be waved through.

Hopper rode up to the guards. This was going to take a lot of words.

"Hello," he said, as instructed by his Silent Voice.

The head of the guards, an Unverified Second Waver, was Bruce Willis, the actor. He told them to stop.

"No one goes into the Burn Zone unless he's in a crew. It's too dangerous with all the charges being set in place."

"What are charges?"

"All of the things that are going to blow up and set everything behind me on fire."

"How do I get in a crew?"

"I'm Security," said Willis. "Check with Inventory." He wasn't hostile; he was just describing his limitations.

"When is it burning?" asked Hopper.

"Soon."

"Ask them how soon," said his Silent Voice.

"How soon?" asked Hopper.

"Hoping tomorrow, expecting the day or three after," said Willis.

Hopper's Silent Voice was so silent when Willis said this that Hopper could feel the Voice's anger. "Why are you mad at me?" Hopper asked him.

"You wasted a day with those children in that school. We should have climbed the wall into this area last night, if not the night before."

In the staging area south of the hotels on Figueroa, a thousand Drifters—men and women—lined up in ranks of a hundred. Hopper left his bicycle at a crowded rack and settled in a middle line as a caravan of pickup trucks, supermarket delivery trucks, and moving vans pulled alongside the curb while supervisors shuttled the workers along. Hopper was pushed into the back of a U-Haul truck. The other five in the truck with him were three women and two men. The driver asked their names but didn't write them down or introduce himself. Hopper told him, "Nole Hazard."

One of the women said, "I really shouldn't be here. This is all a mistake. Listen to me. You can tell from my speech patterns that I've been through rehab, early rehab. I should be in Center Camp. I should be at the parties. I should be climbing up the legs of The Man or asking hard questions of The Woman. I should be wearing costumes from the finest old stores. I know that the stores were fine. How's that for proof my story is true?" She was probably in her late thirties, with something written around her eyes that showed, from the old days, a disappointment that would have progressed into a permanent expression of dismay if she hadn't been rescued from that kind of pain by the hidden blessing of NK3, salvation by forgetting she was ever in love with two men who changed their minds about her. Andy Warhol's portrait of Elizabeth Taylor was tattooed on her right shoulder.

"I'm Siouxsie Banshee. That's what I call myself. My real name is Sonia Pryce, P-R-Y-C-E, which I didn't know until I saw my picture in an art journal at the County Museum. I used to work for Vayler Monokeefe at the County Museum of Art. That was my proof. I tore the picture out of the page but I lost it. I'm Siouxsie Banshee because I needed a name before I found my real name. What's your name?"

"Nole Hazard."

"Nole? Aren't I smart? Isn't Sonia Pryce a real name? Could I make that up? Don't I sound like someone who went through an early rehab?"

"I think so." But he didn't think so. He didn't know.

"Have any of you been on this detail before? You see the reason I'm here is that I have a Strong Feeling about quality. And these so-called experts don't know the difference between a print and a painting."

Bruce Willis waved the truck through the gate into the Burn Zone.

One of the other Drifters in the truck pointed out a stack of red gasoline cans in the middle of an intersection. "Burn soon."

Siouxsie Banshee covered her face with her hands. "Well, that's the level of conversation back here. Isn't that the lowest? All he can do is point and say two words. I don't have to point and I can say a thousand words."

The truck turned right, quickly, no warning, throwing the six Drifters into a packed tangle.

The view from the back had changed. They were in a neighborhood of small houses, and apartments with two or four units. The gardens were dead. Dusty cars were in the driveways.

The truck stopped. No one told them to wait, but they stayed where they were until the driver and his passenger came around.

Siouxsie whispered to Frank, "The driver doesn't even know he's Asian, and the other one may not know she's from Africa."

The driver introduced himself. "I'm Martin Rome, from Inventory, and my partner today is 18 Tee."

"There's a story behind my name," said 18 Tee. "And I'm sure you all want to know it. He's with Inventory but I'm with Systems. I installed Internet cables. I fixed phone lines. I did real things. I worked for AT&T: 18 Tee. Why is Systems doing Inventory? With the Burn coming, Inventory needs help. I hope that answers your questions."

18 Tee carried a manila envelope and set it down on the bed of the truck. She opened the envelope and laid out ten sheets of paper with pictures of valuable furniture, dishware, flatware, and art.

She addressed the group. "This is your job today. We've been assigned ten square blocks. We will work fast. Our committee head, Vayler Monokeefe, expects us to find much that is of value and we must work hard and move things quickly but our first goal is to preserve. If the houses are locked, we break the door open. Some of these houses will have dog doors and some of those houses will have become home to coydogs. They will stink. The furniture will likely be ruined. We will not take it. Look at the printouts. We only want pieces of furniture that look like this. We're looking for American furniture made in the nineteen fifties through the nineteen seventies. We're also looking for record collections, CDs of course but also vinyl albums. They're becoming popular in Center Camp. Unopened bottles of alcohol or wine found in special wine closets in the basements, that's what we want."

Siouxsie Banshee raised her hand.

"Yes?"

"They can't follow what you're saying. I'm the only one who can. Look. Some of this is Stickley furniture and the rest of it is called midcentury modern. This neighborhood is too old to find much mid-century modern. And some of this stuff is just imitation junk."

"How do you know this?" 18 Tee asked.

"I was a curator. I was in rehab to supervise the protection of our heritage. I had a picture that proves this. I knew Vayler Monokeefe."

"Pictures don't prove anything."

"I knew Vayler before things changed."

"That's not verification."

"I'm not in the DMV because I'm from New York City. That's what it said in the article and I looked it up and New York is a long way from here. It's not California, which is what this is or used to be."

18 Tee asked Rome if they should call someone about this. He refused. "We've been told what to select and she's been told to help carry what we select and I'm saying to you both: Don't make trouble. Just do your job."

"This is so unfair," said Siouxsie Banshee.

They went in teams of two into the houses. Hopper followed Siouxsie Banshee, compelled by his Teacher's warnings to stay with people who know about the world, either what it is made from or how it works, those who hold the shredded systems together.

The living room set in the first house matched the pictures. 18 Tee brought the others into the house to carry the furniture to the truck.

"This is all crap," said Siouxsie. "This is all imitation mission, cheap crap from big stores. Look, here, this veneer. Pull it back, see? It peels away and inside, look, wood chips pressed together. Doesn't that verify me?"

18 Tee told Siouxsie not to break the furniture.

"I should kill myself," said Siouxsie.

Hopper said, "Maybe you should. Then they wouldn't bother you. And you wouldn't be angry at them."

"He talks! You talk. You're not like the others. I knew that as soon as I saw you. It's in the eyes. And you have a wedding ring. Don't see many of those."

"Why not?"

"All jewelry was taken off for the magnetic resonance part of the rehab. Then, later, wedding rings . . . Don't you know this?"

"I don't know this."

"The wedding rings were confiscated so that people with rings wouldn't match up with other people with rings. It was called Operation Clean Slate. The order came from the top, from Chief, on June Moulton's recommendations to build a consistent mythology. Look at all the things I know! He didn't want the new society to have divisions left over from the old. The rehab process didn't take couples, only the person who was needed, so very, very few couples made it through together. This house is useless. Let's see how the others are doing." She led him outside.

His Silent Voice warned him: "Don't ask her any more questions about the rings and the past."

In the next house there were four armless chairs with steel legs and leather cushions, and no arms. Couch with bentwood arms. Siouxsie called for 18 Tee to look at it.

"This is the real thing," said Siouxsie. "This is not Ikea. These are designed by Marcel Breuer. I'm surprised to find them here. They're great."

"I don't have a picture of them."

"You don't have to have one."

"But then it can't be verified."

"I'm verifying it for you. You don't need a picture of them. I know what they are."

"I have to have a picture of this kind of chair."

"This area is going to be burned, this will be destroyed, and these are fine pieces."

"That may be so, but you're not verified so you can't verify them, so they stay."

Across the street, two of the crew found a chair that matched the printouts. They called to 18 Tee for her opinion.

"Good work, this is an Eames chair. Put it on the truck."

Siouxsie Banshee stopped them to tilt the chair and look at the mark on the bottom. She offered more of her dismal appraisal that everything bad in the world was aimed at her heart. "That's not an original. It's pretty but it's not really worth anything. Why did they do this to me?"

"Who?" asked Hopper.

"The doctors who saved my life. This is hell. I'm in hell. They should have let me just die. This isn't the life they wanted for me. I don't need the printouts. I'm a museum director. We were nervous people."

The Eames chair was the only treasure that matched anything on the printouts. They wrapped it in furniture blankets and tried to tie it to rings on the floor of the truck. None of them knew how to tie a knot. Hopper knew, but his Silent Voice said, "Don't show them what you can do."

The truck drove to another street, passing a house with gray walls and a flat roof.

"This is the Lukens house," said Siouxsie. "Raphael Soriano was the architect. I know this house, I have pictures of it in my office at the museum. This house shouldn't be burned." But she knew it would be, and was eager to save what she could.

The furniture in the Lukens house wasn't in the printout, but the kitchen held a few matches; dishes, vases, and cutlery. Siouxsie

Banshee was happy with what they found. The crew wrapped the dishes in shirts and towels taken from drawers and closets, then put them in suitcases and loaded them into the truck.

After a lunch of canned sardines and oranges, they moved to the center of the zone, a neighborhood of older large bungalows. "The people who lived here took great care of these old houses," said Siouxsie Banshee. "The roofs are new. The paint is good. The concrete in the driveways isn't badly cracked. Every other car is a Lexus or a BMW or a Prius. This must have been a pleasant place to live."

The truck stopped. Siouxsie Banshee yelled at 18 Tee. "Why does all this have to be burned? A Neutra house over there, and here, a street of Greene and Greene–inspired bungalow-style houses from the nineteen twenties. This is one of the things I was trained in rehab to know about. I was programmed to save what was beautiful from people who were programmed to make sure I had food to eat and you can't have one without the other! Whose decision is it to destroy all of this?"

"No one is ever going to live here. The old houses and neighbor-hoods take too much energy to maintain for too few people. All of you can live well in the buildings downtown while the power and water are cut off from the old neighborhoods. When and if the population returns, we, or the people of the future, can build new houses here."

Rome led the group to the houses on the west side of the street, but Hopper was drawn to the other side.

Hopper walked down a driveway between two large houses, with stained glass windows and upper decks supported by columns made of river stones set in concrete.

Siouxsie Banshee was impressed. "They had these porches because they didn't have air-conditioning. So people would sit here on hot days and watch the street. The modern houses don't have porches because everyone stayed inside. I'm kind of sick of what I know. I didn't ask for it."

Rome led the group into the house. Hopper walked through the living room to the kitchen and the back of the house and opened the back door. There was a one-lane swimming pool, almost the length of the yard; water long gone, it was filled instead with leaves and palm fronds. There was a redwood fence at the end of the yard.

The three-story house on the other side of the fence was painted a dark green with brown trim at the windows. There was a redwood play set in the backyard with two swings and a tower. Three sets of metal wind chimes hung from brass chains on the eaves of the house's ample back porch.

Hopper pulled himself up and over the fence, into the house's backyard. 18 Tee was calling for everyone to come back. He ignored her and went to the back steps of the house, kicked in the door, and went into the kitchen.

He knew where everything was. He reached under a cabinet and touched a key, then another one, hanging on a loop of metal, on a hook. Someone was calling his name again.

He didn't need his Silent Voice to tell him to get out of there quickly. Siouxsie Banshee watched him leave the house and 18 Tee came into that yard just as he was crossing over the fence.

"There's nothing there," he said.

Siouxsie Banshee asked, "You sure? The place is in better condition than most."

"Someone else got it."

18 Tee was unhappy. "What are you doing in houses that aren't on our list?"

Siouxsie Banshee felt something in Hopper that she wanted to protect. "I'm not looking to do more work, either. Martin Rome found some totally crap tables and wants us to take them away."

Rome heard this. "They're on the printout."

"I know that radical inclusion is a big thing in Center Camp, but this is a mistake. It's heavy and it's junk. Why waste our time?"

Hopper saw 18 Tee looking at him as he climbed from the other yard. He wanted to deny her the time to think about his quiet hesitation at the redwood fence.

"What should we take first?" he asked her. She looked through the furniture matches on the printout and led him to the dining room table.

Hopper called for the others to help him and they carried it to the truck.

"It's too long," said Martin Rome.

"It can stick out the back," said 18 Tee.

When they pushed it into the truck the table leg pressed into the suitcase, breaking some of the plates before Siouxsie Banshee stopped them from forcing the table backward any more. The workers, once they were told what to do, didn't always adjust for circumstances.

"Those were Russel Wright dishes," said Siouxsie Banshee. "They had value. This table is junk."

"It matches the picture."

"Not really."

"Who else but you could tell the difference?"

"Nobody else but me. That's why I should be verified. It's not fair. Is it fair? Do you think it's fair?"

Hopper had no opinion about any of this but he knew that Siouxsie had covered for him in the backyard so he agreed with her. "It's not fair."

A dog pack down the street sniffed at the group. Martin Rome shouted at them to go away, but the dogs held their ground. The leader was a thin rottweiler missing patches of hair.

Hopper sat with his feet over the edge of the truck bed and held on to the table as the truck left the curb. He tried to mark the location by fixing the trees on the street as a landmark, but when the truck turned at the corner, he saw that the palm trees were the same height, the same distance from each other. He could find his way back if the dogs stayed quietly in the same place.

Five blocks away the truck stopped. He heard voices outside and a large engine idling. Hopper hopped off the back to see who was talking.

A gasoline delivery tanker was parked in the intersection, and crews were filling twenty-gallon water bottles with gasoline from the tanker and carrying them into the houses.

Rome explained it to the group. "We're in the center of the Burn Zone. The fire crews will set off a big blow here. The fire will spread across the rooftops. To make sure the fire leaps over the streets they're putting more gas at two-block intervals. The houses in the center will burn hot; flames will cross to the next row. The houses at the intersections will be doused with gas to amplify the fire, those houses will blow, the fire will cross the street on fuses made of flammable ropes soaked in tiki torch paraffin, and burn the next block, and so on, until the last four blocks near the firewall. Those will be kept watered down and if the fire manages to break through, the firewall should stop the rest. That's how Encino, Van Nuys, Northridge, and South Pasadena were turned into ash moat. When the fire is out, the wreckers will tear the rubble wall down and level what remained. And then it's on to the next zone until we press the Burn and ash moat from Culver City and Mar Vista to Venice and the beach. That's two or three months away. Not long."

Siouxsie Banshee waved her hand at Rome. "I was the only one listening to you."

"He was listening," said Rome, pointing to Hopper.

His Silent Voice told him to say, "I wasn't."

They unloaded the truck at a movie studio. Three soundstages were designated for the furniture salvaged from the Burn Zone: kitchen, downstairs, upstairs. The Eames chair and the mission table were taken to one stage and the suitcases with the broken dishes were taken to another, unopened. 18 Tee warned Siouxsie Banshee against complaining anymore.

Siouxsie wouldn't give up. "Tee, listen to me and look at what's in here. Something isn't right. I've done the Inventory runs before the other Burns, and we were selective. The building is crowded and I can help make room by getting rid of the stuff that's worthless."

"That's not our business," said 18 Tee. "And you don't have authority."

They carried the table into the soundstage and turned it upside down on another table without a blanket, which was another arrow into her soul. "These tables are just going to get scratched stacking them this way."

"If the furniture is bad as you say, what difference does it make if it's damaged?"

Siouxsie Banshee put her head on Hopper's shoulder. "Thank you for saying so. That makes me feel better. I'm a sensitive person. I know that I'm missing my life. The rest of you don't. Well, not you, maybe. I think you're different. I know I'm different."

She kissed his cheek, then his ear, and licked the back of his neck.

"I like to do that. I think I must have liked that before. I wonder if I had a lover. I hope so. Do you think you had a lover? Silly question. You have a wedding ring."

"Do you know my wife?"

"I could have. I could have known you. I could have been your wife. Maybe you had a family. You're old enough to be a father."

When they were finished unloading the truck, a van drove them back to Figueroa, where the crowds, finished with inventory, were drunk.

# Chief, Shannon, Erin, Helary, Jobe

Erin told Shannon: "If you want to live inside the Fence, you have to belong here. You have to want to belong here. You have to commit to the life. Radical inclusion is radical participation. I want to show you who you were. The more you are who you used to be, the more we can trigger. You had a rehab; you just forgot it. You had skills. You were a performer, so you did the same things over and over. You practiced to be Shannon Squier, and you can be Shannon again."

Erin brought Shannon into the basement screening room. Shannon sat in the front row, playing with the button that ran the motor that raised and lowered the footrest. Erin showed her the six CDs she recorded. "And here are the two DVDs, the collection of your videos, and your Live in Rio concert video. I have a few songs from iTunes that aren't on the records. Your biggest success was 'I (LOVE) YOU.' It's on your third album."

"Play it," said Chief. He was in the back of the room; he'd slipped in quietly. He put a hand on Shannon's shoulder and she jumped up.

"I'm sorry. I was just saying hello."

"We already said hello."

"My mistake. I want to make sure you're comfortable."

"This is a good chair, yes."

"Isn't it? Erin, whenever you're ready."

The song came on, a ballad of pain, a declaration of rage at betrayal, a list of strategies for revenge. After half a minute, Shannon raised her hand. Erin stopped the music.

"That's really me? I don't know how to sing."

"You're singing beautifully on the record."

"That's not me anymore."

"Give yourself a chance to listen."

"Give yourself a chisel in your right eye."

Chief turned to Erin. "That was her most popular song. Is that your favorite song too?"

"I have so many favorites, Chief. All her songs are my favorite."

"Erin, pick one, just pick one."

Erin conferred with Helary and Jobe. "We all like 'Take (My) Night, Please.'"

The song came on, a quiet song, just Shannon and some kind of instrument. Chief couldn't tell what it was, something electronic, like a violin made out of a can.

Nothing changed with this song. Shannon didn't move. Chief stopped it. "Erin, sing along with the song."

"Thank you, Chief," said Erin. It was the worst punishment of her life to sing in front of Shannon, but she recalled the great wisdom of Redwings, "Chief is Chief because there is no other Chief."

Erin went to the front of the room and Jobe started the song. Erin sang along with it, as she had a hundred times, as she had with all of Shannon's songs. Jobe lowered the volume so Chief and Shannon could hear her over the record. Brin had nothing to do, so she did nothing.

Chief moved to the seat next to Shannon's. "Why don't you try that?"

"That's not me anymore."

"So you know that used to be you," said Chief.

She didn't answer.

Erin said, "There's the live concert video. Live in Rio. It's a city in South America. You gave a concert in the stadium, for a hundred thousand people."

The video began with shots of the stage being put together on a platform in the middle of the soccer field.

There were so many people; the city was so full. Even Shannon sat up to see things more clearly.

Searchlights mounted on the walls of the arena scanned the sky and found a plane circling. A paraglider dropped out of the plane, with wings like a squadron of trained fireflies in precise formation. The paraglider took a wide turn over the stadium, sailed over the crowd, and landed on the stage. The searchlights now focused on the sky pilot in a flight suit stripping off her harness and jumpsuit. The cameras replayed this image on screens over the stage and mounted on the walls of the stadium, and revealed Shannon Squier wearing nothing but her tattoos.

Whoever supervised the mix of the DVD had suppressed the presence of the hundred thousand fans in the stadium until the moment Shannon landed on the stage, so that as she stripped, the volume of the audience lifted around the screening room like a flash flood in a narrow canyon.

Chief got a call from Toby Tyler and walked out of the screening room.

Erin tried to stop him. "There's more to see."

"Not now," said Chief.

He turned his attention to Toby.

"Have you talked to Vayler?" she asked.

"About what?"

"The inventory isn't done, he wants another day in the Burn Zone, and I'm already setting the charges. Talk to him. He says he's only following your orders to collect the treasure."

Chief called Vayler.

"Are you going to have time tomorrow to organize the Drifter buses and trucks and get out of downtown before the Burn?"

"Touch and go on that, Chief. There was a lot more of value than we expected. Burn it and it's gone. We'll be fine. It's all good."

# Hopper, Viola, Made In USA

The food trucks along the street were open, the booze carts were full, and the tired workers left their Inventory transports and Burn Brigade details to join the parade. Hopper walked beside Siouxsie Banshee, while she predicted the future. "When the Burn is over they'll resettle a lot of people. Did you know that? Back to the desert, you know what I mean. If there's nothing left to collect, what will they need from Siouxsie Banshee or Nole Hazard? I want to make myself useful. But who do I talk to? You saw how they treat me. Where do you live?"

He pointed to the Hilton.

"Not too bad," said Siouxsie. "I'm in what the sign outside says is a work/loft building. Don't tell anybody but I have some art I found in a storage room at one of the museums. The artist was named Robert Mapplethorpe and he took pictures of penises. Why did I tell you that? What is wrong with me? Don't answer."

From behind them, the naked Shambler Hopper rescued from the Bottle Bangers put a hand on Hopper's shoulder.

"Who is this?" asked Siouxsie.

"I met her on the street."

The naked woman continued to keep pace with Hopper and Siouxsie.

"So you're one of them, a Banger?"

"No," said Hopper.

Siouxsie spoke to the Shambler. "He doesn't want you. Leave us alone." This had no effect on the Shambler. "Is she ignoring me, or does she not understand my simple words?"

Hopper couldn't answer the question.

"I don't want to walk this fast," said Siouxsie. "That's my polite way of saying I hope I see you tomorrow. You could ask why."

"Why what?"

"Why I hope I see you tomorrow, Nole Hazard."

"Why?"

"Because you listen to me. You don't talk but I know you're listening. Good night."

Siouxsie Banshee turned down her street. The naked woman held Hopper's hand.

"What are you doing?" he asked her. She grabbed his other hand. "What do you want? I can't help you. I'm sorry. Please leave me alone."

He walked away but she ran beside him and grabbed his hands again.

His Silent Voice came back: "Get rid of her."

She walked beside him and grabbed his wrist again, so she wouldn't be separated from him in the indifferent crowd. Hopper let the woman hang on as he looked down the side streets they passed until he saw an open clothing store on the ground floor of an office building. The sign painted on the window said **YOU CAN DECOMMODIFY <u>TODAY</u>**. Hopper opened the door enough to talk to the woman who was organizing sweatshirts by size and color. She had abstract tattoos the full length of her left arm.

The woman stopped what she was doing when she saw the naked Driftette.

"Let me guess. She's naked, I run a clothing store, it's a good idea to put us together, yes? I'm Viola, I'm verified, and this was my store and is my store. Take what you want. It's a gift. Accept my apologies for the brands but I sort by style, not by logo, like the hooded sweatshirts, in gray, black, red, and yellow. First priority is style. Second priority is size. Third priority is color within the size stack. No priority by brand. The Founders made a free will offering of the clothes and who are we to treat one brand as more like the Founders than another? I ask everyone to please respect my order, which, being who they are, they often don't. Who are you?"

"I'm Nole. Nole Hazard. She needs clothes."

"Interesting. You've got the tan of a Drifter, but you don't have the attitude of a Drifter. She, on the other hand, she is total full Shamblerina. It doesn't even understand what I'm saying. Does it have a name?"

"Maybe. She can't tell me."

"Then why do you want to dress it?"

"She's naked."

"There's fifty naked women every night trapped by the Bottle Bangers. What's so special about this one?"

"She's the one I know. And she needs shoes."

"Everyone needs shoes. And it doesn't look right to have shoes but no clothes."

Hopper picked up one of the yellow sweatshirts, an S, and held it up against the woman's chest.

"Too small," said Viola. "She's an M. And don't touch her with the shirt; she's just going to get it dirty. I'll pack it for you."

"What shoe will fit?"

"I don't think you should bother. It's not that I'd call it a waste of clothes to dress up the Driftettes, pardon me, *Shamblers*, like these, but I would call it a waste of time. And time is the one thing we can't find in the warehouses and department stores. You ever notice and I'd say this to Chief if he walked into the store, which he doesn't, but he did send Gretel in once. You know Gretel?"

"I don't think so," said Hopper.

"She's Heidi now, or was, that's what they say. But that's her brand, get it, and therefore Chief's brand. I see her on the Playa sometimes, but per Chief, we keep our distance. Radical inclusion? Not around Chief. Watches, you can find watches and clocks, but they don't add any time, you see. They just tell us how much is gone and we have to guess as to how much is left. How much is left for you, Nole Hazard?"

"No one told me."

"It's a thing you have to find out by yourself."

"She needs clothing."

"Look, she's filthy. If I give her the clothes . . . See, this is what I'm saying. Let them put her on the bus, Nole, put her on the bus. Do you understand what I am not trying to be subtle about?"

"I have a bathroom with a shower in my hotel."

"Then let me give you the clothing and shoes. Put them in a bag. I'll give you this bag. It's from American Apparel. That's what this store used to be. You take her back. You clean her up. Then you get her dressed. You see how long before she's walking the city naked again and as a courtesy to her, they put her on the bus. Am I being kind to her or to you? I don't see any reconciliation by act of will that lets me be kind to both of you. It's said of the First Wave that we have heavier traces of old sensitivities, and Chief let me keep the job I had before because I was good at it, but I honestly don't know what to recommend right now."

"I'll take the clothing and dress her after I wash her," said Hopper.

"I don't remember ever seeing someone dress a girl in her condition is what I'm saying. I'm here to be of service to people who understand this. She doesn't care about the clothes. Do you see that?" Viola filled two paper shopping bags with clothing. "Sweatshirts, running pants, underwear, and socks. I gave her exercise clothes, clothes to cover her and help keep her warm. I gave her clothes with zippers, not buttons, because zippers are easier to do up. Granted they're easier to reverse, too. Come here, girl," said Viola to the naked woman, and she found a pair of slip-on canvas shoes with white rubber soles to fit her. "These'll come off easier than the lace-ups, but she'll never learn how to tie a knot and I won't get old trying to teach her."

Hopper's Silent Voice whispered to him: "Obviously shouting doesn't make an impression on you, but you are wasting time."

"You should give her a name. Even if she doesn't answer to it, you should give the girl a name. What do you want to call her?"

"I don't know."

"So it's my choice? Well then, I have a name for her. She won't forget it, because it's in all of her clothing. See?" Viola showed Hopper the label: **MadeInUSA**. "That's what you're going to call her, Madayinoosa, see it? Or maybe it's pronounced Mayday In Oosa. Mad Day in Oosa? That's good. But just say it real quick, Madayinoosa. There you go."

Hopper said it. "Mod Day En Oosah."

"Almost. Mad Day. Mad Day In Oosa. Say it fast. Madayinoosa. Twice more to set it. To be safe."

"Madayinoosa. Madayinoosa."

"Sounds right to me. Friend, you two are good to go."

Hopper took the bag of clothing. He remembered his Teacher and thanked Viola, but it wasn't clear she needed or expected anything from him, except to take the woman out of the store.

Madeinusa held his wrist again as he walked her back down Figueroa to the Hilton. He stopped at a food truck for a bowl of rice. She ate it neatly, with more care than he expected from her.

There was another circle of men banging bottles around another cluster of five hassled women, and Hopper walked faster to get away from them. He didn't want to talk to anyone. He had let this woman make him noticeable, and nothing good would come of it.

He walked her through the lobby of the hotel, past the lobby bar, where First and Second Wavers were dancing to a Shannon Squier song, and pressed the button for the elevator. The Cecilia at the desk said, "You get a limit of one Shamblerina at a time. They're messy, and the cleaners complain."

Once inside the room, he threw the bags of clothing on the bed and turned on the shower. He brought Madeinusa into the bathroom and gave her a bar of soap and a washcloth and she held them without understanding. Hopper had to finish what she could not do. It was a long time before the water ran clear at her feet. He patted her dry with a dirty towel.

Soon she was sitting on the edge of his bed, looking out the window.

He didn't ask her to help him as he lifted her feet and slipped the red underpants over them, pulled the cotton briefs along her legs, pulled them over her knees, pushed her on her back to raise her legs, and pulled them to her waist. Then he rolled up the legs of her sweatpants and pulled the pants up to her waist. Socks went on easily and then the new running shoes. He lifted her arms over her head to put on her black T-shirt. When he pulled the shirt to her chest and touched her breasts, she grabbed him in her arms and pulled him to the bed, holding him.

Her lost language was in her hands, her lost skills, lost family, lost friends, lost education, all of her life made a ruin by NK3 rushed into her hands, which found their way around Hopper's neck, back, around his waist, around his legs. She pressed her face into his neck, chest, pressed her lips against his face. She was trying to say something to Hopper: that she was grateful, but the thing in Hopper that made her grateful was buried as deep as the thing in her that wanted to tell him. They rubbed their bodies together, submitting to something to which they were an audience as much as they were the actors.

When they were done, Hopper said, "Madayinoosa."

The shock of contact did not stimulate any greater clarity. She had no insight, didn't know herself as someone with a past. She still belonged to the eternal present of the Shamblers.

Then she said it too: "Madayinoosa." But Hopper couldn't tell if she was repeating her name or just a sound that mattered to him.

It was eleven o'clock and his Silent Voice set out the plan. "Let her fall asleep. If you fall asleep, I'll wake you up in two hours. That will give you time to get to the house and back before the sun comes up, and be on your way to find your wife. We won't tell her about tonight. You'll leave the woman here. She can find her way down in the morning, and go back to Figueroa and do whatever she does, whatever or however it happens. You have to get to the house tonight, before the Burn."

# Chief, Pippi, Committee Heads, Shannon, Erin,

On either side of each step on the winding path to Chief's terrace, candles in ceramic domes flickered through crescent-moon windows. Not even the heinous ravages of NK3, which ruined so much, could delete the way candles raised everyone's appreciation of themselves. The night's scent—sagebrush and juniper—was wet with the aroma of grilled lamb.

Sinatra walked beside ElderGoth. She was also unhappy about Shannon. "Chief gets excited and expects us all to follow. You know I'm always looking for reasons to complain about him, but enthusiasm seems to me to be a personal matter."

Walking up the path, Monokeefe injected himself into Sinatra and ElderGoth's conversation. "Are we talking about Shannon Squier?"

"Everyone is," said ElderGoth.

"I think I saw Bruce Willis working one of the Burn gates today. Do you know his movies?"

"Why didn't you stop him and bring him to verification?" Elder-Goth asked.

"That's not my job," said Monokeefe. "And it might not have been Bruce Willis. I think most movie stars got out early and they're alive and well breathing safe air on an island in the Pacific, or they're dead because the places they hoped were safe turned out to be infected like home. But I'll say this. I know the two of you resent me. The truth is, if it was Bruce Willis, I bet you that June Moulton would have told me to leave him, the same way she'll tell us that it's a mistake to verify Shannon Squier."

Toby Tyler interrupted them. "Vayler, you're making things difficult."

"How's that?" asked Sinatra.

"You didn't hear? Security has to contain the Drifters now that Vayler isn't taking them out of town."

Vayler explained, "Chief had a big shopping list and there's still a lot of houses to look at. And I know we'll have to let them Burn."

Chief came out of the house, wearing a T-shirt from Shannon's last tour; the back was the tattoo. "We have a few hundred of these, brand-new. They were in a warehouse. Thank you, Vayler."

He bowed to Chief. "At your service."

Sinatra was angry with this. He didn't like Chief, because he didn't really like anyone, but he wanted Chief to keep his power and if Chief was collecting old things because they were rare, he shouldn't be wearing something that any one of a few hundred could put on. He poured a glass of whiskey that was eighteen years old when bottled, but how old was it now? What was the point of protecting this new society if it behaved like the first one? What is this world anyway, he asked himself. Birthed by a weapon from a world of war, how different could it make itself?

Chief held a brass bowl on a small pillow and ran a wooden dowel around the inside of the rim, making the bowl sing. The small crowd settled in a fan around him.

"Thank you all for coming. We're having a little feast tonight in honor of our newest arrival. We don't remember her from before, but we know her music, more than anyone else's, made the leap across the gap between before and now. There's so much from the past that none of us can understand or may ever understand. We know from what we read that a composer named Mozart was supposed to be great. There are thousands of different records of his music, but none of us can hear him in a way that makes sense. Why were the Beatles famous? I'll give a complete set of their music to anyone who wants it. I don't know. As June says, let's not lie to ourselves. There are emotions from the past that music connected to, and since we aren't capable of those emotions, the music can't find its way in. Think of music as a password to what used to be called the soul. We're looking for the passwords to computer systems, but you know what it is to open a drawer and find the passwords to computers that have disappeared. It's like the key to a house after the fire in a Burn Zone. That's what most music is like. So why, of all the musicians of the past, does Shannon Squier still affect us? Because she was already living in the future when she made her music, because NK3 was the expression of the coming rupture, a break in history that was inevitable. She was here before the rest of us, before the world caught up with her. Shannon, please come out now."

Chief led the applause. Sinatra kept one hand on his drink and the other in his pocket.

Pippi and Erin brought Shannon out of the house, dressed only in a plaid skirt like the one in her video.

Erin turned Shannon around so the group could see the Smersh tattoo.

"I don't want to put any pressure on our new friend. I just want you to meet her." He saw the goose bumps on Shannon's arms. "She's cold. Are you cold?"

Shannon didn't say anything.

"Pippi, take her inside and get her dressed in something warm."

"Are you cold?" Pippi asked Shannon.

"A little." Shannon found her eyes meeting the eyes of this woman with red pigtails. "Did they find you the way they found me?"

"I don't think so." Then she added, "I'm waiting for someone."

"Who?"

"I don't know yet."

Pippi took Shannon away, rubbing her back. As the heat built up in her hand, Pippi could feel the colors and lines of the singer's tattoo. It wasn't that the tattoo was giving her another picture of itself. This was a different attribute of the tattoo, discovered only through a warm hand. Pippi ran both hands over Shannon's back, turned her to face the wall, and, with the full tattoo available, drew her fingertips over the dragon until the dragon woke up. The rest was the familiar blur of Center Camp sex, over in a harsh agony that always released just before the tension touched the edges of something that Pippi wanted to last forever.

When they were done, Shannon put her hand on Pippi's )'( brand.

"Why do you have that?"

"Everyone inside the Fence has it."

"Why didn't they give it to me?"

"They're afraid of you."

"I like it. But I won't get it."

When Pippi returned to the group with Shannon wearing one of Pippi's hundred wedding dresses, they were at Chief's long table eating the lamb. Shannon hadn't eaten freshly butchered meat in four years. She picked at the food with her hands. Erin tried to show her how to use a fork, but Chief waved her away.

"This is Center Camp. Not prison. Let her be. Radical expression."

Pippi put the fork in the singer's hand and stabbed the meat with it.

Shannon kissed Pippi's brand scar.

Toby Tyler called out, "Chief, what do you have in mind for our guest? What are you thinking?"

"Nothing, just her company."

"Don't you want her to sing?"

"I wouldn't impose that on her. It's been too long. No pressure."

Shannon ate without reacting to the talk of which she was the center.

"What do you want her for?" It was June Moulton. "For us or them?" Everyone knew that by *them*, the mythologist meant the Second Wavers and the Drifters who lived outside the Fence.

Chief deflected. "Does she have an aura? When you look at her face, can you imagine her doing or being anything other than who she was?"

Moulton didn't answer and asked nothing else.

When dinner was over, they cleared the table and washed the dishes.

Chief removed himself from conversation with the committee leaders and walked away, a withdrawal that caught Sinatra's attention while he was scrubbing a serving platter too large for the dishwasher. He handed the dish to June Moulton and found Chief outside, in the hot tub with Shannon, Pippi, Erin, and Toby Tyler. Sinatra slipped out of his own clothes and sat between Erin and Toby.

Chief's hands played underwater with Erin, who had only had sex with Chief a few times. "Sinatra, what do you think? You saw her first? Was there anything different about her?"

Chief wanted him to say yes. He said, "Absolutely."

Pippi felt Shannon's back again, felt the dragon slipping under her skin, and this time the dragon had a message: "He's on the way."

# Hopper, Madeinusa, Tesla

"Wake up." It was Hopper's Silent Voice. "Time to go." It was an hour past midnight.

Hopper's left foot was between both of Madeinusa's. He moved slowly, and her breathing didn't change as he pulled away and sat on the edge of the bed. His clothes were on the floor. He didn't remember taking them off. He felt rested, and ready.

Figueroa was still busy. He could see the lights of the Burn prep night crews on the other side of the rubble wall. The lights weren't everywhere and he knew how to hide from people who weren't looking for him.

The woman woke up as he was putting on his shoes.

"Madeinusa," she said.

"I'm hungry and I'm going to get some food. I'll bring back enough for both of us, so you can stay here and sleep."

"Madeinusa." She got out of bed and hugged him with stiff arms.

Hopper didn't have enough wire or rope to tie her up. It was better to just take her back down to Figueroa and leave her in the crowd where he found her, but clean now, so maybe no one would bother her.

They took the elevator down and she tried to hug him again and he pushed her away. She watched the numbers run backward and as the elevator passed each floor she said her name, "Madeinusa, Madeinusa, Madeinusa." When the doors opened to the lobby, they could hear the Bottle Bangers.

"Don't worry," said Hopper. They crossed Figueroa to the food truck. A small line waited for spaghetti tossed in oil, while a squad of pigeons at their feet pecked at scraps. Hopper ordered two plates and then moved aside, ignoring what was becoming a stream of hate from his Silent Voice.

"I will punish you Hopper don't make me destroy you let her go I beg you this is bad please Hopper you have a mission I'll protect you don't give up now I'm warning you."

If his Silent Voice had not distracted him, Hopper might have seen Tesla in time to hide before Tesla saw him. He called to Hopper from across the street. "Papa BangBang has a question. He wants to know what are you doing with that Shambler? What's the deal? You can't dress them up."

Hopper's Silent Voice said, "Just walk away from him."

"We're hungry," said Hopper.

"But what are you doing with her all dressed up?"

"I have to go," said Hopper. He felt the pressure to say more, and say it with more words, but he didn't have them.

The server in the truck told Hopper their food was ready. Hopper took the plates and gave one to Madeinusa. She lowered her face to the food and scooped it into her mouth.

"You're actually feeding her? Look at this. She eats like a dog."

His Silent Voice said, "You're on your own. You're a mistake."

"She's hungry," said Hopper, to Tesla, to his Silent Voice.

"You have some rehab. Anyone can see that, but this bitch is running on empty. Has she ever said a word to you?"

"We have to go." He nodded for Madeinusa to follow him, but Tesla stood in his way. The others in the line were watching them.

"I'm First Wave. You, no. Her, definitely no. But I want her. I'm going to take her."

The cook called out to Tesla: "Your order is ready."

Hopper's Silent Voice returned. "Leave her with him."

Madeinusa spilled the potatoes on her shirt. "I have to get her changed," said Hopper and put a hand out for Madeinusa.

"Then good-bye," said Tesla.

Hopper walked Madeinusa back to the hotel while Tesla ate. They were a block away when Tesla caught up with them.

"I was just having fun with you."

They were at the door to the Hilton and Tesla followed them in. The bartender arranging bottles in the lobby bar said hello. The Second Waver vacuuming the lobby rug said hello. The Cecilia said, "Burn tomorrow night. Burn tomorrow night."

Hopper wasn't sure if he'd seen this one before. He needed to get away now that he had only this night, and Tesla wouldn't leave them alone.

"We can have a party with her. I want to have a party with her. We can spit roast her. You take the head or the rear. I'm happy either way. And so is she."

"I have to go," was all Hopper could say.

Hopper pulled her into the elevator and pushed Tesla back.

As the elevator went up, Madeinusa said her name every time the number of the floor changed.

"Madeinusa. Madeinusa. Madeinusa. Madeinusa."

Hopper didn't want to leave her tied up but he didn't see any other way to keep her from following him. When they got into the room, he closed the door. She sat on the bed and reached for him.

"Stay there. That's good."

There was a reading lamp on the room's desk and he yanked the plug from the wall and then tore the wire from the lamp's base. He grabbed Madeinusa's hands as they reached to him and pulled them behind her back and tied them together. He didn't apologize and she didn't fight.

"The cleaners come in the morning. They will find you. They'll let you go. I have to leave now."

He closed the door behind him and it locked automatically. On the ride to the lobby he said his own name a few times as the light blinked at each floor.

When the elevator opened at the lobby, he saw Tesla talking to the Cecilia. Tesla didn't see him and Hopper passed behind him and was out the door when he saw Tesla take the elevator. Hopper went back inside and asked the Cecilia: "What was he doing?"

"He wanted to know your room number and I sent him up."

Hopper went back to the elevator. He said his own name as the numbers changed.

A First Wave couple, dressed as Indians in buckskin outfits taken from the costume warehouse of Universal Studios, came out of the room next to Hopper's as he stood by the door. He could hear Tesla inside, belligerent and indistinct, but wanted the couple to leave before he opened the door. It was too late to pretend he was at the wrong door so he pretended to search his pockets for the key card. They were less interested in Hopper than he was in them, and soon enough they were gone.

He pushed the keycard into the slot, the light turned green, and he was in the room. Madeinusa was naked on the bed, her wrists bound to the legs of the bed by electric cord. Tesla was naked on top of her.

"You have to wait for your turn," said Tesla, as Hopper grabbed the desk lamp and brought the corner of the square base into Tesla's head. Tesla rolled sideways and pushed himself up with his hands. He pulled the lamp from Hopper's hands, but Hopper held on to the cord and wrapped it in his fist. Tesla threw three quick punches at Hopper, but on the third swing, Hopper dropped the lamp and lowered his head, running into Tesla, lifting him and throwing him over the balcony. The man's voice changed pitch as he fell away from the balcony. Hopper watched him hit the ground and when people from the sidewalk looked up to see where the man had come from, Hopper stepped back into the room.

"We have to leave now," said Hopper. He shut the balcony door and pulled the curtain to close it, then turned off the room's light. He slipped Tesla's ID card, his bottle, and his banging stick into the clothing bag.

Taking Madeinusa's hand, he passed the elevator and led her down the fire stairs, past the lobby, to the garage.

The garage was filled with Ferraris, Maseratis, and Bentleys. There were security cameras on the walls. He took Tesla's bottle out of the bag and wrapped his arm around Madeinusa's neck and followed the exit signs up the ramp out of the garage.

It had been five minutes since killing Tesla and there were already sirens. Security was never far away.

"Your plans are ruined," said his Silent Voice. "You will never see your wife."

He told the Voice to be quiet. He didn't need to hear this. If not for Madeinusa, he would have been back in the Burn Zone by now. He would be in his house where he would have found the key and opened the door to the basement.

Instead, he was dragging a mute bottle-banged Shamblerina through downtown and along dark side streets. They stopped at the river, near the bushes where he hid his bicycle.

He led Madeinusa into a stand of trees. He would have to wait until it was night again to return to the house. He promised his Silent Voice: "I will stay here with her until the sun goes down, and then I'll leave her here. I promise."

"We'll see," said his Silent Voice.

# Frank Sinatra, Redwings, Chief

Frank was certain he had never been a friendly man. Suspicion came easily to him, and with an early rehab, more of his personality remained than it did in most people. He guessed at what he had been from imagining his responsibilities around the UCLA campus: with so many things to steal, so many books and chairs, and cash machines, and all of the equipment in the hospital, and all of the cars in the garages, the man in charge of security for a place that large needed to be strong and impartial.

He went back to his house and didn't stay for the orgy after Chief presented Shannon. A return to West Covina on the Audi hunt was out of the question. He was curious about Pippi's silence and wanted to watch her. Pippi almost never joined Chief in a crowded bed.

He had just settled into sleep when Redwings knocked on his door.

"Frank, there was a murder downtown. No ID yet for the perp or the victim. The Burn is tonight and Chief wants to talk to you about this thing."

"How did Chief hear about it before me?"

"That's why he's Chief."

"And why do we know it's a killing?"

"Hotel staff called Security and officer on duty is Gunny Sea Ray. I trust Gunny."

"A good man, a very good man," said Sinatra. Redwings nodded in agreement.

"Yes," said Redwings. "And Gunny Sea Ray goes through the hotel to ascertain if that's the word what room is likeliest for the fellow to have fallen from and comes to a room with bloody sheets, a murder weapon probably, and evidence of a very considerable fight. Plus, Chief says you have to go because you haven't seen it yet."

"Chief went to the scene?"

"Chief doesn't have to go to the scene. Chief knows, Frank. What else does a brother have to say to be understood?"

"Redwings, don't you think Chief should look at the scene himself before pronouncing his opinion, speaking of opinion as we were?"

Frank dressed without showering and was at Chief's house in ten minutes. Chief was in his command center with Toby Tyler and Vayler Monokeefe, listening to the competing voices on the dozen walkie-talkies Tyler used to stay in contact with her crews.

Frank asked Chief: "Why are you so involved in something this small?"

"A murder isn't small when the killer is a Drifter. It's not in them to care enough to kill. It might be contagious, might be a new symptom of the old disease. Look into this."

"Chief, we're burning a fifth of Los Angeles tonight. Vayler, didn't Chief tell you to get the Drifters out of downtown? You're supposed to be moving the Inventory from the storage depots into warehouses downtown."

"Chief, I know I said I'd do that but there was more treasure in the Burn Zone than anyone expected. If there's no Inventory, why have Security?"

Frank persisted. "What about the Drifters panicking?"

"I hate to let the past turn to ash without saving what we can," said Chief.

Vayler thanked him. "You see, Frank, either we put up with some disturbance among the Drifters, or we lose our precious history. Someday people will call us gods for saving what we took from the Burn Zone."

Sinatra saw little choice but to cooperate. "Let me deal with the murder tomorrow, after the Burn. Security still needs everyone on the committee for Drifter crowd control."

"Deal with the murder, too," said Chief. "Don't worry about crowd control. We will have it under control."

"How?"

"That's not your business today. There's a murder: find the killer. He got through. You missed him."

"The bicycle rider?"

"Find him."

On their way downtown, Sinatra interrogated Redwings. "Redwings, why is Chief the Chief?"

"Brother, that's an excellent question, it is, but allow me a piercing inward search for an answer that can be held as fact and not opinion. All right, sir. Chief is Chief because he's a wise man. Chief is Chief because who else is more like a Chief than Chief? He says go here to find something and we find it. He says look here for the good wine and behold, there's the good wine. Other people do have Strong Feelings but brother—nobody has stronger Strong Feelings than Chief. You can say that the feeling his feelings has, has feelings.

So if he has a Strong Feeling about a murder or Shannon Squier, then all I can advise is to watch out."

"Watch out for what, Redwings?"

"That's my sentiment precisely. He has angles within angles but he's never wrong, is he? Consider the wreckage of those pitiful Drifters. He provides for them."

"But that's radical inclusion, Redwings. That's an order from the Founders."

"And asking me without June Moulton to overhear us, or rather you're not asking me but I'm giving you the gift of my opinion, no exchange of value, don't you find that radical self-reliance and radical inclusion butt heads? There's only so many people can climb the great statues on the Playa at one time."

"You're not a stupid man, Redwings."

"I take that as a compliment, sir."

# Chief, The Man, The Woman, Erin

Chief ordered everyone away from the Playa and stood between The Man and The Woman. He was sorry to approach them so close to the dawn, because at night they gleamed in the star light. He had no time to wait for a better effect.

"So he's here. It wasn't the singer you told me about. It was him. That was the message, wasn't it? He's come for Pippi."

In voices no one could hear, but not Silent Voices, The Man said yes. The Woman said no.

"So it's the singer?" he asked The Woman. "Both?"

The Woman told him, in a voice no one else could hear, but not a Silent Voice, not a voice that he carried inside him, a voice that spoke on the Playa only: "Radical self-reliance, radical expression. You're afraid of the Drifters. Trust the Bottle Bangers for once."

"To do what?"

"What they do."

Chief went back to Center Camp and woke up Erin. "I need Shannon. I need her to keep the attention of the Drifters. I have ordered a stage from the motor pool. She is going to perform tonight and you will show her what to do. Otherwise the Drifters will panic."

Erin said, "I don't understand."

"Do what I tell you."

He called Vayler and said the same thing.

⚛

# Eckmann, Marci, Seth, Franz, Spig Wead

Eckmann, standing where it was safe to on the wing, looked down at the men and women who had waited so long for this moment. Seth, Marci, Spig Wead, and Franz watched him from the forward door.

"The Burn Brigades are leaving the Burn Zone. We'll fill up with fuel and leave during the Burn. We'll have enough fuel to cross the country twice, or fly nonstop to Moscow. Or if we go in the other direction, we can get to Hong Kong, but we're not crossing water. Our route will take us over Albuquerque, Dallas, New Orleans, and Florida and then back as far north as Chicago or Seattle. We have enough fuel to be over Orlando at sunrise, and we'll see if it's safe to land there. I don't remember anything about these cities any more than you do. I've read the travel magazines, but I don't think it matters to us now that Santa Fe's best chefs are reinventing the food of Native Americans, or that Chicago is a special place in October. We're probably better off going to a small or isolated city, but the plane was built in Seattle and there might be spare parts. But we can't assume there's jet fuel. What I'm trying to say is: thank you all for helping each other, thank you Dr. Kaplan for fixing up our pilot and thank you Franz for staying alive. Tomorrow is going to be a long day if we make it, and our last day if we don't."

# Frank Sinatra, Gunny Sea Ray, Redwings

Gunny Sea Ray got his name from the three small gothic characters—**GSR**—tattooed in black ink on his left wrist. He was Verified Second Wave, an LA cop, and assigned directly to Sinatra's immediate circle. He was a good shot and it was believed he'd been in the military. He was waiting beside Tesla's naked body, still in the street, still uncovered, when Sinatra arrived with Redwings. Sinatra gave a quick look at the corpse, but there was little that this exploded sack of meat and bones could tell him. The body had landed facedown.

"No ID in the room," said Gunny Sea Ray. "And the face is too broke up to be matched to any database."

"Because there is no face," said Redwings.

"Tesla." It was the night-shift Cecilia, standing nearby. Gunny Sea Ray brought her to Frank and Redwings.

Sinatra asked everyone to step back. "Talk to me."

"Bottle Banger. Papa BangBang. Drifter in Room 2627 and a woman. Bottle Banger."

"He was with them?" asked Frank.

"With them. Room number."

"You gave him the room number. What was the guest's name?"

"Inventory."

"Most everyone down here is Inventory," said Redwings.

She waved her hand to make the gesture of someone writing with a pen.

Gunny Sea Ray ran to the desk for the registry. He opened it for her. She found the name. "Nole Hazard."

"Can you describe him?" This was generally a useless question.

She tried to answer. "Two eyes, nose, mouth, ears, hair."

"Got that," said Redwings, writing it down. "Nole Hazard. Inventory. Two eyes."

After Sinatra gave the order to take the body away, Gunny Sea Ray brought him and Redwings to the hotel room.

Sinatra showed Gunny and Redwings the cord that was still tied around the base of the headboard. "It was cut, but not untied, and why is it here at all?"

Neither of the men could answer the question.

"The mystery man, this missing Drifter, let's get the Inventory crew he was with," said Frank.

"Needle in a haystack," said Redwings.

"Redwings, what's a haystack?"

"Now you go and ask me a question and I don't have the answer in my quiver."

"What's a quiver?"

"I can look it up, if you want, brother."

"Keep a dictionary close by when you're reading your magazines and circle the words you don't understand. It's a good and noble thing you're doing, learning a specific vocabulary that isn't related to work but to the history of character. I applaud this."

"Thank you kindly."

"And call AutoZone at the motor pool. I want to speak to him."

# Frank Sinatra, Siouxsie Banshee,

# Martin Rome, 18 Tee

Inventory Central put out the call over the radio and in an hour, Sinatra and Redwings were at an Inventory dump in Highland Park, three miles away, where Martin Rome and his crew were stacking empty glass bottles into trash cans and loading them onto trucks.

Sinatra didn't want to appear ignorant of something that had the look of organization, and asked Redwings to ask someone to explain what was being accomplished by putting glass bottles back into trash cans and find out which team was Martin Rome's.

"I can ask and they can answer," said Redwings. As he walked away, Sinatra called to him: "Get yourself a new dress, Redwings. This one is ready for the fire."

"It fits me, brother, but when the word comes from you, I expect I always listen."

Sinatra watched the biker in the nurse costume talk to one of the Inventory supervisors. He returned quickly with the answer. "They've been told, on order of Vayler Monokeefe, which I don't doubt is on order of Chief himself, to bag the bottles in the trash cans that you see and then make sure they're distributed along Figueroa, all right away, before sunset. They don't know more than this, and I believe him when he confesses such to me."

"And Martin Rome?"

"The man we seek is the man we shall find. He's over there at the edge of this strange scene and, admit this, Frank Sinatra, a million empty bottles packed for something mysterious is a mystery, and mysteries are strange."

"A million?"

"Could be. We can count them."

"Or not."

Most of the team leaders recognized Sinatra, and no one could be happy with a visit from him without warning. The chimes of the bottles as they were set carefully in the bags, not to break, gave Frank one of those pleasant waves of good feeling that he knew brought him close to the old world. Against his inclination to approach Martin Rome in a way to keep the man nervous, instead he was smiling. He held out a hand: "I'm Frank Sinatra."

"Have we done something wrong?" asked Rome, taking Frank's hand and holding it.

"I just need information."

Siouxsie, standing near them, interrupted him. "I've got information for you. I shouldn't be here. I should be verified. There's been a mistake."

"There's been a lot of mistakes," said Sinatra. "We all have to pay for them one way or another. A Drifter went with you to the Burn Zone. He called himself Nole Hazard. Do you remember him?"

Martin Rome shook his head. "I ask them their names, but I can't match names with faces, usually. Tee, do you remember him?"

"No."

"I remember Nole," said Siouxsie Banshee.

"You shouldn't be listening to us," said Martin Rome, who turned to Sinatra and apologized. "She's good at her work but she's difficult."

Siouxsie growled in frustration. "Maybe I am difficult, but it's my job to remember similarities and differences in classical home furnishings of the postwar era, with a special emphasis on California design as it was influenced before the war by the German avant garde, with an emphasis on the Bauhaus, of course. This training of mine has blessed or cursed me with the ability to recall the faces of people I meet, which proves that I was one of the earliest people in rehab, doesn't it?"

"What did he look like?"

"Can I trade you that description for a privilege?"

Redwings moved closer to her. "You don't bargain with Security, little lady."

To a frustrated museum curator, a trained connoisseur, the promise of danger from a bearded and tattooed outlaw biker in a slut nurse costume has a certain ambiguous glow. She tugged lightly on his beard. "You can push the Drifters and the Unverified Second Wavers around because they don't know they have nothing to lose. That's why they're pliable. But never argue with someone who has nothing to lose and *knows* it."

Sinatra didn't want Redwings to suffer a public embarrassment that could diminish his authority, so even as Siouxsie Banshee's disdain impressed him he grabbed her arm and squeezed until she whimpered. "But you do have something to lose. You have your life. And you know it. And if you did have a thorough rehab, then they restored the old genetic instinct that tells you not to give your life up lightly."

"Well, what do you know? Finally I'm talking to a reasonable man."

"What did Nole look like?"

"Let go of my arm and let's trade."

Sinatra pulled her hair with his other hand, twisting her neck until she was looking up at the sky. "What did he look like?"

"You think I don't like this?" she said, smiling. "I know from some of my reading that museum curators were often sexual masochists. It was the fetish of art strapped to the fetish of wealth, and that kind of humiliation creates a kinky tension that is cured, for a short time, only by the theater of shame. Rinse and repeat. So pull harder, Frank Sinatra. If I can't get privileges, I can still have fun."

"If you tell me something useful, I'll return the favor, but I decide if it helps. So I set the value. And if you're such an inventory specialist, you know what I mean by value, don't you? Do you understand me?" He pulled harder and she liked it.

"I do."

"So, tell me, my annoying ambassador from the lost high culture, what did Nole Hazard look like?"

She said it quickly. "Long black hair, brown skin lighter than yours, with what I'd say was a recent sunburn, likely a Hispanic or a Native American. Or he had a bit of that Aztec grandeur that comes through some mestizo faces. Six feet. A hundred and eighty pounds, maybe less. Strong."

"How do you know?"

"It was an Inventory trip. He lifted things that were heavy. And though you haven't asked, he was more alert than a typical Drifter."

"What did he say?"

"Almost nothing."

"So how do you know so much about his mind?" He pulled her hair again.

"Pay me."

"When was the last time you saw him?"

"Listen to me. Who else gave you a description of him that you can use? What's the value on that? Just give me something that I couldn't have without your help. Please. Do something for me."

"I can get you into the Ritz-Carlton with a good view of the Burn. There's a party on the roof, with a buffet from Center Camp."

Martin Rome heard this and rang a small alarm. "Chief won't like that, will he? The Ritz-Carlton is First Wave only."

Redwings nodded. "Brother Rome is right, probably."

Siouxsie Banshee spoke up for herself. "You're trying to catch a killer. If I help, I deserve this."

Sinatra liked the idea that Chief would be unhappy with letting this woman into the Ritz-Carlton. "What else can you tell me about Nole Hazard?"

Siouxsie said what she knew. "After we were dropped off at the staging area, I was talking to him as I do, talking a lot, and he wasn't paying attention, which is no special surprise. Welcome to the world of Siouxsie Banshee and Sonia Pryce. A naked Driftette came out of the crowd, following him. One of the Bottle-Bang Shamblerinas. She took his hand. He knew her."

"And she just walked up to him out of the crowd?"

"Like I said, she knew him."

"And Nole Hazard, what did Nole Hazard do?"

"He tried to get away from her but she stayed with him. I was talking to him but he was trying so hard to get away that he was running, and she kept up with him. That was the last I saw of him."

"What did she look like?"

"Matted and tangled black hair below her shoulders. Five four, hungry, like a lot of people at the fringes, you could see her ribs. Two skinned knees, barefoot, legs cut up. I didn't see her eyes, don't know the color."

"Was he trying to get away from you or from her?"

"What does that mean?"

"Were you talking this much to Nole Hazard and was he trying to get away from you?"

"I don't talk too much. It's everybody else who doesn't talk enough. The world is more than welcome to interrupt me when it tells me something interesting."

"You spent time with him in the Burn Zone. What was he like there?"

"That's what I mean by interesting, that question. Yes. He didn't talk much but he was listening to me. He stayed closer to me than any of the others. And he was looking around more, paying attention to where we were. Most Drifters just look for the food or look where you point them. Nole Hazard looked where he wanted to look."

"And then he disappeared," said 18 Tee. "Don't forget that part."

"Disappeared where?" asked Sinatra.

"We called for him and he wasn't there. But Siouxsie saw him," 18 Tee said.

"We were finishing up at a house and he went into the backyard, all the way back and climbed over the back wall into the yard of the other house, and stood there, looking at the house."

"Do you know what street?"

Martin Rome answered. "No. We were just cruising up and down, looking for houses that matched the guidelines."

"Stupid guidelines," said Siouxsie.

Sinatra knew that they were at the end of their knowledge.

"Martin Rome, were you surprised that Nole Hazard didn't show up today?"

"I have bigger things to be surprised by than whether a Drifter keeps to his assignments."

Siouxsie offered a quiet thought. "You look unhappy about this."

"Why did he line up for work? He could have gotten away without working."

"It's obvious to me," said Siouxsie. "He wanted to see the Burn Zone and didn't want anyone to know he was here."

Redwings approved of this. "Very logical thinking, Frank. She has me convinced."

"So did I help you?" she asked. "What's the value of what I gave you today?"

"Siouxsie Banshee," he said, with a sincerity he seldom felt, "I'm sorry about your verification problems. I wish there was something we could do about that, but there's not. If you're interested, I can use you, even if I can't bring you into Center Camp."

"Use me how? Take off my clothes and make me dance in the street? Should I find some plastic chopsticks and an empty bottle of Tanqueray?"

"You'd never let anyone do that to you."

"I've thought of joining those circles. For the attention. You get desperate enough sometimes, when you're out here."

"Redwings?"

"Yes, brother?"

"Tell the Ritz-Carlton that I say to give her a room."

"For the night?"

"No, tell them to give her a room with a view, full time. That's a fair trade. She has a good eye for detail and Redwings . . ."

"Yes, Frank?"

"Can't Security use someone with a good eye for detail?"

"Every day, brother."

Siouxsie hugged the fearsome head of the Security Committee. Sinatra stopped Redwings, his loyal protector, from pulling her away until she broke the hug herself.

"And I'll know where you are," said Frank. And with that, he walked away with Redwings.

"Boss, what are you thinking?"

"Nothing yet."

# Chief, Pippi

Pippi heard Chief's side of the conversation with Frank Sinatra: "Do you have his name? Nole Hazard, no, I've never heard it . . . With what crew . . . And who's the woman . . . She's not verified . . . Yes . . . If she helped you . . . Get her a room there, fine. I don't care. Tell them I said so. Yes, she can come to the roof, but you're responsible for her, and you have a lot to worry about tonight . . . No, that's true: I've never seen you worry. I'll be down in an hour."

# Frank Sinatra, AutoZone

AutoZone spoke to Sinatra.

"I saw the body. That's Tesla. He worked with me."

"You know that even without his face?"

"It was Tesla. I know his tattoos."

"Were you friends?"

"Not hardly."

"Did he have any enemies?"

"Who has enemies?"

"Why was he downtown instead of at the garage?"

"He asked if he could go."

"Did you know he was a Bottle Banger?"

"Yes."

"You didn't like that, did you?"

"How can you tell?"

"You're not sorry he's dead."

"Who misses the dead?" He missed Hey You, and wondered if by missing her, it meant she wasn't dead.

AutoZone was on his way back to the motor pool when Chief called him. They'd only spoken a few times.

"AutoZone, I need your help."

☢

# Eckmann, Franz, Spig Wead, Consuelo

Eckmann sent Consuelo on a search through the terminals to find pilot uniforms to fit Franz and Spig Wead. "It would be nice to find something from Singapore Airlines, but what's really important is for Franz and Spig Wead to see the epaulets on each other's shoulders. Each needs to believe that he's with another pilot."

She returned with three jackets from a closet in the forward bulkhead of a LAN Airbus at the International Arrivals terminal. One was too small for either of them, the other two had probably belonged to the same pilot, and they were the same size and too big for both Franz and Spig Wead. Eckmann said it didn't matter.

"Even if it's a bit large, this looks good on you," said Consuelo.

Franz looked at himself in the plane's bathroom mirror.

"I remember him."

"He's handsome," said Consuelo, putting a hand on his shoulder. He pushed her away.

She protested. "I said something nice about you."

Eckmann, though, was delighted, really for the first time since Franz's arrival at the hangar. "No, no, did you see? You covered his stripes. He doesn't like you touching the jacket. This is what we wanted."

Eckmann guided Franz back into his seat, and then the two pilots continued going through the preflight checklist.

# Chief, Pippi

Chief found Pippi in her dressing room, dotting her cheeks with red freckles. He came up behind her and kissed the top of her head.

"I need another five minutes," she said.

He spoke quietly. "I don't think it's a good idea for you to go to Figueroa, Pippi. The Drifters may riot like they did for the last Burn. You'll have Go Bruins and Royce Hall for protection, not that you'll be in any danger. It's just a precaution." He didn't often call her by her new name. He preferred Heidi.

She knew there was nothing to negotiate. Chief was Chief, but even so, she had to say something. "If the Drifters riot, it's because their mythology isn't working. When you're verified, you have a story about yourself. The story that June Moulton pushes on the Drifters doesn't have any power over them. Do they really believe that once upon a time there were Founders who built all of this for us? That food was left for them as a gift? Do they really believe that life inside the Fence is a world of nothing but hard work, and they wouldn't like it?"

"What should we say instead, Pippi?" Her concern about Fence politics surprised him. He thought she didn't care.

"Maybe nothing makes any difference."

"That's something I'd expect to hear myself saying. I don't expect that from you."

"I watch. I'm quiet. I listen."

"What do you see? What do you hear? About the committee heads."

"You need Sinatra but he doesn't know himself, doesn't know what he really wants. You need ElderGoth in Verification, because she just wants to do a good job and you appointed her and she's jealous of anyone getting close. So as long as you favor her, she'll do what you want."

"And Vayler Monokeefe?"

"He knows what's out there, and how much of it is left. He keeps his own books. Did you know that he found a Costco in Reseda that he hasn't told anyone about? Not even Sinatra knows this."

"How do you know about it?"

"Three Inventory tabulators have disappeared. He said they're drunk on Figueroa. Maybe it's true. Maybe not. Nobody pays attention."

She expected Chief to ask more about this, but instead he asked about Toby Tyler. "What do you think of the way Toby Tyler runs Systems?"

"Couldn't be better at her job and she'll do the best for anyone in charge, and she's not replaceable right now because she won't train anyone to know as much as she knows. Give her a few more years to get her crews to learn from her, and then she could be replaced, but now, no."

"Why haven't we talked like this before?"

"I didn't want to, Chief."

"Why don't I like to hear you call me that? Why do I not want to be your Chief?"

"Tell me your old name."

"That's the only name I have."

"Are you really going to stop me from going downtown and joining all my friends on the roof of the Ritz-Carlton to watch the Burn?"

"I don't want you caught up in a disaster."

"What are you scared of, Chief? What's making you so scared today? The Burn? Shannon Squier?"

"I have to be extra careful with you, because I don't want to lose you."

"Why does it sound like you're telling me the truth, but about something else?"

"But this is why I love you."

"Because I don't have the thing you say you have, so that I can love you the way you say you love me?"

"You have to be alive to love me the way I love you."

This made her tired. She didn't know what to think now. She wanted to go to the Playa and send one of those messages by sling-shot over the Fence. Darling . . . she didn't know how to finish the sentence. She could ask The Man and The Woman for help, but if she did, The Woman might tell Chief about Pippi's secret messages.

"I'm going downtown now. I'll see you tomorrow."

After he left, the two guards joined her on the deck.

"Nice telescopes," said Royce Hall. "You can see everything from up here."

"We'll see the fire," said Pippi.

"He wants you inside."

At this insistence, Pippi knew what to tell The Man and The Woman, either or both of them. She wrote it on a piece of paper and folded it inside one of her cigarette boxes, and when the time was right, she would approach the two mute guardians of the Playa, climb into The Man's chest and whisper the message, or maybe just think it loudly. And then she would scale the outside of The Woman and show The Woman what she told The Man: "I have a secret. It's the only thing I have. And I don't know what it is."

☢

# Siouxsie Banshee, Redwings

Siouxsie Banshee's small room at the Ritz-Carlton looked east from the fifteenth floor, a dull view to a Drifter dormitory. It was the best that her patron could negotiate for her in a hotel meant for the exclusive use of the First Wave, but the Sony played sex movies on a closed circuit, the whiskey on the shelf was Johnnie Walker Black, the towels in the bathroom were clean, and the Pellegrino water in glass bottles still had some fizz. Sipping bubbles from the deleted past was as close as she could imagine to a religious experience. Until then she had nothing more important to do than the nothing she was doing. Naked, she lay back on the bed, pleased with the novelty of her friendship with Sinatra and grateful for the result. This was the kind of luxury that Sonia Pryce deserved.

Redwings knocked on the door and announced himself. She opened the door, without covering herself, because she'd heard about the parties inside the Fence and knew that among themselves, First Wavers didn't hide behind clothing. Redwings, in a starched nurse uniform, not a slut costume, introduced himself, as he always did.

"Redwings with news from Frank. First, are you happy with your facilities here?"

"Thank you, Redwings, yes, the room is fine."

"Regretfully we can't get you a view toward the ocean. Now I have to tell you this: the Security command post is the top of this very building and you're invited to join us if you'll just be careful and let us go about our business as it commences. There's a fine chow line and plenty of things to drink."

"Good, because I'm hungry and thirsty."

"What do you have to wear?" asked Redwings. "It gets a bit windy up top."

"The only clothing I have is what I wore for Inventory today."

"There's a conference room on the second floor of the hotel where the ladies of the First Wave get their clothing when they stay downtown. I've gotten some of mine there, as you see."

"Redwings, can I ask you a question?"

"You just did. So you can ask another."

"Does Frank have a woman?"

"I'm not with him all the time, if you know what I mean. But the demands on Frank Sinatra are a remarkable thing to see. He has the safety of our lives in his keeping."

"You look like you can take care of yourself."

"Apparently I spent time in prison but we don't know for what. You can see from this tattoo," he said, pulling up his skirt to show her his thick thigh and the portrait, drawn in fine small lines like the picture on a dollar bill. But instead of George Washington it was Jesus strapped to a lethal injection gurney. "I was probably a violent man. Now, I'm a strong man, but not much of a fighter, to tell the truth. Also, to be warned fairly, Frank is busy but he knows you're there. The man has many eyes. Show starts after sundown."

# Shannon, Erin, Jobe, Helary, Toffe

On Chief's orders, Inventory and Systems assembled a stage on top of a bus made for rock-and-roll tours. AutoZone was driving and Carrera was along for the ride. The bus had a bedroom suite in the back with a shower, another room with couches that could be used as beds, and a kitchen and dining room behind the driver. Above the dining room table, the workers cut a hole three feet across so Erin could stand on the table and give directions to Shannon on the stage, which was the length of the bus and five feet wider, braced and bolted in place. Transport Service workers, diligent as always, hung large flat-screen Sonys and Samsungs, side by side, to the bottom of the stage and connected them on the bus's Wi-Fi to a laptop in Helary's hands.

Chief told Erin not to explain too much to Shannon, but Erin didn't know how to explain what Chief wanted Shannon to do without telling her the stage was for her to dance on as the bus moved down Figueroa, distracting the Drifters. A concert on a normal stage that stayed in one place and was the focus of a crowd—that made sense. But Chief said the Drifters were dispersed and needed a traveling distraction. Erin told him: "Driving slowly down Figueroa is an invitation to catastrophe, and I'm afraid that even though this isn't my idea, I'll take the blame for failure."

Chief didn't offer comfort. "You're right. You will be blamed."

AutoZone could see that Erin was miserable. "Don't worry about the hole in the roof or the platform on top. We have about thirty of these motor coaches in the parking lot at Paramount studios and we keep them in working order."

Erin didn't care if this had been the only bus, irreplaceable, precious as whatever it is that AutoZone cared about most.

"You understand what we're doing?" she asked him.

"Carrying that girl down the street while she puts on a show." He hated Erin's type, the Center Camp First Wave Sparkle Pony princess who looks down on the people who do the real work, which made him think of Hey You and her clunky Driftette dancing, the way she seemed to live only to help improve the days of the men who made fun of her and didn't notice or care that they were cruel. He wanted her to come back. He'd give her a better name, like Jeep or Lincoln, a name for a good dependable American car. Nothing Japanese and nothing Korean, of course. He was glad Tesla was dead. He couldn't make fun of Hey You anymore.

Now he had this job driving the bus because people close to Chief trusted him to do it the right way, and he wouldn't waste his words trying to get Erin to respect him. All he'd been told was that

Chief would tell Erin when it was time to move and she would tell AutoZone.

While the crew worked on the stage, Erin stayed inside the tour bus with Shannon, Helary, Jobe, Brin, and quiet Toffe. Shannon was wearing their best approximation of her Live in Rio bodysuit costume: with green and red electroluminescent wires sewn into the fabric and three battery packs held between her shoulder blades with duct tape.

☢

# Chief, Toby Tyler

The Security radio scanners picked up the chatter among all the teams spread around the city. There were the fire trucks at the Burn barrier, Inventory and Security supervisors along Figueroa. Chief watched from the roof, doubting his plan. He asked for a moment with Toby Tyler.

"Is it too late to put this off for a few days? Look at them."

Drifters who seemed to come from nowhere filled the sidewalks behind the yellow barricades marked **LAPD DO NOT CROSS**. The Shamblers in the crowd were pressed backward by the crowd into the storefronts or, if they were lucky, spread into the cross streets.

"We have to burn tonight, Chief. The charges are set. Uncontrolled sparks can set them off. Rain can put them out. I'll do what you want because you're the Chief, but Vayler wants to protect our resources. We have to do this now. And night is an hour away."

# Eckmann, Marci, Consuelo

At the hangar, Eckmann started to make a ceremony out of opening the big door. "My friends, when I open this door I'm opening the future." But Marci shook her head in disapproval, to say that he was undermining his leadership by acting like the leader. He let Consuelo push the button that started the motor that turned the gears and the door complained with creaks and rumbles as it slid open after being shut for over two years.

"Chief is going to piss his pants," said Spig Wead. "I wish I could see his face after all these years when he sees us. Want to bring this baby over downtown and buzz the fuckers, is what I want to do. Eckmann, don't you want to fuck with them after all this time?"

"Sun sets in an hour," said Eckmann.

# Hopper, Madeinusa

Madeinusa, naked again, walked into the Los Angeles River to her knees. The water reflected the colorless sky. Three white herons lifted together and settled like a lost argument on the other side. A brown duck bobbed her head underwater, with no concern for the woman standing in the shallow part of the stream.

After Hopper changed into his black pants and shirt, he rested the bicycle upside down on its seat and handlebars, dampened a rag with lubricant, and cranked the pedal to run the chain through the rag, shifting the gears. He knew it wasn't necessary. The chain was clean and he'd only ridden a hundred miles on it, but he needed to do something while he thought about Madeinusa. Whatever happened after he went to the house and returned with its secret was going to lead him away from her. His Silent Voice said, "You tried." But this didn't solve the problem, if it even was a problem. *Maybe there are no problems*, thought Hopper, hoping for his Silent Voice to either agree or show him where the idea collapsed from the weight of the evidence of the world. Madeinusa took two more steps in the water toward the duck. The duck was sensible enough to glide away.

The river was faster where Madeinusa was standing. She spread her feet for balance and bent to let her fingers slice the surface.

Hopper called her name. She didn't turn around. There were still a few power bars in his backpack. He left them for her, wrapped in her clothing from American Apparel. He biked away without saying good-bye.

☢

# Shannon, Erin, Toffe

Shannon looked through the hole in the stage and pointed to quiet Toffe. "I want her to stand on the stage where I'm going to be. I want to see what I'm going to look like."

Toffe shook her head no, but Shannon insisted. "Get on the stage. You don't say or do anything to help, so do this for me now."

Toffe began to cry, silently, but Shannon had no reserve of sympathy. "Get up there."

Erin helped Toffe climb through the hole and then Shannon dropped through and left the bus to see Toffe clearly.

Quiet Toffe stood in the middle of the platform.

"Move around the stage and dance," said Shannon. Toffe either didn't hear her or pretended not to, and Shannon yelled at her: "Dance!"

She wasn't going to get Toffe to actually dance no matter how loudly she yelled, but the quiet girl walked the stage from side to side and end to end. Shannon waved to Toffe to come down from the stage. Erin asked her, "Did you see what you needed to see?"

"I don't know." She climbed back up to the roof and told Erin to tell everyone else to leave her alone until it was time to dance.

A few high clouds trapped the gold of the setting sun, but on Figueroa, in the shadows of the tall buildings, it was already dusk. And in the fading light, Shannon's electroluminescent wire had an intensity that was even more vivid, more compelling, than in the dark.

☢

# Hopper

Hopper rode south, parallel to the firewall three blocks to his west with his headlamp turned off. Fire trucks were spread out along the wall where it was closest to downtown in case the flames jumped the barrier. When he had passed the last truck, he turned toward the Burn Zone. It was dark enough now so that no one would see him climbing the rubble pile. The carbon fiber bike was light and he kept the wheels from snagging on the wreckage.

He slipped, twisting an ankle in the gap between a polished wood front door and a steel bed frame.

When he reached the top, he could smell the gasoline.

He pulled a mop handle from the rubble and used it to steady himself as he slipped down the ragged slope to the street.

Hopper turned on his headlamp. In the first intersection he came to, there was an assembly of electric cables leading from a junction box linked to a thick cable that ran down the middle of the street toward the north wall. His Silent Voice told him: "Take them apart wherever you see them."

☢

## Eckmann, Crew

Eckmann greeted the LAX crew as they walked up the rolling stairs and into their seats on the jet.

There weren't many smiles for him, but he didn't expect them to smile, not when death might be only a few hours away. Awful, thought Eckmann, for the plane to crash at night, not to see the sun again. And then, a different idea: better for the plane to crash at night, not to see the ground coming up. So he wasn't the only one on the plane thinking about the insanity of what they were about to try. No one was talking to anyone else.

☢

## Chief, Pippi, Frank Sinatra, Redwings, June Moulton, Toby Tyler, Erin, Shannon Squier, Gunny Sea Ray

Siouxsie Banshee—in red high heels and a white dress she knew from a catalog on costumes was meant for a Mexican girl's fifteenth birthday party—rode the elevator to the roof. She wanted to tell Frank that she hadn't worn high heels in at least four years but that she could walk in them easily, which meant, or proved—as if she needed any more support for her claims—that she had been a sophisticated woman. When the doors opened to the roof, she saw her grand benefactor, busy with Chief and the others. He glanced at her long enough to let her know he knew she was there and she had his permission, and with that assurance she went to the bar, poured a glass of a champagne, and felt, finally, that she was home.

The observers lined up between the hotel's swimming pool and the edge of the roof. In a referee's chair taken from a tennis club, Chief sat eight feet above the command posts. To his right, Sinatra and Redwings stayed in contact with Gunny Sea Ray on the ground. In front of him, Toby Tyler was the busiest, with ten coordinators on the roof talking to the fire crews that were spread around the Burn Zone. To his left, Vayler Monokeefe stayed in contact with the Inventory crew on Figueroa, directing them to hand out the empty bottles and spoons they'd stored in trash cans along the street.

Chief called Pippi. She answered but didn't say anything. He listened to her breathing. "Don't be mad at me," he said.

"Why not?"

"I don't have control tonight. I wanted Vayler to take a hundred busloads of Drifters on a big Inventory hunt away from downtown but the Burn Zone took too much time. So now they're here and all I have to hold them in place is Erin's singer. It wasn't my idea. I listened to The Man and The Woman and they said this would work, but Shannon Squier is not going to distract the Drifters when they see the fire. Drifters see a fire and they want to run away. They'll spread out across the city again like a herd of cattle after lightning."

"I've never seen that."

"I was in Bakersfield two years ago, getting the farms organized. There's ranches there. I saw a billion cows panic in a thunderstorm."

"A billion is a lot."

"Well, a lot, yes. It's better to keep them in one place during a storm. Keep them in the barn."

"What's a barn?" She knew the answer. There were barns in the Heidi books.

"A house for animals."

"I'm locked up now. Is this a barn? Am I an animal?"

"No. You're the woman I love, the woman I don't want to lose. It may not be safe. I'm protecting you. I'll be home in the morning."

"How could you lose me if I was at the hotel with you?"

"A hundred million Drifters are on the street."

"A hundred million, that's a lot of Drifters."

June Moulton, in a red sari trimmed with a gold border, walked out of the elevator, refused an offer of binoculars, and sat on her special throne: a wing-backed rattan chair surrounded by plastic lilies sprayed with a heavy perfume.

"Hello, June," said Sinatra, cautiously. Having a conversation with June Moulton was like holding a soap bubble on a hot needle.

"Everything is going to change tonight, Frank."

"We've had Burns before."

"You'll see. Our way of life can't go on like this and it won't, not after tonight. Stories will be written. You'll see."

Frank knew that to ask her what she meant would just shut her down, so he waited for her next prediction. The oracle was best approached with subtlety, but Redwings pressed the question. "June Moulton, sister, what are you saying? What do you see?"

Sinatra slapped Redwing's shoulder. "She said what she's going to say, Redwings," and the old biker made an unhappy sound.

June Moulton surprised him. "No, Frank, I'm not finished. Tell me about the Drifter who killed the man from the motor pool. Tell me about Nole Hazard."

"How do you know about this, June?"

"I keep track of things. I listen. Everything has to be recorded by someone and that's my job. That's what the Mythology Committee of one is here to do, record everything and then put it in a package of generalizations that can travel through time. The old myths don't work for us because we're not those people anymore. We're new people. We are missing the old neural dramas that in former times were represented symbolically by the old stories that explained metaphysical properties of human character, and the pace and meaning of life. This is to say that you can't be a narcissist when you have no Narcissus."

"Who?"

"Just my point. We may see a stranger in the mirror, but the stranger isn't what used to be called beautiful. That was the myth, as I understand it. The face in the reflection was beautiful. We fell in love with ourselves. Now, the face in the mirror scares us."

Redwings pressed his question. "How do you know Nole Hazard is not a real name?"

She held up a hand for him to be quiet. "Look at Chief. He's getting ready to give the signal."

Chief called Toby Tyler to his white wooden throne. "Toby, is your crew ready?"

"Ready, Chief."

Chief called Erin. "Erin, is she ready?"

Erin said, "We won't know until she starts."

Chief summoned Frank with a discreet nod.

"So we should be ready to start. Frank?"

Sinatra walked slowly to Chief. "Sir?"

"Let's take a look at the crowd."

He climbed down from his chair. Toby Tyler joined them without asking permission. They went to the rail of the deck.

"Vayler, are your people ready?"

"Strictly speaking, Drifters aren't anyone's people, Chief. They're ours to share."

"They're yours tonight, Vayler. Hand out the bottles."

# Shannon, Erin, Helary, Jobe, Toffe

Shannon lay back on the platform and looked up at the office towers. She didn't want to move. She didn't want to do whatever it was that they were expecting of her. All of the preparation to get the stage built so quickly and to give her a costume—it was for something large. She knew that. She knew that they needed her for something, the way she needed her chisel.

Chief called Erin.

"Is the Burn starting?" she asked.

"Not yet. I want to give Shannon Squier the crowd's attention first."

"I think this is a bad idea, Chief. She's not who you want her to be."

"Should I talk to her? If there's any chance that talking to me would get in her way, tell me." He knew that Erin would know he was scared but he had no choice.

"I don't know what we're doing. Neither does she. Wait until the show is over."

Chief wanted to encourage Erin. "That's good thinking, Erin. Your father would be proud of you."

"Thank you, Chief. I hope that would be a good thing."

"It would be. So start now."

"I want to say this again: I don't think we're ready, Chief." She felt herself losing her argument.

"Start now. Right now, not in ten minutes, but now. This second, go! I want to hear the music!"

Chief did not finish the order with a threat to kill her or banish her if she didn't meet the challenge. He needed her. She dropped down from the stage into the bus and told Helary to hit Play and AutoZone to start rolling even before telling Shannon. AutoZone, thankful to finally have something to do, let the bus go without thinking about the girl on the stage. And Shannon, not braced for movement, fell and rolled to the edge of the platform, scraping her hands. Erin yelled at AutoZone to slow down as Erin rose again to tell Shannon that it was time. "Right now. Dance." As the bus made its left turn down Figueroa, meeting the crowd, the sound of the cheering fans in Brazil blasted from the sides and rear of the bus, bounced off the buildings around them, and returned to Shannon blended and muddy, provoking no associations, no memories of movement connected to the rhythms of Carnival. The crowds of Drifters had no central beat to draw them into banging.

Erin told her: "Stand up. You just have to stand up. And move to the music."

From the roof of the Ritz-Carlton, Chief could see the bus, followed by the crowd.

"We shouldn't wait anymore," said Toby.

Chief gave a little wave of his hand, all the order that Toby needed.

Tyler made the call and in thirty seconds the Burn Zone exploded.

Shannon moved to the disorganized echoes of her old song.

# Go Bruins, Royce Hall

In Chief's house, Go Bruins called Gunny Sea Ray for an update. "When does the Burn begin, Gunny?"

Gunny Sea Ray answered, "I don't know. They're taking the Drifters out for a parade."

"I'm going to the observation terrace," said Go Bruins to Royce Hall.

"We were told to stay inside with Pippi."

"You can't do things just the way Chief says. You have to do what he means even if he doesn't know that what he says isn't what he should mean."

Royce Hall closed his eyes to concentrate. "Say that again."

Go Bruins said it again, and Royce Hall kept his eyes shut to figure things out. Go Bruins knew he was smarter than Royce Hall but suspected that Hall was better looking. In the present circumstances,

Go Bruins's intelligence gave him the advantage if there was anything worth using it for and he could see Royce Hall's mind slow down as he thought about the consequences of challenging an order from Chief. Go Bruins wanted to see the fire and hear the music if it traveled this far. He didn't like staying up on the hill when everyone worth knowing was downtown.

He saw the Burn Zone light up.

# Hopper, Silent Voice

Hopper knew he was lost. Even with the headlamp, everything looked different in the dark and nothing looked right. The houses, the palm trees, the dead cars, the cracks in the pavement—only the smell of gasoline gave any shape to this abandoned neighborhood.

Standing in the middle of an intersection with four stop signs and another tangle of cables that led to the houses at each corner, he thought about what the Teacher might say to him when he came back alone to Palm Springs. Would the Teacher tell him: "What matters is that you did your best"? Or would the Teacher say: "You had the chance and you weren't paying attention"?

Three of the four houses on the corner exploded, and at other intersections beyond them other houses blew up, as flame ran on paraffin fuses down the sidewalk, linking to other fuses leading to the other houses, grids of fire on the block as the neighborhood itself was a grid of fire. The already-dry wood of the houses, the dead palm trees, the remaining fumes in the tanks of cars left on the sidewalk or in garages: everything that had been potential only was now released and expanding to fulfillment.

Even his Silent Voice could only say, "What is this?"

In the light of the fire, Hopper could tell his Silent Voice: "I know where we are now." His Silent Voice was scared, wanted to give Hopper directions back to the firewall, but they were six blocks from the house, through the fire.

The flames spread as the fire drew air through broken windows, crawling up window curtains, curling around overhanging eaves.

The coyotes and the dog packs that escaped the Inventory crews ran from their hidden dens in the old houses. Rats dropped from their nests at the top of burning palm trees, ignored by the feral cats bewildered by the smoke.

# Eckmann, Franz, Spig Wead

When he saw the flames, Eckmann took his seat in the cockpit behind Franz and Spig Wead and signaled the tow truck shackled to the front wheel of the jet to pull it out of the hangar. Seth and Marci stayed in the first-class galley, looking over Eckmann's shoulder.

Franz started the right engine, then the left.

The taxiway led past the terminals with the airplanes that no one would ever fly, beasts from a mythology beyond June Moulton's imagination, eating from the trough and disinterested in the departure of one of their kind.

The front cabin door stayed open, waiting for the tow driver to climb in after he centered the jet at the head of the runway. The jet could have made it to the runway on its own power, but Franz asked that the engines not be used to roll the plane until takeoff, saying, "I can't promise to know how to make the plane move slowly."

The runway lights for the first hundred yards were green, followed by white, and at the end of the runway, red. It was the white lights that worried Spig Wead. "They can see those lights from Center Camp if they know what to look for."

Eckmann wasn't worried. "Spig Wead, old friend, don't be afraid of Chief tonight. His fire is in the way. They may plan on hitting us tomorrow or the tomorrow after that, but by then we'll be somewhere else, with its own set of challenges, no doubt, but not these challenges anymore."

Eckmann congratulated Franz for doing so well.

"I haven't done anything yet, Eckmann. We're being pulled."

The tow truck disengaged and the driver parked it past the edge of the right wing and carried a ladder so he could climb back into the plane. He leaned the ladder into the doorway and climbed up, shaking Eckmann's hand.

# Pippi, Go Bruins, Royce Hall

It made Royce Hall a happy man to see Go Bruins disobey Chief's order and bring Pippi to the observation terrace because an advantage would yield to him when Chief found out. He'd been looking at the Burn through the strongest telescope and he stepped away from it for Pippi.

"It's set for downtown. You might want to change the focus."

Pippi adjusted the lens. "I know how this works."

The compulsion to send messages over the wall grabbed her and she turned the telescope toward a point deep in the Burn Zone. She felt a confused message coming to her from one particular burning house, a few of those little Thought Pictures that weren't like dreams, but fragments of a disconnected story, a story about a little girl.

☢

# Hopper, Silent Voice

Hopper passed five houses, until he saw the house where the Inventory truck had stopped to load furniture and behind it, on the next block, the house with the hidden key ring. He dropped the bike on the driveway, adjusted his headlamp, climbed over the wall, kicked in the kitchen door, went straight to the cabinet beside the sink, pulled on the second drawer until it was off the rollers, spilling a tray of knives on the floor, reached into the back of the space, and grabbed the key ring hanging from the hook. There were two keys on the ring, one longer than the other. The shorter key fit the locked door to the cellar. He put the longer key into his pocket. He walked down the stairs to the basement. He turned his head to sweep his light around the room. The far wall was hidden behind shelves full of cardboard banker's boxes. He tossed the boxes aside, uncovering a sledgehammer hidden behind them. He swung the hammer into the wall, which was drywall, not brick, and fell forward, pulled by the momentum of the force he thought he needed.

He cleared enough of a hole to step through and grab the rope handle on a wooden crate. He pulled the crate out and then knew where to find the crowbar and how to crack the crate's lid open.

He knew to grab the backpack from inside the crate.

"Get out of here now," said his Silent Voice. "The house can kill you."

Hopper ran up the stairs, his ankle buzzing in light pain from his stumble on the rubble wall. The kitchen curtains were burning, the fire spreading up the wall and across the ceiling. The living room was on fire.

He slipped his hand into his pocket to be sure that he still had the longer key. The only way out was through the flames feeding on the air coming in from a broken window.

The tar in the street bubbled and the dry brush on the front lawn was burning now, too. His bicycle on the concrete driveway was surrounded by flame. The frame was hot.

His Silent Voice came back to him. While he was in the cellar, he hadn't even thought of the Silent Voice. "I can't give you any help, not here. This has nothing to do with me. This is yours to solve if you want to live."

Solve? The only solution was riding as hard as he had since Palm Springs. The fire was in all directions at once, but between the flames he found gateways.

He watched himself ask the fire for the skill to choose the right way out of the fire and this dependence on something outside of the Silent Voice, outside of the shadow of the Teacher in Palm Springs, was so curious to him that the fire lost its power compared to the marvel of all the strange ways he had been not just Hopper but someone else, someone on the way to either taking over from Hopper or making Hopper into someone new, something that had never been before.

He was a block ahead of the fire, then two, then three, and then out of it, then to the foot of the firewall, then up the firewall with the bike and the bag, and then down to the street. He heard the distant sound of the Bottle Bangers.

# Shannon, Bottle Bangers, Drifters,

# Siouxsie Banshee, Frank Sinatra

Siouxsie Banshee pushed her way through the crowd on the Ritz-Carlton roof to watch the bus with the dancer wrapped in strands of light come slowly down Figueroa. The exploding Burn Zone was hidden from anyone who wasn't forty stories above the street. She grabbed Frank Sinatra's hand. "This is art, Frank. Do you understand?"

He pointed to the fire and the smoke cloud rising over it and coming toward them. "I don't know about art. I just want to know what's going to happen when the ash starts to fall on Figueroa."

As the bus approached Wilshire Boulevard, Shannon smelled the fire. She stood tall and stopped dancing to locate the flames so she could run from them.

Chief called Erin. "Why did she stop?"

"I'll take care of it."

Erin crawled out onto the stage.

"Shannon, you have to dance."

"There's a fire."

"Yes, there's a big fire."

"We should run."

"We'll be fine. It's not close and there's a wall to keep it from spreading."

"I don't like fire."

"Nobody does. Just stay where you are," said Erin as she dropped back into the bus and asked Brin for a glass bottle and a knife or spoon. "Empty and clean."

AutoZone said, "There's some bottles in the bedroom in the back." Toffe took a steel knife out of the drawer.

Jobe found three full bottles of Tito's vodka.

"I just need one," said Erin. "And give me a table knife." She stood up on the table and poked her head through the hole again.

Shannon watched the skyline for flames. Erin gave her the bottle and the knife to bang it with.

"Drink the bottle. Drink all of it." Shannon swallowed a mouthful.

Erin told Helary to turn off the loudspeakers.

With the push of a button, the music stopped and the change in sound was like a change in creation. The silence scared the Bottle Bangers. Instead of making more noise, they made less.

Erin told AutoZone to keep rolling. "Slowly, AutoZone, slowly, slower, slower, that's it, thaaaat's it. Slow."

She climbed out of the portal and dropped to her knees before Shannon. Erin was a fan and she knew that Shannon's obligation to the world started with making each fan happy. As Shannon wrote in her autobiography, Erin's all-time favorite book, "All good things start with one person loving another person and I love my fans, one fan at a time."

"You are Shannon Squier. Shannon Squier is not scared of smoke."

"Chisel Girl is afraid of smoke."

"Chisel Girl is here no more, only you, Shannon Squier, only you. Just get up and bang the bottle, that's all you have to do. You don't have to sing. You don't have to dance."

"Fire," said Shannon. "Run. You can smell it. Run. Can't you smell it?"

"Yes, so can everyone else. And you're going to make them forget it, because you're going to have fun now, Shannon Squier. Now you're going to show them who you really are and, when you do, if you've forgotten who you are, they'll tell you. That's how this works, how it's going to work. But you have to do this quickly, because the Drifters smell the fire, too."

Yes, the Drifters could, too, and the First and Second Wavers among them, immune to panic about fire, weren't immune to panic about a Drifter stampede. The Drifters broke car windows, threw bottles at Shannon on the bus, looked for Shamblerinas to strip. The Shamblers made their humming sound as they massed together.

Siouxsie Banshee watched the two women through her binoculars. "What are they doing?" she asked Redwings.

"Sister, I don't know. Truthfully, I don't. But as I wrote in my old journal, six years ago, 'Even the best of us hit the same pothole twice.'"

Chief climbed down from the referee's chair. "Sinatra, we're going down to the street. Everyone else stay here."

Sinatra knew that Chief wasn't used to Figueroa at night, and never without a swarm of protectors around him. "We stay here, Chief."

Which is what Chief wanted him to say.

*   *   *

In the street around the bus, a wave of order passed with the sound; the Bangers around them felt it before Sinatra and Chief could see Shannon clearly, tapping the neck of her Tito's bottle, one, two, three/four, one, two, three/four, with a slight increase in speed between the third and fourth beat and a tiny hesitation before the repeat.

The Bangers and Drifters closest to her followed her beat exactly, and those next to them followed the precise pattern.

Shannon shifted her weight while raising the bottle overhead and keeping the beat, and some banged their bottles with such ferocious approval that they shattered from exuberance instead of dread.

A delirious Banger beat his own head with metal chopsticks. Every time his face turned in Erin's direction she wanted him to stop and just look at her.

She said, "Daddy."

Helary asked her, "Why'd you say 'Daddy'?"

"That's my father. I know that face. It's on the pictures of my father. He has my father's face. That's my father."

"He has a beard. I know the pictures of your father, and he doesn't have a beard."

"His eyes, Helary. Stop the bus!"

AutoZone knew that if he stopped, the crowd would make it impossible to move forward again. "No, I have to keep moving."

"But, my father. Daddy."

She watched him turn into the crowd, which closed around him with another surge toward the bus.

She pulled herself through the hole in the stage and Shannon, even in her trance, separated from her performance and tapped her foot on the side of Erin's head to force her back into the bus.

"But I saw my father, Shannon. I saw him."

Shannon kicked her harder and Erin let go of the stage and fell back into the bus.

Erin remembered that she was here to do a job. The feeling about her father dribbled away quickly. It wasn't as though she remembered his qualities and his love. She remembered the face in the pictures and maybe it wasn't her father. Her father didn't have a beard.

A Transport Service worker with a bottle of Grey Goose in his hand was close to the stage and offered her another drink. Shannon reached for the bottle and seemed to balance herself with her left foot pressed against the free air beyond the limit of the stage. She took another mouthful and raised the bottle to the sky like it was the head of a wolf she'd just killed with her chisel, like it was bleeding.

She tapped the bottle with the spoon and then cupped her ear with a hand. The Bottle Bangers understood her. No woman in the center of their circles had ever banged the bottle in return.

Shannon banged the bottle and danced and the crowd banged their bottles and danced, returning the old love and restoring something that Erin, so close to Shannon, felt first, as her concentration on the singer turned inward. Erin saw nothing but her mother and father lighting candles at the dining room table and then saw what others around the bus were seeing, as Shannon's energy bounced from the stage into their frayed brains. She danced and gave one man an image of a girl in white in a yellow garden on a red blanket with a birthday cake and another man saw a dozen roses and a dog in the snow and a Driftette saw the Virgin of Guadalupe with her shining robe covered in the crude stars with their emanations of indulgence.

Erin saw this in Drifter eyes. Each of them danced and remembered something, their concentration on Shannon also turning inward.

*If this is happening to me*, thought Erin, *it is happening to them*. It was small at first and not even known to them as a memory but it was there.

They were recovering torn pages of a shredded album that had been carried away by a hurricane four years ago. Erin slowed down to think about what Shannon was like when she was young and famous out of nowhere, nothing left to prepare because everything after that first ascension was going to be shocking and beautiful.

The clumsiest Shamblers, doomed for the desert bus ride, felt the return of lost images, meager and majestic at once.

And then above the sound of the rattling bottles, above the thick notes of the Burn, they heard the loudest sound in four years.

☢

# Eckmann, Marci, Seth Kaplan, MD

Eckmann told Marci to push the ladder away and close the door.

As Seth watched Marci reach to do what she'd been told, a small idea unpacked itself between two breaths, as he thought about who he might have been before NK3, the kind of man he might have been, Seth Kaplan, MD, expert in pediatric oncology, a man who often had to tell the parents of his patients that their children would die soon and in pain. He thought about not just who he had been specifically but who else he had been like, his similarity to other doctors and the lives other doctors lived that had been like his. Of all the grievances he held against Eckmann for stealing him at gunpoint from the hospital inside the Fence, the largest part of his hatred for the man took the shape of the wife he once had and the children they once shared and the life they'd known in Los Angeles and the places they'd visited when they had time to spend the good money he earned. Now—on the plane, about to take off—this family mattered to him, not that he remembered them in any way. Of course it was too late for that, but doctors worked hard for their good lives, and he'd seen family pictures in most of the doctors' offices he explored in the UCLA medical buildings. Here on the plane he wasn't with anyone he had ever traveled with before, and it was that, more than his fear of the plane crashing, that inspired him to hold Marci's hand before she could knock the ladder to the runway, too far to jump without hurting themselves.

Marci and Seth looked at each other, and then touched the backs of their hands together, feeling each other's warmth. Just that.

"I'm going," said Seth. "I don't want to be with these people. Come with me."

"Do I love you?" Marci whispered. "Is that what this is?"

Eckmann again told Marci to close the door.

She went ahead of Seth, stepping down the ladder and dropping the last three rungs. She held it steady while Seth followed and then pulled the ladder down as Eckmann yelled to them: "What are you doing?"

Marci took Seth's hand and they ran past the wing.

Saying nothing else, not calling after them this time, Eckmann sealed and locked the door. They saw Eckmann in the cockpit talk to Franz and Spig Wead.

The jet rolled away on thunder.

"Shouldn't you be going faster?" asked Eckmann.

Franz throttled back and stopped the plane.

"Am I the pilot?" asked Franz.

"You're the pilot, yes. You're the pilot."

"Do you think you can fly the plane?"

"No. I can service the plane, but I can't fly the plane."

"Then why are you asking me questions that you can't answer?"

"I'm being cautious."

"Because of you I almost died."

"I know that."

"And the doctor has run away. He doesn't think I can fly the plane, does he?"

"I didn't talk to him. I don't know why he left the plane."

"He left because he thinks we're going to die. Maybe yes, maybe no. You want to go to Phoenix?"

"First, yes."

"All the airports are in the computer. We're going to fly over the ocean, turn around, and when we do, Spig here will tell the plane which airport you want to go to, and the plane will take us there at the speed and altitude I select. The plane can land automatically once we tell it where to go."

The jet was heavy with fuel and the holds were full and Eckmann thought, *It won't fly, it won't fly, it won't fly.* Because his memory of flight had been erased.

Marci screamed, "No, don't go! Come back! Come back! I want to go with you!" as the plane rolled away from them.

Franz let Eckmann call out the speed of the plane while he held on to the wheel, waiting to pull it back. From 60 to a 125 to 150. The end of the runway wasn't visible except on the panel, and he looked down at the controls and not out the windows, to avoid being confused by reality.

Eckmann couldn't help himself. "Now? Shouldn't you start flying now? Aren't you supposed to pull back? Aren't you supposed to bring the nose of the plane up? Do you know what you're doing?"

Marci chased the plane as it lifted and kept running until it was over the ocean. She dropped to the runway, whipped by regret. "I made a mistake," she whispered. "I made a mistake. I made a mistake."

"No," said Seth. "We love each other."

"We better go," said Marci. "There's nothing for us here."

# Pippi

The telescope was sharp and Pippi saw the lights shining on the jet's tail. The sound didn't cross the basin until the plane was lifting off the ground.

## Eckmann, Spig Wead, Franz

The plane banked over the ocean and turned back over the city. They followed the bright beads of light along the Fence. There was the wide lagoon of fire across the Burn Zone and, beyond that, the lights of Figueroa.

Franz said to Spig, "You want to take a look?"

"That's just what I was thinking."

Eckmann protested. "You can't go over downtown. The fire, the smoke, the ashes, they can hurt the engines."

He was ignored as Franz lowered the plane to three thousand feet.

## Shannon, Chief, Bottle Bangers

Shannon saw the plane and dropped her bottle and then the sound came, the whine of jet turbines mixed with thunder mixed with the windstorms of fire rising from the Burn Zone.

Erin saw the visions snap shut, the Virgin of Guadalupe disappear.

Now the jet was overhead, banking at a harsh angle, wing almost pointing straight to the ground. The Drifters stopped their banging. Some threw their bottles at the plane, as it continued to pivot around a stem of energy rising out of the chaos below.

Erin saw in the crowd's puzzlement that they needed Shannon to tell them what to do, that they didn't want her to separate herself from the coincidence of her performance and the plane's arrival. They wanted her to enlarge her role by leaving nothing in the immediate arrangement of the world outside of her intentions. So they blamed her for the plane, blamed her for their fear.

Bottles were thrown at Shannon, at the bus.

From the roof, Chief called Erin's phone but there was no answer.

Looking down at the crowd, Franz slapped Spig Wead on the back. "This is great. This is fucking great."

"The best," said Wead.

They watched the Drifters retreat from Figueroa, run into the shadows between the buildings, and disappear into the underground parking lots.

Shannon called for the Drifters to come back.

Erin said, "They can't hear you."

The plane stopped circling and flew north, away from city and the Burn Zone.

"Fuck them all," said Spig Wead. "Just fuck them all. Franz, let's go over them one more time, all the way fast. A hundred thousand miles a minute."

"We'll burn fuel," said Eckmann.

"We'll go slow after this."

On the roof: Chief knew that if he blamed anyone for the failure to stop Eckmann, someone would tie him to a bus and drag him to the desert. Or that's what he wanted to do to himself.

On the street: Erin had seen what the heads of the committees missed by staying on the roof. The ash from the Burn Zone was falling over them, maybe, she thought, drawn from the Burn Zone by the vortex of the spiraling airplane.

The plane turned over the San Fernando Valley and Franz pushed the throttle full forward as he brought the jet lower to a straight run over Figueroa to the Ritz-Carlton.

On the hotel roof: the Fence elite lowered their heads to save themselves from the leading edge of the wings. Only Siouxsie Banshee, standing alone with a bottle of red wine in her right hand and a glass in her left, didn't bother with more than the quick glance she might give a squeaking hinge.

After passing over the crowd, Franz turned the jet to the east and set it to climb to thirty thousand feet. The cockpit door was open and he looked backward down the length of the cabin for the first time since leaving the ground. He went on the public address system and read from the manual: "The seat belt light is off which means it is now safe to walk about the cabin, but for your safety, please keep the belts buckled in case of unexpected turbulence. Thank you for flying Singapore Airlines. Relax and enjoy your flight."

# Pippi

The smoke cloud over the fire, blown southwest by the wind, did not obscure the jet or muffle the sound. From the prison of her terrace in the hills, Pippi—with Royce Hall and Go Bruins—was the last person in Los Angeles to see the jet before it disappeared. Go Bruins and Royce Hall continued to gripe about missing the Shannon Squier concert.

Watching the jet made Pippi want to change her name again. Her stiff red pigtails belonged to someone who had little idea of what she really wanted from life and now that she had seen the jet, she needed to shift the idea of herself to be someone who wasn't waiting for rescue. She had to choose a name and story for herself that didn't come from the wallpaper in a child's room. She wanted to name herself secretly and let them call her Pippi. It didn't matter what they called her and maybe it was even better that they called her a name she no longer called herself. That was her mistake from the beginning of this second consciousness after rehab and after Chief claimed her.

She laughed at the thought and Go Bruins asked her what was funny. She knew that whatever she told a guard would be told immediately to Chief, but she still answered with what she was thinking. "I made the mistake of identifying with my identity. If that's not a mistake, I don't know what is."

For the first time in this part of her life, she thought about the future.

# Chief, Vayler

Chief called for Vayler but no one could find him. "This wouldn't have happened if he'd done as I asked and sent a few thousand Drifters on a simple overnight run to carry back supplies. Where is he?"

# Erin, Shannon

Erin brought Shannon into the rear bedroom of the tour bus and helped her out of the costume and into a dress for the party on the roof. "Although I doubt there's going to be a party now," she said. Shannon ignored her.

AutoZone brought the bus to the hotel's front door, where Security protected them as they walked from the bus to the elevators. Chief was in the lobby. He thanked Shannon. "I'm sorry to put you through this exercise. The Drifters should have been out of the city, but Vayler Monokeefe wanted them and of course I was right and they couldn't take the noise."

Erin carefully asked him, "Did you feel anything before the jet, from the crowd?"

"Once I saw the plane, I had other things to worry about than the music."

"It was too far to see anything, and it doesn't matter."

Erin didn't want to tell him that Shannon restored old feeling, or rather, she wanted to tell him, because he was Chief, but found it better to lie.

"Let's go to the party," said Chief.

When they got to the roof, Toby Tyler stopped them. Erin expected Chief to turn away from her but he let her stay, which showed that he trusted her now.

"Toby, tell me."

"Report on the Burn. It jumped the barrier in three places, and the fires were put out. The center of the Burn Zone is already ashes. It'll smolder for a week, and we'll smell it for a long time."

"At least something went right. And we're better off with Eckmann and company gone. Planes are a distraction; escape is pointless."

"Gunny Sea Ray gave me his report and he told me to tell you that a Drifter who'd been trapped inside the zone rode his bicycle through the fire."

"Did anyone try to stop him?"

"Too hot."

☢

# Frank Sinatra, Siouxsie Banshee, June Moulton, Chief, Shannon

Frank Sinatra asked Redwings to find Vayler. "What does he need from Security to get the Drifters back and settled?"

"This was a night to be ashamed of, Frank, if you were to ask me what I thought."

"And why is that?"

"First, we missed that they had a plane. Second, we didn't get the Drifters out of the area."

"There's always a lesson, Redwings. Radical self-reliance means radical self-examination so the next time isn't just the next time."

Siouxsie Banshee offered Sinatra a glass of wine. "This is expensive, Sinatra. I checked it on the wine menu. Eight hundred dollars a bottle. It's from Australia."

"Is it good?"

"It gets the job done."

"I can't move you to my house inside the Fence, but this is pretty close."

"This is nice, Sinatra, but it's just another downtown publicity party. People in good clothes smiling at each other. You see the pictures in the old magazines."

"I don't read those magazines and doubt I ever did."

"That's why you're not the conversationalist you could be."

"Everyone here knows everyone else except for you. They assume you've just been verified. Otherwise you wouldn't be here, but a recent verification is embarrassing. It reminds them that they owe their place to luck, that they wouldn't be here if they hadn't been in the system. That, and someone else's opinion of them."

"Opinion or evaluation."

"Well said. Evaluation, judgment, estimate of worth. They're watching me talk to you, which makes you interesting to them in a way that you hadn't been interesting before."

"Why aren't they talking about the plane that almost hit the building?"

"In a world without memory, it's easy to forget things even while they're happening. Not just easy, convenient."

"You haven't forgotten the Drifter who threw a man from that hotel." She pointed to the Hilton where Hopper killed Tesla.

"Maybe I have, but Chief hasn't. We don't get many murders around here."

"And what about the people killed when the pilot was kidnapped?"

"That's not murder. That's war."

"You kill Drifters when you drive them to the desert and leave them there. Is that war?"

"Self-defense."

"Why not shoot them?"

"Chief doesn't want to give anyone a taste for blood."

"They still die."

"But we don't see them die. Radical self-reliance. That's what Chief calls it. They're on their own."

"Sinatra, don't lie to your Siouxsie. Siouxsie wants the truth. Siouxsie hears you personally shoot Drifters on the spot if they match certain criteria."

"That's also self-defense."

"You're not really on Chief's side."

"How do you get to that thought?"

"You have a detached sense of the world. That's why you like talking to me."

"And how are you the expert on my loyalty, or lack of it, to Chief? You're not an expert on politics. You know art and furniture."

"Yes, exactly, I'm an expert on artifacts made in the past and I can see that you were made in the past. You have a frame that's authentically old, not pressboard like everyone else in this new version of the world and you're a work of art, Sinatra. You want to know things for their value that only other experts can appreciate. Chief's taste, you know it's bogus. He's looking at art books. He's looking at the things that people collected. But he'd never come down here and walk through the warehouses to separate the good from the bad from the ugly. Not him. But you? Yes, you. You know the difference."

"Tell me more about the Drifter who killed the Bottle Banger."

"I knew he was different."

"How?"

"He didn't talk but he wasn't stupid. He didn't like the Drifters any more than I did. And he didn't like the people who were giving the orders. The people who work for the Fence. He tolerated them. Drifters don't get impatient with First Wavers. They don't have a sense of time's passage so there's no sense of time's waste. He was looking for something."

"How do you know?"

"Because he found it."

"What did he find?"

"Something in one of the houses."

"Furniture, art?"

"I don't know."

"So how do you know he found something that you know he was looking for?"

"He walked away from us and went into one of the houses. Then he came back and he did his job better than he had before."

"Do you know which house?"

"No. And even if I did, what good will that do you? It's smoke, Sinatra."

"Someone was seen inside the Burn Zone riding a bicycle out of the fire. It could have been your friend."

"It could have been a Drifter who'd fallen asleep in a house he'd claimed for shelter."

"It's my experience as chief of Security that the Drifter's degraded condition subtracts from him the energy to save his own life."

"There she is! That's really her."

Shannon Squier was at the entrance with Chief and Erin.

"So jets don't impress you but Shannon Squier does?"

"Why not both?" said Siouxsie Banshee, not afraid of any shifts in Sinatra's opinion of her.

Chief raised a hand for everyone's attention. He was in a mood to tell lies that his people believed.

"The Burn is going well. The Drifters are coming back. And we're done with the problem of LAX. They had a pilot. They had a pilot all along and then when we verified a pilot they came up here and killed him in an ambush. Why did they do that? I'll tell you why.

They didn't want anyone to follow them. Let them go. We have a fine thing here that we made for ourselves and keep making but you'd all rather bang your bottles than protect yourselves. You like parties more than work."

"Everyone likes parties more than work," said Shannon Squier. "And you threw the party so why are you complaining?"

"He gets this way," said Erin. "It's just him."

Chief smacked Erin on the side of her head with an open hand. No one, at least in this life she'd known since waking up from rehab, had ever hit her, and the insult to a dignity she only discovered with the slap hurt more than the modest pain.

"You shouldn't have done that," said Shannon. "That was not a good thing to do."

Chief saw it in her eyes, a knowing defiance that didn't need to act on its justifications but could wait.

He said, simply, "I'm sorry."

Erin saw the way Chief relented. This was something new, as was the way Chief turned his own embarrassment into anger at Sinatra.

"There was a murder, Frank Sinatra. What have you done to find the killer?"

Siouxsie spoke: "He's done a lot."

Chief looked to Sinatra and asked, "This is the one you told me about?"

"My name is Siouxsie Banshee. I'm an art curator with a specialty in midcentury modernism and I do a better job at finding what you want than the people who work for you."

"And that makes you the specialist on finding the murderer of a First Wave motor pool mechanic?"

"I have great taste."

"That still doesn't make you one of us."

"She should be one of us," said Sinatra.

"We're not in the Fence," said Siouxsie Banshee. "There's no rule against my being here, is there?"

"Technically, no," said Chief.

Sinatra took control. "I can find the killer for you, Chief. And I apologize for the way our guest is speaking."

"If she can help you find the murderer, she can live," said Chief.

Sinatra saw that June Moulton was right. Yes, everything in the world of the Fence was about to change, because Chief was scared.

He would respect Chief's insistence on proving that a mysterious stranger affected their world. Chief would demand that he stay on the phantom's pursuit so long as Sinatra relayed to Chief his confident assurance that the case was going to break any day.

And then, if Chief was right and there was someone out there who wanted to harm him, would it be so terrible for Frank and Siouxsie if they allowed the stranger to find his way through the Fence?

He now had to convince Chief that he took this threat seriously. But to do that, he had to believe it, or else Chief would suspect him. Chief was shrewd and his insight severe.

# Vayler

Vayler Monokeefe knew they would look for him, and he knew they would find him. But he had already worked a plan to delay the inevitable.

# Hopper

The ash-filled sky blurred the dawn when Hopper came back to the river. He sat down next to Madeinusa's clothing, neatly folded under a layer of gray flakes. Tucked inside the folds were the three power bars he'd left for her. His Silent Voice asked, "Do you think she's dead?"

Hopper said, "We haven't seen anything to say she is or she isn't. We just haven't found her yet. I didn't expect to find her in the house."

"Not your wife, I meant Madeinusa."

"She could be swimming."

"She hardly knew how to walk. And she couldn't dance. How is she going to know how to swim?"

Hopper tore the wrapper off one of the power bars, chewing slowly while he played with the toggle on the zipper of the bag.

"Are you afraid to open the bag?" asked his Silent Voice.

"You're talking too much."

"Are you afraid to open the bag? You shouldn't be."

"I'm not afraid."

"What are you? You're something, otherwise you'd just open the bag and see the thing that pulled you across the desert."

"You wouldn't understand."

"That's not possible."

All the life he really knew for certain had been focused on finding this bag and when he pulled the zipper open, he would no longer be living in anticipation. Everything that still compelled him to seek an answer would be pushed aside by whatever reality demanded of his present attention. He would need something new. Changed desire. Changed motive.

He pulled the zipper slowly. A beach towel was rolled tightly and held in place by a leather belt. Something round and hard was tucked deeply in the bundle. Under the towel was a pistol.

He left the gun in the bag, and loosened the leather belt. With the belt off, the roll released. Inside the beach towel he found a child's bones, a small skull, ribs, hands, hip. A gold ring was pinned to a small pink satin ball gown with short sleeves and puffy shoulders. Inside the dress was a letter and a photograph, both of them burned:

Darling,

She's dead. I'm sorry. We tried. All of the children died. I'm sorry. I buried her here because they're outside now burning the bodies and I don't want to throw her into a fire with other bodies. But you're here now, you're reading this, you remember.

Say no more. When you see me, don't say, "I'm sorry." You don't have to. I'm already forgetting what happened. I wrote it down but I forget where I put the paper.

Find me even if I forget you and I won't forget you. Because if you are reading this, then you remember.

And if anyone else is reading this, please, please, I ask you to put this back where you found it.

Remember mercy?

Love, all love,
Robin

The photograph showed a little girl held in the arms of a man. Her face blocked his. She was in the pink ball gown. The other half of the picture was lost to the fire, except for a woman's left arm, reaching around the little girl, right over the girl's left shoulder. The woman was wearing a wedding ring.

"That's her," said his Silent Voice. "You found her. Very good. We have to leave now. I know where to go next."

Hopper took the ring off the pin. It fit the small finger on his left hand.

# Chief, Go Bruins, Pippi, Shannon, Erin

Chief gave Shannon the front passenger seat of the Hummer and sat behind her with Erin, who would know from his silence to leave him alone. When the Fence gates closed behind them and he was on the road back to Center Camp, Chief wanted to reorganize his life and the life of the world he ruled so that he could keep a promise to himself never to leave the Fence again, never to be stupid about anything ever again, starting with the stupidity of caring for the Second Wave and the Drifters. The fever, he had allowed the fever of the big Burn to infect his brain. *Maybe I have an NK3 relapse*, he worried. Maybe it's a mutation of the mutation—the slow-acting, slow-onset stupidity of leadership.

Back at Center Camp, Erin kissed Chief's hand. "This is the hand that hit me," she said. "And what makes me happy is that I was mad at you and you let me be mad at you, so I can't complain about the pain. Shannon, can I complain about the pain?"

"You can complain about anything."

"When you say 'you,' do you mean me myself or do you mean 'you' in a general way?"

"Yes."

Chief left the car at Erin's and walked up the hill to his palace. It probably wasn't healthy to force his lungs to work harder with the air so dirty, but he welcomed the ordeal as punishment.

He found Pippi in the kitchen, making tea for him.

"It's called Throat Coat. We don't have much left and I asked Vayler to find some. He promised there's more out there and he'd save it all for me."

"Thank you."

"The jet," she said. "That was exciting."

"I'm glad you were here. It might have crashed on us."

"Aren't we happy it didn't?"

# Eckmann, LAX Crew

Singapore Airlines Flight 1 was climbing through the darkness above the San Gabriel Mountains when it started to bounce like a car on a cracked highway. The shaking started without warning and increased. Eckmann screamed at Franz: "Stop doing that! Why is it doing that? Why is the plane bumping on the road? I don't see the road. I don't see the bumps! Make it stop!" Nothing on the gauges indicated a problem with any of the systems.

Franz didn't want to tell Eckmann that he didn't know what he had done wrong, because the plane was on autopilot. Spig Wead looked through the manuals for a remedy to the problem. "Maybe we hit a cloud," he said.

Eckmann locked himself in the bathroom.

Spig Wead watched the radar and as the beam swept the circle, he tried to understand the green mass ahead of them.

"Is that weather?" he said, asking himself more than anyone else.

"I think it's clouds," said Franz. "Or a storm."

"But we can't see it."

"The radar is picking up a wider area than we can see."

Franz knocked on the bathroom door. "Eckmann, you should come out and look at this. We think the problem isn't the plane. It's winds from a storm."

Eckmann said something Franz couldn't hear. "Could you say that again, Eckmann?"

This time Franz heard the word: "Stupid."

"You're not stupid, Eckmann."

"I'm finished."

"Finished with what, my friend?" Franz didn't know why he called Eckmann his friend. He wasn't his friend. Eckmann screamed when he should have been quiet; he scared others when he should have made them feel safe. He had lost their trust. He knew that.

The plane was shaking again, harder than before the pilot had lost control.

"Why are we shaking like that?"

"I think it's the wind, Eckmann. It doesn't look like anything that you did wrong in getting the plane ready to fly.

"But that doesn't matter now. Are you there?"

"Of course I'm here. I can see the cockpit and I can talk to you at the same time."

They were above the clouds. The ground was gone.

"We need to go below the clouds," said Spig Wead. "Unless we go down we won't know what's there."

The radar display showed them over Indio, California.

"We'll have to go slowly," said Franz. "We don't know how high the clouds are above the ground."

The cabin was quiet. Franz pushed the button for everyone to hear.

"We're flying into storm clouds. We can't land in the dark but we're heading toward Arizona and the sun. Keep your seat belts fastened."

# Frank Sinatra, Siouxsie Banshee

"Tell me about art," said Frank. "What was it for?"

"People didn't like blank walls at home. Even here, this is just a hotel room, and there's a photograph of the Hollywood sign before the letters fell down. And that's a picture of a movie star named Marilyn Monroe. Does it do anything to you when you look at her?"

"It makes me wonder if she'd be verified."

"That's Frank the Security person talking. But is there anything else about the picture? Like, does it speak to you about changing ideas of femininity?"

"I want to understand what you're saying," said Frank. "And it makes me angry that I can't."

"I don't want to make you angry."

"Not angry at you. But there are millions of pictures all over the city, and they're different. Big houses, small houses, old motels, big hotels like this, which was very expensive, they all have art. And you know what was good and what wasn't? How can you tell?"

"I don't think I can. I think I only know what I was trained to know, and I don't know what's good. I know what's authentic, not a copy, and only from a limited time. There's not a lot of very old art in Los Angeles so I was sent here because I was an expert in the twentieth century."

"It makes me sorry that you can't be verified."

He didn't say anything after that. He was thinking about sex with her. He was thinking about friendly sex, something new to him. She'd had friendly sex, which seemed to come with knowing about art, since there was a lot of nakedness in art. So she kissed him. She didn't like what he did with his tongue. It filled her mouth without moving, without searching for a hidden Siouxsie that words couldn't express and any other touch couldn't reach, so she pulled away to kiss the edges of his mouth, his neck, his eyes.

They agreed that this was a good way to be together but were soon interrupted by a knock on the door.

"Redwings?" asked Frank.

"I'm here with Chief. He wants to powwow. We have a problem."

When he was in the room, Chief told Frank to send Siouxsie away.

Siouxsie said, "I'm not leaving. As soon as you're gone he's going
to tell me what you said, and whatever the problem is, and obviously
there's a problem because you wouldn't be here, I'll help him figure
it out, which will be good for you, Chief."

"She's right, Chief."

"Then tell me what you're thinking."

"You thought Vayler was just doing his job by making sure he did
a complete inventory of the Burn Zone right up to the Burn, so it was
too late to send a thousand Drifters to the food storage warehouses
that are more than a few hours away. So in preparation for all the
Drifters being downtown, you brought in the singer."

"As insurance."

"So you knew something was wrong about Vayler's refusal to get
them away from Figueroa. I think I know why he didn't. In order to
bring back the supplies he says are out there, he needed a few thousand Drifters. To keep them in line, he needed at least a hundred
Security people. He didn't want Security to go with him; he didn't
want them to see that the warehouses are empty. I've seen it, Chief,
on the way to Covina, a Chinese supermarket with a green triangle
that wasn't crossed off with red, and it was empty. And I talked about
it with Vayler and he said it was emptied for convenience."

"Frank, bring Vayler back quietly."

"I don't think I can find him quietly. He'll know we're looking
for him and he'll keep moving. We still have a lot of sections of the
city that aren't burned."

"Our lives, Frank. Everything depends on knowing what we have
left. We can't eat food that isn't there."

"We don't know yet. It may be that Vayler Monokeefe is hoarding
the food and he's going to hand it out only to people loyal to him."

Redwings interrupted. "That's got to be the truth."

Frank, accustomed to Redwings's sometimes grand unfounded
conclusions, asked him why he thought so.

"Because I wouldn't have thought of that myself and because
you went right to the gnarliest conjecture."

"Two words I'm not sure of, Redwings. The last words you just said."

"I put them together. 'Gnarly' means gnarly, and 'conjecture' means guess."

Frank told Chief he would do what he could.

"Be quiet about this, but take a ride around the inventory depots. It's possible you'll find that what the Founders left us is still there."

"Not likely," said Siouxsie.

"All the more reason we need to talk to Vayler."

# Shannon, Erin

Erin sat behind Shannon in the tub and massaged the singer's back with slick, soapy fingers. Erin was jealous of the people who had Silent Voices, though she'd met few of them because most were inadequately rehabbed and didn't live in Center Camp.

"What are you thinking about?" Erin asked the star.

"What's your name?"

"Erin. I'm Erin."

"I miss my chisel."

"We can always find another at a hardware store or in the supplies depot."

"It's not the same."

After that, Shannon stopped talking and got out of the tub. Erin wrapped the singer in a towel. "You had a long night. You must be tired."

Shannon didn't agree or disagree, but went to her bedroom and shut the door. Erin knocked and Shannon knocked back, and Erin understood to leave her alone.

❖

# Hopper, Visitors

Hopper sat on the riverbank and watched the two white herons that yesterday had flown away from naked Madeinusa. Now they were back on his side of the river, facing upstream. He felt the throbbing pressure to honor his Teacher and keep finding things until those things led him to his wife. He thought that if he stopped trying to solve the puzzle of what to do next, all the obligations that made him ache might scatter like the pieces of burned houses that formed the morning's cloud.

He took the pink dress and photograph from the bag and set them on Madeinusa's clothing, then brushed the loose granules of rotting concrete and made a clear area for the bones. He was careful with the skull, and took it out first, forcing himself to keep the eye sockets toward him. The skull rolled to the left and he braced it with a few small stones. Then he took out the rest of the bones, in no special order, and laid them out evenly. His Silent Voice said, "I don't like looking at this. Can you cover them up?"

Hopper set the pink ball gown neatly on the ground beside them and then shifted the bones one piece at a time until they were inside the gown.

The label in the pink gown with the puffy shoulders was DISNEY. So her name was Disney.

The man in the photograph wore a long-sleeve shirt. "Is this me?" Hopper asked his Silent Voice.

"Yes."

"Is that woman on the other side of Disney my wife?"

"Yes."

"What's her name?"

"I'd have to look at the label in one of her dresses."

A voice in the brush alarmed the herons and as they took off, Hopper heard a woman say, "Is he talking to himself?"

She wasn't Madeinusa and he had to fight that disappointment to give himself the energy to protect Disney's bones. And as he rolled the bones inside Disney's dress and stuffed it back into the backpack he pulled out the pistol, pointing it toward the bushes where the woman was hiding. The gun reminded him of what his Teacher promised: "What you need will come to you."

A man stood up, his hands raised.

"Careful, Seth," said the woman.

"Who else is there?"

"Just us," said Seth.

"Come out, hands up."

"My name is Marci. I don't know my real last name and nobody ever gave me one. This is Dr. Seth Kaplan. He's verified. I'm not."

Seth tried to explain himself. "We've been walking up the river all night. Did you see the jet?"

Hopper didn't answer

"There was a jet," said Seth.

"We were supposed to be on it," said Marci.

Hopper said their names. "Marci and Seth."

"That's right," said Seth. "That's us. Marci and Seth. We were supposed to be on it, but we didn't want to die."

Hopper was puzzled by Marci's anger at Seth. "And then it took off without us and flew over the ocean and came back. We saw it fly over the city. Fly very low over the city and then climb. Without crashing."

"It's one thing to get a plane into the sky and another thing, entirely different, to land a plane, especially a big plane," said Seth. "So they got it up. That's sort of easy. Can they land it safely?"

"I lost faith," Marci said to Hopper. "Eckmann never failed to do what he promised."

"Tell that to Franz," said Seth.

"He didn't promise Franz anything until he promised him a doctor."

"He didn't promise me anything except that unless I saved Franz, he'd kill me."

"He didn't mean that. Did you see him kill anybody?"

"Other than all those people he took into the sky?"

"You didn't see them die, Seth. You saw them fly away under control. They had enough fuel to cross the country three times."

"Then they had enough fuel to stay up until the plane dropped out of the sky. The longer they stay up, the longer they delay what they can't control. Franz practiced taking off, not landing. We did the right thing. We jumped off the plane to save each other's lives because we love each other."

"Love," said Hopper.

"Yes," said Seth. "What else could it be?"

"A mistake," said Marci. "But who are you, really? What are you doing here? What are you hiding under that dress? Whose dress is it?"

"When a man you don't know is pointing a gun at you, don't ask so many questions," said Seth.

Hopper put the gun in his waistband. "I can show you."

He opened the bag and unrolled Disney's pink ball gown. He arranged the skeleton. Marci looked to Seth to say something, and he started, with a sound that could have turned into any of a thousand words, but wasn't sure of any of them. Hopper covered the bones with the dress again.

"Where did you find that?" asked Seth.

"Her," said Marci. "It's the bones of a girl. Where did he find the little girl?"

"Last night. In the fire. The house is gone now," said Hopper. "This is all that's left. Her name was Disney." He showed them the tag in the pink puffy dress. "I found the house and I found her this way."

When Marci touched the label, Hopper pulled it back.

"How old was she?" asked Seth.

"I don't know."

"You're not verified, are you?"

"No."

"But you're not a Drifter, either. You're something else."

"I'm looking for my wife. I have to keep walking up the river until I know where to turn."

Hopper rolled the bones in the towel and tightened the wrap with the belt before putting it back in the bag.

"And when we leave the river, where are we going?" asked Seth.

"We'll find it. My Silent Voice will tell me."

Marci tugged on Seth's hand and whispered to him. "Seth, what do you mean 'we'?" asked Marci. "What are you talking about? You want to follow this Drifter with a child's bones and a gun?"

"What else are we going to do? He has some kind of goal. We don't. I'd rather follow a man with a goal than walk around without one."

"I'd rather not follow a man who can't put seven words together, especially if he's carrying the skeleton of a child and thinks her name is Disney. Disney is the label. It's the name of a movie company, and it's not her name. There were Disney gifts in every gift shop in the airport."

"Well why didn't you tell him? It's not good to let him get a name wrong."

"It's not good to correct anything this man is doing when he's pointing a gun at us."

"We don't have to whisper," said Seth. "He's not trying to listen. What do you want to do? We can't stay here." Seth put his arm around Marci's shoulders. "We don't have a choice. Treat this like conscious drifting. A force we don't understand is moving us. We have impulse but no memory. That makes life so much easier than the other way around."

"When did we ever live with memory but no impulse?" asked Marci.

"I don't remember," said Seth. Marci thought of pointing out all the ways she could disassemble his confusion, but when she tried to form a thought with branches, she came back to the bad choice she made on the runway at LAX. She couldn't trust her powers of discrimination and with no confidence in her own judgment, and no light of intuition, there was nothing better to do except to follow their new leader, as Seth wanted, and drift with him. After her years at the airport and her months in the garage serving AutoZone, the opportunity to take a walk beside a quiet river toward mysterious Burbank, a place that was new to her, seemed in itself to be worth the risk to her life. Perhaps more than that, a stroll in support of a stranger's quest to find his destiny could provoke forces of mercy to release her from the burden of fighting every day for herself. And in return for the sacrifice of her freedom, she'd find both peace and power. She had a glimmer of her cosmic helplessness. If aiding Hopper meant that her spirit of mercy offended the malevolence that had already punished the world with NK3, then fine. Let a gesture of goodness aggravate a supernatural wrath to destroy her where she stood today. She had regrets now: regret for lying to AutoZone, which evoked a memory of his affection, regret for kidnapping Seth, regret for leaving the plane, regret for staying on with Seth when everything he did annoyed her, regret for not having the courage to go out on her own. She felt sick about herself, a feeling that might have once been her general condition but was new to her, and painful enough to make her wish to be erased.

# Frank Sinatra, Siouxsie Banshee

Frank didn't like BMWs the way he loved Audis, but Audi didn't make a convertible like the BMW 650i, and he owned, or claimed for himself, a light blue model with a few hundred miles on the odometer. He knew that Siouxsie would like the convertible and he didn't bother offering a choice.

It was a fast, bad trip from one empty warehouse and box store to another. A hundred and fifty locations were marked and after looking at thirty they found eight that were full.

# Vayler

In the first year, Chief told Vayler to count all the boats at Marina del Rey, the concrete lagoon south of Santa Monica, built below the bluffs that defined the lower wall of the Los Angeles basin. The airport was a few miles beyond the bluffs, and Chief said it was best not to let people wander there. But there might come a time when the boats would be useful if the First Wave ever needed to escape by sea, and he wanted a full inventory. Four years later, the hulls of 5,246 boats in Marina del Rey were heavy with barnacles and green beards of algae, food for the fish that attracted the seals and dolphins that fed on them.

The boat yards had the equipment to scrape the boats and the chemicals and paint to clean the hulls, but the boats needed to be hauled out of the water to get that work done, and the hoists needed electricity, and even if Toby Tyler herself brought power back to the Marina, she didn't have the dredging barges to clear the silt that blocked the entrance to the main channel. The tide couldn't flush the rot into the bay, so the Marina stank of dead fish mixed with the acrid white droppings of the gulls and cormorants that nested on the masts.

There were a few massive yachts over a hundred feet long, with marble floors and large wine lockers. The beds were comfortable and the decks were too far above water for the sea lions to settle in, but Vayler made a den for himself in an empty condominium facing an interior garden. He didn't want anyone to see the light from his propane lanterns and he had an arsenal of guns.

From his first discovery of the shortages, Vayler had siphoned enough food from the existing supplies to fill every room of every apartment unit on his floor, so that if he never left the condominium, he could stay fed for over a year, enough time to outlast the looming famine. He was proud of his self-control, not to make himself too comfortable.

# Hopper, Seth, Marci

Marci watched Seth work hard to keep his balance as he trailed Hopper on the steep banks of the river, slipping in the ash. Hopper moved easily, and was no more a real Drifter than she had been a real Driftette. Marci knew she could run ahead of Seth but then he'd ask her to slow down and she was tired of him, tired of his fear. Where was Eckmann now? Where were her friends from the airport? They weren't chasing anyone carrying bones and pink dresses.

She missed pretending to be a Driftette. *That's it*, she thought. She was happy being stupid, happy dancing badly for the First Wavers in the garage. She didn't like to spy on anyone. That wasn't the good part of each day of those months living so simply. The good part was the job, the work of sweeping the garage, arranging the tools, sorting through the loose hardware on the garage floor, being laughed at, bullied, and teased, being ignored, and being fed good enough food. She felt badly for betraying the trust of the men in the motor pool. She didn't know if her deception was discovered after she left without saying good-bye, but only another Shambler would be stupid enough not to see that she disappeared the same the day the doctor was kidnapped from the hospital. She betrayed people who had been kind to her. *I betrayed Eckmann and I betrayed AutoZone, Carrera, and Tesla. Whoever I was in the days before NK3*, she thought, *I must have hurt a lot of people.*

She caught up with Seth, fifty feet behind Hopper, who moved along the uneven path as though every obstacle was there to help push him along.

"Seth, I have to talk to you."

"This isn't the time."

"Yes it is. I have to say something to you."

"We can't stop until he stops."

"We can stop whenever we want. I'm stopping now. This is where I say good-bye." She called out to Hopper. "Disney!"

Hopper looked back but didn't stop.

"I'm leaving now, Disney."

He half raised a hand to wave good-bye but kept his pace.

Seth stopped, waiting for Marci to catch up with him, so he could talk her out of going.

"No, Seth, I'm not following this man. You can if you want. I'm going back down the river."

Hopper was on the level path at the top of the riverbank. Seth wanted to say more to Marci than just good-bye, but every word he might have said would put him that much farther behind a man who didn't care what he did. Marci cared, but she wasn't inviting him to go with her.

"Good luck," he said, and ran up to the path.

"Good luck," she called after him, although luck was a theology that Eckmann discouraged in Camp LAX. "Luck can't fly an airplane," he told the crew when they started. "There's a difference between patience and luck, and don't confuse them. We will find a pilot. I don't know when, but there will come a day when we will leave here, wheels up." She couldn't think of anything that Seth could consciously wait for, so patience was a wasted virtue to wish for him. It was right to wish him luck, the gift of an unexpected rescue by a force she couldn't imagine, because luck is a free deliverance from bad circumstance, and Seth's circumstance now was vapor. Whatever would pull him into coherence was more complicated than a wounded pilot's need for a doctor. What does a frightened doctor need? Seth was gone around the bend in the river, on the road to Burbank, and Marci's own hard breathing had settled before she realized that Seth was right to leave her without negotiating the terms of the parting, or without trying to convince her to stay with him. The man with the children's bones is probably going to be shot, and Seth knows this and wants to be there to remove the bullet and save another life. Getting Marci off the plane was his way of saving her because he couldn't stop the plane from leaving. Maybe he only said he loved her because without that, she would have stayed on the plane.

How many choices do I have? she asked herself. That's all any-one can ask herself in these times. What are my choices? Stay or go.

Then she saw she had no choice, and this made her happy because she knew the worst of her troubles were over. She crossed the shallow river, sure of herself that when there is only one thing to do, there is no choice. The herons and ducks in the water ignored her splashes. Like them, she was a safe part of nature.

With his last look at the river, Hopper saw that the woman was gone but the man still followed and his Silent Voice advised him: "Don't worry. He's not going to hurt you. He may stop chasing you but if he doesn't, leave him alone." A question took shape but Hopper didn't want to ask it out loud. The thought was more complicated than Hopper was used to working through, but the general shape of the idea depended on a few clear features.

He was following a particular path in a particular order.

He was compelled to do this without knowing why.

The first part of this compulsion brought him safely across the desert.

The second part led him to the house.

The third part of the compulsion was so powerful that he walked through fire to retrieve the package.

He had felt no impulse to follow this river until after he had uncovered the bones. If he had not found the bones, he wouldn't be here. Something was waiting for him in a place he had yet to discover only because he had passed through the stages to get where he was without dying. His Silent Voice recognized the steps in a sequence only when the next goal in that sequence was met.

Instead of feeling secure, though, the neat order of this mission woke another voice that was behind and superior to the Silent Voice, and this voice couldn't be named because it didn't use words or sound.

"Please don't leave me," said Seth. "I want to help you." He waited for Hopper to accept him or push him away, but Hopper said nothing, and Seth panicked in the silence. "I'm a doctor. I can't help without a bag of medicine and surgery knives, and I don't have any, but if we get some, I'll know what to do with it. Can you walk more slowly?"

Seth told Hopper about the airport and Franz and the decision to climb down the ladder instead of staying with the insane crew and crashing into a mountain. "It's not as though life as a Drifter was good but here I am, still alive and even if I haven't been alive for very long by the standards of our present experience of life, I don't want to give it up. I've gotten used to the idea that life is surprising. One day here, the next day there, whatever life wants from me, I say, Let life have it. I don't remember my wife and children. How long will I remember Marci?"

Hopper said, "I remember her."

"Well, of course, that's because she was just here. Now she's going back toward the city, and that strikes me as a dangerous idea. You're running in the other direction and that strikes me also as dangerous, but dangerous with new conditions, so I choose to take the surprise of whatever comes to us, even if it's awful, over returning to the city and getting nabbed by someone with the authority to hurt me. I don't want to tell myself, 'Seth, you knew this was going to happen but you came here anyway.' Now the same bad thing can happen but I won't tell myself that I knew it was bound to find me. The plane was doomed. How could they expect to land safely? They were crazy, weren't they?"

Hopper didn't answer and Seth took this as his sullen revulsion at a man who would give in to fear and pass up the chance for a life where the Fence didn't rule. Seth lost all the power of his conviction of the plane's doom, and with that he replaced the silent image of the jet's nose buried on a mountaintop with a noisy movie of all the members of Camp LAX safely landed in Seattle and eating fresh meat with advanced people whose purpose in life now was to help survivors of NK3 enlarge their capacity for sympathy and, with it, restore their lost memories. This thought propelled him to continue talking about it with Hopper. "But don't you think that if they got their memories back, they might be more unhappy than any of us are now? If you remembered everyone in your life who was dead, wouldn't you feel terrible for living?"

They were in an area of small factories, metal-plating shops, and plumbing-supply stores. Inventory had passed through and left a green triangle on the doors of the inspected buildings but no one had yet come for the construction supplies inside.

Seth asked Hopper, "Are we in the right place?"

"I don't know."

Hopper, who didn't hear any caution from his Silent Voice not to tell Seth something of the time he could remember since leaving Palm Springs. "I have a Teacher. He sent me here and on the way I saw the buses. I was on the way here from Palm Springs."

"What kind of teacher?"

"He taught me how to ride a bicycle."

"And he sent you here to find the bones?"

"He said that when I got here I'd know what to do. My Silent Voice would tell me."

"Like I knew how to take the bullet out of the pilot. It came back to me. So what do you feel here?"

And by now, so recently brought together, Seth felt closer to Hopper than he did to the doctor at the UCLA hospital or any of the people at the airport. Friendship made him feel light, even if the good feelings of affection went in only one direction.

"This way," said Hopper, turning at an intersection. They stopped at a mini storage, three stories tall with a freight elevator that needed power and had none.

Hopper took the stairs and Seth followed.

He stopped at a locker with a heavy combination lock.

"Here," said Hopper. He did what his Silent Voice told him. "Right four times to 36, left three times to 51, right two times to 7, left to 44."

Inside the locker there were three bicycles, three cases of Fiji Water, a stack of boxes with bulk containers of freeze-dried food, changes of clothing in three sizes, knives, rope, power bars. The bicycles matched the bike the Teacher had given Hopper in Palm Springs.

There was a leather briefcase, locked, for which there were no keys. Seth, the surgeon, snapped it with the screwdriver blade from a bicycle's tool kit.

Inside the case was a photograph, the other half of the photograph Hopper found in the burning house. It was cut to leave off Hopper but here she was, her arm extending out of frame, the child half in her arms and half out of the picture.

Hopper took the charred picture out of his pack. The edges matched.

"I saw her," said Seth. "She was inside the Fence. Her hair is different but I remember the face."

"How is it different?" asked Hopper.

"It's light brown in the picture but that was then and now it's red and sticks out to the side."

There was another photograph in the box, of two cargo containers on a train. Another train was visible in the space between the two cars. One of the cars had a number and symbol that matched the other number that until now had not yielded any clues.

"Why three bikes and three boxes with changes of clothing in different sizes?" asked Seth. "One photograph, three bikes, three different sets of clothing. This isn't a good sign."

"There hasn't been a good sign in four years," said Hopper's Silent Voice. Hopper kept that to himself.

"You just heard something, didn't you?" asked Seth. "What did your Voice tell you?"

"Nothing useful, but I don't think I'm the only one looking for my wife."

"Who set up this locker?"

"I think I set up this locker."

"You think?"

"Yes. Before I lost my memory. I set this up so I would have supplies for the people who are going to help me."

"Well, I'm helping you."

"No," said Hopper. "I wasn't looking for you."

Seth didn't like the way he felt after Hopper said this. "What I mean is that you needed someone to help you on your search, and here I am."

"My Teacher said I was going to need luck and he tried to explain it to me. He said that something could happen that shouldn't happen when it does, and this would help me when everything else was against me. He said that was how to know I was lucky."

"And that's me. It's your good luck that I'm with you. And it's my good luck, because Marci was already sorry she didn't stay with the plane. And everyone on that plane was going to need luck for the plane not to crash."

"Who told *you* about luck?"

"Here are three bikes and we're tired of walking. What do you call that?"

"I call it three bikes and we're tired of walking."

"Then let's take two bikes and find the train so we can find your wife."

# Hopper, Seth, Stranger

The lines of engines and containers went in either direction, trains hundreds of cars long. Between the cars, the tracks were filled with small trees and brush that had found its way through the crushed rock. In the rush to rehab the people who knew how to run things, Systems had overlooked the people who understood the trains. The two men examined the picture of the railroad yard again, confused, until Hopper said, "Between the train cars, there's a boxcar and beyond it, the flagpole on top of a building." They found the pole, and from there, it didn't take long to find the car.

The handle was not locked. He pulled the handle up to release the door, and it opened quietly. "There's no rust," said Seth.

"Stay here." The front of the container was stacked with rolls of tar paper. Hopper pulled himself into the container. He tossed a few rolls on the ground and, at the end of the container, found stacks of green metal crates stenciled with: **PROPERTY OF THE US MARINE CORPS**.

Seth opened the first box. There were rifles and bullets.

"You put these here?" asked Seth.

"I don't remember." He was on his knees beside one of the crates when he felt the air stir as someone came into the container. A man. Seth stood up and the man threw Seth out of the car and rolled the door shut.

The stranger lifted Hopper and rushed him backward. Neither of them could see the wall or know when they would hit. Hopper pushed his thumbs into the man's eyes but lost his grip when he was slammed into the wall.

Everything he tried was matched as though by a mirror and Hopper wasn't sure who was thinking of the next move first. They tumbled without being able to stand up because neither could overpower the other. Hopper didn't know how long they were like this. When he pulled his hand away, it was grabbed by the other man and when the other man slipped away, Hopper caught him. He felt the other wanting to ask him the same question he was ready to ask: *Why are we fighting?*

Then he stopped. He thought about his Teacher and what his Teacher would tell him to do and he went limp, curled up on the floor, and covered his head with his hands. The other didn't move either. Was the other doing the same thing?

Hopper let the other move first, hit first, grab first. The other wrapped his hands around Hopper's throat and this time Hopper heard his voice ringing in the container as he roared. The other's grip weakened by a fraction and Hopper's hands were on the other's throat, until the other stopped moving, until the other was dead. He slid the door open. Seth was there.

"I found his bike. It has a map in the saddlebag. You have to see it."

It was a good bike, with a carbon fiber frame, a rear wheel rack with a saddlebag, and a label from a bike shop in Palm Springs. Hopper knew the store. It was like the bike the Teacher had given him. Inside the saddlebag was a map of Los Angeles, with the Fence drawn in black marking pen, and a red star and the words STORM DRAIN where the Fence crossed Westwood Boulevard.

Hopper went back into the container. The dead man was about Hopper's size and age, and he wore a gold wedding ring.

His Silent Voice finally spoke. "I'm thinking that each of you thought the other was there to steal the weapons. But the weapons were for both of you. That's what I'm thinking."

"That means the Teacher sent him?"

"It seems so but that's a leap we don't have to make. And maybe he was here to stop you from taking the guns. He didn't ask who you were or what you were doing here."

"He had food," said Seth. They ate two of the stranger's power bars and artichoke hearts.

Hopper looked at the map. "This is where we are," he said, putting his finger on the rail yards. "This is where we have to go."

☢

# Frank Sinatra, Security Committee, Pickle

Frank gathered all the Unverified Second Wavers who helped with Security, the ones with rehab but no trace in the DMV.

"Vayler Monokeefe was our good friend and we're worried about him. We haven't seen him for a while. We think he might have hurt himself and that scares us. We care so much about him. So we're asking for help. And in return, the person, or persons, who find him, whether he's safe or not, or even alive or not, will be granted verification. Start here, keep walking, and don't follow anybody else. You can go in groups of five, no more than that. The last place we saw him was on Figueroa, and he's not inside the Fence. We wish, but he's not. Start right away."

"I want to look for him, too," said Siouxsie Banshee. "I bet I can find him. Tell me what you know about his habits and hobbies."

"He has the habit of lying. And he has the hobby of running away from punishment."

Pickle, the Inventory driver who was there when Shannon was discovered, knew the city as well as anyone and he remembered the first Inventory runs to Santa Monica, Venice, and the Marina. He was sure that Vayler would go to the Marina because Vayler was a man of little imagination, no matter that he was once in charge of a museum. Pickle thought of asking someone else to help, because the best place to look for Vayler would be from a shallow draft rowboat going up and down the channels of the harbor, and the best thing to look for would be a light, so the best time to hunt for him would be when it was dark. Another set of eyes would be useful, but Pickle wanted to live in Center Camp and get a promotion to assistant committee head and for that it was best to share this with no one.

There were dinghies around the Marina, with paddles or oars. Pickle didn't know how to row but it couldn't be too difficult. Vayler might not be there, but if he was, there'd be no competition for the reward.

☢

# Mr. and Mrs. AutoZone

AutoZone unlocked the garage door and pushed it up on its track. Since the Burn, Inventory was busy and Frank Sinatra was looking for Tesla's murderer. He didn't miss Tesla.

The life of the Fence didn't call to AutoZone's body or his spirit. When he turned around and saw the girl that Tesla and Carrera named Hey You he felt a double happiness, because she wasn't Tesla's killer come to bag another mechanic, and because he had missed her. She disappeared in the days of confusion after the cars had been stolen, and the doctor was kidnapped and the pilot was killed, and he respected her impulse to run away from the tension. For however long she had graced the periphery of life in the motor pool—and not even rehabbed First Wavers could safely gauge units of passed time—the Shamblerette had given the crew the simple entertainment of her primitive vitality.

"Where have you been?" he asked her.

She waved her hands in the air to let him know that she had been everywhere.

"You?" she asked him. He waved his hands the same way and hopped from one foot to the other in imitation of the little jig he hadn't seen in weeks.

She danced the jig in return and he clapped his hands to give her a beat. She wanted to tell him: "This is like drowning, in a good way." But to do this she would have to show him Marci, and she was tired of being Marci. The name meant nothing anyway. What was a Marci other than letters on an airline name tag? Maybe it meant something in the past, but if it did, the substance was gone. The more often she repeated the name to herself, the less it meant anything familiar. She whispered her name so quietly that even she couldn't hear it, until it became two syllables with the stress shifting from Mar to See and back, marSEE, MARsee, marSEE, MARsee and then they decoupled from each other and became two random sounds: mar see mar see mars ee mar seem arms eem ar seem ar sss eee mmm. That was when she stopped being Marci and became . . . no one. She was what she wanted to be, nameless and ready for a new life in a world where all the best people had names that told the world something about their rank, habits, or mistakes. She thought that Jiggy or Jigs would fit her nicely, but this was the choice AutoZone would have to make for her. So she continued to dance, remembering with every sloppy kick not to let AutoZone see her moving too close to the beat. When she was certain that her awkwardness was solid, she asked him: "My name?"

"Let me think about that," said AutoZone. He couldn't remember anyone asking him for a better favor, and with no one there to make a joke of this request, he wanted to give her a name that she deserved. He was sure she'd wander away again and that when she did, this time he'd find her. He looked around the garage at the labels on tires and cans of oil. He thought of calling her Valvoline, but pretty as it was, and Valvoline would fit this Driftette nicely, if she wandered, the name wouldn't bring her back. So he gave her his second choice for a name, not so pretty, but it might help bring her back to him if she got lost. And maybe it was a silly name, but like everything he stocked in the motor pool, it would have a function. "All right," he said. "From now on, I'll call you Mrs. AutoZone. Can you remember that?"

"Mrs. AutoZone."

"That's who you are."

# Shannon, Erin

Shannon stayed in her room. When she wanted food she yelled at Erin to bring her something, but there was no other contact. She listened to her songs and read her autobiography. There were pictures of her with her mother and father when she was little, pictures of her in school plays, with her high school band, backstage. She learned about her boyfriends and girlfriends, about the couple she dated.

She heard Erin at the door and didn't want to answer; there was nothing to say. She knew that Erin had seen what happened on Figueroa before the jet broke the spell but she wasn't ready to talk about it with her. Shannon wanted to keep the door shut against the possibility that Erin might read her mind, since she didn't yet know what she wanted to put in her mind. Erin sent the Stripers, one at a time and then as a chorus. Toffe, who never spoke, spoke.

"Shannon? This is Toffe. Are you okay? We miss you. Nothing is fun now without you. If Erin said things the wrong way, tell me. I used to say things the wrong way and I stopped the saying of anything, but I have to say now we miss you."

"I want to think," said Shannon. "I need to be alone. Leave me alone."

Shannon took a bicycle and rode slowly through Center Camp, trying to see it as she would have when she was protecting herself from men who just wanted to steal her food and fuck her.

She pedaled up the hill out of Center Camp and down the long steep street to the Playa. She wanted to go fast. It was a relief to do something dangerous. Center Camp's comforts had taken from her that thoughtless but contented life of basic survival.

\*     \*     \*

There was a flamethrower party on the Playa, cowboys and cowgirls taking turns burning plywood houses set up for the game of destruction. The peanut butter and jelly bus was parked at the perimeter handing out sandwiches. A golf cart redecorated as a neon bumblebee rolled past Shannon to join a parade of art cars circling The Woman, huge teapots in a line like circus elephants, a rolling skull made of Christmas lights, the driver and passenger in the eye sockets.

Shannon parked her bike and walked among the First Wavers. Everyone she passed said hello, said her name, and clapped hands for her. She made life better for them just by looking at them, just by smiling. There was a way of looking at life behind the Fence that didn't make it immediately awful, the hub of evil in the ruined world, the source of destruction. Whose fault is the world's condition? The world outside the Fence had been ugly and so long as it stayed that way, what could she hope to do inside?

Stilt walkers stopped to drink at a bar built ten feet tall, just for them. She was recognized. The barmaid tossed her a can of prized Tecate beer and a lime. A stilt walker offered her a hand to take an elevated seat beside him.

The beer was cold, the lime wasn't too dry, and it had enough juice to give the beer a fresh tickle. Cool Breeze, a stilt walker with sparse gray hair and deep lines in his face, introduced her to Bullet and Venus DePlaya. Bullet was Erin's age, with long hair wrapped in a bun on his head, secured with chopsticks. Venus wore a leopard-print bodysuit with a hood and leopard makeup, so it was impossible to even guess at what she might look like underneath the costume.

"I'm not used to being with people who know who they are," she told them.

"We're mostly our functions. We're the Burn Brigade; some call us Burners. We make fire. We're attached to Toby Tyler's Systems Committee and also do Inventory, but mostly we just love to make things burn. The way you love to make people dance."

"Or maybe just make people look at me."

"That's an achievement," said Bullet. "I have to put on stilts to be looked at."

Venus DePlaya asked, "Are you going to sing for us the way you sang for the Drifters?"

"I didn't really sing to them," said Shannon.

"We want to hear you," said Bullet, and they all agreed with him.

"Before the food runs out," said Cool Breeze.

Venus made a gesture to him not to say more.

Cool Breeze ignored it. "She's one of us now. She lives in Center Camp. She helped keep the Drifters from going completely out of control at the Burn, and look at how beautiful she is. So she should know that Vayler is missing."

"I don't know who Vayler is," she told them.

"You will."

"And the food?" Shannon asked.

"We don't really know," said Cool Breeze. "We hear things. Our attitude from the beginning of NK3 has been the world died and there is nothing we can do to restore it. Life in some form will continue without us. Maybe the storytelling animal will be gone. We can only save those who think the way we do, and have the competence we all need to make things work as well as possible. And there was a way of doing things in the past that brought the world to the way it is. And we reject that way of doing things."

"In faaact," said Venus, drawing out the word, "in faaact, to tell the truth, we do not remember that way of doing things. So we just do as feels right to us. And you feel right to us. You really do. Give me a kiss."

Shannon kissed her, a deep kiss. Then Bullet said, "Next!" And Shannon kissed them all.

She finished her beer and they lowered her to the ground. She continued inside the perimeter toward The Man and The Woman.

Now she ignored the people who greeted her, and she found that no one was bothered by her disinterest.

She climbed into The Woman's upper chamber and looked at the world through The Woman's eyes. The Woman told her this:

"Shannon, the life of the Playa would make sense if it were once a year for a week, but a festival cannot sustain a culture."

# Hopper, Seth Kaplan, Paolo Piperno

Hopper and Seth, both wearing headlamps, followed the dead man's marked map through the storm drain. The floor of the tunnel was wet and there were shallow pools behind dams of muck.

"I like it in here," said Seth. "There's just the map and you and me."

A heavy black line on the map marked the Fence, but there was nothing to mark it in the drain and they weren't sure they were past that threshold until they heard cars and saw torch light shining through the gutters.

"We'll keep walking," said Seth. Hopper had said nothing for a long time and Seth had stopped asking him what he was thinking.

"How far from Center Camp when we get out of the tunnel?"

"Everything is close, but you have to be careful. You can't just walk up to Center Camp with a bag of bones looking for the woman who lives with Chief. I can do you a service, Hopper."

The tunnel came to a junction where the storm drains of four canyons met. From here the tunnels turned steeply uphill. Seth pointed to the second from the left and traced it on the map.

They walked another two hours. It was after midnight when they came to a grid of iron rebar wrapped in a tangle of long dead tree roots that had pulled the concrete apart.

They heard voices and music.

They pulled at the loose soil and used a broken piece of the rebar to dig more of it away. In a few minutes, they were looking up an angled column outlined in long strands of colored lights.

"We came up underneath The Man," said Seth. "We're looking up his leg. The one with the stairs. We're in the middle of the Playa. And it's packed. People will see us. "Turn off your headlamp." He pulled himself through the hole and looked straight into the eyes of Helary and Jobe.

"What's down there?" asked Helary.

"Nothing much," said Seth.

Jobe offered a hand. "You need help?"

"Thank you," said Seth. "We were just exploring."

"How far down?" asked Helary.

"Not very."

"Is that a tunnel?" asked Jobe. "Does Security know?"

"I can tell them," said Seth. "But I don't think it goes far. No more exploring." He helped Hopper out.

Helary and Jobe moved on.

The giant statues were full of lights tonight and the oil lamps around the perimeter flickered in the breeze but didn't go out. The stilt walkers juggled fire and someone was playing a Shannon Squier record on the loudspeakers mounted in both statues.

The two men left the Playa and walked past the burned-out mansions of the Holmby Hills. From there they crossed to the UCLA campus.

When they were in sight of the UCLA Medical Center, Seth took Hopper's hands in his. "You know how to keep an eye on me without being found. I know you can do that. When I'm ready for you, I'll open my office window. You'll see me. I'll meet you back here. This is where I have to say good-bye now. But I'm going to help you because without you, I wouldn't be back here. If I had to tell them about the airport, they might not believe I was forced to help. If they don't punish me for disappearing, I'll be at work quickly, I'm certain. You just have to keep moving until I can figure out how to make things safe for you, so you can search openly for your wife, and find her and then, together with her, finally bury Disney." It made Seth feel good to put all those words into one sentence. "I'm going to tell them I had help. I'm going to tell them a Transport Service worker found me."

Seth walked through Westwood to the hospital.

He'd never learned the names of the nurses, but the one with leather pants and a vest with no top was behind the reception desk in the emergency room when he approached the door, setting off the mechanism that drew the door aside automatically.

If he didn't remember her name, she had no trouble remembering his. "Dr. Kaplan, Dr. Kaplan, it's you. You're back."

"I am?"

"You've been away."

"I have?"

"Where were you? We were so worried."

"I walked. I know I walked. I went into houses and ate the food that was there. The man helped me find my way back. And now I'm back. Where's Dr. Piperno?"

"I know he wants to see you. He told me to call him if you ever came back. Don't go away, not again. Don't go away again."

She made a call.

"Dr. Piperno, Dr. Kaplan is back. Yes, I'm sure. I'm looking at him right now. I'll tell him. Yes." She asked Seth a question. "Dr. Kaplan, Dr. Piperno wants you to stay here and wait for him. He asked me to see if you're hungry or hurt. Are you hungry or hurt?"

"I'm hungry."

"We have microwave popcorn. It never goes stale. Would you like popcorn?"

"I don't know if I've ever had popcorn."

She put the bag into a microwave. They stood by and watched and listened while the popcorn popped.

Piperno arrived, shouting at Seth. "Where have you been, Dr. Kaplan? We have looked everywhere for you."

"I went for a walk and I think I got lost."

"Lost enough for no one to see you for a month?" Then he turned to the nurse. "How long has he been away? Six weeks? A few days? It's always so hard to keep track."

"Well, the popcorn is ready and he was here before I started it."

"I was in a house somewhere," said Seth. "I was lost. And then I slept in the bushes. You can see how dirty I am."

"And how did you unlose yourself, Dr. Kaplan?"

"I can't say I unlost myself by myself. A man helped me."

"Where is he now?"

"I don't know. He had work."

"So do we."

"Dr. Piperno, I'm ready for that. I'm hungry. I didn't eat very much. But I did think a lot about medicine."

When Piperno heard this he softened. "What did you think?"

"That I'm ready to be a doctor now. That I remembered my medicine and want to help people who are hurt and sick."

"But where did you go?

"I started drifting again, but inside the Fence. I know how to hide. It's something you learn when you're drifting, and I stayed hidden. I woke up while I was drifting this time. I remembered what I'm supposed to do. Dr. Piperno, you gave me good training and I came back to be helpful instead of what I think I was doing, falling into the old way of drifting."

"You must be tired."

"That's true."

"Your operating table is waiting for you. Get some rest."

Seth returned to where he had started and fell asleep in his clothing. A few hours later, Piperno woke him up. "We have a badly cut patient. I've been drinking and my hand isn't steady. It's time for you to sew."

The patient was Hopper, with a deep red stripe on his left arm, the bleeding already stanched by the nurse's tourniquet.

"This is the man who found me!" said Seth. "This is the man who brought me back to the hospital when I was lost. I told you about him, Dr. Piperno. Do you remember when I told you about the man who found me when I was lost, the Transport Service worker?"

"Remember? I think so. We're grateful he helped you. Now, let's return the favor. What happened to you here?"

"I was bicycling and not paying attention and hit a curb and cut myself."

"And scraped your brand off," said Seth, for Piperno to hear him. "That's not supposed to happen. I'll have to get you back down to the DMV."

"That can wait," said Piperno. "We'll clean that with some disinfectant and Dr. Kaplan will sew you up. I'll watch."

Kaplan took the threaded suture and, pinching the two sides of the cut together, pressed the needle through both parts and pulled the thread. It took him twelve turns to finish the job. He didn't talk to Hopper but looked to Piperno for approval. "Is that good?"

Piperno looked closely at the stitches.

"Good work, Dr. Kaplan. Tell your patient to watch where he's going. Good-bye."

Piperno walked away.

Seth growled at Hopper. "You hurt yourself so you could see me. You did this to yourself, didn't you?"

"Is my wife in Center Camp? Have you seen her?"

"I haven't been to Center Camp. I just got here. With you."

"Take me to Center Camp."

"You need an invitation to Center Camp. You need a reason. And this is why I said you were a Transport Service worker. They come and go. Nobody keeps close track of them if they're already inside the Fence. I can send you to Center Camp on a supply mission. You can go there seeing if they need anything from the hospital. I think that's what you should do. That's what I would do."

"You're speaking too quickly."

"I'm exploring a few possibilities for you that won't get us into trouble. Tell them you're doing inventory for the hospital. Inventory is all that anyone really cares about up there or down here. Hospital staff all had picture IDs on lanyards. I can give you a dead man's ID.

There's a drawer filled with them. Nobody recognizes faces. If they see there's no **)'(** brand, you'll have trouble. Get yourself a long-sleeved green uniform from the laundry and you'll look like you work here and everything will be fine."

"Will it?"

"My patients were very sick children. I believe that I spent a lot of time telling them they were getting better. I can lie. It seems to come as easily to me as cutting through a man's skin. And you'll need a clipboard with a pad of paper so you can write things down."

"I don't know how to write."

"You can read. You showed me the letter."

Hopper's Silent Voice said to him: "Do what he says."

"Just tell me what to do."

"There are printed lists all over the hospital, lists of medicines, lists of patients, schedules. We'll put a few of those lists on a clipboard, I'll give you a few pens, different colors, and you can check things off. And you need a name. That's the easy part." Seth went through a list of the names of the dead. "I have the name of a First Waver, from Inventory, which is good. He died three years ago. Kraft Serviss."

Hopper said it to hear it. "Kraft Serviss. Kraft Serviss. What did he die of?"

"It doesn't say why because they probably didn't know, especially three years ago when everyone was just waking up. So now you're Kraft Serviss. I'll call Center Camp and tell them I'm sending you up."

"Kraft Serviss needs a new backpack for the bones. This one smells like fire."

Seth wanted to tell Kraft Serviss not to bring the bones to Center Camp, but he knew that Hopper wouldn't listen.

❖

# Pickle

Pickle talked to himself. "This goddamn place stinks. But I am here on the water at night in a warm jacket I found in a sailboat and I am smoking old cigarettes and drinking good enough tequila and eating from a can of emergency rations and I realize that if he's here he's not on a boat because it's so goddamn cold out here. So he's where it's warm. Where it's warm and he can't be seen, so keep rowing—not that hard to figure out—except the part about looking backward as you row so you have to turn your head a lot. I see his light, shining. I'm on Frank Sinatra's Security Committee, and you're just Inventory, and tonight, Vayler, Inventory loses."

❖

# Pickle, Vayler

"Here's the deal," said Pickle, at the door to Vayler's hideout. "There are fifty men behind me and unless you want to kill yourself now, come out with your hands up."

The door opened and seeing Pickle's gun, Vayler raised his hands. "I don't see fifty people," said Vayler.

"I lied."

"I hope you will believe this was just an awful mistake."

❄

# Chief

Pickle delivered Vayler, his hands bound with zip ties, to Frank, who delivered him to Chief, who put him in a locked room in the house across the street, guarded by Royce Hall and Go Bruins.

❄

# Redwings, Gunny Sea Ray,

# Frank Sinatra, Siouxsie Banshee

Redwings called Frank. "Frank, sir, you have to hear this from Gunny Sea Ray himself."

"Pickle found Vayler Monokeefe. I know about that."

"You don't know this part, which has nothing to do with the other part. Gunny Sea Ray is right here beside me. I'm giving him my radio."

"Gunny Sea Ray here, Frank."

"What have you found?"

"Sir, first we found nothing. We were looking for Vayler, and we went along the riverbank. Hidden in the bushes we found a road bike, with absolute minimal wear on the tires. They were new tires, sir. You know how when you find a bike store and you see the tires on the bikes, they have little points of rubber that get worn down by riding? Well, Frank, these were fresh tires."

"The bicycle could have been there for a few years, Gunny. Someone hid it there after riding ten miles, and he never returned for it."

"If you're testing my judgment, sir, I'm pushing back. The bike is new. The chain has fresh oil. Nothing was growing across it or through it."

"Fine, Gunny, well reasoned and I accept what you say. So now you have a new carbon fiber bicycle, but you didn't call me for that."

"Sir, the bike's condition and quality convinced me to look harder and we then spread out along the riverbank and we picked up a trail of footprints where the ash stuck. We followed the trail and that led to a pack of dogs fighting in the rail yards, which led to a body, sir, a dead body, and then a boxcar full of weapons."

"How did the man die? What I expect won't change what I see. Murdered, yes? How?"

"Beaten to death."

"And the dogs, what did they do?"

"Et him a little, not much."

"Where's the body now?"

"I'm in the rail yards."

"I'll be there. Cover him from the sun."


Nobody recognized the dead man.

"That's not Nole Hazard," said Siouxsie.

"You saw him when he was alive. Now his face is swollen and gray," said Frank. "How can you be so sure?"

"I'm not going by that. I'm going by his hair. Nole's hair was naturally dark. This man's hair is dyed black. You see the roots. Pull down his pants."

Sinatra opened the man's belt and pulled his pants to his knees, and then rolled down his underwear. Redwings applauded Siouxsie. "Look at that, look at that. She knew, Frank. Gunny, would you call that light brown or red?"

"That's light brown, Redwings."

"Do we see many men with dyed hair?" Frank asked.

"Bright colors, sometimes, on light-colored hair, or bleached, sometimes, usually First Wave. Never Drifters. They don't know what they look like so they don't have anything to change."

Gunny Sea Ray called to them from underneath the next rail car.

"The doors were locked but doing my job I looked under the rail car here and found this, a hole on the bottom."

Inside, the container was empty except for an air mattress and clothing hanging from hooks on the wall, two backpacks, a tandem bicycle, and a carton of bags of Corn Nuts.

"He liked Corn Nuts," said Gunny Sea Ray.

"Why so many changes of clothes, Siouxsie?" Frank asked her.

"So he could go to Figueroa and if anybody noticed him, he'd be wearing something different the next time. That's why the wigs, but it's odd that his hair was dyed, too."

"Take everything apart," said Frank. "Take it apart and bring it outside."

"What do you see that we don't?" asked Siouxsie Banshee.

"The same as you. A man who was killed and he wasn't a Drifter. This was a hiding place. Look for what's hidden."

Inside one of the backpacks they found handcuffs with a key in each of the locks. Gunny could feel paper folded inside a compartment in the backpack and cut it open with his knife. He took it aside to show Frank and Redwings. It was another map of the city, with the red line crossing the black circle.

"That's the Fence," said Frank.

"Sagacious man," said Redwings.

"At least someone here is adding to his vocabulary," said Frank. "Now we have to see what the red line is doing here. It goes into Westwood from West Los Angeles, from the next Burn Zone. Until we know what this is, don't talk about it with anyone. There's enough going on about running out of food."

"A tandem bike with handcuffs," said Siouxsie. "Don't you want to talk about that, Frank?"

"It's obvious to me. Isn't it obvious to you?"

"Someone was taking a prisoner hostage? But how can you ride a bicycle when you're handcuffed?"

Frank told Redwings to tell Chief to meet them at the DMV.

# Chief, ElderGoth, Frank Sinatra, Siouxsie Banshee, Redwings, Gunny Sea Ray

ElderGoth hated official visits. The equipment was her responsibility and she had good reason to be scared that one day someone would enter the building who would make the unimaginable mistake of cutting the line to that vital distant and hidden server. And then what would Chief do to her? What value could she claim for herself that deserved privilege? Vayler was doomed, whatever the propaganda. She knew that, and she didn't expect much better for herself.

Now Chief was here because Frank had an idea.

"Chief, what Frank wants to try, it won't work. I can't verify a dead man."

"Have you ever tried?"

"No one has ever asked me. I don't know if the cameras work if the eyes are closed. It's about the distance between the eyes."

"Right," said Frank. "Do you have any Scotch tape?"

Chief studied the dead man's face. Frank didn't expect him to say that he knew the man without some kind of verification. "Do I know you?" Chief asked the dead man.

Frank and Gunny Sea Ray taped the dead man's eyes open and tied him upright to the back of the chair. He still slumped over but ElderGoth said it wouldn't matter if someone stood behind him and put a hand on his head to face him toward the camera. Siouxsie signaled to Frank that she wanted the job.

"Siouxsie can do that."

She wondered if she had ever felt so useful when she was curating at the museum.

ElderGoth took the picture. "It can take a few minutes to search for a hit."

Waiting for the results, no one talked until Siouxsie Banshee said, "Can we cover up the man's body or put him back on the stretcher?"

"Good idea," said Frank.

While they untied the man the computer told them who he was: Reuven Abarbanel, thirty-two. He lived in Silver Lake. He was a lawyer.

Frank asked Chief, "Does that mean anything to you?"

"No," said Chief.

"It may be a false reading, Frank," said ElderGoth. "Dead, he may look like someone else."

"Do you ever get false matches?"

"Chief, how would we know?"

"Admit it, ElderGoth. There have to be a few false verifications wandering around Center Camp."

Siouxsie couldn't restrain herself. "And that's what is so unfair."

Chief told her, "Enough. You've said enough. Thank you all, I'm going back. It's a false reading."

When Chief drove away, ElderGoth said, "I thought she was Verified Second Wave, Frank."

"It's an experiment," said Frank. "There are skilled people among the Drifters and some of them, like my friend Siouxsie Banshee here, can offer the verified community the kind of help we can't get from anyone else."

"What do you give in trade?"

"The chance to work. The chance to be useful. And a good room in a good hotel. Thanks for your help, ElderGoth. I'll make the report to Chief. And you know the rules about Security. Do not discuss this matter with anyone."

This rule was something Frank often invoked, though it had never been formally announced and not often enforced, because it didn't need to be. But at the moment, in the DMV, ElderGoth knew Frank had more to say. She put her mouth to his ear and cupped her hand and whispered so only he could hear. "Whatever Chief is interested in, and as you say he's interested in everything, why, Frank my friend, why is he interested in a dead Drifter when we have two weeks of food left?"

"We don't know. But it's more than that."

"The problem is that we count but don't understand the numbers. We're not used to time so we can't divide what we have by how many we are and estimate how much we use in a day. We have numbers without feeling. And don't tell me we're not running out of food for another two months. We withdraw to give ourselves a far horizon without seeing how little we really have left. Two months. We're running out of food. And everyone blames Tyler, but I blame June Moulton, because our mythology has made us weak just where we thought it made us strong. No surprise, really, as I look at the empty houses of worship around our great city: churches, synagogues, and mosques. I'd say that the previous leaders of the city also wasted their time listening to keepers of mythology, and that their mythology, of which I admit I understand very little, seems to have been about preparation for death. We need a mythology for the preservation of our lives."

"When you say 'our lives,' ElderGoth, who do we save?"

"If I had to choose committees, I'd say keep Systems and Security, and me. Feed them and take the rest to the desert along with June Moulton. Mythology can die; the rest of us can do Inventory. Inventory is a failure. Systems and Security, that's all you and I need to keep up our gracious way of life."

They left the DMV.

# Chief, Go Bruins

It was midnight and Chief crossed the street to talk to Go Bruins. He ignored Vayler screaming in the background, begging to be released, saying it wasn't his fault.

He told Royce Hall he was doing a fine job and needed Go Bruins for something else.

Go Bruins came back to Chief's terrace.

"I hope I'm not disappointing you, Chief."

"Never, Go Bruins. That's why I need you to do a mission for me, right now. I need your silence. I tell you now that I don't expect it, but I need it. So when you break my trust, keep in mind that I can't be mad at you for doing what I expected you'd do, but that you can be disappointed in yourself. Is that ornate enough of a thought? Do you want me to say something more complicated about duty?"

"You don't have to," said Go Bruins.

"Do you have any idea what you did at the university, what your job was?"

"I don't think about it."

"Your hands were calloused."

"So I worked in maintenance, most likely."

"Or you were a professor and at the same time, one of those men with a lot of tools in his garage or basement, one of those men who did a lot of work around the house or had a hobby restoring old cars, and worked on engines."

"I'd like to know I was that, sure."

"Smart and capable, respected and self-respecting. Handy."

"That's a nice word. We're all handy now, though, aren't we? Isn't that who was saved, the people who could do things with their hands?"

"Hands and minds together, that's what you have, the best of us, and not all of us."

"Do you need somebody killed?"

"No, I need someone protected. I need you to take someone north of Bakersfield, and leave her where she won't be found if someone other than me is looking for her."

"Pippi."

"Yes, Pippi."

"Why not just kill the person who's looking for her?"

"We're looking for him, and when we find him, we will, but until then, she has to be someplace far away and safe."

"She doesn't want to do this, does she?"

"She doesn't know the danger she's in."

☢

# Pippi, Go Bruins

Even though she was in the back of a U-Haul truck, blindfolded and bound to the wall, Chief probably wasn't sending her somewhere to die.

Pippi reviewed the evidence. When the First Wavers came back from the Ritz-Carlton, nobody wanted to talk about what they'd seen and heard.

Chief had come to her bedroom and told Go Bruins and Royce Hall to leave them.

"I saw the plane, Chief. I watched it take off. I watched it fly over downtown. How close was it?"

"Could you hear Shannon Squier?"

"Not over the sound of the plane. Was she what you wanted her to be?"

"Different."

"So she wasn't what you wanted?"

"It was a mistake."

"You never admit mistakes. Did you tell that to June Moulton or Frank Sinatra?"

"It was obvious to everyone."

"Are you going to kill her?"

"I have to find a way to use her before she uses me."

"This isn't what we're really talking about, Chief. You're talking about something else but you're not saying it. You're using the feeling of the thing you're not saying and you're telling me about that feeling through the story of Shannon Squier, but I don't think you're telling me the truth about her. You're telling me the other thing using whatever you can, from whatever is happening with Shannon."

"That's complicated."

"You're complicated, Chief."

Why blindfold someone in the darkness of a sealed truck? She knew that Chief's reasons were clouded, and when he came to her in the bedroom he was already planning this adventure for her when he told her: "I'm sorry for keeping you inside the house. That wasn't fair of me. I'm glad you managed to talk your way out of the bedroom and onto the deck so you could watch. And I'm sorry I didn't bring you with me. I needed you there. It would have been better."

"You didn't trust me. Who could blame you?"

"I don't trust anyone. I can't lock them all up."

Then he wanted sex, and with the expectation of her imminent death, she felt hungrier for the simple solid fact of his body than repulsion for anything so minor as his obvious intention to kill her by proxy in his typically remote way, finding someone else to take the action that would end in her death. She was clear enough now to formulate a question, even though nobody could answer it. "Is it the result of NK3 to be both scared and detached from what is happening to me, or is it the nature of who or whatever I was before to want to make love to the man who wants to kill me?" The question had come to her as she made love not to Chief the killer but to the part of him she could most easily touch: to his guilty desire for her. Her tenderness wasted, she was tied up in darkness.

She couldn't remember Chief's last words to her before he left, because she didn't know he was leaving. He might have said, "I'll see you later."

She was asleep when Go Bruins gagged her, tied her hands behind her back, and covered her head in a sack before carrying her to the truck parked in the driveway and chaining her inside. He stopped driving after half an hour and removed the gag.

The truck stopped on a steep downgrade. Go Bruins rolled the door up and cut the zip tie holding her hands and unlocked the chain that bound her to the wall. He took off the blindfold. A Yamaha motorcycle was strapped to the floor.

"I have to pee so I figure you do, too. Aim downhill." Go Bruins gave her a roll of toilet paper and a bottle of hand sanitizer.

They were in the middle of the road. There was no traffic to avoid. The smoke from the Burn didn't cross the mountains and the stars here were bright. She wanted a telescope more than she wanted to relieve herself. But she squatted as Go Bruins had instructed, with her back to the valley.

She thought she might have been a farm girl, once, by the easy way she gave up the ease of a bathroom for splashing on the ground. A farm girl or a soldier. Or someone who hiked in the outdoors. Did people who hiked in the outdoors work in special effects, if that was her job? She didn't know what her life had been before she came to Los Angeles.

When she stood up, she wasn't sure of direction. *I can run*, she thought. But where do I go?

Go Bruins offered her a quarter-full bottle of Jack Daniel's.

She tilted her head back three times and the bourbon was gone. "Is this in honor of the jet that made fun of the Burn?" There was enough alcohol in the bottle to give her a good dose of amused confidence. "This is not the end of the line for me?"

"No."

He offered her a plate of Chinese water chestnuts, a can of salmon with fresh lemon squeezed on it, four thick carrots, and a bottle of French white wine, wet from the cooler where it had chilled on ice.

"I thought we were headed for the desert and that you were going to dump me like a Drifter, but this is the I-5 freeway to Bakersfield, isn't it? What's the plan?"

"He's not killing you. He's protecting you from people who want to hurt him. He's afraid that if they can't hurt him, they'll hurt you."

"They're going to miss me in Center Camp. They're going to wonder where I went."

"You were mad at Chief for locking you up in the house. You're jealous of Shannon Squier. You hated Center Camp. We'll say you stole a truck. You ran away."

"Won't Chief want to send someone to find me?"

"But he did. Me. I followed you on that motorcycle. And I lost your trail. None of this makes sense to me, but I will get extra privileges because I'm not that curious."

"Do I have to stay inside the truck for the rest of the ride?"

"You can sit in front, but I have to tie your wrists. That's not Chief's order. That's me making sure I get you where you're supposed to go. Until then, eat."

They finished the food and the wine. He gave her the passenger seat and tied her wrists in front of her and with a loop through the door handle, making certain she couldn't give him trouble. They went back to the freeway. Neither had more to say. She recognized in him the possibility of sex, that he wanted it and might have asked for it or even taken it, but loyalty to Chief kept him in check. She said it: "You'd like sex but you know that when Chief asks you if you did have sex with me, you want to answer him truthfully."

"But if I didn't care about lying? How would you feel about that?"

"You'd still have to lie, and I don't want you to lie about sex."

They left the I-5 for the 99, into the farmland beyond Bakersfield.

Go Bruins turned off the freeway at an exit that didn't have signs for a gas station or motel. Then they continued west through fifteen miles of orchards and fields, stopping at a crossroads in the orange groves. There was a lumberyard, a church with a short steeple, and a trailer park. He left Pippi in the front seat while he opened the back of the truck. He pulled a ramp into place and rolled the motorcycle to the ground. Then he cut the plastic ties that held her to the door.

"He gave me a message for you, and he told me to hold it until we were here." Go Bruins opened the glove compartment and took out a cigarette pack weighted with a stone wrapped inside a piece of paper.

As she opened the message, Go Bruins stepped away from her. "You didn't read this?" she asked.

"Chief told me not to."

"And you obeyed?"

"It was in my rehab."

The message was in Chief's hand:

> Darling, I love you. Stay there for your own safety. There is no one but me.

"Do you have any questions?" Go Bruins asked.

"Nothing that anyone can answer."

Go Bruins started the motorcycle, which woke up a dog somewhere close by.

"Good luck," he said, and rode away.

The dog came fast from the lumberyard, howling.

# Hopper

Hopper took the shuttle bus to Center Camp, past the Playa. A woman in a wedding gown ran backward, lifting a kite to the sky. He felt his Silent Voice ready to say something favorable about what they were seeing, but neither had the words to understand the kite.

His Silent Voice said, "She's here. I know she's here." But there was a private urgency to the Voice that Hopper didn't recognize, as though his Voice wanted to race ahead of him, didn't care about him.

The bus stopped at the gate. Hopper showed his clipboard to the security guard and the guard looked up Hopper's name on the list. "Kraft Serviss?"

"That's me."

The guard waved him through.

"We're here," said his Silent Voice. "We're late but we're here. Start at the first house and just knock on every door and see what they need. Ask to go into the house. Tell them you want to get out of the sun."

The first house belonged to the water purity engineers. The door was open but Hopper rang the bell to announce himself. It was one of the only houses with a baby, and at the sound of the bell the baby started crying. A woman came to the door.

Hopper showed her his clipboard. "I'm Kraft Serviss. I have questions about the things you need. Can we talk? Can I come in?"

"I'm Season Witch. What kind of questions?"

"What-do-you-need-from-the-hospital questions."

Hopper hadn't seen a child since leaving the school in Redlands. *Inch odge. Inch odge.* The baby had a small head, like a ball with a face painted on it, and even though the head was small, the baby couldn't hold it up, so the head dropped.

"Does the baby have a name?"

"I don't know. It won't tell me. And you're from the hospital?"

"Do you need any of these things?" He showed her his clipboard and stepped into the house. There were blank spaces on the wall, outlined in grime, where there used to be paintings and photographs.

"We don't need towels or pillowcases or rubber tubing or any of this. We're well provisioned."

"Have you seen the woman with the red hair that sticks out from her head?"

"Yes. That's Pippi."

"I was told to ask her if she needs anything."

"Ask her yourself, if you can talk to her. He never lets her out of the house." She pointed to the big house at the top of the hill.

Chest to the floor, the baby dragged himself forward to Season's feet and held her leg. Season looked at the list on the clipboard one more time. "I don't see diapers." She took Hopper's pen and wrote the word on the form. "I have enough for three months. There's no rush. And I could use more baby food, but I don't see it on the list."

"If it's not there, we'll find it." His Silent Voice said, "Good answer."

Season turned without shutting the door and the baby fell back down on its bottom, and then on all fours crawled after her.

Hopper pulled the door behind him, not sure if that was expected, not sure if it mattered. It was good to know that his wife was Chief's prisoner. One more day and he could free her.

☢

# Shannon, Erin, Toffe, Brin

Quiet Toffe didn't believe the rumors that they were running out of food and said so to the group. "I've gone on some Inventory runs. I've seen lots of food."

Brin and Helary were satisfied that the surplus was permanent and didn't see anything to be scared of. Jobe believed in the rumors, with no proof, just a feeling.

It was after one of these discussions that Erin asked Shannon to walk with her, and Shannon was impressed with Erin's confident urgency when Erin said, "Say there isn't a shortage. Say there's twenty-five years of food left. That's still not forever and we're physically young and don't want to run out of food. So if it's true or if it's not, we'll have to take over from Chief someday and why wait? You could be the new Chief. And don't tell me you haven't thought about this yourself."

Shannon told Erin she was being stupid. "If we're running out of food and supplies, what's the use of having any power over the First Wave? We'll be drifting like everyone else. And I'll need to be on my own again because none of you are strong. Everyone will be each other's enemies, and I know what that world is like. I think it makes more sense to leave now. Or . . . no." Shannon held up a hand and Erin watched the expression on Shannon's face as it went from quarrelsome and impatient to neutral, empty of opinion, before changing, as Shannon considered a fresh possibility. Few people in Center Camp ever changed their minds, and to observe this in Shannon was more proof to Erin of the singer's power, except that what Shannon had decided to do was something she wasn't going to share with Erin. This too was legible in Shannon's expression.

Erin tested it. "Shannon, what are you thinking?" Shannon didn't answer and Erin said, "That night on Figueroa, you were on top of the bus, and you were leading the Bottle Bangers, and I felt something. Everyone close to you did. And then the jet came and the feeling stopped. Were you so inside it that you couldn't feel it?"

"I didn't just feel things. I saw things."

"Could you do that again?"

"I didn't like being on the bus."

"Not for the Drifters, for us."

"The plane scared me."

"The plane is gone. Could you bring back those, I don't know what to call them, little stories, pictures, memories?"

"I think so."

"Just seeing you dancing and bottle banging made things different. What if you could sing?"

"My voice is gone."

"You haven't really tried. I have the karaoke disks of your songs in my room. Try singing the songs you used to sing to the music you used to know. It's a lot to ask of you, I'm sorry, but I have to. If you know what I'm thinking about, you'll do it."

Shannon agreed.

Back in her room, Erin played a karaoke track and Shannon followed the lyrics on her SONY screen. Then they played the original recording. They went back and forth between the copy and the original. Shannon's voice was hesitant at first, but she learned to sing along with herself.

How many times had she performed this live? It was habit now, no different than Toby Tyler's automatic ease with a welding torch. Singing along with the karaoke band was like walking into her own house. Erin banged a bottle in time with the music, and Shannon's voice expanded like the sound of the jet over the city.

Shannon kicked the karaoke machine to stop the music. She was sweating and had to catch her breath. She put a hand on Erin's shoulder and pulled her close.

"What?" asked Erin.

"You're not stupid."

"I hope not."

"No, you're smart. You understand. More than I did."

"That's what I've been trying to tell you. I'm your biggest fan. Fans always know more."

"This is a weapon."

"Shannon, you're the weapon."

# Frank Sinatra, Siouxsie, Redwings, Gunny Sea Ray

Frank let Siouxsie drive the BMW, with Redwings following on his motorcycle, carrying Gunny Sea Ray in the sidecar.

With the Burn Zone behind them they followed the boulevards south of the Fence, past the museum where Siouxsie had worked, down the quiet streets with the dead stores and restaurants and broken glass.

The map led them to a concrete trench twenty feet across, with water moving slowly in a little channel down the middle. A block upstream, the water drained from the side of a hill, behind a locked iron gate.

"The lock is rusted," said Redwings. "Nobody's been through here. Let's keep walking."

They found a loose manhole cover above a shaft with handholds.

"All of the storm-drain covers were supposed to have been welded shut," said Frank. "That was one of my jobs during rehab and fence construction. Someone missed this. Could have been a mistake; could have been on purpose."

"If it was on purpose," said Gunny Sea Ray, "then don't you think it would have been used before now?"

"Maybe it has been used and you don't know it," said Siouxsie. "Or maybe someone was waiting for the right time to use it, and that time is now."

Frank agreed with her but didn't say so. "If this map is right, Gunny Sea Ray and Redwings, then the two of you should be able to walk right under the Fence and come up in any one of twenty places behind the Fence and keep on walking until you get to wherever this leads. You have your radios. Call when you're at the end and we'll meet you on the other side. And don't tell anyone what we've seen here today. The news about Vayler's lies is bad enough. Add the threat of a breach and we'll get nothing done. I'll meet you at the other end when you call me. And for now, Siouxsie, you're going back to the Ritz-Carlton. I'll take you there before I go back to Center Camp and tell Chief about our day."

She accepted Frank's order, knowing that she had no choice and wanting to save the right to quarrel for a better day.

As Gunny Sea Ray and Redwings climbed down into the storm drain, Frank stopped them to give one last instruction. No one else could hear him. "Whatever you find, I want you to come back down here and say you couldn't get through. If there's been a breach, I don't want anyone to know about it. Not anyone. Not Chief. Mark the exit and we'll get into it from the other side."

"We'll come back here and find our way out," said Redwings. "Then we can meet you inside the Fence and take you to whatever we find—if there really is anything to find."

Frank drove fast but kept the car in second gear on the ride back to the Ritz-Carlton, to stretch out the engine's whine, the sound that Siouxsic loved.

He left her at the entrance and drove back, slowly, to Chief's house.

☢

# Frank Sinatra, Chief,

# Go Bruins, Royce Hall

Go Bruins stood beside Chief, playing the role of menacing protector as Frank had taught him. Two years after rehab, Frank had released Go Bruins and Royce Hall to Chief's full-time guard and kept Redwings and Gunny Sea Ray for himself how much time either of the men he trusted could spend with Chief so that Chief would overlook their value, while thinking better of Go Bruins and Royce Hall.

Chief showed the pictures of the dead man to Go Bruins. "Familiar?"

"Not to me. The license picture was taken when?"

"Twelve years ago," said Frank. "The license was good for ten years from issue. And he was rehabbed. He was too clean to be a Drifter. Are you sure you don't recognize him? A lot of years have passed."

Chief said, "Not so many, really. It's not from young to old; it's from young to a little older. I would recognize him if he was someone I once knew."

"So there's no chance this is the man from Palm Springs?"

"No. Now we have a second killing. I want a meeting of the committee heads as soon as possible. Before it gets dark."

Alone with Frank, Chief said, "Guns, bicycles, Tesla's murder, the dead body, the food running out. Are we any different from the way things used to be?"

# Pippi

The padlock was heavy, the chain was heavier, the orange trees were tall, and Pippi, who could not move far, was happy. There was nothing she could do to change her situation except to wait for a better moment. She knew Chief didn't want her dead, and for now, without him but still alive, she felt a better connection to life than she could ever remember having. How many things did she know about that she could think about? She wanted to send messages over the Fence, but she was the prisoner of the people who picked the oranges and would stay their prisoner until Chief released her.

# Frank Sinatra, Gunny Sea Ray, Redwings, The Man

Gunny and Redwings came to the end of Hopper and Seth's storm drain and saw The Man above them. "Redwings," said Gunny Sea Ray. "Shouldn't Frank know about this now?"

"Did he make an allowance for us to call him if by chance the exit to this tunnel was point zero: the Playa?"

"No he did not."

"Then back we go, content we should be with the knowledge that until we share this result with Frank, we are in sole possession of some special information that lesser men wouldn't handle with the caution to which we've agreed to abide by."

"No," said Gunny. "As much as I respect my Redwings, I'm getting on the walkie-talkie and telling him where we are. Right now." Gunny called Frank. "Take the tunnel, stay to the middle where the storm drains meet, and you will be surprised."

Frank went into the drain with his flashlight the way he'd gone into the container at the rail yard, chasing the same man. Again he wanted to be alone with his thoughts. He had so few of them and they didn't often link to new ideas. Tracking down Drifters was easy. They were out there living their obvious Drifter lives, but now he was after someone cleverer than himself. Not far from the end, where he could see the light coming through the exit at The Man's foot, he found an empty bag of Corn Nuts.

When he reached the Playa, he asked the men if they'd seen it when they came through.

"We didn't, sir," said Redwings. "But that doesn't mean it wasn't there. We weren't looking at the ground, so to speak. We were looking for a way out."

Gunny Sea Ray added a useful observation. "But we know from the rail yard that someone liked these Corn Nuts. So speaking for myself, if Redwings or I had seen the wrapper, we're trained well enough by you, Frank, sir, to make note of it and we would have saved it and marked its position here in the drain."

Frank told them to continue to keep this a secret, and unlike anyone working for Toby Tyler or Vayler, he knew they would.

He also knew that Redwings was wrong about something. They didn't see the Corn Nuts bag because the Corn Nuts bag hadn't been there when they came through.

"We are always being followed by someone smarter."

# Hopper

When Piperno complained that Chief had called a meeting of the committee heads and once again refused to have the head of the UCLA hospital there to advise on medical matters, Hopper went to Center Camp with his inventory requisitions list.

# Chief, Frank Sinatra, ElderGoth, Toby Tyler, June Moulton, Vayler, Hopper

Chief was alone on the terrace with his eyes closed, walking slowly in a circle as he knew he must have done when he was a child. He trusted that these small treasures of feeling went back to something that must have been ordinary. There weren't enough people in the world now to know what was typical. But in the past—throughout the known cities—so many backyards and parks had structures for children to play on, swings and slides and wooden castles and forts. Chief liked riding on seesaws with Pippi. No one ever had them in their homes, so he went to them in playgrounds. The empty playgrounds were empty of children but also of their parents. He knew of seesaws outside the Fence and went on them with Go Bruins and Royce Hall. Almost everyone now was an orphan. His thoughts went to the ingenious scientists, who mastered the complexity of the human material to design a weapon so strategically ornate in its subtle and total viciousness. Burning the world with thermonuclear weapons had no art, just a love of death. NK3 was made of spite.

When he wasn't sure of what to do, he liked to explore the texture of darkness, self-imposed or natural. Blind circle walking helped him clear many general doubts. In bed at night when the curtains were closed so that no light came through, he held his hands in the air and asked Pippi, "How many fingers am I holding up?" She would answer with a number, but he wouldn't say if she was right or wrong. He missed her now but felt certain that she was safer away from the expanding chaocracy that was so close and would be even closer once the meeting started.

With Vayler locked in the house across the street, all the committee heads were on the way. He told Toby to arrive early. Toby had sent word back that she wanted to bring the crew that always orbited around her, but Chief wanted only the heads today, no staff. He heard her coming up the steps and opened his eyes but continued walking in a circle. There were six chairs around a table set with twelve bottles of red wine with the labels soaked off.

"What's all this for?" she asked, starting to pour a glass.

Chief told her to put the wine down.

"The labels are missing. Is there something special about these bottles I should already know?"

"No."

"Am I early?"

"No, I wanted you first. You can wait until the others arrive."

"Why?"

"I want to honor Systems, Toby Tyler. I give you the right to choose your seat at the table."

"They're going to ask me what you said to me."

"You can tell them that I wanted to just share a quiet moment together, because it's the truth. I like you, Toby, and we don't often say that to each other."

He turned his back on Toby and looked at LAX through Pippi's favorite telescope, wondering what she had seen at the airport that she hadn't told him about.

June Moulton was the second to arrive. Toby tried to start a conversation with her, but June took her usual position at the edge of the terrace and waited for Chief to come to her.

"Is everyone inside the Fence now scared of the Inventory problem?" asked Chief, drawing her into the dry remains of the garden, and even there, whispering.

"Everyone," said the mythologist. "Unless you have a surprise."

"I have an impulse but I'm not sure what to do with it yet. It might surprise you."

"That can't happen. Nothing surprises me completely. A mythologist such as myself watches the reactions of others, not her own. Where you, Chief, might be surprised at someone's reaction to an event, and by 'event' I mean a sudden change in the flow of energy that divides time into sections, I have no personal need for a specific resolution of the inequity in disturbances. At most I have an opinion. Call it the difference between inducing knowledge from a set of responses and determining from them a principle, or starting with a series of principles and from them, deducing and anticipating a particular outcome. I'm sure you understand."

"You didn't say what anger begins with."

"Justified anger expands from justified causes, from the violation of a principle, which begins with the betrayal of trust. And we're here because Vayler broke trust. But right now stop talking to me. It will make you look like you're getting my advice, and everyone who heads a committee wants to think their advice is better than anyone else's. And here comes ElderGoth with Frank Sinatra. See? Sinatra is excusing himself from ElderGoth and she's conceding that he has the right to talk to you now, so I'll withdraw."

ElderGoth stopped to let Sinatra come to Chief.

"Why didn't you tell me that Pippi stole a truck and left you?"

"My personal problems don't matter now, not with the crisis of Inventory."

"And Go Bruins couldn't catch her?"

"I'm upset about this, Frank. But like I say, I have so much to do and it's just not important now. Let's join everyone."

"There are twelve bottles of wine on the table," said Chief. "And the labels have been taken off. Instead of looking up the value of the wines in the wine books and magazines, we have to guess what is good. June, will that work?"

"That's not a question for Mythology."

"Of course it is. The myth is that the more it costs, the better it tastes. Any bottle of wine will get you drunk if you have enough to drink, but you wouldn't know what its rating was in the past. You won't know if, five or six years ago, this bottle was three dollars and ninety-nine cents on the shelf at Trader Joe's or if this bottle is from Erin's father's wine cellar and it cost him three thousand dollars at auction. You'll have to trust your own sense of quality. ElderGoth, do we trust our own sense of quality?"

"That's not my department, Chief."

"But of course it is. You have to trust your sense of the quality of the people you verify."

"The machine does that."

"But what if the machine broke? We'd have to trust our senses. Why would we need the DMV and all of Verification to tell us who among the living survivors of the catastrophe deserves membership in our community and who, for general incompetence or specific disorder, belongs out there beyond the ash fields?" He pointed toward the south and then slapped ElderGoth across the top of her head. "That was a question, ElderGoth. Answer me."

"What's the question?" Her eyes were wet.

"Who else heard my question? Toby Tyler?"

"You can't compare wine tasting to the valuation of those who can help us and deserve to be included in the life of Center Camp."

"Why not?" asked Chief, threatening to slap Toby Tyler as he had just slapped ElderGoth. "We've been going by labels."

Sinatra knew it was time to make his first gesture. "You're right, Chief. The DMV is a failure. We need to find other ways to rank the Drifters, but I don't think that's what we're here to talk about. You're trying to make a comparison between the quality of unknown wine bottles and what Vayler did. You're not asking about Vayler because we all know he lied about Inventory and Chief does not yet want to discuss this except by methods that only June Moulton understands. June, what does Chief want us to understand about bottles of wine that don't have labels?"

But June, still looking to where Chief had pointed south before hitting ElderGoth, wouldn't answer Sinatra, which cost him the little advantage he thought was his. And this impressed upon him the need to avoid any approach to the problem that might be called clever. Clever didn't work around Chief.

No one else wanted to speak, which was Chief's intention from the start.

"We have all heard what Vayler Monokeefe has done or not done. I'm scared and so should you be. When we have a new head of Inventory, we'll have only a little time to calm the fears of the community before everyone reacts separately instead of as the group that we have so successfully been."

Toby Tyler raised a hand but spoke before she was invited. "How much do we think is there now, Chief. Or are the numbers all fucked up?"

"Assume the numbers are all fucked up."

Sinatra raised his hand too. "But does that mean we're out of food in a week or a month or two years?"

"We don't know. We need June to tell us what we should say without knowing the answer. June?"

"Each of you drink from the unlabeled wines and tell us what you think of them, and then I'll answer."

Toby Tyler reached for the nearest bottle and Sinatra knocked her hand away. "No, we won't do this," he said. "We don't have the skill to know the difference. You'll prove nothing, June, and it won't help us help Chief. We have bigger problems than our lost selectivity. Speaking for Security, I see a war over food between Center Camp and the Drifters, and if we win that war, and I have no doubt we can beat them, then after that I see a war inside Center Camp. And each of us, Security, Mythology, Inventory, and Verification, has a network of allegiances that we'll try to use against everyone else."

Chief said, "You left out Systems."

"Yes," said Sinatra. "Because Toby Tyler will rule. She has the rest of us at her command, and she's never used her power against us. But now, I think she will, which is why she reached for the wine so eagerly."

"This will shock some of you but I don't know anything about wine," she said. "You're right, Frank. I just wanted a drink to reward myself for being in such a good position, for being in the best position of all of you."

ElderGoth poured herself a glass of wine and drank it quickly, holding up a hand to let the others know she was about to say something. When the glass was empty she said, "Don't ask me if it's good. I don't care. It gets me drunk. Drink, all of you, we need it."

June spoke. "Toby and the Systems crews can live without the rest of us. She would actually be better off without the rest of us. They're the best organized. Their vulnerability, though, is that Toby has never spread her authority among them. So that if we removed Toby, we could replace her with someone who would not try to elevate

Systems above the rest of us. So it isn't in Toby's interest to be the rebel. We have more cause than ever to stand together, against everyone. ElderGoth, do you see?"

"I do."

"We want to maintain our privilege," said June. "That's what I'm here for. That's why a Mythology Committee, even a committee of one person, was established during our rehab, in anticipation of the end of our resources. People will kill for food. If the committees fight, they'll produce leaders from among the people on our teams who we already trust, and they'll challenge each of us. And if they get rid of us, the factions among the factions will split, and they'll destroy whatever chance the people at this table have to continue not just leading but living. You've seen me apart from you all. You've wondered about my long silences, my meaningless games, and the mystery of June Moulton that I develop and improve. I didn't understand all of it about myself until this table was set. Chief, what did you plan to tell us tonight? Were you going to tell us about Vayler and how you want to punish him?"

"Pour yourselves a sip of wine from each bottle and tell me what you think."

Ten minutes passed as the committee heads tasted the wines.

Frank resisted because he expected that this was a trick. Toby Tyler was first to rap a knuckle on each bottle when she was done with them all. "Good, bad, better, okay, okay, best. Okay, Chief, am I right or wrong?"

"Anyone else? ElderGoth?"

"I think this one is the best." And she tapped Toby's fourth choice.

"All of the bottles are the same," said Chief. "Same wine, same year. That was the only way to conduct a fair test. It's French, Gigondas, close to Burgundy. The wine was considered a good but not a particularly great wine, it cost seventy dollars a bottle five years ago, and it's aged. But it wouldn't cost a thousand dollars if the world hadn't changed. It would be a hundred, maybe. My point is that it was good enough for you to like, but not good enough to be so distinctive that someone might get a perfect score. I wanted to see if any of you were strong enough to resist the temptation to see difference because you were expecting it. So, the question is: what do we do with Vayler Monokeefe, who didn't keep track of the things in this world that all of us need, to sustain the paradise we've made out of the dust, but, worse than that, knowing that we were in trouble, kept a reserve for himself? ElderGoth, would you answer?"

ElderGoth asked, "Why me first?"

"Because you have the most limited perspective of the committee heads. You don't have power over a large team. So, what should we do with Vayler?"

"Hang him in public."

"So, there's the first sentiment. Kill him. That's one. Next, Frank Sinatra, from the needs of Security, what should we do with Vayler?"

"Until I know the real situation with how much we have left, I can't recommend any action."

"Fair enough," said Chief.

ElderGoth raised her hand to speak. "I could have said the same thing."

"You didn't. June?"

"Not ready to answer."

"Toby Tyler, what does Systems think we should do?"

"Systems is only interested in what is practical, not political. Systems needs to see things as they're happening without taking our own emotional reactions into consideration. So, we're facing a shortage. We want the water and electricity to flow. We don't want downtown to get dark at night. We don't want the motors that control the Fence gates to freeze up because they have no power. Lock stuck open, lock stuck closed, bad news either way. So Systems wants to roll back protection of the periphery systems to the essential points. That is, Systems wants help from Security to protect the main electrical switching stations and the main valves and pumps that control the water, and leave the rest of the grid under enough supervision to warn us if it's damaged. We don't fight for everything. We fight for what we can't afford to lose."

June stood up and walked from the table, adjusting her shawl.

Chief called to her. "June, we need everyone."

She walked to the telescopes and stood up on the low stone wall just beyond them.

Toby Tyler said, "She doesn't have to support us. She just can't publically disagree with it or argue with you."

"She never does that," said Chief.

June liked to hear them talk about her as though she couldn't make sense of their words, like a cat or someone who was deaf. June remembered more than the other committee heads about the days following the first recognized symptoms. She was one of the earliest to get sick and, as the mistress of Erin's father, she was given special treatment at the same time as Erin. Erin hadn't known who June was to her father, and now June only knew of the love affair because when she went into rehab, Erin's father had left her a loving letter with his picture, reminding her of who he was to her. It wasn't clear from the letter if he had already separated from his wife or if his wife had walked out on him or if she had lost her mind to NK3. June found the house that had been hers, on a steep street in an area of older small houses close to downtown, and, when she went back to it after rehab, recognized nobody in any of the pictures except, sort of, herself. Her computer at home did not need a password to open the files and in a subfolder called Taxes 2016 she found a photograph of herself naked on a bed with Erin's father, tangled together on red sheets, the phone with the camera in it pointed at the mirrored ceiling. They were smiling, just a couple of buddies. June had not taken a lover since rehab, because she had no desire for someone else's body and over the four years came to see that she was still in love with the married president of Warner Bros.

Her house was filled with screenplays, none with her name on them, and a few movie posters, also none with her name on them. It seemed from the clues that she'd been some kind of film executive at the studio, although possibly in marketing, not in production. She had never married, or if she had been married, that had been in another house and years earlier to someone who left no traces. Perhaps she had deleted that husband the way the Korean weapon snipped all the old human connections for a variation on the same reason.

Something tied the scripts and movie posters to her appointment as mythologist, but no one could explain it to her. The myths she read about had no attachment to the world anymore. Churches with Jesus writhing on the cross or churches with empty crosses, synagogues with scrolls in elaborate closets on the pulpit, Scientology halls, a few mosques, houses with Wiccan shrines, all of this difference in religion told her that nobody preaching about God or religion knew what they were doing, that the effective leaders of those religions shared the secret of religion, that it was arbitrary. All the religions of the past had failed to save anyone. None of them continued and none of their symbols had yet drawn anyone in the world back to the worship chambers with renewed or revived faith in the symbols of the god of each dead domain. Her Silent Voice—a distant entity that as for most First Wavers rarely had anything to tell her and sometimes went weeks without a sound—returned to an old argument between them: "It won't work anymore. That's why you were chosen, because you didn't believe in it then."

"What did I believe in?"

"You believed in the movies."

"But I don't like movies."

"Not anymore, but you used to."

"But that doesn't answer my question."

"The Founders had the idea that the world needed a new myth to control the Drifters. That the old churches would be filled with people worshipping a new set of gods, and this was meant to control them. Center Camp had no use for a unifying mythology, since mythologies mask the legend of a crime and once the DMV was established and a screening process established, half the story was all anyone needed to hear. Mythology gives pleasant answers to the basic questions of human curiosity, and among the attributes missing from humanity after NK3 is curiosity. You could tell the First Wave the truth about who the Drifters were and what we owe them, and no one would care. They won't feel shocked or guilty when they know who the Drifters really are."

"We don't talk about that," said June. "And you shouldn't talk about it either. Right now, I need to know, now, as things are starting to fall apart, what if anything I'm supposed to do to fulfill the mission that was assigned to me during my rehab. I stand here at the edge of the terrace to make them think I have insights too brutal to share, and that whatever I do say is really just a way to give shape to things that can't be experienced by anyone but me."

"Yes, that is your role. You're doing what you're supposed to do. If all that remains of myth's traditional power is the suggestion of enigma, keep standing here and impressing upon the world that you know something they don't. The only knowledge that matters is that, first, you know the depth of your own ignorance, and second, you have sympathy for everyone else's confusion. Exploit it if you have to, betray them if you have to, but start with sympathy. Everyone isn't as full of life as you, June Moulton. I know you want to tell me you're lonely, but you know what I say to that. I say you have what you always wanted. You're living in his house, watching over his daughter."

"But I don't remember him."

"The astronauts in the space station were weightless, but still in the sphere of gravity's influence. The connection is invisible and insensible to the weightless astronauts, but even so, there's an orbit. So it is with you and Erin's father."

"The astronauts are dead."

"And the heads of committee need your opinion on what to do about Vayler."

The Silent Voice was gone and June, familiar with the Voice's habits of visitation, didn't expect to hear from her again for two months. Usually little changed between visits from her Silent Voice. But she knew that change was going to be all the fashion now, since what was usual had only lasted for about two and a half years, and all the experience that felt like a vast continent, experience and memory filling up the available space, was really just a tiny island in time.

So, to keep the theater of her franchise, she returned to her seat and poured another glass of wine. She held the stem in her fingers, lightly, without lifting the glass or drinking the wine.

"In the way the world used to be, there was a mythology of history, call it legend, and the mythology of festivals, the scripts for the rituals of the festivals, call it magic. Inside the Fence we live for the festival. The Woman talks about the festivals. She says we don't have gods and we don't have heroes. The tortured man on the cross, man or god, if he died for our sins, those sins belong to the past. He's nothing to us. The Buddha with his eyes half closed, we've seen the shrines, we've seen the statues in the gardens, but who is he to us? Why are his eyes like that? What does he not want to see? We woke up to the world as it is and were given the life we share, the community we share. We know that people prayed to them, but we don't know prayer. I mean we know the words but no one who says those words to God has ever heard God talk back. And God is not the Silent Voice."

"Anything that gives us, those of us in Center Camp, time to prepare ourselves for the end of the Founders' gifts and to protect ourselves from everyone else, late Verified Second Wavers, Drifters and Driftettes, if that's what it comes to, is what we have to do, because we're all Drifters now. So it's essential that we don't punish Vayler, that we keep him as head of Inventory, with discreet supervision by Security. You can't punish him. The story we tell has to be about a mistake, a simple accounting mistake. We get out the word that Vayler went back over the books and everything is fine."

Sinatra asked, "How much can we say is left, how many years of food?"

"Twenty-five years. The bigger the lie, the more time it buys us."

"Thank you, June Moulton. I know you work for the community. So do we all."

"We work for ourselves, Chief," said June Moulton. "The rest is myth. And don't expect everyone to believe it. The end of the endless food supply is real, and justifies panic."

Chief thanked June. "Frank Sinatra, please go across the street and bring Vayler back. And we need an extra chair at this table."

ElderGoth raised a hand, "I still don't know how we're not going to starve to death."

"I do," said Chief.

# Frank Sinatra, Vayler Monokeefe, Hopper

Vayler Monokeefe—stretched out on a living room couch, resting before the final part of his life began—began to cry when he saw the head of Security walking up the path to his prison. He'd never seen Sinatra kill anyone but others had and they said he never changed expression from his usual deliberate stare. Monokeefe rolled to his feet as Go Bruins let Sinatra in. When the door opened, Monokeefe's attention went to a man at Chief's door. He was in hospital clothes, with an Inventory requisitions clipboard in his hands, talking to Redwings. Sinatra closed the door and faced Vayler.

"Well, Vayler, so here we are and I have to say I'm sorry to be in this position."

"What position is that, Frank?"

"A position of judgment. A position of punishment. A position of disruption not of my choosing."

"Do you often choose disruption, Frank? I didn't know that."

"You have to be strategic, not tactical, Vayler. Do you know the difference?"

"I don't, Frank. Tell me."

"Tactics win battles. Strategies win wars."

"That's a wise thought, Frank."

"I don't think you understand it."

"I'm not so good, Frank. I'm sorry I let everyone down." Vayler looked past Frank at the man with the clipboard. He wished he were just a man with a clipboard.

"What have you learned from this?"

"Not to keep secrets."

"Everyone has secrets, Vayler. Is that all you learned from lying to your friends and stealing from them?"

"I don't think I know what I've learned and I don't expect to have the time to figure all of that out and then fix the things I've broken."

"You'll have the time, Vayler. Your days are numbered but not over. Come to Chief's house. We want to talk to you."

Across the street, Redwings looked at Hopper's inventory lists. "And you want to take inventory in Chief's supply closets?"

"That's what I was told to do," said Hopper.

"Get out of Frank's way," said Redwings, pulling Hopper aside to let Sinatra and Vayler through.

Sinatra looked at Hopper, trying to place him.

Redwings said, "He's from the hospital, Frank. He's checking supplies."

Vayler wanted to say that if Hopper was working for Inventory, he'd never seen him before, but this would probably come back to him as an example of his own inability to manage the Inventory Committee after three years of active consciousness. And then the implications of a house-to-house inventory in Center Camp meant that no accounting under Vayler's supervision could be trusted. He expected a bad death.

When Frank Sinatra brought Vayler to the terrace, Redwings called for Royce Hall to show Hopper around the house. Hall wanted to watch the meeting and pointed Hopper toward the garage. "We don't keep many supplies here," he said to Hopper. "But I know we could use more toilet paper and hand soap."

*   *   *

Hopper left the kitchen and walked through the house. In Palm Springs the house where the Teacher kept him was one level, shaped like a squared-off U, with a swimming pool in the center. Chief's house was three stories with a large central hall. The house wasn't clean like the house in Palm Springs. There were dirty boot prints on the marble tiles. There was dust on the glass that covered some of the art. Hopper only noticed this because the Teacher's house was clean and no one was allowed to wear shoes inside.

He found the Pippi Longstocking room on the second floor overlooking the meeting on the terrace. Pictures of a little girl with flying red pigtails were on everything, from the wallpaper to the sheets. She was even on the curtains. Hopper opened the curtains just enough to see the committee heads around the table. He closed the curtains and lay down on the bed.

"Vayler," said Chief. "I could hang you now. Or I could send you to the desert, but that's not going to help us. It's not true that we're running out of food, and you know it. Don't you?"

"No, Chief. We're running out of food."

"We're not. This rumor has gone wild because you made a mistake, didn't you?"

"Not a math mistake."

"Vayler, try to follow what I'm hinting at. Didn't you make a counting error? If it was deliberate, we'd have to kill you. So, I'm asking you: what is the mistake?"

"I overlooked twenty Costcos and fifty Walmarts, and underestimated the size of the cattle herd in Bakersfield."

"All you had to do was count some cows, Vayler."

"They move around. Most of them look the same."

"So we have enough for how many years?"

"Whatever you want me to say."

"Toby Tyler?"

"Best to move everyone to Bakersfield and expand the farming, but that would mean leaving the Fence. And that would put an end to our way of life. I want to protect our way of life."

Vayler asked if he could speak.

"Only to clarify what you're supposed to say and do. Not to give us any advice."

"I understand. I still want to help. I want to be of service, as we used to say."

Chief slammed the table. "We don't talk about what we used to say."

"Then I'll do what you tell me."

"The Unverified Second Wave is worried about food? They're scaring the Drifters? Prepare a feast like they've never had on Figueroa. Show them surplus. You, personally, making sure the food trucks are stocked, with everything you can. Bring out the best wines. Bring out the oldest whiskey. You have costumes in storage?"

"From the movie studios, yes."

"Hand them out. Put all the Drifters in costume."

"Yes, Chief. When?"

"Tomorrow night. That's what I want you to do. That's all I want you to do."

"You're a good Chief, a kind Chief. I'll feed the people myself. I'll show them we have more than enough food."

"I'm not done, Vayler. Inventory and Verification have all the buses, right, ElderGoth?"

"We do."

"And Frank, Security provides protection for the buses that are used when we leave the Drifters to themselves in the desert."

"We're in charge of that, yes, Chief."

"Get enough buses for two thousand Drifters, if we have that many on Figueroa, and park them a block away from the food trucks. Get the Inventory trucks there, too. Feed the Drifters, get them drunk, and get them on the buses. Drive them to the desert and let them go. Systems?"

Toby Tyler raised her hand. "What can we do?"

"After we finish with what I'm talking about, we may not have enough Drifters for the next Burn. Can you manage without that?"

"Make the Burns smaller. The Burns were better when they were smaller. This last one pushed us too hard."

"You're right. June?"

"Yes, Chief."

"What would the Founders say about this?"

"A trip to the desert calls for radical self-reliance."

In the bedroom, Hopper ran his hands over the quilt. The pillowcase was soft, and the fabric was thin where his wife had rested her head.

He pressed the side of his face into the pillow and saw a few long strands of bright-red hair. He wrapped one long hair five times around the tip of his forefinger, then buried his face in the pillow and breathed deeply, searching for her scent. He licked the hair on his finger. Something of Robin was there. He smelled the back of his hand, to see if he could find the difference between Robin and himself and it was there. He fell asleep with her red hair around his finger.

The gun barrel stuck into his cheek woke him up two hours later. Go Bruins stood over him, with Chief beside him.

Chief said, "Who are you?"

The note of caution in Chief's tone surprised Go Bruins, who expected rage.

"I fell asleep."

Go Bruins moved the gun barrel along Hopper's jaw. "We know you fell asleep. That's why we could wake you up, because you fell asleep. That's how it works."

Frank asked, "Who are you?"

"I'm Kraft Serviss. With Inventory."

"I've never seen you before," said Chief.

"I was assigned to the hospital. You can ask Dr. Kaplan."

"The doctor who disappeared?"

"I'm the one who found him and brought him back to the hospital. I found him in the hills. I hurt myself and Dr. Piperno fixed me."
He showed the bandage over his scar.

Chief looked to Sinatra to ask the next question, but Sinatra saw
in Chief's concerns the same fear he'd seen after the Bottle Banger
was thrown off the balcony. "Who told you to go in this room and lie
down in this bed?"

"I was tired. I'm sorry. I'll go back to work now."

"Are you alone?"

"Alone. Yes."

"Frank, get Dr. Kaplan up here again, with Piperno."

Seth held to the simple story. "Serviss found me wandering and he brought
me back to the hospital. I'd heard there were shortages and I wanted
to help Center Camp prepare, so I sent him up here to take inventory."

Piperno supported Kaplan. "It's all I hear these days: inventory
this, inventory that, and all sorts of shortages. We want to protect
people before they get hurt or sick. Don't we, Dr. Kaplan? He was
hurt. We sewed him up."

Seth agreed with him. Piperno added, "I'm not familiar with the
man who found Dr. Kaplan but he's a hero for bringing him back. And
the sooner he can finish the Center Camp med supplies inventory,
the sooner I, as chief of Medicine, a position I still say deserves to
be included as a separate committee of which I should be the head,
can get back to the work of medicine."

Chief asked Hopper if he was finished in the house.

"Yes, I am," said Hopper.

Frank waited to be alone again with Chief. "We're really running out of food. Don't be worried about a man who fell asleep in a
comfortable bed."

Frank asked Go Bruins to find a camera.

"There's a few in the house, what kind?"

"The one that's closest."

# Pippi, oranges chief

Pippi could put another five oranges into the basket without any falling out, but no one recorded the weight and she wasn't being paid, so she climbed back down the ladder, her chain rattling on the metal steps. She unloaded the basket in the big wagon behind the tractor, which carried the oranges to the storage sheds.

In the morning before work, the chief of the people, who wasn't called Chief, assembled all the workers in the white cinder-block church. Everyone joined a line leading to where he stood beneath the man nailed to the cross, a circle of thorns sticking into his head, a bleeding knife wound on his side, cloth tied around his waist, his mouth open, probably crying in pain, and looking up to the sky, maybe not to be embarrassed in front of any friends if they were on the ground looking up at him. One by one the people waited their turn to stand in front of their chief, where they opened their mouths and stuck out their tongues at him. Drawing from a can of Garlic Seafood–flavored Pringles, he put one—just one—of those Pringles on each extended tongue. Then he waved his hand in front of their faces a few times, and then they pointed a finger at themselves, tapping their chests four times in a diamond pattern.

Pippi wasn't sure she was pointing at herself in the right places, but no one showed her how to do it any other way.

The chief was the only one who spoke to her in words she could understand. She was certain that a few times, when no one knew she was nearby, they spoke the way she spoke, but when they saw her, they talked that other way. And they used that other way of talking even when showing her how to do the work they assigned her.

She was locked in her trailer at the end of the day and someone brought food to her. They had a lot of vodka, tequila, and wine, and they gave her enough to pass out. There were two magazines called *People*, but she didn't know any of the people in them. There was a pack of cigarettes under the bed.

☢

# AutoZone, Mrs. AutoZone

Eckmann's ambition, Eckmann's reason for living, the source of his charisma, the intensity of his devotion: if Mrs. AutoZone could talk to Eckmann now, she would have told him—nothing. Mrs. AutoZone would never tell anything to anyone but AutoZone himself, but not because she might say anything to unmask her. There was nothing more to know about her now except her name. The only thing in life that she was sure of was that AutoZone loved her because she was everyone he had forgotten. He could see the ghosts of the forgotten in her attention to him, her concern for order in the hidden corners of the garage. They liked to get on the floor and pick up trash together. Until the Driftette—Shamblerina—returned from wherever it is she went, no one had ever worried about the elements of AutoZone's life that distracted him from his own capacity for happiness. As AutoZone made love to her when she came back to the motor pool after the Burn, he worried that she was just acting as the toy of some fuckhead Bottle Banger who had used her and abandoned her, that she was doing what was expected of her instead of what she wanted and could give by choice. But she seemed to like what he did to her and like what she did to him. There was nothing awkward or clumsy about her. She didn't come like a Driftette, that tiny shudder.

He said to her, "Inside of you, you're verified."

# Siouxsie Banshee, Frank Sinatra

Frank drove downtown again to show Siouxsie the picture of Kraft Serviss.

"That's him," she said. "Nole Hazard."

"No question?"

"He's the one Chief has been waiting for."

"Seth Kaplan was lying about how he met Hazard. Why? The dead body in the rail yard, Tesla's fall from the hotel balcony, maybe Pippi's disappearance, all that connects to Nole Hazard. But if he was here to attack Chief, why did he go to sleep in that bedroom? Why was he taking inventory up and down Center Camp? Chief didn't recognize him. Chief didn't recognize Reuven Abarbanel, the dead lawyer from Silver Lake, either. I wanted to arrest this man but Chief said no. Why wouldn't Chief arrest this man? Even as a precaution. What do you think Chief is accomplishing by not arresting him? Help me, Siouxsie."

"Because it's over for him. He failed to protect the Fence."

Frank was quiet. "I'm head of Security. That's my job, more than Chief's."

"Look at what we really are. What can we really do?"

"I want to save your life."

"Well that's a comfort. From who or what?"

"Stay in the hotel tomorrow night. Don't go out on Figueroa. I'm not supposed to tell you this, but Chief is sending all the Drifters out to the desert."

"All of them?"

"As many as he can. We can't feed them anymore."

"When they're gone will there be enough food?"

"I don't know."

"Do me a favor, Frank."

"If I can."

"Fuck me."

# Hopper, Seth, Piperno

Back at the hospital, Piperno told Seth, "Don't do anything on your own again. Ask me first." He looked at the requisition lists on Hopper's clipboard. "This is useless, all of it. These aren't good lists. We'll send someone else. Stay away from Center Camp."

After Piperno left for wherever he was going, Hopper said goodbye to Seth. "I have to follow Chief."

"You can't follow Chief. He's Chief. He's in charge. He has people around him all the time."

"He knows where Robin is. That's why her room hasn't changed. I have to follow him until she comes back."

"She's with Chief. She won't want to be with you."

"She's my wife and she wants to be with me."

"I wanted Marci to be with me. She's not."

"She wasn't your wife."

"Chief doesn't want to see you in Center Camp again."

"I know how to hide."

"Really? If you knew how to hide you'd still be in Chief's house."

Hopper's Silent Voice made a new sound, a long howl of malicious delight. "Haaa! He's right, he's right!"

"What?" asked Seth. "You're listening to it again. I can tell."

Hopper understood that something was over. He said to his Silent Voice: "You're not going to help me anymore."

"No. You found her."

"Not yet. I haven't seen her."

"I can't get you any closer."

# Shannon, Erin, the Stripers

On the day of the Feast, as the buses were parked off Figueroa and the food trucks lined up on either side of the street, Shannon, Erin, and the Stripers left Center Camp dressed for the Playa: in motorcycle goggles, long silk scarves, top hats, fingerless gloves, sequin vests, and platform boots laced to the knee. They carried the usual black leather backpacks for food and water. Chief saw them from his window—Shannon no different than the others—and thought of this as a sign that Shannon's charm had faded and she now had no more than an equal share of whatever it was that made the Stripers interesting.

At the Playa, the group climbed into The Woman's lower chamber.

"We'll wait until the sun goes down," said Shannon, tilting an ear upward and scanning the air for the advent of new sounds. "The crowds have their ideas tonight."

"The crowds aren't here," said Jobe.

"I can hear them," said the singer. "It's in the air, the way they're going to align with my music."

Helary taped the microphone to Shannon's cheek and tested the connection to the Playa sound system, the speakers hidden in The Man and The Woman. They plugged in the karaoke machine with Shannon's songs, and with the volume low, Shannon sang a verse. The system worked. Jobe offered Shannon a bottle of Grey Goose and Shannon pushed it away.

"I don't need it now. What I need now is for all of you to be quiet. Nobody look at me. Leave me alone. Don't talk to me. Let me do what I'm going to do. Erin, get the music ready."

"It's ready." As she said this, she gave Shannon a new chisel.

"Don't hit Play until you know it's time."

"How will I know it's time?"

"I'll tell you."

"What's the signal?"

"Erin, are you stupid or scared? I'll count down from ten. Now, all of you, go."

Shannon kissed the chisel.

The official Shannon Squier autobiography, published two months before the first American case of NK3, listed all the concerts she'd given on her last tour, by date, city, venue, size of audience. There were 151 concerts in arenas and stadiums. Every seat was sold at every concert. She wrote, "My tour netted $142,580,400. More than any woman has made on a single tour. The stage is as much my home as the ocean is home to the dolphins, and please my beauties, if you have to eat something that was alive, only eat line-caught tuna, because our friends the dolphins are trapped and killed in big fishing nets." She understood her own importance as a simple fact, not an opinion. She was more important than Chief, more important than June Moulton or Frank Sinatra or anyone else who might bring fear to the Drifters. She knew this. "Erin!"

"Ready?"

"Not yet. Why did I sing?"

"Because there was nothing else for you."

"How do you know?"

"It's in your book."

Jobe said, "Maybe you sang for money."

"No, money is a simplification. I sang for something, a thing, something money can buy."

Erin said, "You sang because there was nothing else for you. You sang because you loved the people who loved you, people like me. That's what you wrote."

Quiet Toffe spoke up. "Erin is right. You sang for love."

Shannon was about to tell Helary to turn on the music but stopped herself. "I'm going to start without the music. Turn it on only when I signal you, Helary."

Helary asked, "Shannon, how will I know the signal?"

"I'll point to you and nod. Will that work? Until then, let me do this my way." Shannon put a finger to her lips for everyone to be quiet and climbed the narrow ladder through The Woman's torso until she reached the head. She sat cross-legged, looking at the Playa through The Woman's eyes. The Man, her stiff companion, looked forward and backward, but at nothing in particular.

# Pippi

She sat in the orchard while the family picked oranges from trees four rows away. She could hear them, but they spoke that other language. One of the women brought her lunch.

She could have told them that their precautions didn't fit the situation. But she didn't know how to explain that situation to herself, so how could she describe it to anyone else? Chief wanted her safely out of Center Camp and here she was. And for now she had to trust Chief's choice for her, or pretend to trust it.

Or not. She had the cigarette pack under the bed, small stones were everywhere, and she could ask for a pen and paper, but what would she write and where would she throw it? She was on the other side of the Fence, and so, she understood, was he, whoever he was.

She couldn't look for him if she couldn't walk and even if she could walk, she didn't have the key to the padlock that kept her chained to the orange tree.

❂

# Siouxsie Banshee, Frank Sinatra

Sinatra stayed downtown with Siouxsie Banshee. There was nothing
for him to do now except stand on the hotel roof with her and watch
as the buses were parked a block from the lines of food trucks on
Figueroa. They watched Inventory workers push racks of costumes
onto sidewalks. The Drifters put them on: aliens, cowboys, firemen,
zombies, baseball players, football players, doctors, nurses, hippies,
punks, soldiers of a dozen different armies, Arab terrorists in suicide
belts, nuns, priests, Klansmen, slaves. "I wouldn't have met you if
everything wasn't so strange," she said.

"Did you study why there are two kinds of Jesus?" he asked her.

"Religious art? I don't think so. What are you thinking about?"

"There's two kinds of crosses. A cross with Jesus and a cross
without. What scared Jesus off the cross? Or did the empty cross
mean that there were two versions of the story? In one version—and
I can't call it the first version because I don't know if one story is older
than the other—the cross is empty because Jesus knows the only way
to stay on the cross is if his hands are nailed to the cross beam. So
is the empty cross the cross of expectation of torture, or the cross of
escape? But on the empty crosses, there's no trace of the hardware,
the nails through the palms, no streaks of red to show he was bleeding. In the other version, where Jesus gets nailed to the cross, is that
the church for people who like to watch him die?"

"I know furniture. But I'd like to know more."

Frank tried to inspect the dry ravines in his brain, the places
eroded by NK3, where he once might have easily found the answer
to the riddle of the two crosses, but he was at the uncomfortable
limits of his intuition. In the church of the empty cross, what would
they have prayed for?

They went back to her room, got undressed, and made each other smile.

Redwings knocked at the door and announced himself. "Frank, sir, it's Redwings."

"I know your voice, Redwings."

"Yes sir, and I need to notify you personally, sir, of the conditions surrounding the Playa."

Frank let him in. "Shannon Squier is in The Woman's head with Erin and the Stripers below and she's going to sing and the word has gone around and everyone inside the Fence, and what is troubling and the reason I am interrupting your time here with Siouxsie Banshee is that from my reports when I say everyone I mean everyone, is on their way to the Playa by foot, art car, Segway, and bike. And she hasn't made a sound yet but still, folks are making a circle around The Woman, just waiting for Shannon Squier to sing. And Erin did not check this first with Security or Chief. Those who were there at the Burn and saw Shannon dancing have been bragging about it to those who didn't go, which was most everyone, and on the reputation of the excitement of that event, no one wants to miss Shannon's return. I say partly that excitement was for the big plane that flew above our heads but I see their point. We can have an observation team on top of the Wilshire Towers condo looking over the Playa, but no crowd control. I got everyone in the Security team on Figueroa, getting ready to move the Drifters to the buses."

"Redwings, you have the bike with the sidecar?"

"Yes sir."

"My trusted friend, always ready. Siouxsie, I can use your help here if you go to the roof and watch the street. Redwings will set you up with communications."

"I want to be with you."

"You will be."

"Thank you, Frank."

"For needing your help?" He kissed her and left her.

✴

# Gunny Sea Ray, Hopper

Gunny Sea Ray called Frank to tell him he'd watched Hopper, in green hospital clothing, take a charged electric bicycle from the rack outside the hospital.

"Gunny, wherever this Kraft Serviss or Nole Hazard goes, stay close to him. If he goes to the Playa, stay near him. If he goes back to Center Camp, stay near him. Let the man go where he wants. He's working with someone else, or being protected by someone else. Serviss-Hazard wants something from Chief, and it's not Chief's life. And see if anyone else is watching him, following him the way you're following him. I think he has a partner. He might be eating Corn Nuts."

Gunny Sea Ray followed on his Segway, forced to go slowly so that Hopper wouldn't see him. The traffic was heavy toward the Playa and Gunny was certain Hazard didn't know he was being followed. Gunny Sea Ray lost him on the road up to Center Camp but found him again, hiding in bushes with a view of Chief's terrace. The green hospital clothes were not camouflage and his binoculars reflected light. Gunny called Redwings with his report.

"He's watching Chief's house with binoculars."

"See a weapon?"

"No."

"Then you don't have to do anything now. Call right away if something changes, but otherwise, keep me posted every thirty. Frank and I are on the way to oversee the unfolding events on the Playa."

# Vayler

Vayler walked through the Drifter crowds lining up for their last meal and wondered about his basic mistake. He should have worked closely with Toby Tyler, he thought. She always wanted extra Drifters to do the heavy work, because she believed in the endless surplus. If she knew what Vayler kept hidden, she would have understood the need to leave most of the Drifters in the desert instead of sharing the food with them. It would have meant harder work for the First Wave, but the resources would have sufficed.

He stopped at a Korean truck for thin slices of gristled and fatty barbecued beef. The Drifters had never looked happier. A few of the regular Bottle Bangers stood naked pretending to be Shamblerettes, dancing badly to the bottle banging of their friends.

Everything was in place, waiting for word from Chief.

# The Woman

The sun was low over the Fence.

Erin climbed to Shannon. "You have to start singing."

"I will."

"When?"

"Not yet."

"You see the crowd. They're waiting. Impatient."

"No one has to stay."

"Frank Sinatra and Redwings are here. They're on top of that building, on the roof, watching us."

Erin waved to them.

"They can't see you."

"Call the Lamplighter Guild."

Soon, the Lamplighter Guild, in their double file procession, faces hidden in their heavy cowls, came from their encampment bearing torches. A shrouded Lamplighter lit the first fuel-soaked tiki torch and the Lamplighter to her right touched flame to the torch, and then the next Lamplighter followed in solemn ceremony, and then the next.

When a hundred torches were burning, Shannon tested her voice and sang one note, a low O, extending it without raising the pitch. Shannon was only introducing the song, expecting to signal for the music, but the crowd wasn't returning the usual involuntary cheer sucked from them by theatrical habit. No one had heard a voice alone like this in four years. They didn't know what to do. The crowd settled, everyone sat down.

# Shannon, Helary, Erin

Redwings was telling Sinatra: "This is the biggest assembly we've had inside the Fence, Frank. In all the four years I don't recall a crowd this big. I didn't know there was this many of us."

"What would that change if you did know there were so many of us?"

"Frank, sir, as I proposed the thought, I'm ashamed that I can't comprehend an answer. You're probing the limits of my understanding."

Frank was about to say, "Good friend, your limits are limitless," when Shannon's voice reached them. The long O continued and Frank waited to hear the singer break the note to take a breath, but it continued, a sound that was clear and rough and human. He couldn't speak.

Shannon was gone, the Playa was gone, Frank was with three other boys, on bicycles, on a path beside the ocean. He was in a desert war, he was in the Hollywood Bowl filled with people singing along to *The Sound of Music*.

☢

# Chief

Chief's house. He couldn't hear Shannon clearly, wasn't sure if she was singing a song or making it up, but as he picked the music out of the night's ambient background, he remembered a woman in a restaurant. They weren't going to see each other again. She asked for a last kiss and he said he couldn't. He didn't think the woman was Pippi, but she might have been. Then a new memory: he was on a boat, there's a shark following, and a man said, "We're going to need a bigger boat."

He remembered looking for the mayor, to kill him.

☢

# The Playa

Shannon was invisible to the crowd. From the Playa, there was no Shannon, there was only the miracle of The Woman, singing.

Shannon watched the crowd as she went from a loud and sustained high note to a note halfway down the scale, in the safe middle of her range, where she could hold the note gently and quietly, not recovering from the high note's strain but distributing the high note's power throughout her body and absorbing it into her blood. She looked down at Helary and Jobe. Their eyes were closed.

She didn't know what she was doing. She was just singing because it felt amazing to let her voice go on without intention.

She sang: a long OOOOO.

Shannon looked at the crowd's closed eyes as her reflection. She was the only real weapon inside the Fence and for all she knew the only weapon in the world.

She sang it again: OOOOO.

When she had performed for the Drifters and Bottle Bangers in the street on Figueroa the night of the Burn—without her voice, with only her rhythm to provoke them—isolated feelings were all that she could release with the encouragement of her bottle banging. But the verified and rehabbed First and Second Wavers surrounding her on the Playa were getting more from her than just the beat.

Shannon saw that the crowd was not a series of concentric circles like the rings of a tree, but a coil, a single line starting at The Woman's feet, wrapping around The Woman and The Man, spiraling away as newcomers took the next place, extending the serpent's tail.

On the night of the Burn, the jet had broken the connection between Shannon and the Figueroa Drifters, but here on the Playa, in the open field ten miles from downtown, as she sang in her own voice for the First Wave, there was that feeling and then a series of pictures. No one knew that some of the pictures belonged to their old lives and some of them belonged to movies and television. They couldn't make out the difference between the memory of crying at a fifth birthday party and crying over the act break in any one of all those episodes of television they'd watched. The sadness they could feel now might be about the loss of someone they loved in their real lives before NK3 or it might be the memory of a child dying in an episode of *ER*. They didn't know the difference between their dead or drifting parents or baskets of puppies on YouTube.

Erin thought of one of the pictures in her bedroom, standing between her father and mother, with their arms around her shoulders. They were on a high point overlooking a lake, with pine trees everywhere. She remembered her father asking someone else to use his camera to take the picture. Just that: "Excuse me," her father said. "Could you take our picture? You just have to push this button."

⠀

⠀

## Siouxsie Banshee, Vayler Monokeefe

On the roof of the Ritz-Carlton, Siouxsie Banshee heard Shannon's voice and saw the Drifters moving. She called Frank.

"Something is happening. The Drifters are moving toward Wilshire. They're dropping their food and leaving Figueroa and they're on the way to the Fence. I'm coming with them. I'm coming to you."

"If they try to open the Fence, they'll be shot."

"She's calling everyone to join her, Frank. I can feel it. If it weren't for you, I'd . . . I don't know. I'm confused. Shamblers, Drifters, Driftettes, Verified and Unverified Second Wave. That's what I see from the roof here, Frank. Bottle Bangers dressed as bleeding Driftettes, food-wagon chefs in gun-shop camouflage suits, and squadrons of Transport Service workers in high school cheerleader uniforms. They're on their way, walking down Wilshire, all dressed up, everyone but me."

"A soldier. I think that's what I was. I made a mistake in not bringing you inside."

"This is the end of the Fence, tonight."

"Why? How?"

"Because all of civilization, every civilization, every country, collapses under the weight of its own stupidity when the conditions it ignored put on costumes and march in a parade that cannot be stopped."

As the Drifters left the food trucks, as the people working in the trucks left them, too, as the Security detail left Figueroa for the march to the Fence, Vayler wanted to call Chief to say, "It's not my fault." But he knew he was wrong. This was all his fault. He tried to run ahead of the crowd, to stop them before they attacked the East Gate, because Chief would never forgive him if the grand buffet turned into fuel for a revolution.

"Turn back," he tried to say, but he couldn't hear his own voice anymore. As the crowd approached the Fence, Shannon sent the message to open the gate, and the Drifters, after four years of exclusion, poured through the Fence, and Vayler disappeared under their feet.

## Chief, Go Bruins

Go Bruins asked Chief: "What's Shannon singing? Is that a song? We should go to the Playa and hear it."

"Not a good idea, Go Bruins. I can tell from what I hear she's put something in the song, like a poison. We're safe here, but only a little."

"If it's dangerous, you can stop it."

"You think so?"

"You're Chief."

"That's true. I was once the chief of police of Los Angeles. The last chief of police."

"I did not know that."

"I was one of the first ten people through rehab. The mayor, the chief of police, the head of the fire department, the head of medicine at County General Hospital, the head of the California National

Guard. That was Toby Tyler, but her name was different. We were the first two to wake up. We made some choices. They weren't all the smartest choices. The mayor ran away. I don't know where he went or what happened to him. Perhaps he died."

"A lot of people died."

"And more will die, Go Bruins," said Chief, pointing toward the crowds on the Playa. "Look at them." He showed Go Bruins how to focus the strongest telescope. "Can you lead them, Go Bruins?"

"Me, Chief?"

"No one but you knows where to find Pippi, right?"

"Unless you change your mind, sir, no one else will know."

"Then I charge you with this, Go Bruins. While I go to Pippi to bring her back, I want you to be the Chief. I know you can do that. You believe what I tell you, don't you?"

"Always, Chief."

"Then those people are yours to manage while I'm gone." While Go Bruins searched for faces in the crowd—impossible at this distance—Chief went into the house, took one of the handguns from the closet in his bedroom, returned to the terrace, and shot Go Bruins in the side of the head, to keep bullet or blood from the telescope.

# Hopper, Gunny Sea Ray

Was it a gunshot? Gunny Sea Ray had a better view of Hopper than of Chief's house on the hill. Most of the big houses in Center Camp were made of stone and the single crack of the explosion bounced around the mansions. Frank Sinatra had taught his men not to expose themselves until they were certain of a gun's placement. In the early days of their recovered consciousness the Security teams were not yet certain that attackers could come from any direction, and that snipers could hide from Inventory squads on the search for box stores that hadn't been looted. But Gunny was sure that the gunshot came from Chief's.

When Gunny saw the man he knew as Nole put his binoculars back in his bag and move through the brush toward Chief's, he called Redwings, but Redwings didn't answer.

Gunny thought about Frank, and what advice Frank would give, and then, what Frank would say to Gunny for making the wrong choice here. And Gunny's idea of what would make Frank angry with him was simple. If Gunny Sea Ray knew that someone in Chief's house had fired a gun while a stranger was breaking into the house, he needed help.

# Chief

With Go Bruins dead, no one but Chief knew where to find Pippi. So that was it. After sending so many Drifters on their final bus rides to the desert—to keep as much death as possible away from the city—now there was a murder in Center Camp.

All he had left in the world was Pippi, and he wanted to be with her. Yes, she resented him or hated him, but he would go to her now, while everyone was away and no one needed him or wanted him. "This is how things collapse," he said to Go Bruins's body. "This is what it means to be human now. It used to mean something else. Or maybe that's vanity. Maybe it was always this way. I don't know. Things feel wrong. I pretended they felt right, but that was all it was. I encouraged myself to believe in my plan and I had enough of the aura of confidence to convince others that their self-doubts were true, and that anyone who trusted himself over me was doomed. So long as they didn't know that things were ever different, they didn't have a cause to panic. They left that to me. I wasted my time with the dual project of Burn and preserve. Burn to protect the community of the Fence, and preserve what had value and would again. Rather than? We learned how to plant food. That was all we needed to know. There are things we overcomplicate, Go Bruins. No, not we, me. Blame it on me. There are things I overcomplicated. The Founders? We were the Founders."

Hidden behind the terrace wall, Hopper listened to Chief talking to the body. Gunny Sea Ray couldn't hear Chief and wanted a better view of Hopper. Hidden from both of them, Gunny Sea Ray felt safe leaving the protection of the brush to move quietly up the sidewalk.

Born before the plague as Felipe Louma and after the plague reborn as Gunny Sea Ray, he was about to die again, but in this edition of his life, there would be no sequel. There was a man behind him with a knife and a gun. There was nothing personal in Felipe/ Gunny's death, but the man with the knife and gun wanted to follow Hopper, since Hopper was on his way to Robin, to the woman he believed was his wife. To get closer to Hopper he'd have to be ahead of Gunny Sea Ray, and having come this far, what was one more death? He crept up on Gunny Sea Ray and slit his throat.

# Siouxsie Banshee

Siouxsie saw that the gate constricted the long parade of costumed Drifters and that as her area of the line approached the threshold into the once forbidden city, the crowd around her thickened. The distant music tickled an associated image out of her brain: she was waiting in the line in a supermarket at Thanksgiving, waiting to pass through customs at the airport in Moscow, waiting in the lunch crowd line at In-N-Out Burger.

The immediate group around her was spun away from the current, the central human stream to her left pushing her away to the right. She could only join that flow by kicking the legs of a Drifter in a county sheriff's brown shirt. He hit back at her and she moved into the gap he opened when he returned the pain she'd given him. She accepted the pain and, moving on through the line, she slapped heads, pinched and twisted ears, kicked at the backs of knees to force her new enemies down. And at the gate, her feet lifted from the ground and then she was through. She was inside the Fence, and she was running forward with room around her, all the room she needed so that nothing would get in her way now.

In the Playa, the new arrivals settled at the fringes of the seated thousands, finding their place at the end of the coil, keeping their faces turned toward Shannon like the mirrors around the solar heating plant in the desert, all the sun's bright rays shining on the central column that turned the light to heat and the heat to steam, which spun the turbine, which generated the electricity, which Shannon didn't need because now she was her own generator.

When Siouxsie Banshee passed the cover of the last tall building before the Playa, the sound of Shannon's voice hit and she lost her balance as all the music she'd ever heard came back to her like the bass sounding through the subwoofer of a car beside her at a stoplight and none of this was conscious except the flux of the way what started as pain turned into charm, and she too wanted to find her space in the curved line surrounding the woman at the center of this delivery system. But she had a lover, and the forgotten love songs contained within the waves of Shannon's O increased her love for Frank, so Siouxsie left the line and rode on Shannon's power toward the tower where Frank was waiting for her.

On the condo rooftop, Redwings couldn't get through to Gunny Sea Ray. "Frank, sir, it scares me to say this but I have to share with you my concern about Gunny Sea Ray not calling me for the last two hours, which is not like him when he's on assignment. He's an independent man of course but he's also a man bound by connection to us to keep us aware of what he's doing. Many times I've heard from him when he just had nothing more to say than that he was where he was supposed to be, doing what was expected of him, and that whatever the task, there was no new information except that things were steady."

"Call him again."

"It appears to worry you as well that Nole Hazard may have discovered he was being followed."

"And did what with that discovery? Kill Gunny Sea Ray? Anything is possible but I can't help feeling that I've taken a measure of the man and that by putting Gunny Sea Ray in place to study him, I was not putting Gunny's life at risk."

"Then why have him hide?"

"I don't have a satisfying answer for that, good Redwings, except that keeping track of Nole Hazard let me keep track of Chief without Chief seeing my deputy."

Redwings wanted Sinatra to say more but the word from below was that Siouxsie Banshee had been seen crossing into the Playa from the breach in the Fence, and after that was lost in the crowd.

# Chief, Hopper, Shannon Squier

*If I give up now*, Chief thought, *if I go to Pippi, I can't come back to the city. Someone will replace me tonight if I haven't already been replaced.*

He passed through a shifting series of moments of melancholy, as though he knew what he should regret, which slowed time by taking him away from his responsibility to lead a confused and frightened . . . people . . . city . . . the confused and frightened people of a city besieged by the living shrouds of its former aristocracy, called to the Playa by a song, and in the fog of the vanity of aimless sorrow he forgot that just because he was Chief, he had authority. He was one thing only now, his own distraction by a torment from Shannon that she had planned on.

In the Playa, Shannon could feel what Chief was thinking. She could feel what everyone was thinking, a total simultaneous clair-voyance. She did nothing more than make one clear tone to release everyone from the fantasy that Shannon was important while they were nothing.

Siouxsie Banshee cried to herself, "Will I ever see him again through all of this mess?" And she was answered by Shannon. "He's on top of that building, on the roof, where he always goes when there's a big event like this. Don't cry; don't be scared."

Shannon told Sinatra that Siouxsie was on the Playa.

Sinatra sent Redwings to find her.

Shannon told Redwings where to look. He grabbed Siouxsie's hand and pulled her away from the crowd.

Shannon remembered a conversation she'd had with Stephen Colbert on *The Late Show*, about her belief in ESP and God. "Think about the freeway and all the cars going seventy miles an hour so close to each other, and that most of the accidents are caused by drunk drivers. This tells me that the roads are safer when everyone is sober because everyone on the road and in life is in psychic connection, and alcohol breaks the connection while making you feel like the connection has never been better, and that in the boozy connection, everyone on the road is giving you permission. But it's the other way around. This is why people who drive drunk are so dangerous, because they're disconnected from the human flow. I wish I could write a song about this, but I truly believe the reason I connect to my audience is that I never sing in any condition other than truly sober. I hope that what I'm saying makes sense. One love."

Colbert said, "Thank God for Uber, then."

And while she remembered this moment from her first life of celebrity, in the center of that coil of all those First Wavers, Second Wavers, and Drifters, Driftettes, Shamblers, Shamblerinas, and Bottle Bangers, all that remained of their human distinction was washing up on the sands of the Playa, which absorbed those distinctions like they were the last slick of the lather of broken waves.

She wanted to wake up the world and be its leader but it was too late to wake up the world.

She thought she was there to give them power, but they were melting.

She would sing and they would listen to her until they all starved to death.

Running up the fire stairs to the roof, Siouxsie Banshee asked Redwings, "Is there any food up there, Redwings?"

"Wherever Chief goes food goes, but Chief himself is missing from the observation area. I very much hope that we can find a few old protein bars, because otherwise to my regret I am at a loss as to how to get you or any of us fed quick tonight. We were supposed to be at the big food trough on Figueroa. If you haven't put this thought in your thought quiver, what Shannon Squier has pulled off with her strange concert this night of nights is nothing less than a profound revelation into the essence of things being sorely fucked up inside the Fence. Save your breath—it's twelve more floors we have to go up."

"Redwings," Siouxsie asked him. "What about you? Aren't you hungry, too?"

"I don't know," he answered. He pushed his mind through his body, inspecting himself for hunger. It was there. "I suppose I am. This could be a problem. We were ordered to say that Vayler counted wrong and there's plenty for years to come. But at the same time, who are we going to say that to now? The evidence is to the contrary."

"Is this the end of Center Camp?" asked Siouxsie.

"Center Camp as a specific place or Center Camp as a state of mind, like being a true biker is a state of mind, a brotherhood, not a locale?"

"As an art person, as Sonia Pryce, I would have wanted to preserve Center Camp as a construct of organization, as a subject of contemplation, as a relic, if you see what I'm saying. But as Siouxsie Banshee . . ."

"Which is the only way I know you. And sorry for the interruption. Go on."

"I always wanted to see Center Camp the way I saw the hotel roof garden the night of the Burn, for the privilege of privilege. I'm really very simple, underneath the stuff that's been left in a jumble of unrelated discernments."

"I regret the thought to say that you may have missed your opportune moment to have known Center Camp in its spectacular privacy before the crowds took over, Siouxsie Banshee. And the Burns were better."

"Oh noble Redwings, my life is one missed opportunity. Except for you and Frank Sinatra."

Redwings felt an old but so long unfamiliar flood of good feeling for Siouxsie; he loved her like knowing her was the same as going to the movies with your buddies not to see the movie that's playing but only to see the first trailer for *Star Wars*. She was parole, she was Mendocino weed from a brother Angel in Yucaipa before he crossed the edge and hit a wall, and she was the sound of a shovel full of graveyard dirt on his casket. Only an Angel can throw dirt on another Angel and there's a long line of brother Angels from America and not just America but the world, to pay their respects and more.

Redwings took the woman's hand like it was a funeral for a child.

With his other hand he pushed open the stairwell door and they were on the roof.

"Frank, I found her. And she's hungry. And I'm hungry, Frank."

Frank couldn't hear them, because Shannon Squier had just made contact with him. "Frank, are you sorry you found me?"

"Why?"

"Because I'm taking it all down. The world you built. Are you sorry about that?"

"Somewhat, yes. Are you sorry I found you?"

"I could have run. Chisel Girl was good at getting away."

"Why did you stay?"

"I was hungry. The way I'm hungry now, the way they're all hungry."

"You don't have to die."

"Of course I do. And so do they. I'll take them across to whatever's on the other side, and we'll all go gently. Wherever we go. Who didn't have to die is Go Bruins. Chief killed him and now he's driving north. Gunny Sea Ray died, too."

"Who killed him?"

"He's called the Teacher."

"Thank you."

The contact was over. Frank told Redwings what Shannon had just told him. Redwings said, "Then I bid that noble princess a grand sincere adios, and however you say good-bye in the mother tongue of the man whose signature of SMERSH we have inscribed in our flesh. Siouxsie Banshee, dear Siouxsie, do you know how to say good-bye in Russian?"

"Maybe I used to, Redwings, but I don't anymore."

"Perhaps we'll have the chance to study up on it."

Frank kissed Siouxsie and then Redwings, and said, "We have work to do."

# Chief

*Places have moods,* thought Chief. *Some things I never forget.* A little more memory, a better sense of the *circumstances,* what surrounds the moment and the place, these things I have. What I have, am, is imperfect compared to before, but I can see just that much that others can't, especially their need for anyone to take my position. Things I can't talk about with anyone, although I might have with Sinatra.

His time at Center Camp finished, Chief took the biggest car, a Dodge Ram truck, and filled the back with food and two crates of vodka. He put two rifles, a shotgun, and three pistols on the backseat, and another pistol under his seat. He expected to be followed and had no plan beyond getting to Pippi first and taking her north, no matter who was there or if NK3 was still dangerous.

Hopper watched from the hill across from the house and while Chief loaded the truck, there was time to find a Lincoln Navigator with a full tank of fuel. When Chief drove away, Hopper followed with his lights off. Chief drove to the ridge road overlooking the San Fernando Valley, then down Coldwater Canyon, then to the freeway. Chief drove fast and Hopper followed easily. There were no other cars on the road.

Chief turned north on the 405, toward Bakersfield.

## Frank Sinatra, Siouxsie Banshee, Redwings

They found Gunny Sea Ray and then Go Bruins. They carried the bodies into the house and set the house on fire.

"I was commanded by Chief to find the man who killed Tesla."

Redwings asked him, "What about the man who killed Go Bruins and Gunny Sea Ray?"

"That's two people, Redwings. Shannon told us where to look for one. Perhaps we'll find the other."

They went north, as Shannon told them, in the Audi RS7 Frank kept in Center Camp. They drove as fast as the car could go.

# Shannon Squier, Erin

Shannon felt Frank and his crew drive away, leaving the outer reaches of her awareness. Erin sent her a thought: "Do you need anything?"

She thanked her. "No."

As the Drifters linked to the end of the coil, the panic from the unwelcome invasion subsided. First Wave and Shamblers together, everyone committed to their shared fate as Shannon stopped thinking about anything except her beloved audience, her millions of fans, and what they wanted from her. She raised the pitch of her endless wordless song, drawing everyone's fragments into the shape of a sphere, and amplified her concentration until the hidden associations inside everything reached everyone at the same time, as though light had no speed limit and so all light arrived at once, and everything was like God's face, impossible to see.

# Hopper

Hopper, in his Navigator, saw a car in his rearview mirror, the headlights off. The car was only visible at the crest of a hill, a shadow against the stars.

"Someone is following me," said Hopper, hoping his Silent Voice would help him. There was no answer.

⚛

# Pippi

She woke up when she heard the oranges chief unlock her door. She was ready to have sex with him if that's what he wanted. It was something she missed. He asked her if she was awake.

"You can see that I am."

"I'm taking off your chain now."

He had the key in his pocket. When he took off the padlock, he put it on a table.

"Because it's over. The Fence is down. Center Camp is finished. They can't do anything for us, and we can't do anything for them. We have no one to talk to there. Your door is open now. No more lock. You're here now. One of us. If you want. Pippi."

"What are you going to do when you run out of Pringles?"

"When I run out of Pringles, I'll tell them that the Founders had this in their plan and that after the Pringles ran out, the Founders wanted us to take a special slice of orange. And if we run out of oranges, I'll find something else that the Founders left for us. Maybe celery. I could cut up a stick of celery and use it for ten people. But for now come for your Pringle. You need it."

"The Founders were here, too?"

"That's the story."

She followed him to the church. He rang the bell and the people came from their cabins and trailers to line up for their Pringles. Pippi was the first in line. The oranges chief wore a green-and-gold shawl over a white robe. He had special Pringles today, Original Flavor, and lifted the can and opened it so everyone could see that the Pringles were fresh.

He waved the open can in front of Pippi. "That smell was put in there before the changes," he said. He directed this to her. "Open wide." He brought the saddle-shaped potato chip to her tongue, and when she tried to close her mouth over it, he drew it back. "Let it sit there, feel it, taste it. They say this is what God tastes like. Have you ever heard of God?"

She shook her head no. He lowered the Pringle to her tongue again. "This time just let it sit there."

# The Teacher

It doesn't matter who was the father. That's what he wanted to tell Robin, even though she wouldn't know what he was talking about. And the little girl was dead. Robin didn't have to run away from him just because he ran away from her.

Do you remember buying the house? We wanted a craftsman house, the green bungalow with a front porch, wanted those green shutters and the stained glass, wanted the fireplace tiles of farm scenes and hay wagons, wanted the yard with the three-legged rescue dog and the redwood swings and the swimming pool. We wanted and we had what we wanted.

I ran away. I stayed in the desert.

I trained the men to find you and bring you back. I could have forced myself to stop thinking about you but I kept your memory alive even if you don't remember any of it. The bones of the little girl. That's my last hope. That you'll see the bones and the pink dress and remember something. She was mine, not his. We knew that. Our child.

I trained him. He was nothing to you, only to me. I had a plan. All that remains of a civilization, human hieroglyphics, rehab, the reconstruction of manifold humanity, single-purpose entities trailing loose ends that spark when dragged across the concrete road.

I returned to the city and walked through the world that nobody there remembered. A look in the eye sometimes, did they know? Couldn't be sure.

She will love me. She will remember me because I'm in there. I can show her the picture.

He slowed down to look at the picture. That is me, that is Robin, that is our baby. Proof.

# Robin

The Pringle was hers now and she closed her mouth over the thing. She kept it on her tongue as the oranges chief directed, and the chip softened. No need to chew. She didn't need the oranges chief to tell her what was next, and she pointed at her chest four times.

"Good-bye," he said.

She was going to tell him that she'd see him later, but the line was long and he had a few hundred Pringles to give away.

She went back to the trailer. The padlock and key were where he'd left them. She put them in her pocket along with the empty cigarette pack and wrapped the forty feet of chain over her right shoulder and under her left arm.

It was dark but she knew where she was. She crossed the road into the orchard. The dogs followed her but quietly and, after a few minutes, didn't care for where she was going and turned back.

In every direction, the orderly grid of the orange groves formed straight lines. It felt like there was no center to anything except the spot where she chose to stand, so she walked along different lines of trees for half an hour until she came to the next paved road. She crossed that road and walked into the next orange grove and switched rows there until she came to a damp irrigation ditch. She followed the ditch until she came to a wheel and gear that controlled a small floodgate. The wheel was rusted shut, which meant it wasn't serviced, which meant no one was likely to be here soon.

Robin put the key to the padlock in the cigarette pack and added a few small stones to give it weight. Then she turned in a circle three times and, with her eyes closed, threw the cigarette pack over a row of trees. She wrapped the chain around her waist and over her shoulders and crossed it over her chest and then around her back again. She ran both ends through the rusted wheel and, with her arms behind her, slipped the shackle on the padlock through the two ends of the chain and snapped it into the padlock body. She was bound too tightly to stretch out on the ground. She leaned against the gate. She wasn't so comfortable, but how long would that last?

# Siouxsie, Frank Sinatra, Redwings

The Audi saw a Porsche ahead of them where the freeway descended into the Central Valley.

Frank recognized the car. "I know that Porsche. He stole it from Center Camp."

"Do we call him Nole Hazard or Kraft Serviss?" asked Redwings.

"Let's ask him," said Siouxsie.

"He's slowing down, Frank. Watch out for what he's avoiding."

"He's not stopping."

"Don't you know he can see us? It's stupid to drive without your lights. You can hit something and where are we? No one can help us."

Redwings agreed. "It's not my place, Frank, to quarrel with your strategical tactics so to speak, but you're not a man who has risen to your position by wasting energy on making the wager that someone may not know you're coming. You're a prominently decisive man, the

best-qualified head of committee I've had the obligation to know. I
would never ride any of my Harleys lights out on a road known to be
an obstacle course made of material out of place."

"Good Redwings, that's why we're in my Audi, four wheels on the
road, instead of your motorcycle, because should we hit something
with one wheel, we have three more to balance the ride. This isn't
the time for your choppers. He's not driving like he knows what the
car can do for him. And every wiggle he makes I make, so unless he
can pass through an obstacle I can't, I'm where I want to be. I want
to know something, and he can tell me. I know he can."

Redwings clapped his hands. "The only way you ever surprise
me is when I forget that I should never be surprised by the way you
put two and three together."

Siouxsie rested a hand on Frank Sinatra's shoulder. "You want
to know who you were, don't you?"

"No, I know who I was, not in the particulars of my life, but in
the positive verification of where I worked. I'm Reynaldo Johnston.
I was the head of security for UCLA before the change and no one
ever replaced me, so I'm still that man with an expanded territory. I
want to know who Chief was."

Siouxsie asked him, "Why does it matter?"

"Chief is running from the man who threw the motor pool worker,
Tesla, from the balcony. Before the Fence went down, I had reason
to protect him. Now I really don't. Redwings, what do you say I say
fuck this caution and I turn on my lights?"

"Can't agree more with you, Frank, but not that I'm understanding who or what we're fucking."

Frank turned on his lights. "This is a fast car, Siouxsie. The
Founders left them for us and then disappeared. The Founders built
them in a place called Germany and put them on a ship and sailed
them to Long Beach and put them on trailers and left them in big
parking lots. All we had to do was pump up the tires and add some
gasoline and use fresh batteries."

"That's a lot."

"Worth it."

Frank hit the gas and the Audi responded with a muffled whine. "I love that sound. It's not as pleasant as the steady loud murmur of a BMW but it has its own charm."

Redwings agreed. "Like a Harley at idle, the sound of promise."

Sinatra passed the car ahead of him, the Porsche, driven by a man none had ever seen before.

"Who's that?" asked Siouxsie.

"It should be Nole Hazard," said Frank. "Hang on, though." Frank pulled alongside the other car and then drove closer, until the cars were a foot apart, then closed the gap and brushed the side of the Audi against the Porsche. He pulled ahead and forced the Porsche into the guardrail, where it stopped.

Frank grabbed his gun from the glove compartment and was out of the car, followed by Redwings and Siouxsie Banshee. Frank took the driver out of the car and frisked him while Redwings looked in the car and found the pistol under the driver's seat along with six bags of Corn Nuts.

"Well hello, hello, Reynaldo," said the Porsche driver.

"That's not my name anymore."

"That's what I used to call you. Old habits, you know what I mean, Reynaldo?"

"Siouxsie? Do you know what he means?"

"We haven't had habits in four years. But he knows who you were." She asked the man, "How do you know Frank used to be Reynaldo?"

"I got around."

"If you know Frank's old name, do you know me? Do you know my old name? It's Sonia Pryce. P-R-Y-C-E."

"No."

"Who are you?" she asked.

Frank had a different question. "Why were you in the storm drain following Nole Hazard?"

"I'm still following him. A Lincoln Navigator, up ahead. He's leading me to my wife. We should hurry."

"Did you kill Tesla?"

"Who's Tesla?"

"From the motor pool. I think you threw him from the balcony."

"Not I. I never heard of Tesla. Did you ask Nole?"

"If he did it, why did he do it?"

"No idea. I wasn't there."

"Who was the Shamblerina with Nole Hazard in the hotel room when Tesla was murdered?"

"That's now two questions about a murder, if that's what it was, that I had nothing to do with. I'll tell you this. I saw Nole near the river with a woman, but I don't know who she was."

"But you know him, Nole, yes?"

"Better than he knows himself."

"The woman with him, she was naked and dirty and he dressed her and cleaned her up. She was a Shamblerina. We know that much. And he fed her. Do you know why?"

"I can guess. Residual compassion or something that I didn't see before I sent him to find my wife. He wasn't supposed to do that. If he'd done things the right way he would have led her out of the Fence, brought her to me, and I would have, well, left him behind and gone back to Palm Springs with her."

"The singer told me your name is Teacher."

"People used to call me Mr. Mayor. I was the last elected mayor of Los Angeles. My term has expired. So you can call me Mr. Mayor, but that would be out of deference or kindness, and I can't expect either from you, can I? Very different conditions. But it's why I had to send . . . the one you call Nole. Someone would have recognized me. Chief, or someone around him, Toby Tyler of Systems, the early victors in the race for rehab. Like me. Only one person could be Chief, and I wasn't popular. I ran away to the desert and stayed there waiting to be invited back, but Chief and the rest of you, who were supposed to return power to those of us who were in control before NK3, kept the control. You took over their houses. You put up the Fence. Deny that."

Frank said, "Why should I? We let the rich die or drift and the ones who tried to get back in, homing in on the beacon of their old routines, we drove out to the desert. Like you, Mr. Mayor. The rest we left banging their bottles down Figueroa."

"Is that true?" asked Redwings.

"He's not lying," said Siouxsie. "Frank never lies."

"Amen to that. Frank Sinatra don't lie," said Redwings. "He's a man of his word. That does make me a little sad."

"And what do you want with Nole Hazard or Kraft Serviss?"

"His name is Hopper. Well trained. We won't catch him. So let's find Chief. He erased me from the woman I loved. Keep my guns. Reynaldo, I have no fight with you and you have no claim on me."

"He's not Reynaldo anymore," said Siouxsie. "And I'm not Sonia Pryce. If you want to call yourself the Mayor, I can't stop you. You're looking for the woman who doesn't remember you. What are you going to do to convince her she still loves you?"

"When she sees me, she'll wake up. Hopper is carrying the bones of our child, wrapped in the pink princess dress of her third birthday party. She'll remember."

"One thing I learned by walking through the museum that was left to me is that there was a time when people made paintings that looked like real people and times when paintings were just different ways of mixing colors and shapes." She was about to say more, lifting up toward a larger explanation, something to improve an idea from private theory to public law, to tell the Mayor he was wrong. But that was all she said.

The Mayor spoke into the quiet left by the expectation of more. "And, what does that mean? Why did you say that? How does that apply to the return of the woman who loved me?"

"If I have to explain it, you'll never understand. So think about it."

"I'll think about it, thanks. And Reynaldo, so uncommonly quiet right now, can you give me a lift? You wrecked my car."

"Well allow me to revert to who I am at all times," said Redwings. "So fuck this shit. Let's ride."

⚛

# Chief, oranges chief

There was a light on in the trailer, just where Go Bruins said Pippi would be. She rarely slept well at the house in Center Camp, not even in the Pippi room, and Chief hoped she was awake now, although she'd be angry when she saw him. How to explain that sending her here was the only way to protect her, when the protection was for his sake, not hers?

A dog barked, then another, and a third, in one of the buildings or trailers. Someone would come out soon and ask him questions as though he was obliged to answer.

The trailer door was unlocked. The bed was unmade.

The oranges chief came to the door. "She's gone," he said.

"You were supposed to lock her up."

"I let her go."

"Why?"

"I was taking care of her for a powerful man. You don't have that power anymore."

"Did she know?"

"I told her what I knew. She walked away."

"No. I would have seen her if she was walking back to the city."

"I don't think she wanted to go back."

They heard the Audi come fast down the road and stop, heard the doors open and shut. Frank, Siouxsie, Redwings, and the Mayor ran to him.

"Who are they?" asked oranges chief.

Chief wanted to tell him that in his mythology, everything was as it should be, that Inventory was full, that Verifications were tied to computers that had the entire database, that the Fence was reinforced, that nothing at LAX could fly, that doctors knew what they were doing, that he was Chief, and that she loved him alone, and no one else.

"Where is she?" asked the Mayor.

Chief felt some joy in being able to say, "She's not here. I'm late, and so are you. She's gone."

"That means Hopper took her."

"Who's Hopper?" asked Chief.

"He's the man you were afraid of," said Frank. "The man who killed Tesla. Also called Nole Hazard, also called Kraft Serviss."

"I was afraid of this man," said Chief, pointing at the Mayor. "He's the one who sent Nole Hazard to find me. He's waiting to see her with me," said Chief. "Then Hazard will take her from me, killing me along the way. That's all his rehab was designed to do."

"So where is Nole?" asked Frank.

"Watching us," said Siouxsie. "I met him. I know what he's doing."

Oranges chief said, "Unless he found her already."

"No," said Redwings. "From what I savvy, he can't find her on his own. He has to follow. He'll be close by, but you may not see him. So you can take the risk of finding her and getting away from him. There's a saying I learned in the club. 'Three can keep a secret if two are dead.' I expect the same is true of a woman's heart."

Siouxsie said, "No. She has to choose."

Chief grabbed Siouxsie and hugged her. Redwings, on instinct, pulled him away.

"No, Redwings. What she just said. I have to give her up. The Mayor and Hopper, let them fight over her. I should go back to Center Camp. That's where I'm needed. Maybe I can save them. She's yours, Mr. Mayor, all yours, if you can get ahead of Hopper. I loved her but she was always yours. Frank, can I have your car?"

"Why?"

"It's better than my truck. You can find another one. There's sure to be an Audi dealer in Bakersfield."

"I'm sure there is," said Frank. He tossed the keys to him.

Chief walked to the Audi, got in, adjusted the seat, and drove away.

The Mayor asked the oranges chief, "Which way did my wife go?"

"There." The oranges chief pointed his hand to the west and swept it in an arc to the east.

"When I find her, I'll bring her back," said the Mayor, before running into the orchard and disappearing between the rows, calling out, "Heidi! Gretel! Pippi! Robin! Robin! Robin!"

As he ran away, Hopper walked out of the trees behind the trailer, the bones rattling in his backpack.

Siouxsie said his name. "Nole. Nole Hazard. Remember me?"

"I have to find my wife."

Sinatra asked him, "Why did you kill Tesla?"

"He was hurting Madeinusa."

No one had anything else to say to him.

Tracing what he hoped were his Teacher's steps, Hopper was also soon lost in the grove.

A few men and women who worked in the orchard had been watching this, and they asked the oranges chief some questions in words Frank didn't know.

Frank asked Siouxsie, "Do you understand what they're saying?"

"It's Spanish. I don't speak it, but I know what it is."

"A language."

"Yes."

Frank turned to Redwings. "Redwings, what happened to the plane that left LAX?"

"It flew over the city."

"And then?"

"I don't know. Do you know?"

"No. What's Chief going to find when he gets back to the Playa?"

"Shannon Squier might still be singing," said Redwings. "Erin and Brin, and Toffe, and Helary and Jobe, what about them?"

"They're either good, or not," said Frank.

"What happened to June Moulton? What happened to Elder-Goth?" asked Siouxsie.

"June will manage," said Frank.

"How do you know? Maybe she won't."

"She can ask for help if she can find us," said Frank.

"Yes," said Siouxsie. "This is where we are."

# ACKNOWLEDGMENTS

I do not live in a vacuum.

Over the last seven years I worked on different ways to tell a story about the social structures of a city in distress, with Nick Wechsler, John Schoenfelder, Dawn Olmstead, Marti Noxon, Josh Appelbaum, André Nemec, Jeff Pinkner, Scott Rosenberg, and Sean Daniel. They may be surprised to see their names here, but as someone once discovered, just as marzipan is the best delivery system for sugar and almonds, so one has to find the right form for the thing at hand of any endeavor, and they helped me on the way to Figueroa and the Fence, so thanks are in order. Perhaps those other stories will yet find the right delivery system.

Long before the book was done, Mercedes Martinez asked if I had something she could print in *The Black Rocker*, a journal of the Ashram Galactica, to be handed out as a gift at that arts festival in the Black Rock Desert of Nevada, and I gave her an early chapter. To see one's words in the alienated form of a different font, above the caution, "From A Work in Progress," is a goad to finish. Also thanks to Chris Paine, that great utopian. To Chris Kraus for an early read. To Brett Johnson, for the last few years of creative company. And I won't waste an opportunity to thank Emma Tolkin and Susanna Tolkin.

Gratitude to my publisher, Morgan Entrekin, for his cogent notes, and to his editors Allison Malecha and Paula Cooper Hughes for theirs. And also to my agent Kim Witherspoon.

Finally, a great cheer to Chevalier's Books, of Larchmont Boulevard in Los Angeles. Bert Deixler, Darryl Holter, Filis Winthrop, Liz Newstat, and Erica Luttrell have saved one block in America from becoming nothing but a food court. Stop in, say hi, and buy a book you've heard about, or a book they recommend, or a book whose cover intrigues you.